Honoré de Balzac

A Daughter of Eve and Letters of two Brides

Honoré de Balzac

A Daughter of Eve and Letters of two Brides

ISBN/EAN: 9783744764483

Printed in Europe, USA, Canada, Australia, Japan

Cover: Foto ©Andreas Hilbeck / pixelio.de

More available books at **www.hansebooks.com**

H. DE BALZAC

A DAUGHTER OF EVE

(UNE FILLE D' ÉVE)

AND

LETTERS OF TWO BRIDES

(MÉMOIRES DE DEUX JEUNES MARIÉES)

TRANSLATED BY

R. S. SCOTT

WITH A PREFACE BY

GEORGE SAINTSBURY

PHILADELPHIA

THE GEBBIE PUBLISHING CO., Ltd.

1898

CONTENTS

LIST OF ILLUSTRATIONS

PREFACE.

OPINIONS of the larger division of this book will vary in pretty direct ratio with the general taste of the reader for Balzac in his more sentimental mood, and for his delineations of virtuous or "honest" women. As is the case with the number of the Comédie which immediately succeeds it in Scènes de la Vie Privée, I cannot say of it that it appeals to me personally with any strong attraction. It is, however, much later and much more accomplished work than "La Femme de Trente Ans" and its companions. It is possible also that opinion may be conditioned by likes or dislikes for novels written in the form of letters, but this cannot count for very much. Some of the best novels in the world, and some of the worst, have taken this form, so that the form itself can have had nothing necessarily to do with their goodness and badness by itself.

Something of the odd perversity which seems to make it so difficult for a French author to imagine a woman, not necessarily a model of perfection, who combines love for her husband of the passionate kind with love for her children of the animal sort, commonsense and good housewifery with freedom from the characteristics of the mere *ménagère*, interest in affairs and books and things in general without, in the French sense, "dissipation" or neglect of home,—appears in the division of the parts of Louise de Chaulieu and Renée de Maucombe. I cannot think that Balzac has improved his book, though he has made it much easier to write, by this separation. We should take more interest in Renée's nursery —it is fair to Balzac to say that he was one of the earliest, despite his lukewarm affection for things English, to introduce this important apartment into a French novel—if she had married her husband less as a matter of business, and had regarded him with a somewhat more romantic affection ; and though it is perhaps not fair to look forward to the "Député d'Arcis" (which, after all, is not in this part probably Balzac's work), we should not in that case have been so little surprised as we are to find the staid matron very nearly flinging herself at the head of a young sculptor, and "making it up" to him (one of the nastiest situations in fiction) with her own daughter. So, too, if the addition of a little more romance to Renée had resulted in the subtraction of a corresponding quantity from Louise, there might not have been much harm done. This very inflammable lady of high degree irresistibly reminds one (except in beauty) of the terrible spinster in Mr. Punch's gallery who "had never seen the man whom she could not love, and hoped to Heaven she never might." It was not for nothing that Mlle. de Chaulieu requested (in defiance of possibility) to be introduced to Madame de Staël. She is herself a later and slightly modernized variety of the Corinne ideal —a sort of French equivalent in fiction of the actual English Lady Caroline Lamb, a person with no repose in her affections, and conceiving herself in conscience bound to make both herself and her lovers or husbands miserable. It is true that in order to the successful accomplishment of this cheerful life-programme, Balzac has provided her with two singularly complaisant and adequate helpmates in the shape of the Spaniard-Sardinian Félipe de Macumer and the French-Englishman and lunatic Marie Gaston. Nor do I know that she is more than they themselves desire, being, as they are, walking gentlemen of a most *triste* description, deplorable to consider as coming from the hand that created not merely Goriot and Grandet, but even Rastignac, Flore Brazier, and Lucien de Rubempré. If this censure seems too hard, I can only say that of all things that deserve the name of failure, "sensibility" that does not reach the actual boiling-point of passion seems to me to fail most disagreeably.

There are, however, even for those who are thus minded,

considerable condolences and consolations in "Une Fille d'Eve." It is perhaps unfortunate, and may not improbably be the cause of that abiding notion of Balzac as preferring moral ugliness to moral beauty, which has been so often referred to, that he has rather a habit of setting his studies in rose-pink side by side with his far more vigorous exercitations in black and crimson. "Une Fille d'Eve" is one of the best of these latter in its own way. It is no doubt conditioned by Balzac's quaint hatred of that newspaper press from which he never could quite succeed in disengaging himself; and we should have been more entirely rejoiced at the escape of Count Félix de Vandenesse from the decoration so often alluded to by our Elizabethan poets and dramatists if he had not been the very questionable hero of "Le Lys dans la Vallée." But the whole intrigue is managed with remarkable ease and skill; the "double arrangement," so to speak, by which Raoul Nathan proves for a time at least equally attractive to such very different persons as Florine and Madame de Vandenesse, the perfidious manœuvres of the respectable ladies who have formerly enjoyed the doubtful honor of Count Félix's attentions—all are good. It can hardly be said, considering the nature of the case, that the Count's method of saving his honor, though not quite the most scrupulous in the world, is contrary to "the game," and the whole moves well.

Perhaps the character of Nathan himself cannot be said to be quite fully worked out. Balzac seems to have postulated, as almost necessary to the journalist nature, a sort of levity half artistic, half immoral, which is incapable of constancy or uprightness. Blondet, and perhaps Claud Vignon, are about the only members of the accursed vocation whom he allows in some measure to escape the curse. But he has not elaborated and instanced its working quite so fully in the case of Nathan as in the cases of Lousteau and Lucien de Rubempré. I do not know whether any special original has been assigned to Nathan, who, it will be observed, is something more than a mere journalist, being a successful dramatist and romancer.

"Mémoires de Deux Jeunes Mariées" first appeared in the "Presse" during the winter of 1841–42, and was published as a book by Souverain in the latter year. The Comédie in its complete form was already under weigh ; and the Mémoires being suitable for its earliest division, the Scènes de la Vie Privée were entered at once on the books, the same year, 1842, seeing the entrance.

"Une Fille d'Eve" was a little earlier. After appearing (with nine chapter divisions) in the "Siècle" on the last day of December 1838 and during the first fortnight of January 1839, it was in the latter year published as a book by Souverain with "Massimilla Doni," and three years later was comprised in the first volume of the Comédie.

G. S.

A DAUGHTER OF EVE.

To Madame la Comtesse de Bolognini, née Vimercati.

If you remember, dear lady, the pleasure your conversation gave to a certain traveler, making Paris live for him in Milan, you will not be surprised that he should lay one of his works at your feet, as a token of gratitude for so many delightful evenings spent in your society, nor that he should seek for it the shelter of a name which, in old times, was given to not a few of the tales by one of your early writers, beloved of the Milanese. You have a Eugénie, with more than the promise of beauty, whose speaking smile proclaims her to have inherited from you the most precious gifts a woman can possess, and whose childhood, it is certain, will be rich in all those joys which a harsh mother refused to the Eugénie of these pages. If Frenchmen are accused of being frivolous and inconstant, I, you see, am Italian in my faithfulness and attachments. How often, as I wrote the name of Eugénie, have my thoughts carried me back to the cool stuccoed drawing-room and little garden of the Vicolo dei Capuccini, *which used to resound to the dear child's merry laughter, to our quarrels, and our stories. You have left the* Corso *for the* Tre Monasteri, *where I know nothing of your manner of life, and I am forced to picture you, no longer amongst the pretty things, which doubtless still surround you, but like one of the beautiful heads of Carlo Dolci, Raphaël, Titian, or Allori, which, in their remoteness, seem to us like abstractions.*

(1)

*If this book succeed in making its way across the
Alps, it will tell you of the lively gratitude and respectful friendship of*

Your humble servant,

DE BALZAC.

CHAPTER I.

THE TWO MARIES.

IT was half-past eleven in the evening, and two women were
seated by the fire of a boudoir in one of the finest houses of
the Rue Neuve-des-Mathurins. The room was hung in blue
velvet, of the kind with tender melting lights, which French
industry has only lately learned to manufacture. The doors
and windows had been draped by a really artistic decorator
with rich cashmere curtains, matching the walls in color.
From a prettily moulded rose in the centre of the ceiling,
hung, by three finely wrought chains, a silver lamp, studded
with turquoises. The plan of decoration had been carried
out to the very minutest detail; even the ceiling was covered
with blue silk, while long bands of cashmere, folded across
the silk at equal distances, made stars of white, looped up
with pearl beading. The feet sank in the warm pile of a
Belgian carpet, close as a lawn, where blue nosegays were
sprinkled over a ground the color of unbleached linen. The
warm tone of the furniture, which was of solid rosewood and
carved after the best antique models, saved from insipidity
the general effect which a painter might have called a little
"muzzy." On the backs of the chairs small panels of splendid figured silk—white with blue flowers—were set in broad
leafy frames, finely cut on the wood. On either side of the
window stood a set of shelves, loaded with valuable knick-
knacks, the flower of mechanical art, sprung into being at the

touch of creative fancy. The mantelpiece of African marble bore a platinum timepiece with arabesques in black enamel, flanked by extravagant specimens of old Saxe—the inevitable shepherd with dainty bouquet for ever tripping to meet his bride—embodying the Teutonic conception of ceramic art. Above sparkled the beveled facets of a Venetian mirror in an ebony frame, crowded with figures in relief, relic of some royal residence. Two flower-stands displayed at this season the sickly triumphs of the hothouse, pale, spirit-like blossoms, the pearls of the world of flowers. The room might have been for sale, it was so desperately tidy and prim. It bore no impress of will and character such as marks a happy home, and even the women did not break the general chilly impression, for they were weeping.

The proprietor of the house, Ferdinand du Tillet, was one of the richest bankers in Paris, and the very mention of his name will account for the lavish style of the house decoration, of which the boudoir may be taken as a sample. Du Tillet, though a man of no family, and sprung from heaven knows where, had taken for a wife, in 1831, the only unmarried daughter of the Comte de Granville, whose name was one of the most illustrious on the French bench, and who had been made a peer of the realm after the Revolution of July. This ambitious alliance was not gotten for nothing; in the settlement, du Tillet had to sign a receipt for a dowry of which he never touched a penny. This nominal dowry was the same in amount as the huge sum given to the elder sister on her marriage with Comte Félix de Vandenesse, and which, in fact, was the price paid by the Granvilles in their turn for a matrimonial prize. Thus, in the long run, the bank repaired the breach which aristocracy had made in the finances of the bench. Could the Comte de Vandenesse have seen himself, three years in advance, brother-in-law of a Master Ferdinand, self-styled du Tillet, it is possible he might have declined the match; but who could have foreseen at the close of 1828 the strange upheavals which 1830 was to produce in the political, financial, and moral condition of France? Had Count Félix been told that in the general shuffle he would lose his peer's coronet, to find it again on his father-in-law's brow, he would have treated his informant as a lunatic.

Crouching in a listening attitude in one of those low chairs called a *chauffeuse*, Mme. du Tillet pressed her sister's hand to her breast with motherly tenderness, and from time to time kissed it. This sister was known in society as Mme. Félix de Vandenesse, the Christian name being joined to that of the family, in order to distinguish the countess from her sister-in-law, wife of the former ambassador, Charles de Vandenesse, widow of the late Comte de Kergarouët, whose wealth she had inherited, and by birth a de Fontaine. The countess had thrown herself back upon a lounge, a handkerchief in her other hand, her eyes swimming, her breath choked with half-stifled sobs. She had just poured out her confidences to Mme. du Tillet in a way which proved the tenderness of their sisterly love. In an age like ours it would have seemed so natural for sisters, who had married into such very different spheres, not to be on intimate terms, that a rapid glance at the story of their childhood will be necessary in order to explain the origin of this affection which had survived, without jar or flaw, the alienating forces of society and the mutual scorn of their husbands.

The early home of Marie-Angélique and Marie-Eugénie was a dismal house in the Marais. Here they were brought up by a pious but narrow-minded woman, "imbued with high principle," as the classic phrase has it, who conceived herself to have performed the whole duty of a mother when her girls arrived at the door of matrimony without ever having traveled beyond the domestic circle embraced by the maternal eye. Up to that time they had never even been to a play. A Paris church was their nearest approach to a theatre. In short, their upbringing in their mother's house was as strict as it

could have been in a convent. From the time that they had
ceased to be mere infants they always slept in a room adjoin-
ing that of the countess, the door of which was kept open at
night. The time not occupied by dressing, religious observ-
ances, and the minimum of study requisite for the children of
gentlefolk, was spent in making poor-clothes and in taking
exercise, modeled on the English Sunday walk, where any
quickening of the solemn pace is checked as being suggestive
of cheerfulness. Their lessons were kept within the limits
imposed by confessors, chosen from among the least liberal
and most Jansenist of ecclesiastics. Never were girls handed
over to their husbands more pure and virgin : in this point,
doubtless one of great importance, their mother seemed to
have seen the fulfillment of her whole duty to God and man.
Not a novel did the poor things read till they were married.
In drawing an old maid was their instructor, and their only
copies were figures whose anatomy would have confounded
Cuvier, and so drawn as to have made a woman of the Farnese
Hercules. A worthy priest taught them grammar, French,
history, geography, and the little arithmetic a woman needs
to know. As for literature, they read aloud in the evening
from certain authorized books, such as the "Lettres édi-
fiantes" and Noël's "Leçons de littérature," but only in the
presence of their mother's confessor, since even here passages
might occur, which, apart from heedful commentary, would
be liable to stir the imagination. Fénelon's "Telemachus"
was held dangerous. The Comtesse de Granville was not
without affection for her daughters, and it showed itself in
wishing to make angels of them in the fashion of Marie
Alacoque, but the daughters would have preferred a mother
less saintly and more human.

This education bore its inevitable fruit. Religion, imposed
as a yoke and presented under its harshest aspect, wearied
these innocent young hearts with a discipline adapted for
hardened sinners. It repressed their feelings, and, though

striking deep root, could create no affection. The two Maries had no alternative but to sink into imbecility or to long for independence. Independence meant marriage, and to this they looked as soon as they began to see something of the world and could exchange a few ideas, while yet remaining utterly unconscious of their own touching grace and rare qualities. Ignorant of what innocence meant, without arms against misfortune, without experience of happiness, how should they be able to judge of life? Their only comfort in the depths of this maternal jail was drawn from each other. Their sweet whispered talks at night, the few sentences they could exchange when their mother left them for a moment, contained sometimes more thoughts than could be put in words. Often would a stolen glance, charged with sympathetic message and response, convey a whole poem of bitter melancholy. They found a marvelous joy in simple things—the sight of a cloudless sky, the scent of flowers, a turn in the garden with interlacing arms—and would exult with innocent glee over the completion of a piece of embroidery.

Their mother's friends, far from providing intellectual stimulus or calling forth their sympathies, only deepened the surrounding gloom. They were stiff-backed old ladies, dry and rigid, whose conversation turned on their ailments, on the shades of difference between preachers or confessors, or on the most trifling events in the religious world, which might be found in the pages of "La Quotidienne" or "L'Ami de la Religion." The men again might have served as extinguishers to the torch of love, so cold and mournfully impassive were their faces. They had all reached the age when a man becomes churlish and irritable, when his tastes are blunted except at table, and are directed only to procure the comforts of life. Religious egotism had dried up hearts devoted to task work and intrenched behind routine. They spent the greater part of the evening over silent card parties. At times the two poor little girls, placed under the ban of this sanhedrin, who abetted the maternal severity, would suddenly feel that they could bear no longer the sight of these wearisome persons with their sunken eyes and frowning faces.

Against the dull background of this life stood out in bold relief the single figure of a man, that of their music-master. The confessors had ruled that music was a Christian art, having its source in the Catholic church and developed by it, and therefore the two little girls were allowed to learn music. A spectacled lady, who professed sol-fa and the piano at a neighboring convent, bored them for a time with exercises. But, when the elder of his girls was ten years old, the Comte de Granville pointed out the necessity of finding a master. Mme. de Granville, who could not deny it, gave to her concession all the merit of wifely submissiveness. A pious woman never loses an opportunity of taking credit for doing her duty.

The master was a Catholic German, one of those men who are born old and will always remain fifty, even if they live to be eighty. His hollowed, wrinkled, swarthy face had kept something childlike and simple in its darkest folds. The blue of innocence sparkled in his eyes, and the gay smile of spring dwelt on his lips. His gray, old hair, which fell in natural curls, like those of Jesus Christ, added to his ecstatic air a vague solemnity which was highly misleading, for he was a man to make a fool of himself with the most exemplary gravity. His clothes were a necessary envelope to which he paid no attention, for his gaze soared too high in the clouds to come in contact with material things. And so this great unrecognized artist belonged to that generous race of the absent-minded, who give their time and their hearts to others, just as they drop their gloves on every table, their umbrellas at every door. His hands were of the kind which look dirty after washing. Finally, his aged frame, badly set up on tottering, knotty limbs, gave ocular proof how far a man's body can become a mere accessory to his mind. It was one of those strange freaks of nature which no one has ever properly described except Hoffmann, a German, who has made himself the poet of all which appears lifeless and yet lives. Such was Schmucke, formerly choirmaster to the Margrave of Anspach, a learned man who underwent inspection from a council of piety. They asked him whether he fasted. The master was tempted to reply, "Look at me!" but it is ill work jesting with saints and Jansenist confessors.

This apocryphal old man held so large a place in the life of the two Maries—they became so much attached to the great simple-minded artist whose sole interest was in his art—that, after they were married, each bestowed on him an annuity of three hundred francs, a sum which sufficed for his lodging, his beer, his pipe, and his clothes. Six hundred francs a year and his lessons were a Paradise for Schmucke. He had not ventured to confide his poverty and his hopes to any one except these two charming children, whose hearts had blossomed under the snow of maternal rigor and the frost of devotion, and this fact by itself sums up the character of Schmucke and the childhood of the two Maries.

No one could tell afterward what abbé, what devout old lady, had unearthed this German, lost in Paris. No sooner did mothers of a family learn that the Comtesse de Granville had found a music-master for her daughters than they all asked for his name and address. Schmucke had thirty houses in the Marais. This tardy success displayed itself in slippers with bronzed steel buckles and lined with horse-hair soles, and in a more frequent change of shirt. His childlike gayety, long repressed by an honorable and seemly poverty, bubbled forth afresh. He let fall little jokes such as: "Young ladies, the cats supped off the dirt of Paris last night," when a frost had dried the muddy streets overnight, only they were spoken in a Germano-Gallic lingo: "*Younc ladies, de gads subbed off de dirt off Barees.*" Gratified at having brought his adorable ladies this species of *Vergiss mein nicht*, culled from the flowers of his fancy, he put on an air of such ineffable roguishness in presenting it that mockery was disarmed. It made him so happy to call a smile to the lips of his pupils, the sadness of whose life was no mystery to him, that he would have made himself ridiculous on purpose if nature had not saved him the trouble. And yet there was no commonplace so vulgar that the warmth of his heart could not infuse it with fresh meaning. . In the fine words of the late Saint-Martin, the radiance of his smile might have turned the mire of the highway to gold. The two Maries, following one of the best traditions of religious education, used to escort their master respectfully to the door of the suite when he left. There the poor girls would say a few kind words to him, happy in making him happy. It was the one chance they had of exercising their woman's nature.

Thus, up to the time of their marriage, music became for the girls a life within life, just as, we are told, the Russian peasant takes his dreams for realities, his waking life for a restless sleep. In their eagerness to find some bulwark against the rising tide of pettiness and consuming ascetic ideas, they threw themselves desperately into the difficulties of the musical art. Melody, harmony, and composition, those three daughters of the skies, rewarded their labors, making a rampart for them with their aerial dances, while the old Catholic faun, intoxicated by music, led the chorus. Mozart, Beethoven, Haydn, Paesiello, Cimarosa, Hummel, along with musicians of lesser rank, developed in them sensations which never passed beyond the modest limit of their veiled bosoms, but which went to the heart of that new world of fancy whither they eagerly betook themselves. When the execution of some piece had been brought to perfection, they would clasp hands and embrace in the wildest ecstasy. The old master called them his Saint Cecilias.

The two Maries did not go to balls till they were sixteen, and then only four times a year, to a few selected houses. They only left their mother's side when well fortified with rules of conduct, so strict that they could reply nothing but yes and no to their partners. The eye of the countess never quitted her daughters and seemed to read the words upon their lips. The ball-dresses of the poor little things were models of decorum—high-necked lawn frocks, with an extraordinary number of fluffy frills and long sleeves. This ungraceful costume, which concealed instead of setting off their beauty, reminded one of an Egyptian mummy, in spite of two sweetly pathetic faces which peeped out from the mass of cotton. With all their innocence, they were furious to find themselves the objects of a kindly pity. Where is the woman, however artless, who would not inspire envy rather than compassion? The white matter of their brains was unsoiled by a single perilous, morbid, or even equivocal thought; their hearts were pure, their hands were frightfully red; they were bursting with health. Eve did not leave the hands of her Creator more guileless than were these two girls when they left their mother's home to go to the mayor's office and to the church, with one simple but awful command in their ears—to obey in all things the man by whose side they were to spend the night, awake or sleeping. To them it seemed impossible that they should suffer more in the strange house whither they were to be banished than in the maternal convent.

How came it that the father of these girls did nothing to protect them from so crushing a despotism? The Comte de Granville had a great reputation as a judge, able and incorruptible, if sometimes a little carried away by party feeling. Unhappily, by the terms of a remarkable compromise, agreed upon after ten years of married life, husband and wife lived apart, each in their own suite of apartments. The father, who judged the repressive system less dangerous for women than for men, kept the education of his boys in his own hands, while leaving that of the girls to their mother. The two Maries, who could hardly escape the imposition of some tyranny, whether in love or marriage, would suffer less than boys, whose intelligence ought to be unfettered and whose natural spirit would be broken by the harsh constraint of religious dogma, pushed to an extreme. Of four victims the count saved two. The countess looked on her sons, both destined for the law—the one for the *magistrature assise*, the other for the *magistrature amovible*—as far too badly brought up to be allowed any intimacy with their sisters. All intercourse between the poor children was strictly guarded. When the count took his boys from school for a day he was careful that it should not be spent in the house. After luncheon with their mother and sisters he would find something to amuse them outside. Restaurants, theatres, museums, an expedition to the country in summer-time, were their treats. Only on important family occasions, such as the birthday of the countess or of their father, New Year's Day, and prize-giving days, did the boys spend day and night under the paternal roof, in extreme discomfort, and not daring to kiss their sisters under the eye of the countess, who never left them alone together for an instant. Seeing so little of their brothers, how was it possible the poor girls should feel any bond with them? On these days it was a perpetual, " Where is Angélique ?" " What is Eugénie about ?" " Where can my children be ?" When her sons were mentioned, the countess would raise her cold and sodden eyes to heaven, as though imploring pardon for having failed to snatch them from ungodliness. Her exclamations and her silence in regard to them were alike eloquent as the most lamentable verses of Jeremiah, and the girls not unnaturally came to look on their brothers as hopeless reprobates.

The count gave to each of his sons, at the age of eighteen, a couple of rooms in his own suite, and they then began to

---

* The *magistrature assise* consists of the judges who sit in Court, and are appointed for life. The members of the *magistrature amovible* conduct the examination and prosecution of accused persons. They address the Court standing, and are not appointed for life.

study law under the direction of his secretary, a barrister, to whom he intrusted the task of initiating them into the mysteries of their profession.

The two Maries, therefore, had no practical knowledge of what it is to have a brother.   On the occasion of their sisters' weddings it happened that both brothers were detained at a distance by important cases: the one having then a post as *avocat-général** at a distant court, while the other was making his first appearance in the provinces.   In many families the reality of that home-life, which we are apt to picture as linked together by the closest and most vital ties, is something very different.   The brothers are far away, engrossed in money-making, in pushing their way in the world, or they are chained to the public service ; the sisters are absorbed in a vortex of family interests, outside their own circle.   Thus the different members spend their lives apart and indifferent to each other, held together only by the feeble bond of memory.   If on occasion pride or self-interest reunites them, just as often these motives act in the opposite sense and divide them in heart, as they have already been divided in life, so that it becomes a rare exception to find a family living in one home and animated by one spirit.   Modern legislation, by splitting up the family into units, has created that most hideous evil—the isolation of the individual.

Angélique and Eugénie, amid the profound solitude in which their youth glided by, saw their father but rarely, and it was a melancholy face which he showed in his wife's handsome rooms on the first-floor.   At home, as on the bench, he maintained the grave and dignified bearing of the judge. When the girls had passed the period of toys and dolls, when they were beginning, at twelve years of age, to think for themselves, and had given up making fun of Schmucke, they found out the secret of the cares which lined the count's fore-

* The term is applied to all the substitutes of the *procureur-général* or attorney-general.

head.   Under the mask of severity they could read traces of a kindly, lovable nature.   He had yielded to the church his place as head of the household, his hopes of wedded happiness had been blighted, and his father's heart was wounded in its tenderest spot—the love he bore his daughters.   Sorrows such as these rouse strange pity in the breast of girls who have never known tenderness.   Sometimes he would stroll in the garden between his daughters, an arm round each little figure, fitting his pace to their childish steps; then stopping in the shrubbery, he would kiss them, one after the other, on the forehead, while his eyes, his mouth, and his whole expression breathed the deepest pity.

"You are not very happy, my darlings," he said on one such occasion; "but I shall marry you off early, and it will be a good day for me when I see you take wing."

"Papa," said Eugénie, "we have made up our minds to marry the first man who offers."

"And this," he exclaimed, "is the bitter fruit of such a system.   In trying to make saints of them, they——"

He stopped.   Often the girls were conscious of a passionate tenderness in their father's farewell, or in the way he looked at them when by chance he dined with their mother.   This father, whom they so rarely saw, became the object of their pity, and whom we pity we love.

The marriage of both sisters—welded together by misfortune, as Rita-Christina was by nature—was the direct result of this strict conventual training.   Many men, when thinking of marriage, prefer a girl taken straight from the convent and impregnated with an atmosphere of devotion to one who has been trained in the school of society.   There is no medium.   On the one hand is the girl with nothing left to learn, who reads and discusses the papers, who has spun round ball-rooms in the arms of countless young men, who has seen every play and devoured every novel, whose knees have been made supple by a dancing-master, pressing them against his own, who does not trouble her head about religion and has evolved her own morality; on the other is the guileless, simple girl of the type of Marie-Angélique and Marie-Eugénie. Possibly the husband's risk is no greater in the one case than in the other, but the immense majority of men, who have not yet reached the age of Arnolphe, would choose a saintly Agnès rather than a budding Celimène.

The two Maries were identical in figure, feet, and hands. Both were small and slight. Eugénie, the younger, was fair like her mother; Angélique, dark like her father. But they had the same complexion—a skin of that mother-of-pearl white which tells of a rich and healthy blood and against which the carnation stands out in vivid patches, firm in texture like the jasmine, and like it also, delicate, smooth, and soft to the touch. The blue eyes of Eugénie, the brown eyes of Angélique, had the same naïve expression of indifference and unaffected astonishment, betrayed by the indecisive wavering of the iris in the liquid white. Their figures were good; the shoulders, a little angular now, would be rounded by time. The neck and bosom, which had been so long veiled, appeared quite startlingly perfect in form, when, at the request of her husband, each sister for the first time attired herself for a ball in a low-necked dress. What blushes covered the poor innocent things, so charming in their shame-facedness, as they first saw themselves in the privacy of their own rooms; nor did the color fade all evening!

At the moment when this story opens, with the younger Marie consoling her weeping sister, they are no longer raw girls. Each had nursed an infant—one a boy, the other a girl—and the hands and arms of both were white as milk. Eugénie had always seemed something of a madcap to her terrible mother, who redoubled her watchful care and severity on her behalf. Angélique, stately and proud, had, she thought, a soul of high temper fitted to guard itself, while the skittish Eugénie seemed to demand a firmer hand. There are charming natures of this kind, misread by destiny, whose life ought to be unbroken sunshine, but who live and die in misery, plagued by some evil genius, the victims of chance. Thus the sprightly, artless Eugénie had fallen under the malign despotism of a parvenu when released from the maternal clutches. Angélique, high-strung and sensitive, had been sent adrift in the highest circles of Parisian society without any restraining curb.

CHAPTER II.

SISTERLY CONFIDENCES.

Mme. de Vandenesse, it was plain, was crushed by the burden of troubles too heavy for a mind still unsophisticated after six years of marriage. She lay at length, her limbs flaccid, her body bent, her head fallen anyhow on the back of the lounge. Having looked in at the opera before hurrying to her sister's, she had still a few flowers in the plaits of her hair, while others lay scattered on the carpet, together with her gloves, her mantle of fur-lined silk, her muff and her hood. Bright tears mingled with the pearls on her white bosom and brimming eyes told a tale in gruesome contrast with the luxury around. The countess had no heart for further words.

"You poor darling," said Mme. du Tillet, "what strange delusion as to my married life made you come to me for help?"

It seemed as though the torrent of her sister's grief had forced these words from the heart of the banker's wife, as melting snow will set free stones that are held the fastest in the river's bed. The countess gazed stupidly on her with fixed eyes, in which terror had dried the tears.

"Can it be that the waters have closed over your head too, my sweet one?" she said in a low voice.

"Nay, dear, my troubles won't lessen yours."

"But tell me them, dear child. Do you think I am so sunk in self already as not to listen? Then we are comrades again in suffering as of old!"

"But we suffer apart," sadly replied Mme. du Tillet. "We live in opposing camps. It is my turn to visit the Tuileries now that you have ceased to go. Our husbands belong to rival parties. I am the wife of an ambitious banker, a bad, ever-scheming man. Your husband, sweetest, is kind, noble, generous——"

"Ah! do not reproach me," cried the countess. "No woman has the right to do so, who has not suffered the weariness of a tame, colorless life and passed from it straight to the paradise of love. She must have known the bliss of living her whole life in another, of espousing the ever-varying emotions of a poet's soul. In every flight of his imagination, in all the efforts of his ambition, in the great part he plays upon the stage of life, she must have borne her share, suffering in his pain and mounting on the wings of his measureless delights; and all this while never losing her cold, impassive demeanor before a prying world. Yes, dear, a tumult of emotion may rage within, while one sits by the fire at home, quietly and comfortably like this. And yet what joy to have at every instant one overwhelming interest which expands the heart and makes it live in every fibre. Nothing is indifferent to you; your very life seems to depend on a drive, which gives you the chance of seeing in the crowd the one man before the flash of whose eye the sunlight pales; you tremble if he is late, and could strangle the bore who steals from you one of those precious moments when happiness throbs in every vein! To be alive, only to be alive is rapture! Think of it, dear, to live, when so many women would give the world to feel as I do—and cannot. Remember, child, that for this poetry of life there is but one season—the season of youth. Soon, very soon, will come the chills of winter. Oh! if you were rich as I am in these living treasures of the heart and were threatened with losing them——"

Mme. du Tillet, terrified, had hidden her face in her hands during this wild rhapsody. At last, seeing the warm tears on her sister's cheek, she began—

"I never dreamed of reproaching you, my darling. Your words have, in a single instant, stirred in my heart more burning thoughts than all my tears have quenched, for indeed the life I lead might well plead within me for a passion such as you describe. Let me cling to the belief that if we had seen more of each other we should not have drifted to this point. The knowledge of my sufferings would have enabled you to realize your own happiness, and I might perhaps have learned from you courage to resist the tyranny which has crushed the sweetness out of my life. Your misery is an accident which chance may remedy, mine is unceasing. My husband neither has real affection for me nor does he trust me. I am a mere peg for his magnificence, the hall-mark of his ambition, a tit-bit for his vanity.

"Ferdinand"—and she struck her hand upon the mantel-piece—"is hard and smooth like this marble. He is suspicious of me. If I ask anything for myself I know beforehand that refusal is certain; but for whatever may tickle his self-importance or advertise his wealth I have not even to express a desire. He decorates my rooms, and spends lavishly on my table; my servants, my boxes at the theatre, all the trappings of my life are of the smartest. He grudges nothing to his vanity. His children's baby-linen must be trimmed with real lace, but he would never trouble about their actual needs, and would shut his ears to their cries. Can you understand such a state of things? I go to Court loaded with diamonds, and my ornaments are of the most costly whenever I am in society; yet I have not a sou of my own. Madame du Tillet, whom envious onlookers no doubt suppose to be rolling in wealth, cannot lay her hand on a hundred francs. If the father cares little for his children, he cares still less for their mother. Never does he allow me to forget that I have been paid for as a chattel, and that my personal fortune, which has never been in my possession, has been filched from him. If he stood alone I might have a chance of fascinating him, but there is an alien influence at work. He is under the thumb of a woman, a notary's widow, over fifty, but who still reckons on her charms, and I can see very well that while she lives I shall never be free.

"My whole life here is planned out like a sovereign's. A bell is rung for my lunch and dinner as at your castle. I never miss going to the Bois at a certain hour, accompanied by two footmen in full livery, and returning at a fixed time. In place of giving orders, I receive them. At balls and the theatre, a lackey comes up to me saying, 'Your carriage waits, madame,' and I have to go, whether I am enjoying myself or not. Ferdinand would be vexed if I did not carry out the code of rules drawn up for his wife, and I am afraid of him. Surrounded by all this hateful splendor, I sometimes look back with regret, and begin to think we had a kind mother. At least she left us our nights, and I had you to talk to. In my sufferings, then, I had a loving companion, but this gorgeous house is a desert to me."

It was for the countess now to play the comforter. As this tale of misery fell from her sister's lips she took her hand and kissed it with tears.

"How is it possible for me to help you?" Eugénie went on in a low voice. "If he were to find us together he would suspect something. He would want to know what we had been talking about this hour, and it is not easy to put off the scent any one so false and full of wiles. He would be sure to lay a trap for me. But enough of my troubles; let us think of you. Your forty thousand francs, darling, would be nothing to Ferdinand. He and the Baron de Nucingen, another of these rich bankers, are accustomed to handle millions.

Sometimes at dinner I hear them talking of things to make your flesh creep. Du Tillet knows I am no talker, so they speak freely before me, confident that it will go no further, and I can assure you that highway murder would be an act of mercy compared to some of their financial schemes. Nucingen and he makes as little of ruining a man as I do of all their display. Among the people who come to see me, often there are poor dupes whose affairs I have heard settled overnight, and who are plunging into speculations which will beggar them. How I long to act Léonarde in the brigands' cave, and cry, ' Beware ! ' But what would become of me? I hold my tongue, but this luxurious mansion is nothing but a den of cut-throats. And du Tillet and Nucingen scatter bank-notes in handfuls for any whim that takes their fancy. Ferdinand has bought the site of the old castle at Tillet, and intends rebuilding it, and then adding a forest and magnificent grounds. He says his son will be a count and his grandson a peer. Nucingen is tired of his house in the Rue Saint-Lazare and is having a palace built. His wife is a friend of mine. Ah ! '' she cried, '' she might be of use to us. She is not in awe of her husband, her property is in her own hands ; she is the person to save you.''

'' Darling,'' cried Mme. de Vandenesse, throwing herself into her sister's arms and bursting into tears, '' there are only a few hours left. Let us go there to-night, this very instant.''

'' How can I go out at eleven o'clock at night ? ''

'' My carriage is here.''

'' Well, what are you two plotting here ? '' It was du Tillet who threw open the door of the boudoir.

A false geniality lit up the blank countenance which met the sisters' gaze. They had been too much absorbed in talking to notice the wheels of du Tillet's carriage, and the thick carpets had muffled the sound of his steps. The countess, who had an indulgent husband and was well used to society, had acquired a tact and address such as her sister, passing straight from a mother's to a husband's yoke, had had no opportunity of cultivating. She was able then to save the situation, which she saw that Eugénie's terror was on the point of betraying, by a frank reply.

"I thought my sister wealthier than she is," she said, looking her brother-in-law in the face. "Women sometimes get into difficulties which they don't care to speak of to their husbands—witness Napoleon and Joséphine—and I came to ask a favor of her."

"There will be no difficulty about that. Eugénie is a rich woman," replied du Tillet, in a tone of honeyed acerbity.

"Only for you," said the countess, with a bitter smile.

"How much do you want?" said du Tillet, who was not sorry at the prospect of getting his aristocratic sister-in-law into his toils.

"How dense you are! Didn't I tell you that we want to keep our husbands out of this?" was the prudent reply of Mme. de Vandenesse, who feared to place herself at the mercy of the man whose character had by good luck just been sketched by her sister. "I shall come and see Eugénie to-morrow."

"To-morrow? No," said the banker coldly. "Madame du Tillet dines to-morrow with a future peer of the realm, Baron de Nucingen, who is resigning to me his seat in the Chamber of Deputies."

"Won't you allow her to accept my box at the opera?" said the countess, without exchanging even a look with her sister, in her terror lest their secret understanding should be betrayed.

"Thank you, she has her own," said du Tillet, offended.

"Very well, then, I shall see her there," replied the countess.

"It will be the first time you have done us that honor," said du Tillet.

The countess felt the reproach and began to laugh.

"Keep your mind easy, you shan't be asked to pay this time," she said. "Good-by, darling."

"The jade!" cried du Tillet, picking up the flowers which had fallen from the countess' hair. "You would do well," he said to his wife, "to take a lesson from Madame de Vandenesse. I should like to see you as saucy in society as she was here just now. Your want of style and spirit are enough to drive a man wild."

For all reply, Eugénie raised her eyes to heaven.

"Well, madame, what have you two been about here?" said the banker after a pause, pointing to the flowers. "What has happened to bring your sister to your box to-morrow?"

In order to get away to her bedroom, and escape the cross-questioning she dreaded, the poor thrall made an excuse of being sleepy. But du Tillet took his wife's arm and, dragging her back, planted her before him beneath the full blaze of the candles, flaming in their silver-gilt branches between two beautiful bunches of flowers. Fixing her eyes with his keen glance, he began with cold deliberation.

"Your sister came to borrow forty thousand francs to pay the debts of a man in whom she is interested, and who, within three days, will be under lock and key in the Rue de Clichy. He's too precious to be left loose."

The miserable woman tried to repress the nervous shiver which ran through her.

"You gave me a fright," she said. "But you know that my sister has too much principle and too much affection for her husband to take that sort of interest in any man."

"On the contrary," he replied drily. "Girls brought up as you were, in a very strait-laced and puritan fashion, always pant for liberty and happiness, and the happiness they have never comes up to what they imagined. Those are the girls that make bad wives."

"Speak for me if you like," said poor Eugénie, in a tone of bitter irony, "but respect my sister. The Comtesse de

Vandenesse is too happy, too completely trusted by her husband, not to be attached to him. Beside, supposing what you say were true, she would not have told me."

"It is as I said," persisted du Tillet, "and I forbid you to have anything to do with the matter. It is to my interest that the man go to prison. Let that suffice."

Mme. du Tillet left the room.

"She is sure to disobey me," said du Tillet to himself, left alone in the boudoir, "and if I keep my eye on them I may be able to find out what they are up to. Poor fools, to pit themselves against us !"

He shrugged his shoulders and went to rejoin his wife, or, more properly speaking, his slave.

CHAPTER III.

THE STORY OF A HAPPY WOMAN.

The confession which Mme. Félix de Vandenesse had poured into her sister's ear was so intimately connected with her history during the six preceding years that a brief narrative of the chief incidents of her married life is necessary to its understanding.

Félix de Vandenesse was one of the band of distinguished men who owed their fortune to the Restoration, till a short-sighted policy excluded them, as followers of Martignac, from the inner circle of Government. In the last days of Charles X. he was banished with some others to the Upper Chamber; and this disgrace, though in his eyes only temporary, led him to think of marriage. He was the more inclined to it from a sort of nausea of intrigue and gallantry not uncommon with men when the hour of youth's gay frenzy is past. There comes then a critical moment when the serious side of social ties makes itself felt. Félix de Vandenesse had had his bright and his dark hours, but the latter predominated, as is apt to

be the case with a man who has quite early in life become
acquainted with passion in its noblest form. The initiated
become fastidious. A long experience of life and study of
character reconciles them at last to the second best, when they
take refuge in a universal tolerance. Having lost all illusions,
they are proof against guile; yet they wear their cynicism
with a grace, and, being prepared for the worst, are saved the
pangs of disappointment.

In spite of this, Félix still passed for one of the handsomest
and most agreeable men in Paris. With women his reputation
was largely due to one of the noblest of their contemporaries,
who was said to have died of a broken heart for him ;* but it
was the beautiful Lady Dudley who had the chief hand in
forming him. In the eyes of many Paris ladies Félix was a
hero of romance, owing not a few of his conquests to his evil
repute. Madame de Manerville had closed the chapter of his
intrigues. Although not a Don Juan, he retired from the
world of love, as from that of politics, a disillusioned man.
That ideal type of woman and of love which, for his misfortune, had brightened and dominated his youth, he despaired
of finding again. At the age of thirty, Count Félix resolved
to cut short by marriage pleasures which had begun to pall.
On one point he was determined; he would have none but a
girl trained in the strictest dogmas of Catholicism. No sooner
did he hear how the Comtesse de Granville brought up her
daughters than he asked for the hand of the elder. His own
mother had been a domestic tyrant; and he could still remember enough of his dismal childhood to descry, through
the veil of maidenly modesty, what effect had been produced
on a young girl's character by such a bondage, to see whether
she were sulky, soured, and inclined to revolt, or had remained sweet and loving, responsive to the voice of nobler
feeling. Tyranny produces two results, exactly opposite in
character, and which are symbolized in those two great types

* See "The Lily of the Valley."

of the slave in classical times—Epictetus and Spartacus. The one is hatred with its evil train, the other, meekness with its Christian graces. The Comte de Vandenesse read the history of his life again in Marie-Angélique de Granville.

In thus choosing for wife a young girl in her fresh innocence and purity, he had made up his mind beforehand, as befitted a man old in everything but years, to unite paternal with conjugal affection. He was conscious that in him politics and society had blighted feeling, and that he had only the dregs of a used-up life to offer in exchange for one in the bloom of youth. The flowers of spring would be matched with winter frosts, hoary experience with a saucy, impulsive waywardness. Having thus impartially taken stock of his position, he intrenched himself in his married quarters with an ample store of provisions. Indulgence and trust were his two sheet-anchors. Mothers with marriageable daughters ought to look out for men of this stamp, men with brains to act as protecting divinity, with worldly wisdom to diagnose like a surgeon, and with experience to take a mother's place in warding off evil. These are the three cardinal virtues in matrimony.

The refinements and luxuries to which his habits as a man of fashion and of pleasure had accustomed Félix, his training in affairs of State, the insight of a life alternately devoted to action, reflection, and literature; all the resources, in short, at his command were applied intelligently to work out his wife's happiness.

Marie-Angélique passed at once from the maternal purgatory to the wedded paradise prepared for her by Félix in their house in the Rue du Rocher, where every trifle breathed of distinction at the same time that the conventions of fashion were not allowed to interfere with that gracious spontaneity natural to warm young hearts. She began by enjoying to the full the merely material pleasures of life, her husband for two years acting as major-domo. Félix expounded to his wife very gradually and with great tact the facts of life, initiated her by degrees into the mysteries of the best society, taught her the genealogies of all families of rank, instructed her in the ways of the world, directed her in the arts of dress and conversation, took her to all the theatres, and put her through a course of literature and history. He carried out this education with the assiduity of a lover, a father, a master, and a husband combined; but with a wise discretion he allowed neither amusement nor studies to undermine his wife's faith. In short, he acquitted himself of his task in a masterly manner, and had the gratification of seeing his pupil, at the end of four years, one of the most charming and striking women of her time.

Marie-Angélique's feelings toward her husband were precisely such as he wished to inspire—true friendship, lively gratitude, sisterly affection, with a dash of wifely fondness on occasion, not passing the due limits of dignity and self-respect. She was a good mother to her child.

Thus Félix, without any appearance of coercion, attached his wife to himself by all possible ties, reckoning on the force of habit to keep his heaven cloudless. Only men practiced in worldly arts and who have run the gamut of disillusion in politics and love have the knowledge necessary for acting on this system. Félix found in it, also, the pleasure which painters, authors, and great architects take in their work, while in addition to the artistic delight in creation he had the satisfaction of contemplating the result and admiring in his wife a woman of polished but unaffected manners and an unforced wit, a maiden and a mother, modestly attractive, unfettered and yet bound.

The history of a happy household is like that of a prosperous state; it can be summed up in half a dozen words, and gives no scope for fine writing. Moreover, as the only explanation of happiness is the fact that it exists, these four years present nothing but the gray wash of an eternal love-

making, insipid as manna, and as exciting as the romance of
Astræa.

In 1833, however, this edifice of happiness, so carefully
put together by Félix, was on the point of falling to the
ground ; the foundations had been sapped without his knowledge. The fact is the heart of a woman of five-and-twenty
is not that of a girl of eighteen, any more than the heart of a
woman of forty is that of one ten years younger. A woman's
life has four epochs and each epoch creates a new woman.
Vandenesse was certainly not ignorant of the laws which determine this development, induced by our modern habits, but
he neglected to apply them in his own case. Thus the sound-
est grammarian may be caught tripping when he turns author ;
the greatest general on the field of battle, under stress of fire,
and at the mercy of the accidents of the ground, will cast to
the winds a theoretic rule of military science. The man
whose action habitually bears the stamp of his mind is a
genius, but the greatest genius is not always equal to himself,
or he would cease to be human.

Four years had passed of unruffled calm, four years of tuneful
concert without one jarring note. The countess, under these
influences, felt her nature expanding like a healthy plant in
good soil under the warm kisses of a sun shining in unclouded
azure, and she now began to question her heart. The crisis
in her life, which this tale is to unfold, would be unintelligi-
ble but for some explanations which may perhaps extenuate
in the eyes of women the guilt of this young countess, happy
wife and happy mother, who at first sight might seem inexcusable.

Life is the result of a balance between two opposing forces ;
the absence of either is injurious to the creature. Vandenesse,
in piling up satisfaction, had quenched desire, that lord of the
universe, at whose disposal lie vast stores of moral energy.
Extreme heat, extreme suffering, unalloyed happiness, like all
abstract principles, reign over a barren desert. They demand

solitude, and will suffer no existence but their own. Vandenesse was not a woman, and it is women only who know the art of giving variety to a state of bliss. Hence their coquetry, their coldness, their tremors, their tempers, and that ingenuous battery of unreason, by which they demolish to-day what yesterday they found entirely satisfactory. Constancy in a man may pall, in a woman never. Vandenesse was too thoroughly good-hearted to wantonly plague the woman he loved ; the heaven into which he plunged her could not be too ardent or too cloudless. The problem of perpetual felicity is one the solution of which is reserved for another and higher world. Here below, even the most inspired of poets do not fail to bore their readers when they attempt to sing of Paradise. The rock on which Dante split was to be the ruin also of Vandenesse : all honor to a desperate courage !

His wife began at last to find so well-regulated an Eden a little monotonous. The perfect happiness of Eve in her terrestrial paradise produced in her the nausea which comes from living too much on sweets. A longing seized her, as it seized Rivarol on reading Florian, to come across some wolf in the sheepfold. This, it appears, has been the meaning in all ages of that symbolical serpent to whom the first woman made advances, some day no doubt when she was feeling bored. The moral of this may not commend itself to certain Protestants who take Genesis more seriously than the Jews themselves, but the situation of Mme. de Vandenesse requires no biblical images to explain it. She was conscious of a force within, which found no exercise. She was happy, but her happiness caused her no pangs ; it was placid and uneventful ; she was not haunted by the dread of losing it. It arrived every morning with the same smile and sunshine, the same soft words. Not a zephyr's breath wrinkled this calm expanse ; she longed for a ripple on the glassy surface.

There was something childish in all this, which may partly excuse her ; but society is no more lenient in its judgments than was the Jehovah of Genesis. The countess was quite enough woman of the world now to know how improper these feelings were, and nothing would have induced her to confide them to her "darling husband." This was the most impassioned epithet her innocence could devise, for it is given to no one to forge in cold blood that delicious language of hyperbole which love dictates to its victims at the stake. Vandenesse, pleased with this pretty reserve, applied his arts to keep his wife within the temperate zone of wedded fervor. Moreover, this model husband wanted to be loved for himself, and judged unworthy of an honorable man those tricks of the trade which might have imposed upon his wife or awakened her feeling. He would owe nothing to the expedients of wealth. The Comtesse Marie would smile to see a shabby turn-out in the Bois, and turn her eyes complacently to her own elegant equipage and the horses which, harnessed in the English fashion, moved with very free action and kept their distance perfectly. Félix would not stoop to gather the fruit of all his labors; his lavish expenditure, and the good taste which guided it, were accepted as a matter of course by his wife, ignorant that to them she owed her perfect immunity from vexations or wounding comparisons. It was the same throughout. Kindness is not without its rocks ahead. People are apt to put it down to an easy temper, and seldom recognize it as the secret striving of a generous nature; whilst, on the other hand, the ill-natured get credit for all the evil they refrain from.

About this period Mme. de Vandenesse was sufficiently drilled in the practices of society to abandon the insignificant part of timid supernumerary, all eyes and ears, which even Grisi is said, once on a time, to have played in the choruses of the La Scala theatre. The young countess felt herself equal to the part of *prima donna* and made some essays in it. To the great satisfaction of Félix, she began to take her share in conversation. Sharp repartees and shrewd reflections, which were the fruit of talks with her husband, brought her into notice, and this success emboldened her. Vandenesse, whose wife had always been allowed to be pretty, was charmed when she showed herself clever also. On her return from the ball or concert or rout where she had shone, Marie, as she laid aside her finery, would turn to Félix and say with a little air of prim delight, "Please, have I done well to-night?"

At this stage the countess began to rouse jealousy in the breasts of certain women, amongst whom was the Marquise de Listomère, her husband's sister, who hitherto had patronized Marie, looking on her as a good foil for her own charms. Poor innocent victim! A countess with the sacred name of Marie, beautiful, witty, and good, a musician and not a flirt— no wonder society whetted its teeth! Félix de Vandenesse numbered amongst his acquaintance several women who— although their connection with him was broken off, whether by their own doing or his—were by no means indifferent to his marriage. When these ladies saw in Marie de Vandenesse a sheepish little woman with red hands, rather silent, and to all appearance stupid also, they considered themselves sufficiently avenged.

Then came the disasters of July, 1830, and for the space of two years society was broken up. Rich people spent the troubled interval on their estates or traveling in Europe ; and the salons hardly reopened before 1833. The Faubourg Saint-Germain sulked, but it admitted as neutral ground a few houses, amongst others that of the Ambassador of Austria. In these select rooms legitimist society and the new society met, represented by their most fashionable leaders. Vandenesse, though strong in his convictions and attached by a thousand ties of sympathy and gratitude to the exiled family, did not feel himself bound to follow his party in its stupid fanaticism. At a critical moment he had performed his duty at the risk of life by breasting the flood of popular fury in order to propose a compromise. He could afford therefore to take his wife into a society which could not possibly expose his good faith to suspicion.

Vandenesse's former friends hardly recognized the young bride in the graceful, sparkling, and gentle countess, who took her place with all the breeding of the high-born lady. Mmes. d'Espard and de Manerville, Lady Dudley, and other ladies of less distinction felt the stirring of a brood of vipers in their hearts; the dulcet moan of angry pride piped in their ears. The happiness of Félix enraged them, and they would have given a brand-new pair of shoes to do him an ill turn. In place of showing hostility to the countess, these amiable intriguers buzzed about her with protestations of extreme friendliness and sang her praises to their male friends. Félix, who perfectly understood their little game, kept his eye upon their intercourse with Marie and warned her to be upon her guard. Divining, every one of them, the anxiety which their assiduity caused the count, they could not pardon his suspicions. They redoubled their flattering attentions to their rival and in this way contrived an immense success for her, to the disgust of the Marquise de Listomère, who was quite in the dark about it all. The Comtesse Félix de Vandenesse was everywhere pointed to as the most charming and brilliant woman in Paris; and Marie's other sister-in-law, the Marquise Charles de Vandenesse, endured many mortifications from the confusion produced by the similarity of name and the comparisons to which it gave rise. For, though the marquise was also a handsome and clever woman, the countess had the advantage of her in being twelve years younger, a point of which her rivals did not fail to make use. They well knew what bitterness the success of the countess would infuse into her relations with her sisters-in-law, who, indeed, were most chilling and disagreeable to Marie-Angélique in her triumph.

And so danger lurked in the family, enmity in friendship. It is well known how the literature of that day tried to over-

come the indifference of the public, engrossed in the exciting
political drama, by the production of more or less Byronic
works, exclusively occupied with illicit love affairs. Conjugal
infidelity furnished at this time the sole material of magazines,
novels, and plays. This perennial theme came more than
ever into fashion. The lover, that nightmare of the husband,
was everywhere, except perhaps in the family circle, which
saw less of him during that reign of the middle-class than at
any other period. When the streets are ablaze with light and
"Stop thief" is shouted from every window, it is hardly the
moment robbers choose to be abroad. If, in the course of
those years, so fruitful in civic, political, and moral upheavals,
an occasional domestic misadventure took place, it was exceptional and attracted less notice than it would have done under
the Restoration. Nevertheless, women talked freely among
themselves of a subject in which both lyric and dramatic
poetry then reveled. The lover, that being so rare and so
bewitching, was a favorite theme. The few intrigues which
came to light supplied matter for such conversation, which,
then as ever, was confined to women of unexceptionable life.
The repugnance to this sort of talk shown by women who
have a stolen joy to conceal is indeed a noteworthy fact. They
are the prudes of society, cautious, and even bashful; their
attitude is one of perpetual appeal for silence or pardon. On
the other hand, when a woman takes pleasure in hearing of
such disasters and is curious about the temptations which lead
to them, you may be sure she is halting at the cross-roads,
uncertain and hesitating.

During this winter the Comtesse de Vandenesse caught
the distant roll of society's thunder, and the rising storm
whistled about her ears. Her so-called friends, whose repu-
tations were under the safeguard of exalted rank and position,
drew many sketches of the irresistible gallant for her benefit,
and dropped into her heart burning words about love, the one
solution of life for women, the master passion, according to

Mme. de Staël, who did not speak without experience. When the countess, in a friendly conclave, naïvely asked why a lover was so different from a husband, not one of these women failed to reply in such a way as to pique her curiosity, haunt her imagination, touch her heart, and interest her mind. They burned to see Vandenesse in trouble.

"With one's husband, dear, one simply rubs along; with a lover it's life," said her sister-in-law, the Marquise de Vandenesse.

"Marriage, my child, is our purgatory, love is paradise," said Lady Dudley.

"Don't believe her," cried Mlle. des Touches, "it's hell!"

"Yes, but a hell with love in it," observed the Marquise de Rochefide. "There may be more satisfaction in suffering than in an easy life. Look at the martyrs!"

"Little simpleton," said the Marquise d'Espard, "in marriage we live, so to speak, our own life; love is living in another."

"In short, a lover is the forbidden fruit, and that's enough for me!" laughingly spoke the pretty Moïna de Saint-Héren.

When there were no diplomatic at homes, or balls given by wealthy foreigners, such as Lady Dudley or the Princesse de Galathionne, the countess went almost every evening after the opera to one of the few aristocratic drawing-rooms still open —whether that of the Marquise d'Espard, Mme. de Listomère, Mlle. des Touches, the Comtesse de Montcornet, or the Vicomtesse de Grandlieu. Never did she leave these gatherings without some seeds of evil scattered in her soul. She heard talk about "completing her life," an expression much in vogue then, or about being "understood," another word to which women attach marvelous meanings. She would return home uneasy, pensive, dreamy, and curious. Her life seemed somehow impoverished, but she had not yet gone so far as to feel it entirely barren.

CHAPTER IV.

A MAN OF NOTE.

The most lively, but also the most mixed, company to be
found in any of the houses where Mme. de Vandenesse
visited was decidedly that which met at the Comtesse de
Montcornet's. She was a charming little woman who opened
her doors to distinguished artists, commercial princes, and
celebrated literary men ; but the tests to which she submitted
them before admission were so rigorous that the most exclusive need not fear rubbing up against persons of an inferior
grade ; the most unapproachable were safe from pollution.
During the winter, society (which never loses its rights, and
at all costs will be amused) began to rally again, and a few
drawing-rooms—including those of Mmes. d'Espard and de
Listomère, of Mlle. des Touches, and of the Duchesse de
Grandlieu—had picked up recruits from among the latest
celebrities in art, science, literature, and politics. At a concert given by the Comtesse de Montcornet, toward the end of
the winter, Raoul Nathan, a well-known name in literature
and politics, made his entry, introduced by Émile Blondet,
a very brilliant but also very indolent writer. Blondet too
was a celebrity, but only among the initiated few ; much
made of by the critics, he was unknown to the general public.
Blondet was perfectly aware of this, and in general was a man
of few illusions. In regard to fame, he said, among other
disparaging remarks, that it was a poison best taken in small
doses.

Raoul Nathan had a long struggle before emerging to the
surface. Having reached it, he had at once made capital out
of that sudden craze for external form then distinguishing certain exquisites, who swore by the Middle Ages, and were hu-

morously known as " young France." He adopted the eccentricities of genius, and enrolled himself among these worshipers of art, whose intentions at least we cannot but admire, since nothing is more absurd than the dress of a Frenchman of the nineteenth century, and courage was needed to change it. Raoul, to do him justice, has something unusual and fantastic in his person, which seems to demand a setting. His enemies or his friends—there is little to choose between them—are agreed that nothing in the world so well matches the inner Nathan as the outer. He would probably look even more remarkable if left to nature than he is when touched by art. His worn and wasted features suggest a wrestling with spirits, good or evil. His face has some likeness to that which German painters give to the dead Christ, and bears innumerable traces of a constant struggle between weak human nature and the powers on high. But the deep hollows of his cheeks, the knobs on his craggy and furrowed skull, the cavities round his eyes and temples, point to nothing weak in the constitution. There is remarkable solidity about the tough tissues and prominent bones; and though the skin, tanned by excess, sticks to them as though parched by some fire within, it none the less covers a massive framework. He is tall and thin. His long hair, which always needs brushing, aims at effect. He is a Byron, badly groomed and badly put together, with legs like a heron's, congested knees, an exaggeratedly small waist, a hand with muscles of whip-cord, the grip of a crab's claw, and lean, nervous fingers.

Raoul's eyes are Napoleonic, blue and soul-piercing; his nose is sensitive and finely chiseled, his mouth charming and adorned with teeth white enough to excite a woman's envy. There is life and fire in the head, genius on the brow. Raoul belongs to the small number of men who would not pass unnoticed in the street, and who, in a drawing-room, at once form a centre of light, drawing all eyes. He attracts attention by his *négligé*, if one may borrow from Molière the word used by

Eliante to describe personal slovenliness. His clothes look as though they had been pulled about, frayed and crumpled on purpose to harmonize with his countenance. He habitually thrusts one hand into his open vest in the pose which Girodet's portrait of Chateaubriand has made famous, but not so much for the sake of copying Chateaubriand (he would disdain to copy any one) as to take the stiffness out of his shirt-front. His tie becomes all in a moment a mere wisp, from a trick he has of throwing back his head with a sudden convulsive movement, like that of a race-horse champing its bit and tossing its head in the effort to break loose from bridle and curb. His long, pointed beard is very different from that of the dandy, combed, brushed, scented, sleek, shaped like a fan or cut into a peak ; Nathan's is left entirely to nature. His hair, caught in by his coat-collar and tie, and lying thick upon his shoulders, leaves a grease spot wherever it rests. His dry, stringy hands are innocent of nail-brush or the luxury of a lemon. There are even journalists who declare that only on rare occasions is their grimy skin laved in baptismal waters.

In a word, this awe-inspiring Raoul is a caricature. He moves in a jerky way, as though propelled by some faulty machinery ; and when walking the boulevards of Paris he offends all sense of order by impetuous zigzags and unexpected halts, which bring him into collision with peaceful citizens as they stroll along. His conversation, full of caustic humor and stinging epigrams, imitates the gait of his body ; of a sudden it will drop the tone of fury to become, for no apparent reason, gracious, dreamy, soothing, and gentle ; then come unaccountable pauses or mental somersaults, which at times grow fatiguing. In society he does not conceal an unblushing awkwardness, a scorn of convention, and an attitude of criticism toward things usually held in respect there, which make him objectionable to plain people, as well as to those who strive to keep up the traditions of old-world courtliness. Yet, after all, he is an oddity, like a Chinese image, and women have a weakness for such things. Beside, with women he often puts on an air of elaborate suavity, and seems to take a pleasure in making them forget his grotesque exterior, and in vanquishing their antipathy. This is a salve to his vanity, his self-esteem, and his pride.

"Why do you behave so?" said the Marquise de Vandenesse to him one day.

"Are not pearls found in oyster shells?" was the pompous reply.

To some one else, who put a similar question, he answered—

"If I made myself agreeable to every one, what should I have left for her whom I design to honor supremely?"

Raoul Nathan carries into his intellectual life the irregularity which he has made his badge. Nor is the device misleading: like poor girls, who go out as maids-of-all-work in humble homes, he can turn his hand to anything. He began with serious criticism, but soon became convinced that this was a losing trade. His articles, he said, cost as much as books. The profits of the theatre attracted him, but, incapable of the slow, sustained labor involved in putting anything on the boards, he was driven to ally himself with du Bruel, who worked up his ideas and converted them into light paying pieces with plenty of humor, and composed in view of some particular actor or actress. Between them they unearthed Florine, a popular actress.

Ashamed, however, of this Siamese-like union, Nathan unaided, brought out at the Theatre-Français a great drama, which fell with all the honors of war amidst salvoes from the artillery of the press. In his youth he had already tried the theatre which represents the fine traditions of the French drama with a splendid romantic play in the style of "Pinto," and this at a time when classicism held undisputed sway. The result was that the Odéon became for three nights the scene of such disorder that the piece had to be stopped. The second play, no less then the first, seemed to many people a masterpiece, and it won for him, though only within the select world of judges and connoisseurs, a far higher reputation than the light remunerative pieces at which he worked with others.

" One more such failure," said Émile Blondet, "and you will be immortal."

But Nathan, instead of sticking to this arduous path, was driven by stress of poverty to fall back upon more profitable work, such as the production of spectacular pieces or of an eighteenth-century powder and patches vaudeville and the adaptation of popular novels to the stage. Nevertheless, he was still counted as a man of great ability, whose last word had not yet been heard. He made an excursion also into pure literature and published three novels, not reckoning those which he kept going in the press, like fishes in an aquarium. As often happens, when a writer has stuff in him for only one work, the first of these three was a brilliant success. Its author rashly put it at once in the front rank of his works as an artistic creation, and lost no opportunity of getting it puffed as the " finest book of the period," the " novel of the century."

Yet he complained loudly of the exigencies of art, and did as much as any man toward having it accepted as the one standard for all kinds of creative work—painting, sculpture, literature, architecture. He had begun by perpetrating a book of verse, which won him a place in the pleiad of poets of the day, and which contained one obscure poem that was greatly admired. Compelled by straitened circumstances to go on producing, he turned from the theatre to the press, and from the press back to the theatre, breaking up and scattering his powers, but with unshaken confidence in his inspiration. He did not suffer, therefore, from lack of a publisher for his fame, differing in this from certain celebrities, whose flickering flame is kept from extinction by the titles of books still in

the future, for which a public will be a more pressing necessity
than a new edition.

Nathan came near to being a genius, and, had destiny
crowned his ambition by marching him to the scaffold, he
would have been justified in striking his forehead after André
de Chénier. The sudden accession to power of a dozen
authors, professors, metaphysicians, and historians fired him
with emulation, and he regretted not having devoted his pen
to politics rather than to literature. He believed himself superior to these upstarts, who had foisted themselves on to the
party-machine during the troubles of 1830–3 and whose fortune now filled him with consuming envy. He belonged to
the type of man who covets everything and looks on all success as a fraud on himself, who is always stumbling on some
luminous track but settles down nowhere, drawing all the
while on the tolerance of his neighbors. At this moment he
was traveling from Saint-Simonism to Republicanism, which
might serve, perhaps, as a stage to Ministerialism. His eye
swept every corner for some bone to pick, some safe shelter
whence he might bark beyond the reach of kicks, and make
himself a terror to the passers-by. He had, however, the
mortification of finding himself not taken seriously by the
great de Marsay, then at the head of affairs, who had a low
opinion of authors as lacking in what Richelieu called the
logical spirit, or rather in coherence of ideas. Beside, no
minister could have failed to reckon on Raoul's constant
pecuniary difficulties which, sooner or later, would drive him
into the position of accepting rather than imposing conditions.

Raoul's real and studiously suppressed character accords
with that which he shows to the public. He is carried away
by his own acting, declaims with great eloquence, and could
not be more self-centred were he, like Louis XIV., the State
in person. None knows better how to play at sentiment or
to deck himself out in a shoddy greatness. The grace of
moral beauty and the language of self-respect are at his com-

mand, he is a very Alceste in pose, while acting like Philinte. His selfishness ambles along under cover of this painted cardboard, and not seldom attains the end he has in view. Excessively idle, he never works except under the prick of necessity. Continuous labor applied to the construction of a lasting fabric is beyond his conception; but in a paroxysm of rage, the result of wounded vanity, or in some crisis precipitated by his creditors, he will leap the Eurotas and perform miracles of mental forestallment; after which, worn out and amazed at his own fertility, he falls back into the enervating dissipations of Paris life. Does necessity once more threaten, he has no strength to meet it; he sinks a step and traffics with his honor. Impelled by a false idea of his talents and his future, founded on the rapid rise of one of his old comrades (one of the few cases of administrative ability brought to light by the Revolution of July), he tries to regain his footing by taking liberties with his friends, which are nothing short of a moral outrage, though they remain buried among the skeletons of private life, without a word of comment or blame.

His heart devoid of nicety, his shameless hand, hail-fellow-well-met with every vice, every degradation, every treachery, every party, have placed him as much beyond reach of attack as a constitutional king. The peccadillo, which would raise hue and cry after a man of high character, counts for nothing in him; while conduct bordering on grossness is barely noticed. In making his excuses people find their own. The very man who would fain despise him shakes him by the hand, fearing to need his help. So numerous are his friends that he would prefer enemies. This surface good-nature which captivates a new acquaintance and is no bar to treachery, which knows no scruple and is never at fault for an excuse, which makes an outcry at the wound which it condones, is one of the most distinctive features of the journalist. This *camaraderie* (the word is a stroke of genius) corrodes the noblest minds; it eats into their pride like rust, kills the germ of great deeds, and lends a sanction to moral cowardice. There are men who, by exacting this general slackness of conscience, get themselves absolved for playing the traitor and the turn-coat. Thus it is that the most enlightened portion of the nation becomes the least worthy of respect.

From the literary point of view Nathan is deficient in style and information. Like most young aspirants in literature he gives out to-day what he learned yesterday. He has neither the time nor the patience to make an author. He does not use his own eyes, but can pick up from others, and, while he fails in producing a vigorously constructed plot, he sometimes covers this defect by the fervor he throws into it. He "went in" for passion, to use a slang word, because there is no limit to the variety of modes in which passion may express itself, while the task of genius is to sift out from these various expressions the element in each which will appeal to every one as natural. His heroes do not stir the imagination; they are magnified individuals, exciting only a passing sympathy; they have no connection with the wider interests of life, and therefore stand for nothing but themselves. Yet the author saves himself by means of a ready wit and of those lucky hits which billiard-players call "flukes." He is the best man for a flying shot at the ideas which swoop down upon Paris, or which Paris starts. His teeming brain is not his own, it belongs to the period. He lives upon the event of the day, and, in order to get all he can from it, exaggerates its bearing. In short, we miss the accent of truth, his words ring false; there is something of the juggler in him, as Count Félix said. One feels that his pen has dipped in the ink of an actress' dressing-room.

In Nathan we find an image of the literary youth of the day, with their sham greatness and real poverty; he represents their irregular charm and their terrible falls, their life of seething cataracts, sudden reverses, and unlooked-for triumphs. He is a true child of this jealousy-ridden age, in which a thousand personal rivalries, cloaking themselves under the name of schools, make profit out of their failures by feeding fat with them a hydra-headed anarchy; an age which expects fortune without work, glory without talent, and success without effort, but which, after many a revolt and skirmish, is at last brought by its vices to swell the civil list, in submission to the powers that be. When so many young ambitions start on foot to meet at the same goal, there must be competing wills, frightful destitution, and a relentless struggle. In this merciless combat it is the fiercest or the adroitest selfishness which wins. The lesson is not lost on an admiring world; spite of bawling, as Molière would say, it acquits and follows suit.

When, in his capacity of opponent to the new dynasty, Raoul was introduced to Mme. de Montcornet's drawing-room his spacious greatness was at its height. He was recognized as the political critic of the de Marsays, the Rastignacs, and the la Roche-Hugons, who constituted the party in power. His sponsor, Émile Blondet, handicapped by his fatal indecision and dislike of action where his own affairs were concerned, stuck to his trade of scoffer and took sides with no party, while on good terms with all. He was the friend of Raoul, of Rastignac, and of Montcornet.

"You are a political triangle," said de Marsay, with a laugh, when he met him at the opera; "that geometrical form is the peculiar property of the deity, who can afford to be idle; but a man who wants to get on should adopt a curve, which is the shortest road in politics."

Beheld from afar, Raoul Nathan was a resplendent meteor. The fashion of the day justified his manner and appearance. His pose as a Republican gave him, for the moment, that puritan ruggedness assumed by champions of the popular cause, men whom Nathan in his heart derided. This is not without attraction for women, who love to perform prodigies, such as shattering rocks, melting an iron will. Raoul's moral costume, therefore, was in keeping with the external. He was bound to be, and he was, for this Eve, listless in her paradise of the Rue du Rocher, the insidious serpent, bright to the eye and flattering to the ear, with magnetic gaze and graceful motion, who ruined the first woman.

Marie, on seeing Raoul, at once felt that inward shock, the violence of which is almost terrifying. This would-be great man, by a mere glance, sent a thrill right through to her heart, causing a delicious flutter there. The regal mantle which fame had for the moment draped on Nathan's shoulders dazzled this simple-minded woman. When tea came Marie left the group of chattering women, among whom she had stood silent since the appearance of this wonderful being—a fact which did not escape her so-called friends. The countess drew near the ottoman in the centre of the room where Raoul was perorating. She remained standing, her arm linked in that of Mme. Octave de Camps, an excellent woman, who kept the secret of the nervous quivering by which Marie betrayed her strong emotion. Despite the sweet magic distilled from the eye of the woman who loves or is startled into self-betrayal, Raoul was just then entirely occupied with a regular display of fireworks. He was far too busy letting off epigrams like rockets, winding and unwinding indictments like catherine-wheels, and tracing blazing portaits in lines of fire, to notice the naïve admiration of a little Eve, lost in the crowd of women surrounding him. The love of novelty which would bring Paris flocking to the Zoological Gardens, if a unicorn had been brought there from those famous Mountains of the Moon, virgin yet of European tread, intoxicates minds of a lower stamp, as much as it saddens the truly wise. Raoul was enraptured and far too much engrossed with women in general to pay attention to one woman in particular.

" Take care, dear, you had better come away," her fair companion, sweetest of women, whispered to Marie.

The countess turned to her husband and, with one of those

speaking glances which husbands are sometimes slow in interpreting, begged for his arm. Félix led her away.

"Well, you are in luck, my good friend," said Mme. d'Espard in Raoul's ear. "You've done execution in more than one quarter to-night, and, best of all, with that charming countess who has just left us so abruptly."

"Do you know what the Marquise d'Espard meant?" asked Raoul of Blondet, repeating the great lady's remark, when almost all the other guests had departed, between one and two in the morning.

"Why, yes, I have just heard that the Comtesse de Vandenesse has fallen wildly in love with you. Lucky dog!"

"I did not see her," said Raoul.

"Ah! but you will see her, you rascal," said Émile Blondet, laughing. "Lady Dudley has invited you to her great ball with the very purpose of bringing about a meeting."

Raoul and Blondet left together, and joining Rastignac, who offered them a place in his carriage, the three made merry over this conjunction of an eclectic under-secretary of State with a fierce Republican and a political skeptic.

"Suppose we sup at the expense of law and order?" said Blondet, who had a fancy for reviving the old-fashioned supper.

Rastignac took them to Véry's, and dismissed his carriage; the three then sat down to table and set themselves to pull to pieces their contemporaries amidst Rabelaisian laughter. During the course of supper Rastignac and Blondet urged their counterfeit opponent not to neglect the magnificent opportunity thrown in his way. The story of Marie de Vandenesse was caricatured by these two profligates, who applied the scalpel of epigram and the keen edge of mockery to that transparent childhood, that happy marriage. Blondet congratulated Raoul on having found a woman who so far had been guilty only of execrable red-chalk drawings and feeble water-color landscapes, of embroidering slippers for her husband, and performing sonatas with a most lady-like absence of passion ; a woman who had been tied for eighteen years to her mother's apron-strings, pickled in devotion, trained by Vandenesse, and cooked to a turn by marriage for the palate of love. At the third bottle of champagne Raoul Nathan became more expansive than he had ever shown himself before.

"My dear friends," he said, "you know my relations with Florine, you know my life, you will not be surprised to hear me confess that I have never yet seen the color of a countess' love. It has often been a humiliating thought to me that only in poetry could I find a Beatrice, a Laura! A pure and noble woman is like a spotless conscience, she raises us in our own estimation. Elsewhere we may be soiled, with her we keep our honor, pride, and purity. Elsewhere life is a wild frenzy, with her we breathe the peace, the freshness, the bloom of the oasis."

"Come, come, my good soul," said Rastignac, "shift the prayer of Moses on to the high notes, as Paganini does."

Raoul sat speechless with fixed and besotted eyes. At last he opened his mouth.

"This beast of a 'prentice minister does not understand me!"

Thus, whilst the poor Eve of the Rue du Rocher went to bed, swathed in shame, terrified at the delight which had filled her while listening to this poetic pretender, hovering between the stern voice of gratitude to Vandenesse and the flattering tongue of the serpent, these three shameless spirits trampled on the tender white blossoms of her opening love. Ah! if women knew how cynical those men can be behind their backs, who show themselves all meekness and cajolery when by their side! if they knew how they mock their idols! Fresh, lovely, and timid creature, whose charms lie at the mercy of some graceless buffoon! And yet she triumphs! The more the veils are rent, the clearer her beauty shines.

Marie at this moment was comparing Raoul and Félix, all-ignorant of the danger to her heart in such a process. No better contrast could be found to the robust and unconventional Raoul than Félix de Vandenesse, with his clothes fitting like a glove, the finish of a fine lady in his person, his charming natural ease (*disinvoltura*), combined with a touch of English refinement, picked up from Lady Dudley. A contrast like this pleases the fancy of a woman, ever ready to fly from one extreme to another. The countess was too well-principled and pious not to forbid her thoughts dwelling on Raoul, and next day, in the heart of her paradise, she took herself to task for base ingratitude.

"What do you think of Raoul Nathan?" she asked her husband during lunch.

"He is a charlatan," replied the count; "one of those volcanoes which a sprinkling of gold-dust will keep tranquil. The Comtesse de Montcornet ought not to have had him at her house."

This reply was the more galling to Marie because Félix, who knew the literary world well, supported his verdict with proofs drawn from the life of Raoul—a life of shifts, in which Florine, a well-known actress, played a large part.

"Granting the man has genius," he concluded, "he is without the patience and persistency which make genius a thing apart and sacred. He tries to impress people by assuming a position which he cannot live up to. That is not the behavior of really able men and students; if they are honorable men they stick to their own line, and don't try to hide their rags under frippery."

A woman's thought has marvelous elasticity; it may sink under a blow, to all appearance crushed, but in a given time it is up again, as though nothing had happened.

"Félix must be right," was the first thought of the countess.

Three days later, however, her mind traveled back to the tempter, allured by that sweet yet ruthless emotion which it was the mistake of Vandenesse not to have aroused. The count and countess went to Lady Dudley's great ball, where de Marsay made his last appearance in society. Two months later he died, leaving the reputation of a statesman so profound that, as Blondet said, he was unfathomable. Here Vandenesse and his wife again met Raoul Nathan, amid a concourse of people made remarkable by the number of actors in the political drama whom, to their mutual surprise, it brought together.

It was one of the chief social functions in the great world. The reception-rooms offered a magic picture to the eye. Flowers, diamonds, shining hair, the plunder of countless jewel-cases, every art of the toilet—all contributed to the effect. The room might be compared to one of those show hot-houses where wealthy amateurs collect the most marvelous varieties. There was the same brilliancy, the same delicacy of texture. It seemed as though the art of man would compete also with the animal world. On all sides fluttered gauze, white or painted like the wings of prettiest dragon-fly, crêpe, lace, blonde, tulle, pucked, puffed, or notched, vying in eccentricity of form with the freaks of nature in the insect tribe. There were spider's threads in gold or silver, clouds of silk, flowers which some fairy might have woven or imprisoned spirit breathed into life ; feathers, whose rich tints told of a tropical sun, drooping willow-like over haughty heads ; ropes of pearls, drapery in broad folds, ribbed or slashed, as though the genius of arabesque had presided over French millinery.

This splendor harmonized with the beauties gathered together as though to form a "keepsake." The eye roamed over a wealth of fair shoulders in every tone of white that man could conceive—some amber-tinted, others glistening like some glazed surface or glossy as satin, others, again, of a rich lustreless color which the brush of Rubens might have mixed. Then the eyes, sparkling like onyx stones or turquoises, with their dark velvet edging or fair fringes; and profiles of every contour, recalling the noblest types of different lands. There were brows lofty with pride; rounded brows, index of thought within; level brows, the seat of an indomitable will. Lastly—most bewitching of all in a scene of such studied splendor—necks and bosoms in the rich voluptuous folds, adored by George IV., or with the more delicate modeling which found favor in the eighteenth century and at the court of Louis XV.; but all, whatever the type, frankly exhibited, either without drapery or through the dainty plaited tuckers of Raphael's portraits, supreme triumph of his laborious pupils. Prettiest of feet, itching for the dance, figures yielding softly to the embrace of the waltz, roused the most apathetic to attention; murmurings of gentle voices, rustling dresses, whispering partners, vibrations of the dance, made a fantastic burden to the music.

A fairy's wand might have called forth this witchery, bewildering to the senses, the harmony of scents, the rainbow tints flashing in the crystal candelabra, the blaze of the candles, the mirrors which repeated the scene on every side. The groups of lovely women in costly attire stood out against a dark background of men, where might be observed the delicate, regular features of the aristocracy, the tawny mustache of the sedate Englishman, the gay, smiling countenance of the French noble. Every European order glittered in the room, some hanging from a collar on the breast, others dangling by the side.

To a watchful observer the scene presented more than this gaily decorated surface. It had a soul; it lived, it thought, it felt, it found expression in the hidden passions which now and again forced their way to the surface. Now it would be an interchange of malicious glances; now some fair young girl, carried away by excitement and novelty, would betray a touch of passion; jealous women talked scandal behind their fans and paid each other extravagant compliments.

Society, decked out, curled, and perfumed, abandoned itself
to that frenzy of the fête which goes to the head like the
fumes of wine. From every brow, as from every heart,
seemed to emanate sensations and thoughts, which, forming
together one potent influence, inflamed the most cold-
blooded.

It was the most exciting moment of this entrancing evening. In a corner of the gilded drawing-room, where a few
bankers, ambassadors, and retired ministers, together with
that old reprobate, Lord Dudley (an unexpected arrival),
were seated at play, Mme. Félix de Vandenesse found herself
unable to resist the impulse to enter into conversation with
Nathan. She, too, may have been yielding to that ballroom
intoxication which has wrung many a confession from the
lips of the most coy.

The sight of this splendid pageant of a world to which he
was still a stranger stung Nathan to the heart with redoubled
ambition. He looked at Rastignac, whose brother, at the
age of twenty-seven, had just been made a bishop, and whose
brother-in-law, Martial de la Roche-Hugon, held office, while
he himself was an under-secretary of State, and about to marry,
as rumor said, the only daughter of the Baron de Nucingen.
He saw among the members of the diplomatic body an obscure
writer who used to translate foreign newspapers for a journal
that passed over to the reigning dynasty after 1830; he saw
leader-writers members of the Council and professors peers of
France. And he perceived, with bitterness, that he had taken
the wrong road in preaching the overthrow of an aristocracy
which counted among its ornaments the true nobility of fortunate talent and successful scheming. Blondet, though still a
mere journalistic hack, was made much of in society, and had
it yet in his power to strike the road to fortune by means of
his intimacy with Mme. de Montcornet. Blondet, therefore,
with all his ill-luck, was a striking example in Nathan's eyes
of the importance of having friends in high places. In the

depths of his heart he resolved upon following the example of men like de Marsay, Rastignac, Blondet, and Talleyrand, the leader of the sect. He would throw conviction to the winds, paying allegiance only to accomplished facts, which he would wrest to his own advantage ; no system should be to him more than an instrument ; and on no account would he upset the balance of a society so admirably constructed, so decorative, and so consonant with nature.

" My future," he said to himself, " is in the hands of a woman belonging to the great world."

Full of this thought, the outcome of a frantic cupidity, Nathan pounced upon the Comtesse de Vandenesse like a hawk upon its prey. She was looking charming in a head-dress of marabout feathers, which produced the delicious melting effect of Lawrence's portraits, well suited to her gentle character. The fervid rhapsodies of the poet, crazed by ambition, carried the sweet creature quite off her feet. Lady Dudley, whose eye was everywhere, secured the *tête-à-tête* by handing over the Comte de Vandenesse to Mme. de Manerville. It was the first time the parted lovers had spoken face to face since their rupture. The woman, strong in the habit of ascendency, caught Félix in the toils of a coquettish controversy, with plenty of blushing confidences, regrets deftly cast like flowers at his feet, and recriminations, where self-defense was intended to stimulate reproach.

Whilst her husband's former mistress was raking among the ashes of dead joys to find some spark of life, Mme. Félix de Vandenesse experienced those violent heart-throbs which assail a woman with the certainty of going astray and treading forbidden paths. These emotions are not without fascination, and rouse many dormant faculties. Now, as in the days of Blue Beard, all women love to use the blood-stained key, that splendid mythological symbol which is one of Perrault's glories.

The dramatist, who knew his Shakespeare, unfolded the

4

tale of his hardships, described his struggle with men and things, opened up glimpses of his unstable success, his political genius wasting in obscurity, his life unblessed by any generous affection. Without a word directly to that effect, he conveyed to this gracious lady the suggestion that she might play for him the noble part of Rebecca in "Ivanhoe," might love and shelter him. Not a syllable overstepped the pure regions of sentiment. The blue of the forget-me-not, the white of the lily, are not more pure than were his flowers of rhetoric and the things signified by them ; the radiance of a seraph lighted the brow of this artist, who might yet utilize his discourse with a publisher. He acquitted himself well of the serpent's part, and flashed before the eyes of the countess the tempting colors of the fatal fruit. Marie left the ball consumed by remorse, which was akin to hope, thrilled by compliments flattering to her vanity, and agitated to the remotest corner of her heart. Her very goodness was her snare ; she could not resist her own pity for the unfortunate.

Whether Mme. de Manerville brought Vandenesse to the room where his wife was talking with Nathan, whether he came there of his own accord, or whether the conversation had roused in him a slumbering pain, the fact remains, whatever the cause, that, when his wife came to ask for his arm, she found him gloomy and abstracted. The countess was afraid she had been seen. As soon as she was alone with Félix in the carriage, she threw him a smile full of meaning, and began—

"Was not that Madame de Manerville with whom you were talking, dear?"

Félix had not yet gotten clear of the thorny ground, through which his wife's neat little attack marched him, when the carriage stopped at their door. It was the first stratagem prompted by love. Marie was delighted to have gotten the better of a man whom till then she thought so superior. She tasted for the first time the joy of victory at a critical moment.

CHAPTER V.

FLORINE.

In a passage between the Rue Basse-du-Rempart and the Rue Neuve-des-Mathurins, Raoul had one or two bare, cold rooms on the fourth floor of a thin, ugly house. This was his abode for the general public, for literary novices, creditors, intruders, and the whole race of bores who were not allowed to cross the threshold of private life. His real home, which was the stage of his wider life and public appearances, he made with Florine, a second-rate actress who, ten years before, had been raised to the rank of a great dramatic artist by the combined efforts of Nathan's friends, the newspaper critics, and a few literary men.

For ten years Raoul had been so closely attached to this woman, that he spent half his life in her house, taking his meals there whenever he had no engagements outside nor friends to entertain. Florine, to a finished depravity, added a very pretty wit, which constant intercourse with artists and daily practice had developed and sharpened. Wit is generally supposed to be a rare quality among actors. It seems an easy inference that those who spend their lives in bringing the outside to perfection should have little left with which to furnish the interior. But any one who considers the small number of actors and actresses in a century, compared with the quantity of dramatic authors and attractive women produced by the same population, will see reason to dispute this notion. It rests, in fact, on the common assumption that personal feeling must disappear in the imitative expression of passion, whereas the real fact is that intelligence, memory, and imagination are the only powers employed in such imitation. Great artists are those who, according to Napoleon's definition, can intercept at will the communication established by nature between sensation and thought.　Molière and Talma loved more passionately in their old age than is usual with ordinary mortals.

Florine's position forced her to listen to the talk of alert and calculating journalists and to the prophecies of garrulous literary men, while keeping an eye on certain politicians who used her house as a means of profiting by the sallies of her guests.　The mixture of angel and demon which she embodied made her a fitting hostess for these profligates, who reveled in her impudence and found unfailing amusement in the perversity of her mind and heart.

Her house, enriched with offerings from admirers, displayed in its exaggerated magnificence an entire regardlessness of cost.　Women of this type set a purely arbitrary value on their possessions; in a fit of temper they will smash a fan or a scent-bottle worthy of a queen, and they will be inconsolable if anything happens to a ten-franc basin which their lap-dogs drink out of.　The dining-room, crowded with rare and costly gifts, may serve as a specimen of the regal and insolent profusion of the establishment.

The whole room, including the ceiling, was covered with carved oak, left unstained, and set off with lines of dull gold. In the panels, encircled by groups of children playing with chimeras, were placed the lights, which illuminated here a rough sketch by Decamps; there a plaster angel holding a basin of holy water, a present from Antonin Moine; further on a dainty picture of Eugène Devéria; the sombre figure of some Spanish alchemist by Louis Boulanger; an autograph letter from Lord Byron to Caroline in an ebony frame, carved by Elschoet, with a letter of Napoleon to Josephine to match it.　The things were arranged without any view to symmetry, and yet with a sort of unstudied art; the whole effect took one, as it were, by storm.　There was a union of carelessness and a desire to please, such as can only be found in the homes of artists.　The exquisitely carved mantelpiece was bare except for a whimsical Florentine statue in ivory, attributed to

Michael Angelo, representing a Pan discovering a woman disguised as a young herd, the original of which is at the Treasury in Vienna. On either side of this hung an iron candelabrum, the work of some Renaissance chisel. A Boule timepiece on a tortoise-shell bracket, lacquered with copper arabesques, glittered in the middle of a panel between two statuettes, survivals from some ruined abbey. In the corners of the room on pedestals stood gorgeously resplendent lamps—the fee paid by some maker to Florine for trumpeting his wares among her friends, who were assured that Japanese pots, with rich fittings, made the only possible stand for lamps. On a marvelous whatnot lay a display of silver, well-earned trophy of a combat in which some English lord had been forced to acknowledge the superiority of the French nation. Next came porcelain reliefs. The whole room displayed the charming profusion of an artist whose furniture represents all his capital.

The bedroom, in violet, was a young ballet-girl's dream: velvet curtains, lined with silk, were draped over inner folds of tulle; the ceiling was in white cashmere relieved with violet silk; at the foot of the bed lay an ermine rug; within the bed-curtains, which fell in the form of an inverted lily, hung a lantern by which to read the proofs of next day's papers. A yellow drawing-room, enriched with ornaments the color of Florentine bronze, carried out the same impression of magnificence, but a detailed description would make these pages too much of a broker's inventory. To find anything comparable to these treasures, it would be necessary to visit the Rothschilds' house close by.

Sophie Grignoult, who, following the usual custom of taking a stage name, was known as Florine, had made her debut, beautiful as she was, in a subordinate capacity. Her triumph and her wealth she owed to Raoul Nathan. The association of these two careers, common enough in the dramatic and literary world, did not injure Raoul, who, in his character as a man of high pretensions, respected the proprieties. Nevertheless, Florine's fortune was far from assured. Her professional income, arising from her salary and what she could earn in her holidays, barely sufficed for dress and housekeeping. Nathan helped her with contributions levied on new ventures in trade, and was always chivalrous and ready to act as her protector; but the support he gave was neither regular nor solid. This instability, this hand-to-mouth life, had no terrors for Florine. She believed in her talent and her beauty; and this robust faith had something comic in it for those who heard her, in answer to remonstrances, mortgaging her future on such security.

"I can live on my means whenever I like," she would say; "I have fifty francs in the Funds now."

No one could understand how, with her beauty, Florine had remained seven years in obscurity; but, as a matter of fact, she was enrolled as a supernumerary at the age of thirteen, and made her debut two years later in a humble theatre on the boulevards. At fifteen, beauty and talent do not exist; there can only be promise of the coming woman. She was now twenty-eight, an age which with Frenchwomen is the culminating point of their beauty. Painters admired most of all her shoulders, glossy white, with olive tints about the back of the neck, but firm and polished, reflecting the light like watered silk. When she turned her head, the neck made magnificent curves in which sculptors delighted. On this neck rose the small, imperious head of a Roman empress, graceful and finely moulded, round and self-assertive, like that of Poppæa. The features were correct, yet expressive, and the unlined forehead was that of an easy-going woman who takes all trouble lightly, yet can be obstinate as a mule on occasion and deaf to all reason. This forehead, with its pure unbroken sweep, gave value to the lovely flaxen hair, generally raised in front, in Roman fashion, in two equal masses and twisted into a high knot at the back, so as to prolong the curve of the neck and bring out its whiteness. Dark, delicate eyebrows, such as a Chinese artist pencils, framed the heavy lids, covered with a network of tiny pink veins. The pupils, sparkling with fire but spotted with patches of brown, gave to her look the fierce fixity of a wild beast, emblematic of the courtesan's cold heartlessness. The lovely gazelle-like iris was a beautiful gray, and fringed with black lashes, a bewitching contrast which brought out yet more strikingly the expression of calm and expectant desire. Darker tints encircled the eyes ; but it was the artistic finish with which she used them that was most remarkable. Those darting, sidelong glances which nothing escaped, the upward gaze of her dreamy pose, the way she had of keeping the iris fixed, while charging it with the most intense passion and without moving the head or stirring a muscle of the face—a trick, this, learned on the stage—the keen sweep which would embrace a whole room to find out the man she wanted—these were the arts which made of her eyes the most terrible, the sweetest, the strangest in the world.

Rouge had spoilt the delicate transparency of her soft cheeks. But if it was beyond her power to blush or grow pale, she had a slender nose, indented by pink, quivering nostrils, which seemed to breathe the sarcasm and mockery of Molière's waiting-maids. Her mouth, sensual and luxurious, lending itself to irony as readily as to love, owed much of its beauty to the finely-cut edges of the little groove joining the upper lip to the nose. Her white, rather fleshy, chin portended storms in love. Her hands and arms might have been an empress'. But the feet were short and thick, ineradicable sign of low birth. Never had heritage wrought more woe. In her efforts to change it, Florine had stopped short only at amputation. But her feet were obstinate, like the Bretons from whom she sprang, and refused to yield to any science or manipulation. Florine therefore wore long boots, stuffed with cotton, to give her an arched instep. She was of medium height, and threatened with corpulence, but her figure still kept its curves and precision.

Morally, she was past mistress in all the airs and graces, tantrums, quips, and caresses of her trade; but she gave them a special character by affecting childishness and edging in a sly thrust under cover of innocent laughter. With all her apparent ignorance and giddiness, she was at home in the mysteries of discount and commercial law. She had waded through so many bad times to reach her day of precarious triumph! She had descended, story by story, to the first floor, through such a coil of intrigue! She knew life under so many forms; from that which dines off bread and cheese to that which toys listlessly with apricot fritters; from that which does its cooking and washing in the corner of a garret with an earthen stove to that which summons its vassal host of big-paunched chefs and impudent scullions. She had indulged in credit without killing it. She knew everything of which good women are ignorant, and could speak all languages. A child of the people by her origin, the refinement of her beauty allied her to the upper classes. She was hard to overreach and impossible to mystify; for, like spies, barristers, and those who have grown old in statecraft, she kept an open mind for every possibility. She knew how to deal with tradespeople and their little tricks, and could quote prices with an auctioneer. Lying back, like some fair young bride, on her couch, with the part she was learning in her hand, she might have passed for a guileless and ignorant girl of sixteen, protected only by her innocence. But let some important creditor arrive, and she was on her feet like a startled fawn, a good round oath upon her lips.

"My good fellow," she would address him, "your insolence is really too high an interest on my debt. I am tired of the sight of you; go and send the bailiffs. Rather them than your imbecile face."

Florine gave charming dinners, concerts, and crowded

receptions, where the play was very high. Her women friends were all beautiful. Never had an old woman been seen at her parties ; she was entirely free from jealousy, which seemed to her a confession of weakness. Among her old acquaintances were Coralie and la Torpille; among those of the day, the Tullias, Euphrasie, the Aquilinas, Madame du Val-Noble, and Mariette—those women who float through Paris like threads of gossamer in the air, no one knowing whence they come or whither they go ; queens to-day, to-morrow drudges. Her rivals, too, came, actresses and singers, the whole company, in short, of that unique feminine world, so kindly and gracious in its recklessness, whose bohemian life carries away with its dash, its spirit, its scorn of to-morrow, the men who join the frenzied dance. Though in Florine's house bohemianism flourished unchecked to a chorus of gay artists, the mistress had all her wits about her, and could use them as could none of her guests. Secret saturnalia of literature and art were held there side by side with politics and finance. There passion reigned supreme ; there temper and the whim of the moment received the reverence which a simple society pays to honor and virtue. There might be seen Blondet, Finot, Étienne Lousteau (her seventh lover who believed himself to be the first), Félicien Vernou the journalist, Couture, Bixiou, Rastignac formerly, Claud Vignon the critic, Nucingen the banker, du Tillet, Conti the composer; in a word, the whole diabolic legion of ferocious egotists in every walk of life. There also came the friends of the singers, dancers, and actresses whom Florine knew.

Every member of this society hated or loved every other member according to circumstances. This house of call, open to celebrities of every kind, was a sort of brothel of wit, a galleys of the mind. Not a guest there but had filched his fortune within the four corners of the law, had worked through ten years of squalor, had strangled two or three love affairs, and had made his mark, whether by a book or a vest, a drama or a carriage-and-pair. Their time was spent in hatching mischief, in exploring roads to wealth, in ridiculing popular outbreaks, which they had incited the day before, and in studying the fluctuations of the money market. Each man, as he left the house, donned again the livery of his beliefs, which he had cast aside on entering in order to abuse at his ease his own party, and admire the strategy and skill of its opponents, to put in plain words thoughts which men keep to themselves, to practice, in fine, that license of speech which goes with license in action. Paris is the one place in the world where houses of this eclectic sort exist, in which every taste, every vice, every opinion, finds a welcome, so long as it comes in decent garb.

It remains to be said that Florine is still a second-rate actress. Further, her life is neither an idle nor an enviable one. Many people, deluded by the splendid vantage-ground which the theatre gives to a woman, imagine her to live in a perpetual carnival. How many a poor girl, buried in some porter's lodge or under an attic roof, dreams on her return from the theatre of pearls and diamonds, of dresses bedecked with gold and rich sashes; and pictures herself, the glitter of the footlights on her hair, applauded, purchased, worshiped, carried off. And not one of them knows the facts of that treadmill existence, how an actress is forced to attend rehearsals under penalty of a fine, to read plays, and perpetually study new parts, at a time when two or three hundred pieces a year are played in Paris. In the course of each performance, Florine changes her dress two or three times, and often she returns to her dressing-room half-dead with exhaustion. Then she has to get rid of the red or white paint with the aid of plentiful cosmetics, and dust the powder out of her hair, if she has been playing an eighteenth-century part. Barely has she time to dine. When she is playing, an actress can neither lace her stays, nor eat, nor talk. For supper, again, Florine has no time. On returning from a performance, which now-a-days is not over till past midnight, she has her toilet for the night to make and orders to give. After going to bed at one or two in the morning, she has to be up in time to revise her parts, to order her dresses, to explain them and try them on ; then lunch, read her love-letters, reply to them, transact business with her hired applauders, so that she may be properly greeted on entering and leaving the stage, and, while paying the bill for her triumphs of the past month, order wholesale those of the present. In the days of Saint Genest, a canonized actor, who neglected no means of grace and wore a hairshirt, the stage, we must suppose, did not demand this relentless activity. Often Florine is forced to feign an illness if she wants to go into the country and pick flowers like an ordinary mortal.

Yet these purely mechanical occupations are nothing in comparison with the mental worries, arising from intrigues to be conducted, annoyances to vanity, preferences shown by authors, competition for parts, with its triumphs and disappointments, unreasonable actors, ill-natured rivals, and the importunities of managers and critics, all of which demand another twenty-four hours in the day. .

And, lastly, there is the art itself and all the difficulties it involves—the interpretation of passion, details of mimicry, and stage effects, with thousands of opera-glasses ready to pounce on the slightest flaw in the most brilliant presentment. These are the things which wore away the life and energy of Talma, Lekain, Baron, Contat, Clairon, Champmeslé. In the pandemonium of the greenroom self-love is sexless ; the successful artist, man or woman, has all other men and women for enemies.

As to profits, however handsome Florine's salaries may be, they do not cover the cost of the stage finery, which—not to speak of costumes—demands an enormous expenditure in long gloves and shoes, and does not do away with the necessity for evening and visiting dresses. One-third of such a life is spent in begging favors, another in making sure the ground already won, and the remainder in repelling attacks; but all alike is work. If it contains also moments of intense happiness, that is because happiness here is rare and stolen, long waited—a chance godsend amid the hateful grind of forced pleasure and stage smiles.

To Florine, Raoul's power was a sovereign protection. He saved her many a vexation and worry, in the fashion of a great noble of former days defending his mistress; or, to take a modern instance, like the old men who go on their knees to the editor when their idol has been scarified by some five-centime print. He was more than a lover to her; he was a staff to lean on. She tended him like a father, and deceived him like a husband; but there was nothing in the world she would not have sacrificed for him. Raoul was indispensable to her artistic vanity, to the tranquillity of her self-esteem, and to her dramatic future. Without the intervention of some great writer, no great actress can be produced; we owe la Champmeslé to Racine, as we owe Mars to Monvel and Andrieux. Florine, on her side, could do nothing for Raoul, much as she would have liked to be useful or necessary to him. She counted on the seductions of habit, and was always ready to open her rooms and offer the profusion of her table to help his plans or his friends. In fact, she aspired to be for him what Madame de Pompadour was for Louis XV.; and there were actresses who envied her position, just as there were journalists who would have changed places with Raoul.

Now, those who know the bent of the human mind to opposition and contrast will easily understand that Raoul, after ten years of this rakish bohemian life, should weary of its ups and downs, its revelry and its writs, its orgies and its fasts, and should feel drawn to a pure and innocent love, as well as to the gentle harmony of a great lady's existence. In the same way, the Comtesse Félix longed to introduce the torments of passion into a life the bliss of which had cloyed through its sameness. This law of life is the law of all art, which exists only through contrast. A work produced independently of such aid is the highest expression of genius, as the cloister is the highest effort of Christianity.

Raoul, on returning home, found a note from Florine, which her maid had brought, but was too sleepy to read it. He went to bed in the restful satisfaction of a tender love, which had so far been lacking to his life. A few hours later, he found important news in this letter, news of which neither Rastignac nor de Marsay had dropped a hint. Florine had learned from some indiscreet friend that the Chamber was to be dissolved at the close of the session. Raoul at once went to Florine's, and sent for Blondet to meet him there.

In Florine's boudoir, their feet upon the fire-dogs, Émile and Raoul dissected the political situation of France in 1834. On what side lay the best chance for a man who wanted to get on? Every shade of opinion was passed in review—Republicans pure and simple, Republicans with a president, Republicans without a republic, Dynastic Constitutionalists and Constitutionalists without a dynasty, Conservative Ministerialists and Absolutist Ministerialists; lastly, the compromising right, the aristocratic right, the Legitimist right, the Henriquinquist right, and the Carlist right. As between the party of obstruction and the party of progress there could be no question; as well might one hesitate between life and death.

The vast number of newspapers at this time in circulation, representing different shades of party, was significant of the chaotic confusion—the "slush," as it might vulgarly be called —to which politics were reduced. Blondet, the man of his day with most judgment, although, like a barrister unable to plead his own cause, he could use it only on behalf of others, was magnificent in these friendly discussions. His advice to Nathan was not to desert abruptly.

"It was Napoleon who said that young republics cannot be made out of old monarchies. Therefore, do you, my friend, become the hero, the pillar, the creator of a Left Centre in the next Chamber, and a political future is before you. Once past the barrier, once in the Ministry, a man can do what he pleases, he can wear the winning colors."

Nathan decided to start a political daily paper, of which he should have the complete control, and to affiliate to it one of those small society sheets with which the press swarmed, establishing at the same time a connection with some magazine. The press had been the mainspring of so many fortunes around him that Nathan refused to listen to Blondet's warnings against trusting to it. In Blondet's opinion, the speculation was unsafe, because of the multitude of competing papers, and because the power of the press seemed to him used up. Raoul, strong in his supposed friends and in his courage, was keen to go forward ; with a gesture of pride he sprang to his feet and exclaimed—

"I shall succeed ! "

"You haven't a penny ! "

"I shall write a play ! "

"It will fall dead."

"Let it," said Nathan.

He paced up and down Florine's room, followed by Blondet, who thought he had gone crazy ; he cast covetous glances on the costly treasures piled up around; then Blondet understood him.

"There's more than one hundred thousand francs' worth here," said Émile.

"Yes," said Raoul, with a sigh toward Florine's sumptuous bed ; "but I would sell patent safety-chains on the boulevards and live on fried potatoes all my life rather than sell a single patera from these rooms."

"Not one patera, no," said Blondet, "but the whole lot ! Ambition is like death ; it clutches all because life, it knows, is hounding it on."

"No ! a thousand times, no ! I would accept anything

from that countess of yesterday, but to rob Florine of her nest ? "

" To overthrow one's mint," said Blondet, with a tragic air, " to smash up the coining-press, and break the stamp, is certainly serious."

" From what I can gather, you are abandoning the stage for politics," said Florine, suddenly breaking in on them.

" Yes, my child, yes," said Raoul good-naturedly, putting his arm round her neck and kissing her forehead. " Why that frown ? It will be no loss to you. Won't the minister be better placed then the journalist for getting a first-rate engagement for the queen of the boards ? You will still have your parts and your holidays."

" Where is the money to come from ? " she asked.

" From my uncle," replied Raoul.

Florine knew this " uncle." The word meant a money-lender, just as " my aunt " was the vulgar name for a pawn-broker.

" Don't bother yourself, my pretty one," said Blondet to Florine, patting her on the shoulder. " I will get Massol to help him. He's a barrister, and, like the rest of them, intends to have a turn at being Minister of Justice. Then there's du Tillet, who wants a seat in the Chamber; Finot, who is still backing a society paper; Plantin, who has his eye on a post under the Conseil d'État, and who has some share in a magazine. No fear ! I won't let him ruin himself. We will get a meeting here with Étienne Lousteau, who will do the light stuff, and Claud Vignon for the serious criticism. Félicien Vernou will be the charwoman of the paper, the barrister will sweat for it, du Tillet will look after trade and the Exchange, and we shall see where this union of determined men and their tools will land us."

" In the workhouse or on the Government bench, those refuges for the ruined in body or mind," said Raoul.

" What about the dinner ? "

"We'll have it here," said Raoul, "five days hence."

"Let me know how much you need," said Florine simply.

"Why, the barrister, du Tillet, and Raoul can't start with less than one hundred thousand francs a-piece," said Blondet. "That will run the paper very well for eighteen months, time enough to make a hit or miss in Paris."

Florine made a gesture of approval. The two friends then took a coach and set out in quest of guests, pens, ideas, and sources of support. The beautiful actress on her part sent for four dealers in furniture, curiosities, pictures, and jewelry. The dealers, who were all men of substance, entered the sanctuary and made an inventory of its whole contents, just as though Florine were dead. She threatened them with a public auction in case they hardened their hearts in hope of a better opportunity. She had, she told them, excited the admiration of an English lord in a mediæval part, and she wished to dispose of all her personal property, in order that her apparently destitute condition might move him to present her with a splendid house, which she would furnish as a rival to Rothschild's. With all her arts, she only succeeded in getting an offer of seventy thousand francs for the whole of the spoil, which was well worth one hundred and fifty thousand. Florine, who did not care a button for the things, promised they should be handed over in seven days for eighty thousand francs.

"You can take it or leave it," she said.

The bargain was concluded. When the dealers had gone, the actress skipped for joy, like the little hills of King David. She could not contain herself for delight; never had she dreamed of such wealth. When Raoul returned, she pretended to be offended with him, and declared that she was deserted. She saw through it all now; men don't change their party or leave the stage for the Chamber without some reason. There must be a rival! Her instinct told her so! Vows of eternal love rewarded her little comedy.

Five days later, Florine gave a magnificent entertainment. The ceremony of christening the paper was then performed amidst floods of wine and wit, oaths of fidelity, of good fellowship, and of serious alliance. The name, forgotten now, like the "Libéral," the "Communal," the "Départemental," the "Garde National," the "Fédéral," the "Impartial," was something which ended in *al*, and was bound not to take. Descriptions of banquets have been so numerous in a literary period which had more first-hand experience of starving in an attic, that it would be difficult to do justice to Florine's. Suffice it to say that, at three in the morning, Florine was able to undress and go to bed as if she had been alone, though not one of her guests had left. These lights of their age were sleeping like pigs. When, early in the morning, the packers, commissionaires, and porters arrived to carry off the gorgeous trappings of the famous actress, she laughed aloud to see them lifting these celebrities like heavy pieces of furniture and depositing them on the floor.

Thus the splendid collection went its way.

Florine carried her personal remembrances to stores where the sight of them did not enlighten passers-by as to how and when these flowers of luxury had been paid for. It was agreed to leave her until the evening a few specially reserved articles, including her bed, her table, and her crockery, so that she might offer breakfast to her guests. These witty gentlemen, having falling asleep under the beauteous drapery of wealth, awoke to the cold, naked walls of poverty, studded with nail-marks and disfigured by those incongruous patches which are found at the back of wall decorations, as ropes behind an opera scene.

"Why, Florine, the poor girl has an execution in the house!" cried Bixiou, one of the guests. "Quick! your pockets, gentlemen! A subscription!"

At these words the whole company was on foot. The net sweepings of the pockets came to thirty-seven francs, which

Raoul handed over with mock ceremony to the laughing
Florine. The happy courtesan raised her head from the pil-
low and pointed to a heap of bank-notes on the sheet, thick as
in the golden days of her trade. Raoul called Blondet.

"I see it now," said Blondet. "The little rogue has sold
off without a word to us. Well done, Florine!"

Delighted with this stroke, the few friends who remained
carried Florine in triumph and *déshabillé* to the dining-room.
The barrister and the bankers had gone. That evening Florine
had a tremendous reception at the theatre. The rumor of her
sacrifice was all over the house.

"I should prefer to be applauded for my talent," said
Florine's rival to her in the greenroom.

"That is very natural on the part of an artist who has never
yet won applause except for the lavishness of her favors," she
replied.

During the evening Florine's maid had her things moved
to Raoul's flat in the Passage Sandrié. The journalist was to
pitch his camp in the building where the newspaper office was
opened.

Such was the rival of the ingenuous Mme. de Vandenesse.
Raoul's fancy was a link binding the actress to the lady of
title. It was a ghastly tie like this which was severed by that
Duchess of Louis XIV.'s time who poisoned Lecouvreur; nor
can such an act of vengeance be wondered at, considering the
magnitude of the offense.

CHAPTER VI.

LOVE VERSUS SOCIETY.

Florine proved no difficulty in the early stages of Raoul's
passion. Foreseeing financial disappointments in the hazard-
ous scheme into which he had plunged, she begged leave of
absence for six months. Raoul took an active part in the

negotiation, and by bringing it to a successful issue still further endeared himself to Florine. With the good sense of the peasant in La Fontaine's fable, who makes sure of his dinner while the patricians are chattering over plans, the actress hurried off to the provinces and abroad, to glean the where-withal to support the great man during his place-hunting.

Up to the present time the art of fiction has seldom dealt with love as it shows itself in the highest society, a compound of noble impulse and hidden wretchedness. There is a terrible strain in the constant check imposed on passion by the most trivial and trumpery incidents, and not infrequently the thread snaps from sheer lassitude. Perhaps some glimpse of what it means may be obtained here.

The day after Lady Dudley's ball, although nothing approaching a declaration had escaped on either side, Marie felt that Raoul's love was the realization of her dreams, and Raoul had no doubt that he was the chosen of Marie's heart. Neither of the two had reached that point of depravity where preliminaries are curtailed, and yet they advanced rapidly toward the end. Raoul, sated with pleasure, was in the mood for Platonic affection ; whilst Marie, from whom the idea of an actual fault was still remote, had never contemplated passing beyond it. Never, therefore, was love more pure and innocent in fact, or more impassioned and rapturous in thought, than this of Raoul and Marie. The countess had been fascinated by ideas which, though clothed in modern dress, belonged to the times of chivalry. In her rôle, as she conceived it, her husband's dislike to Nathan no longer appeared an obstacle to her love. The less Raoul merited esteem, the nobler was her mission. The inflated language of the poet stirred her imagination rather than her blood. It was charity which wakened at the call of passion. This queen of the virtues lent what in the eyes of the countess seemed almost a sanction to the tremors, the delights, the turbulence of her love. She felt it a fine thing to be the human providence of Raoul.

How sweet to think of supporting with her feeble, white hand this colossal figure, whose feet of clay she refused to see, of sowing life where none had been, of working in secret at the foundation of a great destiny. With her help this man of genius should wrestle with and overcome his fate; her hand should embroider his scarf for the tourney, buckle on his armor, give him a charm against sorcery, and balm for all his wounds.

In a woman with Marie's noble nature and religious up-bringing this passionate charity was the only form love could assume. Hence her boldness. The pure in mind have a superb disdain for appearances, which may be mistaken for the shamelessness of the courtesan. No sooner had the countess assured herself by casuistical arguments that her husband's honor ran no risk, than she abandoned herself completely to the bliss of loving Raoul. The most trivial things in life had now a charm for her. The boudoir in which she dreamed of him became a sanctuary. Even her pretty writing-table recalled to her the countless joys of correspondence; there she would have to read, to hide, his letters; there reply to them. Dress, that splendid poem of a woman's life, the significance of which she had either exhausted or ignored, now appeared to her full of a magic hitherto unknown. Suddenly it became to her what it is to all women— a continuous expression of the inner thought, a language, a symbol. What wealth of delight in a costume designed for *his* pleasure, in *his* honor! She threw herself with all simplicity into those charming nothings which make the business of a Paris woman's life, and which charge with meaning every detail in her house, her person, her clothes. Rare indeed are the women who frequent dress stores, milliners, and fashionable tailors simply for their own pleasure. As they become old they cease to think of dress. Scrutinize the face which in passing you see for a moment arrested before a store-front: "Would he like me better in this?" are the words written plain in the clearing brow, in eyes sparkling with hope, and in the beaming, angelic smile that plays upon the lips.

Lady Dudley's ball took place on a Saturday evening; on the Monday the countess went to the opera, allured by the certainty of seeing Raoul. Raoul, in fact, was there, planted on one of the staircases which lead down to the amphitheatre stalls. He lowered his eyes as the countess entered her box. With what ecstasy did Mme. de Vandenesse observe the unwonted carefulness of her lover's attire! This contemner of the laws of elegance might be seen with well-brushed hair, which shone with scent in the recesses of every curl, a fashionable vest, a well-fastened tie, and an immaculate shirt-front. Under the yellow gloves, which were the order of the day, his hands showed very white. Raoul kept his arms crossed over his breast, as though posing for his portrait, superbly indifferent to the whole house, which murmured with barely restrained impatience. His eyes, though bent on the ground, seemed turned toward the red velvet bar on which Marie's arm rested. Félix, seated in the opposite corner of the box, had his back to Nathan. The countess had been adroit enough to place herself so that she looked straight down on the pillar against which Raoul leaned. In a single hour, then, Marie had brought this clever man to abjure his cynicism in dress. The humblest, as well as the most distinguished, woman must feel her head turned by the first open declaration of her power in such a transformation. Every change is a confession of servitude.

"They were right, there is a great happiness in being understood," she said to herself, calling to mind her unworthy instructors.

When the two lovers had scanned the house in a rapid all-embracing survey, they exchanged a glance of intelligence. For both it was as though a heavenly dew had fallen with cooling power upon their fevered suspense. "I have been in hell for an hour; now the heavens open," spoke the eyes of Raoul.

"I knew you were there, but am I free?" replied those of the countess.

None but slaves of every variety, including thieves, spies, lovers, and diplomatists, know all that a flash of the eye can convey of information or delight. They alone can grasp the intelligence, the sweetness, the humor, the wrath, and the malice with which this changeful lightning of the soul is pregnant. Raoul felt his passion kick against the pricks of necessity and grow more vigorous in presence of obstacles. Between the step on which he was perched and the box of the Comtesse Félix de Vandenesse was a space of barely thirty feet, impassable for him. To a passionate man who, so far in his life, had known but little interval between desire and satisfaction, this abyss of solid ground, which could not be spanned, inspired a wild desire to spring upon the countess in a tiger-like bound. In a paroxysm of fury he tried to feel his way. He bowed openly to the countess, who replied with a slight, scornful inclination of the head, such as women use for snubbing their admirers. Félix turned to see who had greeted his wife, and perceiving Nathan, of whom he took no notice beyond a mute inquiry as to the cause of this liberty, turned slowly away again, with some words probably approving of his wife's assumed coldness. Plainly the door of the box was barred against Nathan, who hurled a threatening glance at Félix, which it required no great wit to interpret by one of Florine's sallies: "Lookout for your hat; it will soon not rest on your head!"

Mme. d'Espard, one of the most insolent women of her time, who had been watching these manœuvres from her box, now raised her voice in some meaningless bravo. Raoul, who was standing beneath her, turned. He bowed, and received in return a gracious smile, which so clearly said: "If you are dismissed there, come to me!" that Raoul left his column and went to pay a visit to Mme. d'Espard. He wanted to be seen there in order to show that fellow Vandenesse that his fame was equal to a patent of nobility, and that before Nathan blazoned doors flew open. The marchioness made him sit down in the front of the box opposite to her. She intended to play the inquisitor.

"Madame Félix de Vandenesse looks charming to-night," she said, congratulating him on the lady's dress, as though it were a book he had just published.

"Yes," said Raoul carelessly, "feathers are very becoming to her. But she is too constant, she wore them the day before yesterday," he added, with an easy air, as though by his critical attitude to repudiate the flattering complicity which the marchioness had laid to his charge.

"You know the proverb?" she replied. "'Every feast day should have a morrow.'"

At the game of repartee literary giants are not always equal to ladies of title. Raoul took refuge in a pretended stupidity, the last resource of clever men.

"The proverb is true for me," he said, casting an admiring look on the marchioness.

"Your pretty speech, sir, comes too late for me to accept it," she replied, laughing. "Come, come, don't be a prude; in the small hours of yesterday morning, you thought Mme. de Vandenesse entrancing in feathers; she was perfectly aware of it, and puts them on again to please you. She is in love with you, and you adore her; no time has been lost, certainly; still I see nothing in it but what is most natural. If it were not as I say, you would not be tearing your glove to pieces in your rage at having to sit here beside me, instead of in the box of your idol—which has just been shut in your face by supercilious authority—whispering low what you would fain hear said aloud."

Raoul was in fact twisting one of his gloves, and the hand which he showed was surprisingly white.

"She has won from you," she went on, fixing his hand with an impertinent stare, "sacrifices which you refused to society. She ought to be enchanted at her success, and, I daresay, she is a little vain of it; but in her place I think I should be more so. So far she has only been a woman of good parts, now she will pass for a woman of genius. We shall find her portrait in one of those delightful books of yours. But, my dear friend, do me the kindness not to forget Vandenesse. That man is really too fatuous. I could not stand such self-complacency in Jupiter Olympus himself, who is said to have been the only god in mythology exempt from domestic misfortune."

"Madame," cried Raoul, "you credit me with a very base soul if you suppose that I would make profit out of my feelings, out of my love. Sooner than be guilty of such literary dishonor, I would follow the English custom, and drag a woman to market with a rope round her neck."

"But I know Marie," said the marquise; "she will ask you to do it."

"No, she is incapable of it," protested Raoul.

"You know her intimately then?"

Nathan could not help laughing that he, a playwright, should be caught in this little comedy dialogue.

"The play is no longer there," he said, pointing to the footlights; "it rests with you."

To hide his confusion, he took the opera-glass and began to examine the house.

"Are you vexed with me?" said the marchioness, with a sidelong glance at him. "Wouldn't your secret have been mine in any case? It won't be hard to make peace. Come to my house, I am at home every Wednesday; the dear countess won't miss an evening when she finds you come, and I shall be the gainer. Sometimes she comes to me before four and five o'clock; I will be very good-natured, and add you to the select few admitted at that hour."

"Only see," said Raoul, "how unjust people are! I was told you were spiteful."

"Oh! so I am," she said, "when I want to be. One has to fight for one's own hand. But as for your countess, I adore her. You have no idea how charming she is! You will be the first to have your name inscribed on her heart with that infantine joy which causes all lovers, even drill-sergeants, to cut their initials on the bark of a tree. A woman's first love is a luscious fruit. Later, you see, there is always some calculation in our attentions and caresses. I'm an old woman, and can say what I like; nothing frightens me, not even a journalist. Well, then, in the autumn of life, we know how to make you happy; but when love is a new thing, we are happy ourselves, and that gives endless satisfaction to your pride. We are full of delicious surprises then, because the heart is fresh. You, who are a poet, must prefer flowers to fruit. Six months hence you shall tell me about it."

Raoul began with denying everything, as all men do when they are brought to the bar, but found that this only supplied weapons to so practiced a champion. Entangled in the noose of a dialogue, manipulated with all the dangerous adroitness of a woman and a Parisian, he dreaded to let fall admissions which would serve as fuel for the lady's wit, and he beat a prudent retreat when he saw Lady Dudley enter.

"Well," said the Englishwoman, "how far have they gone?"

"They are desperately in love. Nathan has just told me so."

"I wish he had been uglier," said Lady Dudley, with a venomous scowl at Félix. "Otherwise, he is exactly what I would have wished; he is the son of a Jewish broker, who died bankrupt shortly after his marriage; unfortunately, his mother was a Catholic, and has made a Christian of him."

Nathan's origin, which he kept a most profound secret, was a new discovery to Lady Dudley, who gloated in advance over the delight of drawing thence some pointed shaft to aim at Vandenesse.

"And I've just asked him to my house!" exclaimed the marchioness.

"Wasn't he at my ball yesterday?" replied Lady Dudley. "There are pleasures, my dear, for which one pays heavily."

The news of a mutual passion between Raoul and Mme. de Vandenesse went the round of society that evening, not without calling forth protests and doubts; but the countess was defended by her friends, Lady Dudley, Mmes. d'Espard and de Manerville, with a clumsy eagerness which gained some credence for the rumor. Yielding to necessity, Raoul went on Wednesday evening to Mme. d'Espard's, and found there the usual distinguished company. As Félix did not accompany his wife, Raoul was able to exchange a few words with Marie, the tone of which expressed more than the matter. The countess, warned against malicious gossips by Mme. Octave de Camps, realized her critical position before society, and contrived to make Raoul understand it also.

Amidst this gay assembly, the lovers found their only joy in a long draught of the delicious sensations arising from the words, the voice, the gestures, and the bearing of the loved one. The soul clings desperately to such trifles. At times the eyes of both will converge upon the same spot, embedding there, as it were, a thought of which they thus risk the interchange. They talk, and longing looks follow the peeping foot, the quivering hand, the fingers which toy with some ornament, flicking it, twisting it about, then dropping it, in significant fashion. It is no longer words or thoughts which make themselves heard, it is things; and that in so clear a voice, that often the man who loves will leave to others the task of handing a cup of tea, a sugar-basin, or what not, to his lady-love, in dread lest his agitation should be visible to eyes which, apparently seeing nothing, see all. Thronging desires, mad wishes, passionate thoughts, find their way into a glance and die out there. The pressure of a hand, eluding a thousand Argus eyes, is eloquent as written pages, burning as a kiss. Love grows by all that it denies itself; it treads on obstacles to reach the higher. And barriers, more often cursed than cleared, are hacked and cast into the fire to feed its flames. Here it is that women see the measure of their power, when love, that is boundless, coils up and hides itself within a thirsty glance, a nervous thrill, behind the screen of formal civility. How often has not a single word, on the last step of a staircase, paid the price of an evening's silent agony and empty talk !

Raoul, careless of social forms, gave rein to his anger in brilliant oratory. Everybody present could hear the lion's roar, and recognized the artist's nature, intolerant of disappointment. This Orlando-like rage, this cutting and slashing wit, this laying on of epigrams as with a club, enraptured Marie and amused the onlookers, much as the spectacle of a maddened bull, covered with streamers, in a Spanish amphitheatre, might have done.

"Hit out as much as you like, you can't clear the ring," Blondet said to him.

This sarcasm restored to Raoul his presence of mind ; he ceased making an exhibition of himself and his vexation. The marchioness came to offer him a cup of tea, and said, loud enough for Marie to hear—

"You are really very amusing ; come and see me sometimes at four o'clock."

Raoul took offense at the word "amusing," although it had served as passport to the invitation. He began to give ear, as actors do, when they are attending to the house and not to the stage.

Blondet took pity on him.

"My dear fellow," he said, drawing him aside into a corner, "you behave in polite society exactly as you might at Florine's. Here nobody flies into a passion, nobody lectures ; from time to time a smart thing may be said, and you must look most impassive at the very moment when you long to throw some one out of the window ; a gentle raillery is allowed, and some show of attention to the lady you adore, but you can't lie down and kick like a donkey in the middle of the road. Here, my good soul, love proceeds by rule. Either carry off Madame de Vandenesse or behave like a gentleman. You are too much the lover of one of your own romances."

Nathan listened with hanging head; he was a wild beast caught in the toils.

"I shall never set foot here again," said he. "This papier-maché marchioness puts too high a price upon her tea. She thinks me amusing, does she? Now I know why St. Just guillotined all these people."

"You'll come back to-morrow."

Blondet was right. Passion is as cowardly as it is cruel. The next day, after fluctuating long between "I'll go" and "I won't go," Raoul left his partners in the middle of an important discussion to hasten to the Faubourg St. Honoré and Mme. d'Espard's house. The sight of Rastignac's elegant cabriolet driving up as he was paying his cabman at the door hurt Nathan's vanity; he too would have such a cabriolet, he resolved, and the correct tiger. The carriage of the countess was in the court, and Raoul's heart swelled with joy as he perceived it. Marie's movements responded to her longings with the regularity of a clock-hand propelled by its spring. She was reclining in an armchair by the fire-place in the small drawing-room. Instead of looking at Nathan as he entered, she gazed at his reflection in the mirror, feeling sure that the mistress of the house would turn to him. Love, baited by society, is forced to have recourse to these little tricks; it endows with life mirrors, muffs, fans, and numberless objects, the purpose of which is not clear at first sight, and is indeed never found out by many of the women who make use of them.

"The prime minister," said Mme. d'Espard, with a glance at de Marsay, as she drew Nathan into the conversation,

MARIE—— HELD OUT HER HAND TO RAOUL.

" was just declaring, when you came in, that there is an understanding between the Royalists and Republicans. What do you say? You ought to know something about it."

" Supposing it were so, where would be the harm ?" said Raoul. " The object of our animosity is the same ; we agree in our hatred, and differ only in what we love."

" The alliance is at least singular," said de Marsay, with a glance which embraced Raoul and the Comtesse Félix.

" It will not last," said Rastignac, who, like all novices, took his politics a little too seriously.

" What do you say, darling?" asked Mme. d'Espard of the countess.

" I ! oh ! I know nothing about politics."

" You will learn, madame," said de Marsay, "and then you will be doubly our enemy."

Neither Nathan nor Marie understood de Marsay's sally till he had gone. Rastignac followed him, and Mme. d'Espard went with them both as far as the door of the first drawing-room. Not another thought did the lovers give to the minister's epigram ; they saw the priceless wealth of a few minutes before them. Marie swiftly removed her glove, and held out her hand to Raoul, who took it and kissed it with the fervor of eighteen. The eyes of the countess were eloquent of a devotion so generous and absolute that Raoul felt his own moisten. A tear is always at the command of men of nervous temperament.

" Where can I see you—speak to you ?" he said. " It will kill me if I must perpetually disguise my looks and my voice, my heart and my love."

Moved by the tear, Marie promised to go to the Bois whenever the weather did not make it impossible. This promise gave Raoul more happiness than Florine had brought him in five years.

" I have so much to say to you ! I suffer so from the silence to which we are condemned !"

The countess was gazing at him rapturously, unable to reply, when the marchioness returned.

"So!" she exclaimed as she entered, "you had no retort for de Marsay!"

"One must respect the dead," replied Raoul. "Don't you see that he is at the last gasp? Rastignac is acting as nurse, and hopes to be mentioned in the will."

The countess made an excuse of having calls to pay, and took leave, as a precaution against gossip. For this quarter of an hour Raoul had sacrificed precious time and most urgent claims. Marie as yet knew nothing of the details of a life, which, while to all appearance gay and idle as a bird's, had yet its side of very complicated business and extremely taxing work. When two beings, united by an enduring love, lead a life which each day knits them more closely in the bonds of mutual confidence and by the interchange of counsel over difficulties as they arise ; when two hearts pour forth their sorrows, night and morning, with mingled sighs ; when they share the same suspense and shudder together at a common danger, then everything is taken into account. The woman then can measure the love in an averted gaze, the cost of a hurried visit, she has her part in the business, the hurrying to and fro, the hopes and anxieties of the hard-worked, harassed man. If she complains, it is only of the actual conditions ; her doubts are at rest, for she knows and appreciates the details of his life. But in the opening chapters of passion, when all is eagerness, suspicion, and demands ; when neither of the two know themselves or each other ; when, in addition, the woman is an idler, expecting love to stand guard all day at her door—one of those who have an exaggerated estimate of their own claims, and choose to be obeyed even when obedience spells ruin to a career—then love, in Paris and at the present time, becomes a superhuman task. Women of fashion have not yet thrown off the traditions of the eighteenth century, when every man had his own place marked out for him.

Few of them know anything of the difficulties of existence for the bulk of men, all with a position to carve out, a distinction to win, a fortune to consolidate. Men of well-established fortune are, at present, rare exceptions. Only the old have time for love; men in their prime are chained, like Nathan, to the galleys of ambition.

Women, not yet reconciled to this change of habits, cannot bring themselves to believe any man short of the time which is so cheap a commodity with them; they can imagine no occupations or aims other than their own. Had the gallant vanquished the hydra of Lerna to get at them, he would not rise one whit in their estimation; the joy of seeing him is everything. They are grateful because he makes them happy, but never think of asking what their happiness has cost him. Whereas, if they, in an idle hour, have devised some stratagem such as they abound in, they flaunt it in your eyes as something superlative. You have wrenched the iron bars of destiny, while they have played with subterfuge and diplomacy —and yet the palm is theirs, dispute were vain. After all, are they not right? The woman who gives up all for you, should she not receive all? She exacts no more than she gives.

Raoul, during his walk home, pondered on the difficulty of directing at one and the same time a fashionable intrigue, the ten-horse chariot of journalism, his theatrical pieces, and his entangled personal affairs.

"It will be a wretched paper to-night," he said to himself as he went; "nothing from my hand, and the second number too!"

Mme. Félix de Vandenesse went three times to the Bois de Boulogne without seeing Raoul; she came home agitated and despairing. Nathan was determined not to show himself till he could do so in all the glory of a press magnate. He spent the week in looking out for a pair of horses and a suitable cabriolet and tiger, in persuading his partners of the necessity of sparing time so valuable as his, and in getting the purchase put down to the general expenses of the paper. Massol and du Tillet agreed so readily to this request that he thought them the best fellows in the world. But for this assistance, life would have been impossible for Raoul. As it was, it became so taxing, in spite of the exquisite delights of ideal love with which it was mingled, that many men, even of excellent constitution, would have broken down under the strain of such distractions. A violent and reciprocal passion is bound to bulk largely even in an ordinary life; but when its object is a woman of conspicuous position, like Mme. de Vandenesse, it cannot fail to play havoc with that of a busy man like Nathan.

Here are some of the duties to which his passion gave the first place: Almost every day between two and three o'clock he rode to the Bois de Boulogne in the style of the purest dandy. He then learned in what house or at what theatre he might meet Mme. de Vandenesse again that evening. He never left a reception till close upon midnight, when he had at last succeeded in snapping up some long watched-for words, a few crumbs of tenderness, artfully dropped below the table, or in a corridor, or on the way to the carriage. Marie, who had launched him in the world of fashion, generally got him invitations to dinner at the houses where she visited. Nothing could be more natural. Raoul was too proud, and also too much in love, to say a word about business. He had to obey every caprice and whim of his innocent tyrant; while, at the same time, following closely the debates in the Chamber and the rapid current of politics, directing his paper, and bringing out two plays which were to furnish the sinews of war. If ever he asked to be let off a ball, a concert, or a drive, a look of annoyance from Mme. de Vandenesse was enough to make him sacrifice his interests to her pleasure.

When he returned home from these engagements at one or two in the morning, he worked till eight or nine, leaving scant time for sleep. Directly he was up, he plunged into consultations with influential supporters as to the policy of the paper. A thousand and one internal difficulties meantime would await his settlement, for journalism nowadays has an all-embracing grasp. Business, public and private interests, new ventures, the personal sensitiveness of literary men, as well as their compositions—nothing is alien to it. When, harassed and exhausted, Nathan flew from his office to the theatre, from the theatre to the Chamber, from the Chamber to a creditor, he had next to present himself, calm and smiling, before Marie, and canter beside her carriage with the ease of a man who has no cares, and whose only business is pleasure. When, as sole reward for so many unnoticed acts of devotion, he found only the gentlest of words or prettiest assurances of undying attachment, a warm pressure of the hand, if by chance they escaped observation for a moment, or one or two passionate expressions in response to his own, Raoul began to feel that it was mere Quixotism not to make known the extravagant price he paid for these "modest favors," as our fathers might have called them.

The opportunity for an explanation was not long in coming. On a lovely April day the countess took Nathan's arm in a secluded corner of the Bois de Boulogne. She had a pretty little quarrel to pick with him about one of those molehills which women have the art of turning into mountains. There was no smiling welcome, no radiant brow, the eyes did not sparkle with fun or happiness; it was a serious and burdened woman who met him.

" What is wrong ? " said Nathan.

" Oh ! Why worry about trifles ? " she said. " Surely you know how childish women are."

" Are you angry with me ? "

" Should I be here ? "

" But you don't smile, you don't seem a bit glad to see me."

6

"I suppose you mean that I am cross," she said, with the resigned air of a woman determined to be a martyr.

Nathan walked on a few steps, an overshadowing fear gripping at his heart. After a moment's silence, he went on—

"It can only be one of those idle fears, those vague suspicions, to which you give such exaggerated importance. A straw, a thread in your hands is enough to upset the balance of the world!"

"Satire next!—— Well, I expect it," she said, hanging her head.

"Marie, my beloved, do you not see that I say this only to wring your secret from you?"

"My secret will remain a secret, even after I have told you."

"Well, tell me——"

"I am not loved," she said, with the stealthy side-look, which is a woman's instrument for probing the man she means to torture.

"Not loved!" exclaimed Nathan.

"No; you have too many things on your mind. What am I in the midst of this whirl? You are only too glad to forget me. Yesterday I came to the Bois, I waited for you——"

"But——"

"I had put on a new dress for you, and you did not come. Where were you?"

"But——"

"I couldn't tell. I went to Mme. d'Espard's; you were not there."

"But——"

"At the opera in the evening my eyes never left the balcony. Every time the door opened my heart beat so that I thought it would break."

"But——"

"What an evening! You have no conception of such agony!"

"But——"

"It eats into life——"

"But——".

"Well," she said.

"Yes," replied Nathan, "it *does* eat into life, and in a few months you will have consumed mine. Your wild reproaches have torn from me my secret also. Ah! you are not loved! My God, you are loved too well."

He drew a graphic picture of his straits. He told her how he sat up at nights, how he had to keep certain engagements at fixed hours, and how, above all things, he was bound to succeed. He showed her how insatiable were the claims of a paper, compelled, at risk of losing its reputation, to be beforehand with an accurate judgment on every event that took place, and how incessant was the call for a rapid survey of questions, which chased each other like clouds over the horizon in that period of political convulsions.

In a moment the mischief was done. Raoul had been told by the Marquise d'Espard that nothing is so ingenuous as a first love, and it soon appeared that the countess erred in loving too much. A loving woman meets every difficulty with delight and fresh proof of her passion. On seeing the panorama of this varied life unrolled before her, the countess was filled with admiration. She had pictured Nathan a great man, but now he seemed transcendent. She blamed herself for an excessive love, and begged him to come only when he was at liberty; Nathan's ambitious struggles sank to nothing before the glance she cast toward heaven! She would wait! Henceforth her pleasure should be sacrificed. She, who had wished to be a stepping-stone, had proved only an obstacle. She wept despairingly.

"Women, it seems," she said with tearful eyes, "are fit only to love. Men have a thousand different ways of spending their energy; all we can do is to dream, and pray, and worship."

So much love deserved a recompense. Peeping around, like a nightingale ready to alight from its branch beside a spring of water, she tried to make sure whether they were alone in this solitude, and whether no spectator lurked in the silence. Then raising her head to Raoul, who bent his to meet her, she allowed him a kiss, the first, the only, contraband kiss she was destined to give. At that instant she was happier than she had been for five years, while Raoul felt himself repaid for all that he had gone through.

They had to return to their carriages, and walked on, hardly knowing whither, along the road from Auteuil to Boulogne, moving with the even rhythmic step familiar to lovers. Confidence came to Raoul in that kiss, tendered with the modest frankness that is the outcome of a pure mind. All the evil came from society, not from this woman, who was so absolutely his. The hardships of his frenzied existence were nothing now to him; and Marie, in the ardor of her first passion, was bound, womanlike, soon to forget them, since she could not witness from hour to hour the terrible throes of a life too exceptional to be easily imagined.

Marie, penetrated by the grateful veneration, characteristic of a woman's love, hastened with resolute and active tread along the sand-strewn alley. Like Raoul, she spoke but little, but that little came from the heart, and was full of meaning. The sky was clear; buds were forming on the larger trees, where already spots of green enlivened the delicate brown tracery; while the shrubs, birches, willows, and poplars showed their first tender and still unsubstantial foliage. What heart can resist the harmony of such a scene? Love was now interpreting nature to the countess, as it had already interpreted the ways of men.

"If only I were your first love!" she breathed.

"You are," replied Raoul. "We have each been the first to reveal true love to the other."

Nor did he speak falsely. In posing before this fresh young

heart as a man of pure life, he became affected by the noble sentiments with which he embroidered his talk. His passion, at first a matter of policy and ambition, had become sincere. Starting from falsehood, he had arrived at truth. Add to this that all authors have a natural instinct, repressed only with effort, to admire moral beauty. Lastly, a man has but to make enough sacrifices in order to become attached to the person demanding them. Women of the world know this intuitively, just as courtesans do, and it may even be that they unconsciously act upon the knowledge.

The countess, after her first burst of surprised gratitude, was delighted to have inspired so much devotion and been the cause of such astounding feats. The man who loved her was worthy of her. Raoul had not the least idea to what this playing at greatness would commit him. He forgot that no woman will allow her lover to fall below her ideal of him, and that nothing paltry can be suffered in a god. Marie had never heard that solution of the problem which Raoul had disclosed to his friends in the course of the supper at Véry's. His struggles as a man of letters, forcing his way upward from the masses, had filled the first ten years of early manhood; now he was resolved to be loved by one of the queens of the fashionable world. Vanity, without which, as Chamfort said, love has no backbone, sustained his passion, and could not fail to augment it day by day.

"Can you swear to me," said Marie, "that you are nothing, and never will be anything, to another woman?"

"My life has no space for another, even were my heart free," was his reply, made in all sincerity, so completely had Florine dropped out of sight.

And she believed him.

When they reached the road where the carriages were waiting, Marie let go the arm of Nathan, who at once assumed a respectful attitude, as though this were a chance meeting. He walked with her, hat in hand, as far as the carriage, and then followed it down the avenue Charles X., inhaling the dust it raised, and watching the drooping feathers swaying in the wind.

In spite of Marie's generous resolutions of sacrifice, Raoul, spurred on by passion, continued to appear wherever she went ; he adored the half-vexed, half-smiling air with which she vainly tried to scold him for wasting the time he could so badly spare. Marie began to take Raoul's work in hand, laid down what he was to do every hour in the day, and remained at home herself, so as to leave him no excuse for taking a holiday. She read his paper every morning, and she trumpeted the praises of Étienne Lousteau the feuilletonist, whom she thought charming, of Félicien Vernou, Claud Vignon, and all the staff. It was she who advised Raoul to deal generously with de Marsay when he died, and she read with dizzy pride the fine dignified tribute which he paid the late Minister, while deploring his Machiavellianism and hatred of the masses. She was, of course, present in a stage-box at the Gymnase on the first night of the play, to which Raoul was trusting for the funds of his undertaking, and which seemed to her, deceived by the hired applause, an immense success.

"You did not come to say farewell to the opera?" asked Lady Dudley, to whose house she went after the performance.

"No ; I was at the Gymnase. It was a first night."

"I can't bear vaudeville. I feel to it as Louis XIV. did to a Teniers," said Lady Dudley.

"For my part," remarked Mme. d'Espard, "I think they have improved very much. Vaudevilles now are charming comedies, full of wit, and the work of very clever men. I enjoy them immensely."

"The acting is so good too," said Marie. "The play to-night at the Gymnase went capitally ; it seemed to suit the actors, and the dialogue is spirited and amusing."

"A regular Beaumarchais business," said Lady Dudley.

"Monsieur Nathan is not a Molière yet, but——" said Mme. d'Espard, with a look at the countess.

"But he makes vaudevilles," said Mme. Charles de Vandenesse.

"And unmakes ministers," retorted Mme. de Manerville.

The countess remained silent; she racked her brains for pungent epigrams; her heart burned with rage, but nothing better occurred to her than—

"Some day perhaps he will make one."

All the women exchanged glances of mysterious understanding. When Mme. de Vandenesse had gone, Moïna de Saint-Héren exclaimed—

"Why, she adores Nathan !"

"She makes no mystery of it," said Mme. d'Espard.

CHAPTER VII.

SUICIDE.

With the month of May, Vandenesse took his wife away to their country seat. Here her only comfort was in passionate letters from Raoul, to whom she wrote every day.

The absence of the countess might possibly have saved Raoul from the abyss over which he hung had Florine been with him. But he was alone amongst friends, secretly turned to enemies ever since his determination to take the whip hand became plain. For the moment he was an object of hatred to his staff, who reserved, however, the right of holding out a consoling hand in case he failed, or of cringing to him should he succeed. This is the way in the literary world, where people are friendly only to their inferiors, and the rising man has everybody against him. This universal jealousy increases tenfold the chance of mediocrities, who arouse neither envy nor suspicion. Like moles, they work their way underground, and, with all their incompetence, find

more than one snug corner in the official lists, while really
able men are struggling and blocking each other at the door
of promotion. Florine, with the inborn gift of such women
for putting their finger on the real thing among a thousand
presentments of it, would at once have detected the under-
hand animosity of these false friends.

But this was not Raoul's greatest danger. His two partners,
the barrister Massol and the banker du Tillet, had conceived
the idea of harnessing his energy to the car in which they
should loll at ease, with the full intention of turning him
adrift as soon as his resources failed to keep the paper going,
or of wresting it from his hands the moment they saw their
way to using this powerful instrument for their own purposes.
To their minds, Nathan represented so much capital to run
through, a literary force, equal to that of ten ordinary writers,
to exploit.

Massol belonged to the type of barrister who takes a flux of
words for eloquence and can weary any audience by his pro-
lixity, who in every gathering of men acts as a blight, shrivel-
ing up their enthusiasm, yet who is determined at all costs
to be a somebody. Massol's ambition, however, no longer
pointed to the ministry of justice. Within four years he had
seen five or six men clothed with the robes of office, and this
had cured him of the fancy. Meanwhile he was ready to
accept, as something in hand, a professorship or a post under
the Council, with of course the cross of the Legion of Honor
to season the dish. Du Tillet and the Baron de Nucingen
had guaranteed him the cross and the desired post if he fell
in with their views; and as he judged them to be in a better
position than Nathan for fulfilling their promises, he followed
them blindly.

The better to hoodwink Raoul, these men allowed him to
exercise uncontrolled power. Du Tillet only made use of the
paper for his stock-jobbing interests, which were outside
Raoul's ken. He had, however, already given Rastignac to

understand, through the Baron de Nucingen, that this organ was ready to give a silent adhesion to the Government, on the one condition that the Government should support du Tillet's candidature as successor to M. de Nucingen, who would be a peer some day, and who at present sat for a rotten borough, where the paper was lavishly circulated, gratis. Thus was Raoul jockeyed by both the banker and the barrister, who took a huge delight in seeing him lord it at the office, pocketing all the gains, as well as the less substantial dues of vanity and the like. Nathan could not praise them enough; again, as when they furnished his stables, they were " the best fellows in the world," and he actually believed that he was duping them.

Men of imagination, whose whole life is based on hope, never will admit that in business the moment of danger is that when everything goes to a wish. Such a moment of triumph had come for Nathan, and he made full use of it, letting himself be seen both in political and financial circles. Du Tillet introduced him to the Nucingens, and he was received in a most friendly way by Mme. de Nucingen, not so much for his own sake as for that of Mme. de Vandenesse. Yet, when she alluded to the countess, Nathan thought himself a marvel of discretion for taking refuge behind Florine, and he enlarged with generous self-complacency on his relations with the actress, which nothing, he declared, could break. How could any man abandon an assured happiness for the coquetry of the Faubourg Saint-Germain?

Nathan, beguiled by Nucingen and Rastignac, du Tillet and Blondet, lent an ostentatious support to the doctrinaire party in the formation of one of their ephemeral cabinets. At the same time, wishing to start in public life with clean hands, he refused, with much parade, to accept any share in the profits of certain enterprises, which had been launched by the help of his paper. And this was the man who never hesitated to compromise a friend, or was hampered by a scruple in his relations with a certain class of business men at critical moments! Such startling contrasts, born of vanity and ambition, may often be found in careers like his. The mantle must make a brave show to the public, but scraps raised from a friend will serve to patch it.

But in the very midst of all his successes, Nathan was roused to some uneasiness by a bad quarter of an hour which he spent over his business accounts two months after the departure of the countess. Du Tillet had advanced a hundred thousand francs. The money given by Florine, the third part of his original capital, had gone in government dues and in the expenses of starting the paper, which were enormous. The future had to be provided for. The banker assisted him by accepting bills for fifty thousand francs at four months, and thereby fastened a halter round the author's neck. Thanks to this subvention, the paper was in funds again for six months. In the eyes of many literary men, six months is an eternity. Further, by dint of puffs and by sending round canvassers, who offered illusory advantages to subscribers, they managed to raise the circulation by two thousand. This semi-triumph was an incentive to cast his latest borrowings into the melting pot. One more effort of his wits, and a political lawsuit or a sham persecution might give Raoul a place among those modern Condottieri,* whose ink has to-day taken the place of gunpowder.

Unfortunately, these steps were already taken when Florine returned with about fifty thousand francs. Instead of setting this aside as a reserve, Raoul, confident of a success which was his only safety, humiliated at the thought of having once before accepted money from the actress, feeling that his love had raised him to a higher plane, and dazzled by the specious plaudits of his flatterers, deceived Florine as to his situation, and obliged her to spend the money in setting up house again. Under present circumstances, a smart and dashing style was,

* Mercenary Italian soldiers.

he assured her, essential. The actress, who needed no spurring, got into debt for thirty thousand francs. Instead of a flat, Florine took a charming house in the Rue Pigalle, where her old friends came about her again. The house of a woman in Florine's position supplied a neutral ground, most convenient for pushing politicians, who, following the example of Louis XIV. with the Dutch, entertained at Raoul's house in Raoul's absence.

Nathan had reserved for the return of the actress a play, the chief part in which suited her admirably. This vaudeville-drama was intended as Raoul's farewell to the theatre. The newspapers, by an attention to Raoul which cost them nothing, planned beforehand such an ovation to Florine that the Comédie-Française began to speak of engaging her. Critics pointed to her as the direct successor of Mlle. Mars. This triumph threw the actress so far off her balance as to prevent her examining carefully the state of Nathan's affairs; her life was a whirl of banquets and revelry. Queen in a horde of bustling suitors, each with something to push—a book, a play, a ballet-girl, a theatre, a company, or an advertisement—she reveled in the delights of this press influence, which she pictured as the dawn of ministerial patronage. In the mouths of those who frequented her house, Nathan was a politician of high standing. His scheme would succeed, he would be elected to the Chamber, and beyond doubt have a turn at office, like so many others. Actresses are rarely slow to believe what flatters their hopes. How could Florine, lauded in the notices, mistrust the paper or its contributors? She was too ignorant of the mechanism of the press to be uneasy about its resources, and women of her stamp look only to results.

As for Nathan, he no longer doubted that in the course of the next session he would come to the front, along with two former journalists, one of whom, already in office, was anxious to strengthen his position by turning out his colleagues. After six months of absence, Nathan was glad to see Florine again, and lazily fell back into his old habits. The coarse web of his life was covertly embroidered by him with the loveliest flowers of his ideal passion and with the pleasures scattered by Florine. His letters to Marie were masterpieces of love, elegance, and style. He made of her the guiding star of his life; he undertook nothing without consulting his good genius. Miserable at being on the popular side, he was tempted at times to join the aristocrats; but, with all his skill in turning his back on himself, it seemed impossible to make the leap from left to right; it was easier to get office.

Marie's precious letters were kept in a portfolio with secret springs, an invention either of Huret or Fichet, the two mechanics who carry on a war of emulation in the newspaper columns and on the walls of Paris as to the comparative efficacy and unobtrusiveness of their locks. The portfolio lay in Florine's new boudoir, where Raoul worked. No one is more easily deceived than the woman who is used to frankness; she has no suspicions, because she believes herself to know and see all that goes on. Moreover, since her return the actress took her part in Nathan's daily life, which appeared to go on just as usual. It never would have occurred to her that this writing-case, which she had barely noticed, and which Raoul made no mystery about locking, contained love tokens in the shape of a rival's letters, addressed, at Raoul's request, to the office. To all appearance, therefore, Nathan's situation was of the brightest. He had plenty of nominal friends. Two plays, at which he had worked jointly with others, and which had just made a success, kept him in luxuries and removed all anxiety for the future. Indeed, his debt to his friend du Tillet never gave him a moment's uneasiness.

"How can one suspect a friend?" he said, when now and again Blondet would give utterance to doubts, which were natural to his analytic turn of mind.

"But we have no need to fear our enemies," said Florine.

Nathan stood up for du Tillet. Du Tillet was the best, most good-natured, and most honorable of men.

This life upon the tight-rope, without even a steadying pole, which might have appalled a mere onlooker who had grasped its meaning, was watched by du Tillet with the stoicism and hard-heartedness of a parvenu. At times a fierce irony broke through the genial cordiality of his manner with Nathan. One day he pressed his hand as he was leaving Florine's, and watched him get into his cabriolet.

"There goes our dandy off to the Bois in tiptop style," he said to Lousteau, the very incarnation of envy, "and in six months he may be laid by the heels in Clichy."

"Not he!" exclaimed Lousteau; "think of Florine."

"And how do you know, my good fellow, that he'll keep Florine? I tell you, you're worth a thousand of him, and I expect six months will see you in the editorial chair."

In October the bills fell due, and du Tillet graciously renewed them, but this time for two months only, and the amount was increased by the discount and by a new loan. Confident of victory, Raoul drained his till. An overmastering desire to see him was bringing the countess back to town a month earlier than usual—within a few days, in fact—and it would not do to be crippled for lack of funds when the moment had come for entering the field again.

The pen is always bolder than the tongue, and the letters she received had raised the Comtesse de Vandenesse to the highest pitch of excitement. Thoughts clothed in the flowers of rhetoric can express so much without meeting a repulse. She saw in Raoul one of the finest intellects of the day, a delicately strung and unappreciated heart, which in its unstained purity was worthy of adoration. She watched him put forth a bold hand upon the citadel of power. Ere long that voice, so tuneful in love, would thunder from the tribune. Marie was now entirely absorbed in that life of intersecting circles, which resemble the orbits of the planets, and revolve around the sun of society as their centre. Finding no flavor in the calm pleasures of home, she received the shock of every agitation in this whirling life, brought home to her by the pen of a literary artist and a lover. She showered kisses on letters which had been written in the thick of press combats, or purloined from hours of study. She realized now what they had cost and was well assured of being his only love, with no rivals but glory and ambition. Even in the depths of her solitude she found occupation for all her powers and could dwell with satisfaction upon the choice of her heart. There was no one like Nathan.

Fortunately, her withdrawal into the country and the barriers thus placed between her and Raoul had silenced ill-natured gossip. During the last days of autumn, therefore, Marie and Raoul were able once more to begin their walks in the Bois de Boulogne, their only meeting-place until the season opened. Raoul had now a little more leisure to enjoy the exquisite delights of his ideal life, and also to practice concealment with Florine; his work at the office had ceased to be so hard since things were well in train there and each member of the staff understood his duty. Involuntarily he made comparisons which, though always favorable to Florine, did the countess no injury. Exhausted once more by the various shifts to which his passion, alike of the head and of the heart, for a woman of fashion impelled him, Raoul put forth superhuman energy in the effort to appear simultaneously on three different stages—society, the office, and the greenroom. While Florine, always grateful and taking almost a partner's share in his work and difficulties, appeared and vanished as required, and showered on him a wealth of substantial and unpretentious happiness, which called forth no remorse, the unapproachable countess, with her hungry eyes, had already forgotten his stupendous labors and the trouble it often cost him to get a passing glimpse of her. Florine, far from trying to impose her will, would let herself be taken up and put down with the good-natured indifference of a cat, which always falls on its feet and walks off, shaking its ears. This easy way of life is admirably fitted to the habits of brain-workers; and it is only in the artist's nature to take full advantage of it, as Nathan did, whilst not abandoning the pursuit of that fine ideal love, that splendid passion, which delighted at once his poetic instincts, the germ of greatness in him, and his social ambitions. Fully aware how disastrous would be the effect of any indiscretion, he told himself it was impossible that either the countess or Florine should find out anything. The chasm between them was too great.

With the beginning of winter Raoul once more made his appearance in society, and this time in the heyday of his glory; he was all but a personage. Rastignac, who had fallen with the Government which went to pieces on de Marsay's death, leaned upon Raoul, and in return gave him the support of his good word. Mme. de Vandenesse was curious to know whether her husband had changed his opinion of Raoul. After the lapse of a year she questioned him again, in the expectation of a signal revenge, such as the noblest and least earthly of women do not disdain; for we may be sure that the angels in heaven have not lost all thought of self as they range themselves round the throne.

"That he should become the tool of unscrupulous men was the one thing lacking to him," replied the count.

Félix, with the keen insight of a politician and a man of the world, had thoroughly gauged Raoul's position. He calmly explained to his wife how the attempt of Fieschi had resulted in rallying many lukewarm people round the interests threatened in the person of Louis-Philippe. The comparatively neutral papers would go down in circulation as journalism, along with politics, fell into more definite lines. If Nathan had put his capital into his paper, he would soon be done for. This summary of the situation, so clear and accurate in spite of its brevity and the purely abstract point of view from which it was made, and coming from a man well used to calculate the chances of party, frightened Mme. de Vandenesse.

"Do you take much interest in him then?" asked Félix of his wife.

"Oh! I like his humor, and he talks well."

The reply came so naturally that it did not rouse the count's suspicions.

At four o'clock next day at Mme. d'Espard's, Marie and Raoul held a long whispered conversation. The countess gave expression to fears which Raoul dissipated, only too glad of this opportunity to damage the husband's authority under a battery of epigrams. He had his revenge to take. The count, thus handled, appeared a man of narrow mind and behind the day, who judged the Revolution of July by the standard of the Restoration, and shut his eyes to the triumph of the middle-class, that new and substantial factor to be reckoned with, for a time at least if not permanently, in every society. The great feudal lords of the past were impossible now, the reign of true merit had begun. Instead of weighing well the indirect and impartial warning he had received from an experienced politician in the expression of his deliberate opinion, Raoul made it an occasion for display, mounted his stilts, and draped himself in the purple of success. Where is the woman who would not believe her lover rather than her husband?

Mme. de Vandenesse, reassured, plunged once more into that life of repressed irritation, of little stolen pleasures, and of covert hand-pressings which had carried her through the preceding winter; but which can have no other end than to drag a woman over the boundary-line if the man she loves has any spirit and chafes against the curb. Happily for her, Raoul, kept in check by Florine, was not dangerous. He was engrossed, too, in business which did not allow him to turn his good fortune to account. Nevertheless, some sudden disaster, a renewal of difficulties, an outburst of impatience, might at any moment precipitate the countess into the abyss.

Raoul was becoming conscious of this disposition in Marie when, toward the end of December, du Tillet asked for his money. The wealthy banker told Raoul he was hard up, and advised him to borrow the amount for a fortnight from a money-lender called Gigonnet—a twenty-five per cent. providence for all young men in difficulties. In a few days the paper would make a fresh financial start with the new year, there would be cash in the counting-house, and then du Tillet would see what he could do. Beside, why should not Nathan write another play? Nathan was too proud not to resolve on paying at any cost. Du Tillet gave him a letter for the money-lender, in response to which Gigonnet handed him the amount required and took bills payable in twenty days. Raoul, instead of having his suspicions aroused by this accommodating reception, was only vexed that he had not asked for more. This is the way with men of the greatest intellectual power; they see only matter for pleasantry in a grave predicament, and reserve their wits for writing books, as though afraid there might not be enough of them to go round if applied to daily life. Raoul told Florine and Blondet how he had spent his morning; he drew a faithful picture of Gigonnet and his surroundings, his cheap *fleur-de-lys* (lily-flowered) wall-paper, his staircase, his asthmatic bell, his stag's-foot knocker, his worn little door-mat, his heart as devoid of fire as his eye; he made them laugh at this new "uncle," and neither du Tillet's professed need of money nor the facility of the usurer caused them the least uneasiness. One can't account for every whim!

"He has only taken fifteen per cent. from you," said Blondet; "he deserves your thanks. At twenty-five they cease to be gentlemen; at fifty, usury begins; at this figure they are only contemptible!"

"Contemptible!" cried Florine. "I should like to know

7

which of your friends would lend you money at this rate without posing as a benefactor?"

"She is quite right; I am heartily glad to be quit of du Tillet's debt," said Raoul.

Most mysterious is this lack of penetration in regard to their private affairs on the part of men generally so keen-sighted! It may be that it is impossible for the mind to be fully equipped on every side; it may be that artists live too entirely in the present to trouble about the future; or it may be that, always on the lookout for the ridiculous, they are blind to traps, and cannot believe in any one daring to fool them.

The end did not tarry. Twenty days later the bills were protested; but in the court Florine had a respite of twenty-five days applied for and granted. Raoul made an effort to see where he stood; he sent for the books; and from these it appeared that the receipts of the paper covered two-thirds of the cost, and that the circulation was going down. The great man became uneasy and gloomy, but only in the company of Florine, in whom he confided. Florine advised him to borrow on the security of plays not yet written, selling them in a lump, and parting at the same time with the royalties on his acted plays. By this means Nathan raised twenty thousand francs, and reduced his debt to forty thousand.

On the 10th of February the twenty-five days expired. Du Tillet, determined to oust Nathan, as a rival, from the constituency, where he intended to stand himself (leaving to Massol another which was in the pocket of the Government), got Gigonnet to refuse Raoul all quarter. A man laid by the heels for debt can hardly present himself as a candidate; and the embryo minister might disappear in the maw of a debtor's prison. Florine herself was in constant communication with the bailiffs on account of her own debts, and in this crisis the only resource left to her was the "I!" of Medea, for her furniture was seized. The aspirant to fame heard on every side the crack of ruin in his freshly reared but baseless fabric. Unequal to the task of sustaining so vast an enterprise, how could he think of beginning again to lay the foundations? Nothing remained, therefore, but to perish beneath his crumbling visions. His love for the countess still brought flashes of life, but only to the outer mask; within, all hope was dead. He did not suspect du Tillet; the usurer alone filled his view. Rastignac, Blondet, Lousteau, Vernou, Finot, Massol, carefully refrained from enlightening a man of such dangerous energy. Rastignac, who aimed at getting back to power, made common cause with Nucingen and du Tillet. The rest found measureless delight in watching the expiring agony of one of their comrades, convicted of the crime of aiming at mastery. Not one of them would breathe a word to Florine; to her, on the contrary, they were full of Raoul's praises. "Nathan's shoulders were broad enough to bear the world; he would come out all right, no fear!"

"The circulation went up two yesterday," said Blondet solemnly. "Raoul will be elected yet. As soon as the budget is through the dissolution will be announced."

Nathan, dogged by the law, could no longer look to moneylenders; Florine, her furniture distrained, had no hope left save in the chance of inspiring a passion in some good-natured fool, who never turns up at the right moment. Nathan's friends were all men without money or credit. His political chances would be ruined by his arrest. To crown all, he saw himself pledged to huge tasks, paid for in advance; it was a bottomless pit of horrors into which he gazed.

Before an outlook so threatening his self-confidence deserted him. Would the Comtesse de Vandenesse unite her fate to his and fly with him? Only a fully developed passion can bring a woman to this fatal step, and theirs had never bound them to each other in the mysterious ties of illicit rapture. Even supposing the countess would follow him abroad, she would come penniless, bare, and stripped, and would prove an added burden.   A proud man, of second-rate quality, like Nathan, could not fail to see in suicide, as Nathan did, the sword with which to cut this Gordian knot.   The idea of overthrow, in full view of that society into which he had worked his way and which he had aspired to dominate, of leaving the countess enthroned there, while he fell back to join the mud-spattered rank and file, was unbearable.   Madness danced and rang her bells before the door of that airy palace in which the poet had made his home.   In this extremity, Nathan waited upon a chance, and put off killing himself till the last moment.

During the last days, occupied with the notice of judgment, the writs, and publication of order of arrest, Raoul could not succeed in throwing off that coldly sinister look, observed by noticing people to haunt those marked out for suicide, or whose minds are dwelling on it.   The dismal ideas which they fondle cast a gray, gloomy shade over the forehead ; their smile is vaguely ominous, and they move with solemnity. The unhappy wretches seem resolved to suck dry the golden fruit of life ; they cast appealing glances on every side, the toll of the passing-bell is in their ears, and their minds wander.   These alarming symptoms were perceived by Marie one night at Lady Dudley's.   Raoul had remained alone on a sofa in the boudoir, while the rest of the company were conversing in the drawing-room ; when the countess came to the door, he did not raise his head ; he heard neither Marie's breath nor the rustle of her silk dress ; his eyes, stupid with pain, were fixed on a flower in the carpet.   "Sooner die than abdicate," was his thought.   It is not every man who has a Saint-Helena to retire upon.   Suicide, moreover, was at that time in vogue in Paris : what more suitable key to the mystery of life for a skeptical society ?   Raoul, then, had just resolved to put an end to himself.   Despair must be proportioned to hope, and that of Raoul could find no issue but the grave.

"What is the matter?" said Marie, flying to him.

"Nothing," he replied.

"Lovers have a way of using this word "nothing" which implies exactly the opposite. Marie gave a little shrug.

"What a child you are!" she said. "Something has gone wrong with you?"

"Not with me," he said. "Beside," he added affectionately, "you will know it all too soon, Marie."

"What were you thinking of when I came in?" she said, with an air that would not be denied.

"Are you determined to know the truth?"

She bowed her head.

"I was thinking of you; I said to myself that many men in my place would have wished to be loved without reserve: I am loved, am I not?"

"Yes," she said.

Braving the risk of interruption, Raoul put his arm around her and drew her near enough to kiss her on the forehead, as he continued—

"And I am leaving you pure and free from remorse. I might drag you into the abyss, but you stand upon the brink in all your stainless glory. One thought, though, haunts me——"

"What thought?"

"You will despise me."

She smiled a proud smile.

"Yes, you will never believe in the holiness of my love for you; and then they will slander me, I know. No woman can conceive how, from out of the filth in which we wallow, we raise our eyes to heaven in single-hearted worship of some radiant star—some Marie. They mix up this adoration with painful questions; they cannot understand that men of high intellect and poetic vision are able to wean their souls from pleasure and keep them to lay entire upon some cherished altar. And yet, Marie, our devotion to the ideal is more ardent than yours; we embody it in a woman, while she does not even seek for it in us.''

''Why this effusion?'' she said, with the irony of a woman who has no misgivings.

''I am leaving France; you will learn how and why to-morrow from a letter which my servant will bring you. Farewell, Marie.''

Raoul went out, after pressing the countess to his heart in an agonized embrace, and left her dazed with misery.

''What is wrong, dear?'' said the Marquise d'Espard, coming to look for her. ''What has Monsieur Nathan been saying? He left us with quite a melodramatic air. You must have been terribly foolish—or terribly prudent.''

The countess took Mme. d'Espard's arm to return to the drawing-room, where, however, she only stayed a few instants.

''Perhaps she is going to her first appointment,'' said Lady Dudley to the marchioness.

''I shall make sure as to that,'' replied Mme. d'Espard, who left at once to follow the countess' carriage.

But the coupé of Mme. de Vandenesse took the road to the Faubourg St. Honoré. When Mme. d'Espard entered her house, she saw the countess driving along the faubourg in the direction of the Rue du Rocher. Marie went to bed, but not to sleep, and spent the night in reading a voyage to the North Pole, of which she did not take in a word.

At half-past eight next morning she got a letter from Raoul and opened it in feverish haste. The letter began with the classic phrase—

''My loved one, when this paper is in your hands, I shall be no more.''

She read no further, but crushing the paper with a nervous motion, rang for her maid, hastily put on a loose gown, and the first pair of shoes that came to hand, wrapped a shawl round her, took a bonnet, and then went out, instructing her maid to tell the count that she had gone to her sister, Mme. du Tillet.

"Where did you leave your master?" she asked of Raoul's servant.

"At the newspaper office."

"Take me there," she said.

To the amazement of the household, she left the house on foot before nine o'clock, visibly distraught. Fortunately for her, the maid went to tell the count that her mistress had just received a letter from Mme. du Tillet which had upset her very much, and that she had started in a great hurry for her sister's house, accompanied by the servant who had brought the letter. Vandenesse waited for further explanations till his wife's return. The countess got a cab and was borne rapidly to the office. At that time of day the spacious rooms occupied by the paper, in an old house in the Rue Feydeau, were deserted. The only occupant was an attendant, whose astonishment was great when a pretty and distracted young woman rushed up and demanded M. Nathan.

"I expect he is with Mademoiselle Florine," he replied, taking the countess for some jealous rival, bent on making a scene.

"Where does he work?" she asked.

"In a small room, the key of which is in his pocket."

"I must go there."

The man led her to a dark room, looking out on a back-yard, which had formerly been the dressing-closet attached to a large bedroom. This closet made an angle with the bed-room, in which the recess for the bed still remained. By opening the bedroom window, the countess was able to see through that of the closet what was happening within.

Nathan lay in the editorial chair, the death-rattle in his throat.

"Break open that door, and tell no one! I will pay you

to keep silence," she cried. "Can't you see that Monsieur Nathan is dying?"

"Ah!" was the only reply.

The man rushed to the compositors' room to fetch an iron chase with which to force the door. Raoul was killing himself, like some poor work-girl, with the fumes from a pan of charcoal. He had just finished a letter to Blondet, in which he begged him to attribute his death to a fit of apoplexy. The countess was just in time; she had Raoul carried into the cab; and not knowing where to get him looked after, she went to a hotel, took a room there, and sent the attendant to fetch a doctor. Raoul in a few hours was out of danger; but the countess did not leave his bedside till she had obtained a full confession. When the prostrate wrestler with fate had poured into her heart the terrible elegy of his sufferings, she returned home a prey to all the torturing fancies which the evening before had brooded over Nathan's brow.

"Leave it all to me," she had said, hoping to win him back to life.

"Well, what is wrong with your sister?" asked Félix, on seeing his wife return. "You look like a ghost."

"It is a frightful story, but I must keep it an absolute secret," she replied, summoning all her strength to put on an appearance of composure.

In order to be alone and able to think in peace, she went to the opera in the evening, and thence had gone on to unbosom her woes to Mme. du Tillet. After describing the ghastly scene of the morning, she implored her sister's advice and aid. Neither of them had an idea then that it was du Tillet whose hand had put the match to that vulgar pan of charcoal, the sight of which had so dismayed Mme. de Vandenesse.

"He has no one but me in the world," Marie had said to her sister, "and I shall not fail him."

In these words may be read the key to women's hearts.

They become heroic in the assurance of being all in all to a great and honorable man.

CHAPTER VIII.

A LOVER SAVED AND LOST.

Du Tillet had heard many speculations as to the greater or less probability of his sister-in-law's love for Nathan ; but he was one of those who deemed the *liaison* incompatible with that existing between Raoul and Florine, or who denied it on other grounds. In his view, either the actress made the countess impossible, or *vice versâ*. But when, on his return that evening, he found his sister-in-law, whose agitation had been plainly written on her face at the opera, he surmised that Raoul had confided his plight to the countess. This meant that the countess loved him, and had come to beg from Marie-Eugénie the amount due to old Gigonnet. Mme. du Tillet, at a loss how to explain this apparently miraculous insight, had betrayed so much confusion, that du Tillet's suspicion became a certainty. The banker was confident that he could now get hold of the clue to Nathan's intrigues.

No one knew of the poor wretch who lay ill in a private hotel in the Rue du Mail, under the name of the attendant, François Quillet, to whom the countess had promised five hundred francs as the reward for silence on the events of the night and morning. Quillet in consequence had taken the precaution of telling the portress that Nathan was ill from overwork. It was no surprise to du Tillet not to see Nathan, for it was only natural the journalist should keep in hiding from the bailiffs. When the detectives came to make inquiry, they were told that a lady had been there that morning and carried off the editor. Two days elapsed before they had discovered the number of the cab, questioned the driver, and identified and explored the house in which the poor insolvent

was coming back to life.   Thus Marie's wary tactics had won
for Nathan a respite of three days.

Each of the sisters passed an agitated night.   Such a tragedy
casts a lurid light, like the glow of its own charcoal, upon the
whole substance of a life, throwing out its shoals and reefs
rather than the heights which hitherto had struck the eye.
Mme. du Tillet, overcome by the frightful spectacle of a
young man dying in his editorial chair, and writing his last
words with Roman stoicism, could think of nothing but how
to help him, how to restore to life the being in whom her
sister's life was bound up.   It is a law of the mind to look at
effects before analyzing causes.   Eugénie once more approved
the idea, which had occurred to her, of applying to the
Baronne Delphine de Nucingen, with whom she had a dining acquaintance, and felt that it promised well.   With the
generosity natural to those whose hearts have not been ground
in the polished mill of society, Mme. du Tillet determined to
take everything upon herself.

The countess again, happy in having saved Nathan's life,
spent the night in scheming how to lay her hands on forty
thousand francs.   In such a crisis women are beyond praise.
Under the impulse of feeling they light upon contrivances
which would excite, if anything could, the admiration of
thieves, brokers, and usurers, those three more or less licensed
classes of filchers who live by their wits.   The countess would
sell her diamonds and wear false ones.   Then she was for
asking Vandenesse to give her the money for her sister, whom
she had already used as a pretext ; but she was too high-
minded not to recoil from such degrading expedients, which
occurred to her only to be rejected.   To give Vandenesse's
money to Nathan !   At the very thought she leaped up in
bed, horrified at her own baseness.   Wear false diamonds !
her husband would find out sooner or later.   She would go and
beg the money from the Rothschilds, who had so much ; from
the Archbishop of Paris, whose duty it was to succor the poor.

Thus in her extremity she rushed from one religion to another with impartial prayers. She lamented being in opposition ; in old days she could have borrowed from persons near to royalty. She thought of applying to her father. But the ex-judge had a horror of any breach of the law ; his children had learned from experience how little sympathy he had with love troubles ; he refused to hear of them, he had become a misanthrope, he could not away with intrigue of any description. As to the Comtesse de Granville, she had gone to live in retirement on one of her estates in Normandy, and, icy to the last, was ending her days, pinching and praying, between money-bags and priests. Even were there time for Marie to reach Bayeux, would her mother give her so large a sum without knowing for what it was wanted ? Imaginary debts ? Yes, possibly her favorite child might move her to compassion. Well, then, as a last resource, to Normandy the countess would go. The Comte de Granville would not refuse to give her a pretext by sending false news of his wife's serious illness.

The tragedy which had given her such a shock in the morning, the care she had lavished on Nathan, the hours passed by his bedside, the broken tale, the agony of a great mind, the career of genius cut short by a vulgar and ignoble detail, all rushed upon her memory as so many spurs to love. Once more she lived through every heart-throb, and felt her love stronger in the hour of Nathan's abasement than in that of his success. Would she have kissed that forehead crowned with triumph ? Her heart answered : No. The parting words Nathan had spoken to her in Lady Dudley's boudoir touched her unspeakably by their noble dignity. Was ever farewell more saintly ? What could be more heroic than to abandon happiness because it would have made her misery ? The countess had longed for sensations in her life, truly she had a wealth of them now, fearful, agonizing, and yet dear to her. Her life seemed fuller in pain than it had ever been in pleasure.

With what ecstasy she repeated to herself: " I have saved him already, and I will save him again! " She heard his cry: " Only the miserable know the power of love! " when he had felt his Marie's lips upon his forehead.

" Are you ill? " asked her husband, coming into her room to fetch her for lunch.

" I cannot get over the tragedy which is being enacted at my sister's," she said, truthfully enough.

" She has fallen into bad hands; it's a disgrace to the family to have a du Tillet in it, a worthless fellow like that. If your sister got into any trouble, she would find scant pity with him."

" What woman could endure pity? " said the countess, with an involuntary shudder. " Your ruthless harshness is the truest homage."

" There speaks your noble heart! " said Félix, kissing his wife's hand, quite touched by her fine scorn. " A woman who feels like that does not need guarding."

" Guarding? " she answered; " that again is another disgrace which recoils on you."

Félix smiled, but Marie blushed. When a woman has committed a secret fault, she cloaks herself in an exaggerated womanly pride, nor can we blame the fraud, which points to a reserve of dignity or even high-mindedness.

Marie wrote a line to Nathan, under the name of M. Quillet, to tell him that all was going well and sent it by a commissionaire to the Mail Hotel. At the opera in the evening the countess reaped the benefit of her falsehoods, her husband finding it quite natural that she should leave her box to go and see her sister. Félix waited to give her his arm till du Tillet had left his wife alone. What were not Marie's feelings as she crossed the passage, entered her sister's box, and took her seat there, facing with calm and serene countenance the world of fashion, amazed to see the sisters together!

" Tell me," she said.

The reply was written on Marie-Eugénie's face, the radiance of which many people ascribed to gratified vanity.

"Yes, he will be saved, darling, but for three months only, during which time we will put our heads together and find some more substantial help. Madame de Nucingen will take four bills, each for ten thousand francs, signed by any one you like, so as not to compromise you. She has explained to me how they are to be made out; I don't understand in the least, but Monsieur Nathan will get them ready for you. Only it occurred to me that perhaps our old master, Schmucke, might be useful to us now; he would sign them. If, in addition to these four securities, you write a letter guaranteeing their payment to Madame de Nucingen, she will hand you the money to-morrow. Do the whole thing yourself; don't trust to anybody. Schmucke, you see, would, I think, make no difficulty if you asked him. To disarm suspicion, I said that you wanted to do a kindness to our old music-master, a German, who was in trouble. In this way I was able to beg for the strictest secrecy."

"You angel of cleverness! If only the Baronne de Nucingen does not talk till after she has given the money!" said the countess, raising her eyes as though in prayer, regardless of her surroundings.

"Schmucke lives in the little Rue de Nevers, on the Quai Conti; don't forget, and go yourself."

"Thanks," said the countess, pressing her sister's hand. "Ah! I would give ten years of my life——"

"From your old age——"

"To put an end to all these horrors," said the countess, with a smile at the interruption.

The crowd at this moment, spying the two sisters through their opera-glasses, might suppose them to be talking of trivialities, as they heard the ring of their frank laughter. But any one of those idlers, who frequent the opera rather to study dress and faces than to enjoy themselves, would be able to

detect the secret of the countess in the wave of feeling which
suddenly blotted all cheerfulness out of their fair faces.
Raoul, who did not fear the bailiffs at night, appeared, pale
and ashy, with anxious eye and gloomy brow, on the step of
the staircase where he regularly took his stand. He looked
for the countess in her box, and, finding it empty, buried his
face in his hands, leaning his elbows on the balustrade.

"Can she be here!" he thought.

"Look up, unhappy hero," whispered Mme. du Tillet.

As for Marie, at all risks she fixed on him that steady magnetic gaze, in which the will flashes from the eye, as rays of
light from the sun. Such a look, mesmerizers say, penetrates
to the person on whom it is directed, and certainly Raoul
seemed as though struck by a magic wand. Raising his head,
his eyes met those of the sisters. With that charming feminine readiness which is never at fault, Mme. de Vandenesse
seized a cross, sparkling on her neck, and directed his attention to it by a swift smile, full of meaning. The brilliance of
the gem radiated even upon Raoul's forehead, and he replied
with a look of joy; he had understood.

"Is it nothing, then, Eugénie," said the countess, "thus
to restore life to the dead?"

"You have a chance yet with the Royal Humane Society,"
replied Eugénie, with a smile.

"How wretched and depressed he looked when he came,
and how happy he will go away!"

At this moment du Tillet, coming up to Raoul with every
mark of friendliness, pressed his hand, and said—

"Well, old fellow, how are you?"

"As well as a man is likely to be who has just got the best
possible news of the election. I shall be successful," replied
Raoul, radiant.

"Delighted," said du Tillet. "We shall want money for
the paper."

"The money will be found," said Raoul.

"The devil is with these women!" exclaimed du Tillet, still unconvinced by the words of Raoul, whom he had nick-named *Charnathan*—carriage-gift.

"What are you talking about?" said Raoul.

"My sister-in-law is there with my wife, and they are hatching something together. You seem in high favor with the countess; she is bowing to you right across the house."

"Look," said Mme. du Tillet to her sister, "they told us wrong. See how my husband fawns on Monsieur Nathan, and it is he who they declared was trying to get him put in prison!"

"And men call us slanderers!" cried the countess. "I will give him a warning."

She rose, took the arm of Vandenesse, who was waiting in the passage, and returned jubilant to her box; by-and-by she left the opera, ordered her carriage for the next morning before eight o'clock, and found herself at half-past eight on the Quai Conti, having called at the Rue du Mail on her way.

The carriage could not enter the narrrow Rue de Nevers; but, as Schmucke's house stood at the corner of the quay, the countess was not obliged to walk to it through the mud. She almost leapt from the step of the carriage on to the dirty and dilapidated entrance of the grimy old house, which was held together by iron clamps, like a poor man's crockery, and over-hung the street in quite an alarming fashion.

The old organist lived on the fourth floor, and rejoiced in a beautiful view of the Seine, from the Pont Neuf to the rising ground of Chaillot. The simple fellow was so taken aback when the footman announced his former pupil, that, before he could recover himself, she was in the room. Never could the countess have imagined or guessed at an existence such as that suddenly laid bare to her, though she had long known Schmucke's scorn for appearances and his indifference to worldly things. Who could have believed in so neglected a life, in carelessness carried to such a pitch? Schmucke was a musical Diogenes ; he felt no shame for the hugger-mugger in which he lived ; indeed, custom had made him insensible to it.

The constant use of a fat, friendly, German pipe had spread over the ceiling and the flimsy wall-paper—well rubbed by the cat—a faint yellow tint, which gave a pervading impression of the golden harvests of Ceres. The cat, whose long ruffled silky coat made a garment such as a portress might have envied, did the honors of the house, sedately whiskered, and entirely at her ease. From the top of a first-rate Vienna piano, where she lay couched in state, she cast on the countess as she entered the gracious yet chilly glance with which any woman, astonished at her beauty, might have greeted her. She did not stir, except to wave the two silvery threads of her upright mustache and to fix upon Schmucke two golden eyes. The piano, which had known better days, and was cased in a good wood, painted black and gold, was dirty, discolored, chipped, and its keys were worn like the teeth of an old horse and mellowed by the deeper tints which fell from the pipe. Little piles of ashes on the ledge proclaimed that the night before Schmucke had bestridden the old instrument to some witches' rendezvous. The brick floor, strewn with dried mud, torn paper, tobacco-ashes, and odds and ends that defy description, suggested the boards of a lodging-house floor, when they have not been swept for a week and heaps of litter, a cross between the contents of the ash-pit and the rag-bag, await the servants' brooms. A more practiced eye than that of the countess might have read indications of Schmucke's way of living in the chestnut scraps, parings of apple-peel, and shells of Easter eggs, which covered broken fragments of plates, all messed with *sauer kraut.* This German detritus formed a carpet of dusty filth which grated under the feet and lost itself in a mass of cinders, dropping with slow dignity from a painted stone fireplace, where a lump of coal lorded it over two half-burnt logs that seemed to waste away before it. On the mantel was a pier-glass with figures dancing a saraband round it ; on one side the glorious pipe hung on a nail, on the other stood a china pot in which the professor kept his tobacco. Two armchairs, casually picked up, together with a thin, flattened couch, a worm-eaten bureau with the marble top gone, and a maimed table, on which lay the remains of a frugal breakfast, made up the furniture, unpretending as that of a Mohican wigwam. A shaving-glass hanging from the catch of a curtainless window, and surmounted by a rag, striped by razor scrapings, were evidence of the sole sacrifices paid by Schmucke to the graces and to society.

The cat, petted as a feeble and dependent being, was the best off. It rejoiced in an old armchair cushion, beside which stood a white china cup and dish. But what no pen can describe is the state to which Schmucke, the cat, and the pipe— trinity of living beings—had reduced the furniture. The pipe had scorched the table in places. The cat and Schmucke's head had greased the green Utrecht velvet of the two armchairs till it was worn quite smooth. But for the cat's magnificent tail, which did a part of the cleaning, the dust would have lain for ever undisturbed on the uncovered parts of the chest of drawers and piano. In a corner lay the army of slippers, to which only a Homeric catalogue could do justice. The tops of the bureau and of the piano were blocked with broken-backed, loose-paged music-books, the boards showing all the pages peeping through, with corners white and dogs-eared. Along the walls the addresses of pupils were glued with little wafers. The wafers without papers showed the number of obsolete addresses. On the wall-paper chalk additions might be read. The bureau was adorned with last night's beer tankards, which stood out quite fresh and bright in the midst of all this stuffiness and decay. Hygiene was represented by a water-jug crowned with a towel and a bit of common soap, white marbled with blue, which left its damp-mark here and there on the red wood. Two hats, equally ancient, hung on pegs,

8

from which was also suspended the familiar blue ulster with its three capes, without which the countess would hardly have known Schmucke. Beneath the window stood three pots of flowers, German flowers presumably, and close by a holly walking-stick.

Though the countess was disagreeably affected both in sight and smell, yet Schmucke's eyes and smile transformed the sordid scene with heavenly rays, that gave a glory to the dingy tones and animation to the chaos. The soul of this man, who seemed to belong to another world and revealed so many of its mysteries, radiated light like the sun. His frank and hearty laugh at the sight of one of his Saint Cecilias diffused the brightness of youth, mirth, and innocence. He poured out treasures of that which mankind holds dearest, and made a cloak of them to veil his poverty. The most purse-proud upstart would perhaps have blushed to think twice of the surroundings within which moved this noble apostle of the religion of music.

"Eh, py vot tchance came you here, tear Montame la Gondesse?" he said. "Must I den zing de zong ov Zimeon at mein asche?"

This idea started him on another peal of ringing laughter.

"Is it dat I haf a conqvest made?" he went on, with a look of cunning.

Then, laughing like a child again—

"You com for de musike, not for a boor man, I know," he said sadly; "but com for vat you vill, you know dat all is here for you, pody, zoul, ant coots!"

He took the hand of the countess, kissed it, and dropped a tear, for with this good man every day was the morrow of a kindness received. His joy had for a moment deprived him of memory, only to bring it back in greater force. He seized on the chalk, leaped on the armchair in front of the piano, and then, with the alacrity of a young man, wrote on the wall in large letters, "*February* 17th, 1835." This movement, so pretty and artless, came with such an outburst of gratitude that the countess was quite moved.

"My sister is coming too," she said.

"De oder alzo! Ven? Ven? May it pe bevor I tie!" he replied.

"She will come to thank you for a great favor which I am here now to ask from you on her behalf."

"Qvick! qvick! qvick! qvick!" cried Schmucke, "vot is dis dat I mosd to? Mosd I to de teufel go?"

"I only want you to write, 'I promise to pay the sum of ten thousand francs' on each of these papers," she said, drawing from her muff the four bills, which Nathan had prepared in accordance with the formula prescribed.

"Ach! dat vill pe soon tone," replied the German with a lamblike docility. "Only, I know not vere are mein bens and baber. Get you away, *Meinherr Mirr*," he cried to the cat, who stared at him frigidly. "Dis is mein gat," he said, pointing it out to the countess. "Dis is de boor peast vich lifs mit de boor Schmucke. He is peautivul, dot zo?"

The countess agreed.

"You vould vish him?"

"What an idea! Take away your friend!"

The cat, who was hiding the ink-bottle, divined what Schmucke wanted and jumped on to the bed.

"He is naughty ass ein monkey!" he went on, pointing to it on the bed. "I name him Mirr, for to glorivy our creat Hoffmann at Berlin, dat I haf mosh known."

The good man signed with the innocence of a child doing its mother's bidding, utterly ignorant what it is about, but sure that all will be right. He was far more taken up with presenting the cat to the countess than with the papers, which, by the laws relating to foreigners, might have deprived him for ever of liberty.

"You make me zure dat dese leetl stambed babers."

"Don't have the least uneasiness," said the countess.

"I haf not oneasiness," he replied hastily. "I ask if dese leetl stambed babers vil plees der Montame ti Dilet?"

"Oh yes," she said; "you will be helping her as a father might."

"I am ver habby do pe coot do her for zomting. Com, do mein music!" he said, leaving the papers on the table and springing to the piano.

In a moment the hands of this unworldly being were flying over the well-worn keys, in a moment his glance pierced the roof to heaven, in a moment the sweetest of songs blossomed in the air and penetrated the soul. But only while the ink was drying could this simple-minded interpreter of heavenly things be allowed to draw forth eloquence from wood and string, like Raphael's St. Cecilia playing to the listening hosts of heaven. The countess then slipped the bills into her muff again, and recalled the radiant master from the ethereal spheres in which he soared by a touch on the shoulder.

"My good Schmucke," she cried.

"Zo zoon," he exclaimed, with a submissiveness painful to see. "Vy den are you com?"

He did not complain, he stood like a faithful dog, waiting for a word from the countess.

"My good Schmucke," she again began, "this is a question of life and death, minutes now may be the price of blood and tears."

"Efer de zame!" he said. "Go den! try de tears ov oders! Know dat de boor Schmucke counts your fisit for more dan your pounty."

"We shall meet again," she said. "You must come and play to me and dine with me every Sunday, or else we shall quarrel. I shall expect you next Sunday."

"Truly?"

"Indeed, I hope you will come; and my sister, I am sure, will fix a day for you also."

"Mein habbiness vill be den gomplete," he said, "vor I

tid not zee you put at de Champes-Hailysées, ven you passed in de carrisch, fery rarely."

The thought of this dried the tears which had gathered in the old man's eyes, and he offered his arm to his fair pupil, who could feel the wild beats of his heart.

"You thought of us then sometimes?" she said.

"Efery time ven I mein pret eat!" he replied. "Virst ass mein pountivul laties, ant den ass de two virst young girls vurty of luf dat I haf zeen."

The countess dared say no more! There was a marvelous and respectful solemnity in these words, as though they formed part of some religious service, breathing fidelity. That smoky room, that den of refuse, became a temple for two goddesses. Devotion there waxed stronger, all unknown to its objects.

"Here, then, we are loved, truly loved," she thought.

The countess shared the emotion with which old Schmucke saw her get into her carriage, as she blew from the ends of her fingers one of those airy kisses, which are a woman's distant greeting. At this sight, Schmucke stood transfixed long after the carriage had disappeared.

A few minutes later, the countess entered the courtyard of Mme. de Nucingen's house. The baroness was not yet up; but, in order not to keep a lady of position waiting, she flung a shawl and dressing-gown around her.

"I come on the business of others, and promptitude is then a virtue," said the countess. "This must be my excuse for disturbing you so early."

"Not at all! I am only too happy," said the banker's wife, taking the four papers and the guarantee of the countess.

She rang for her maid.

"Theresa, tell the cashier to bring me up himself, at once, forty thousand francs."

Then she sealed the letter of Mme. de Vandenesse, and locked it into a secret drawer of her table.

"What a pretty room you have!" said the countess.

"Monsieur de Nucingen is going to deprive me of it; he is getting a new house built."

"You will no doubt give this one to your daughter. I hear that she is engaged to Monsieur de Rastignac."

The cashier appeared as Mme. de Nucingen was on the point of replying. She took the notes and handed him the four bills of exchange.

"That balances," said the baroness to the cashier.

"Egzebd for de disgound," said the cashier. "Dis Schmucke iss ein musician vrom Ansbach," he added, with a glance at the signature, which sent a shiver through the countess.

"Do you suppose I am transacting business?" said Mme. de Nucingen, with a haughty glance of rebuke at the cashier. "This is my affair."

In vain did the cashier cast sly glances now at the countess, now at the baroness; not a line of their faces moved.

"You can leave us now. Be so good as remain a minute or two, so that you may not seem to have anything to do with this matter," said the baroness to Mme. de Vandenesse.

"I must beg of you to add to your other kind services that of keeping my secret," said the countess.

"In a matter of charity that is of course," replied the baroness, with a smile. "I shall have your carriage sent to the end of the garden; it will start without you; then we shall cross the garden together, no one will see you leave this. The whole thing will remain a mystery."

"You must have known suffering to have learned so much thought for others," said the countess.

"I don't know about thoughtfulness, but I have suffered a great deal," said the baroness; "you, I trust, have paid less dearly for yours."

The orders given, the baroness took her fur shoes and cloak and led the countess to the side-door of the garden.

When a man is plotting against any one, as du Tillet did

against Nathan, he makes no confidant. Nucingen had some notion of what was going on, but his wife remained entirely outside this Machiavellian scheming. She knew, however, that Raoul was in difficulties, and was not deceived therefore by the sisters; she suspected shrewdly into whose hands the money would pass, and it gave her real pleasure to help the countess. Entanglements of the kind always roused her deepest sympathy.

Rastignac, who was playing the detective on the intrigues of the two bankers, came to lunch with Mme. de Nucingen. Delphine and Rastignac had no secrets from each other, and she told him of her interview with the countess. Rastignac, unable to imagine how the baroness had become mixed up in this affair, which in his eyes was merely incidental, one weapon amongst many, explained to her that she had this morning in all probability demolished the electoral hopes of du Tillet and rendered abortive the foul play and sacrifices of a whole year. He then went on to enlighten her as to the whole position, urging her to keep silence about her own mistake.

"If only," she said, "the cashier does not speak of it to Nucingen."

Du Tillet was at lunch when, a few minutes after twelve, M. Gigonnet was announced.

"Show him in," said the banker, regardless of his wife's presence. "Well, old Shylock, is our man under lock and key?"

"No."

"No! Didn't I tell you Rue du Mail, at the hotel?"

"He has paid," said Gigonnet, drawing from his pocket-book forty bank-notes.

A look of despair passed over du Tillet's face.

"You should never look askance at good money," said the impassive crony of du Tillet; "it's unlucky."

"Where did you get this money, madame?" said the

banker, with a scowl at his wife, which made her scarlet to the roots of her hair.

"I have no idea what you mean," she said.

"I shall get to the bottom of this," he replied, starting up in a fury. "You have upset my most-cherished plans."

"You will upset your lunch," said Gigonnet, laying hold of the tablecloth, which had caught in the skirts of du Tillet's dressing-gown.

Mme. du Tillet rose with frigid dignity, for his words had terrified her. She rang, and a footman came.

"My horses," she said. "And send Virginie; I wish to dress."

"Where are you going?" said du Tillet.

"Men who have any manners do not question their wives. You profess to be a gentleman."

"You have not been yourself for the last two days, since your flippant sister has twice been to see you."

"You ordered me to be flippant," she said. "I am practicing on you."

Gigonnet, who took no interest in family broils, saluted Mme. du Tillet and went out.

Du Tillet looked fixedly at his wife, whose eyes met his without wavering.

"What is the meaning of this?" he said.

"It means that I am no longer a child to be cowed by you," she replied. "I am, and shall remain all my life, a faithful, attentive wife to you; you may be master if you like, but tyrant, no."

Du Tillet left her, and Marie-Eugénie retired to her room, quite unnerved by such an effort.

"But for my sister's danger," she said to herself, "I should never have ventured to beard him thus; as the proverb says, 'It's an ill wind that blows no good.'"

During the night Mme. du Tillet again passed in review her sister's confidences. Raoul's safety being assured, her reason was no longer overpowered by the thought of this imminent danger. She recalled the alarming energy with which the countess had spoken of flying with Nathan, in order to console him in his calamity if she could not avert it. She foresaw how this man, in the violence of his gratitude and love, might persuade her sister to do what to the well-balanced Eugénie seemed an act of madness. There had been instances lately in the best society of such elopements, which pay the price of a doubtful pleasure in remorse and the social discredit arising out of a false position, and Eugénie recalled to mind their disastrous results. Du Tillet's words had put the last touch to her panic; she dreaded discovery; she saw the signature of the Comtesse de Vandenesse in the archives of the Nucingen firm and she resolved to implore her sister to confess everything to Félix.

Mme. du Tillet did not find the countess next morning; but Félix was at home. A voice within called on Eugénie to save her sister. To-morrow even might be too late. It was a heavy responsibility, but she decided to tell everything to the count. Surely he would be lenient, since his honor was still safe and the countess was not so much depraved as misguided. Eugénie hesitated to commit what seemed like an act of cowardice and treachery by divulging secrets which society, at one in this, universally respects. But then came the thought of her sister's future, the dread of seeing her some day deserted, ruined by Nathan, poor, ill, unhappy, despairing; she hesitated no longer, and asked to see the count. Félix, greatly surprised by this visit, had a long conversation with his sister-in-law, in the course of which he showed such calm and self-mastery that Eugénie trembled at the desperate steps he might be resolving.

"Don't be troubled," said Vandenesse; "I shall act so that the day will come when your sister will bless you. However great your repugnance to keeping from her the fact that you have spoken to me, I must ask you to give me a few days'

grace.   I require this in order to see my way through certain
mysteries, of which you know nothing, and above all to take
my measures with prudence.   Possibly I may find out everything at once !   I am the only one to blame, dear sister.   All
lovers play their own game, but all women are not fortunate
enough to see life as it really is.''

CHAPTER IX.

A HUSBAND'S TRIUMPH.

Mme. du Tillet left Vandenesse's house somewhat comforted.   Félix, on his part, went at once to draw forty thousand francs from the Bank of France, and then hastened to
Mme. de Nucingen.   He found her at home, thanked her for
the confidence she had shown in his wife, and returned her
the money.   He gave, as the reason for this mysterious loan,
an excessive almsgiving, on which he had wished to impose
some limit.

"Do not trouble to explain, since Madame de Vandenesse
has told you about it," said the Baronne de Nucingen.

"She knows all," thought Vandenesse.

The baroness handed him his wife's guarantee and sent for
the four bills.   Vandenesse, while this was going on, scanned
the baroness with the statesman's piercing eye ; she flinched a
little, and he judged the time had come for negotiating.

"We live, madame," he said, "at a period when nothing is
stable.   Thrones rise and disappear in France with a discon-
certing rapidity.   Fifteen years may see the end of a great
empire, of a monarchy, and also of a revolution.   No one can
take upon himself to answer for the future.   You know my
devotion to the legitimist party.   Such words in my mouth
cannot surprise you.   Imagine a catastrophe : would it not
be a satisfaction to you to have a friend on the winning
side ? ''

"Undoubtedly," she replied with a smile.

"Supposing such a case to occur, will you have in me, unknown to the world, a grateful friend, ready to secure for Monsieur de Nucingen under these circumstances the peerage to which he aspires?"

"What do you ask from me?" she said.

"Not much. Only the facts in your possession about Monsieur Nathan."

The baroness repeated her conversation of the morning with Rastignac, and said to the ex-peer of France, as she handed him the four bills which the cashier brought her——

"Don't forget your promise."

So far was Vandenesse from forgetting this magical promise, that he dangled it before the eyes of the Baron de Rastignac in order to extract from him further information.

On leaving the baron, he dictated to a scrivener the following letter addressed to Florine:

"If Mlle. Florine wishes to know what part is awaiting her, will she be so good as come to the approaching masked ball, and bring M. Nathan as her escort?"

This letter posted, he went next to his man of business, a very astute fellow, full of resource, and withal honest.

Him he begged to personate a friend, to whom the visit of Mme. de Vandenesse should have been confided by Schmucke, aroused to a tardy suspicion by the fourfold repetition of the words, "I promise to pay ten thousand francs," and who should have come to request from M. Nathan a bill for forty thousand francs in exchange. It was a risky game. Nathan might already have learned how the thing had been arranged, but something had to be dared for so great a prize. In her agitation, Marie might easily have forgotten to ask her beloved Raoul for an acknowledgment for Schmucke. The man of business went at once to Nathan's office, and returned triumphant to the count by five o'clock with the bill for forty thousand francs. The very first words exchanged with Nathan had enabled him to pass for an emissary from the countess.

This success obliged Félix to take steps for preventing a meeting between Raoul and his wife before the masked ball, whither he intended to escort her, in order that she might discover for herself the relation in which Nathan stood to Florine. He knew the jealous pride of the countess, and was anxious to bring her to renounce the love affair of her own will, so that she might be spared from humiliation before himself. He also hoped to show her before it was too late her letters to Nathan sold by Florine, from whom he reckoned on buying them back. This prudent plan, so swiftly conceived and in part executed, was destined to fail through one of those chances to which the affairs of mortals are subject. After dinner Félix turned the conversation on the masked ball, re-marking that Marie had never been to one, and proposed to take her there the following day by way of diversion.

"I will find some one for you to mystify."

"Ah ! I should like that immensely."

"To make it really amusing, a woman ought to get hold of a foeman worthy of her steel, some celebrity or wit, and make mincemeat of him. What do you say to Nathan ? A man who knows Florine could put me up to a few little things that would drive him wild."

"Florine," said the countess, "the actress?"

Marie had already heard this name from the lips of Quillet, the office attendant ; a thought flashed through her like lightning.

"Well, yes, his mistress," replied the count. "What is there surprising in that ?"

"I should have thought Monsieur Nathan was too busy for such things. How can literary men find time for love ?"

"I say nothing about *love*, my dear, but they have to *lodge* somewhere, like other people ; and when they have no home and the bloodhounds of the law are after them, they lodge with their mistresses, which may seem a little strong to you, but which is infinitely preferable to lodging in prison."

The fire was less red than the cheeks of the countess.

"Would you like him for your victim? You could easily give him a fright," the count went on, paying no attention to his wife's looks. "I can give you proofs by which you can show him that he has been a mere child in the hands of your brother-in-law du Tillet. The wretch wanted to clap him in prison in order to disqualify him for opposing his candidature in Nucingen's constituency. I have learned from a friend of Florine's the amount produced by the sale of her furniture, the whole of which she gave to Nathan for starting his paper, and I know what portion was sent to him of the harvest which she reaped this year in the provinces and Belgium; money which, in the long run, all goes into the pockets of du Tillet, Nucingen, and Massol. These three have sold the paper in advance to the Government, so confident are they of dispossessing the great man."

"Monsieur Nathan would never take money from an actress."

"You don't know these people, my dear," said the count; "he won't deny the fact."

"I shall certainly go to the ball," said the countess.

"You will have some fun," replied Vandenesse. "Armed with such weapons, you will read a sharp lesson to Nathan's vanity, and it will be a kindness to him. You will watch the ebb and flow of his rage, and his writhings under your stinging epigrams. Your badinage will be quite enough to show a clever man like him the danger in which he stands, and you will have the satisfaction of getting a good trouncing for the *juste milieu** team within their own stables—— You are not listening, my child."

"Yes, indeed, I am only too much interested," she an-

* Right Centre.

swered. "I will tell you later why I am so anxious to be certain about all this."

"Certain?" replied Vandenesse. "If you keep on your mask, I will take you to supper with Florine and Nathan. It will be sport for a great lady like you to take in an actress after having kept a famous man on the stretch, manœuvring round his most precious secrets; you can harness them both to the same mystification. I shall put myself on the track of Nathan's infidelities. If I can lay hold of the details of any recent affair, you will be able to indulge yourself in the spectacle of a courtesan's rage, which is worth seeing. The fury of Florine will seethe like an Alpine torrent. She adores Nathan; he is everything to her, precious as the marrow of her bones, dear as her cubs to a lioness. I remember in my youth having seen a celebrated actress, whose writing was like a kitchen-maid's, come to demand back her letters from one of my friends. I have never seen anything like it since; that quiet fury, that impudent dignity, that barbaric pose—— Are you ill, Marie?"

"No! only the fire is hot."

The countess went to fling herself down on a sofa. All at once an incalculable impulse, inspired by the consuming ache of jealousy, drove her to her feet. Trembling in every limb, she crossed her arms, and advanced slowly toward her husband.

"How much do you know?" she asked. "It is not like you to torture me. Even were I guilty, you would give me an easy death."

"What should I know, Marie?"

"About Nathan?"

"You believe you love him," he replied, "but you love only a phantom made of words."

"Then you do know——?"

"Everything," he said.

The word fell like a blow on Marie's head.

"If you wish," he continued, "it shall be as though I knew nothing. My child, you have fallen into an abyss, and I must save you; already I have done something. See——"

He drew from his pocket her guarantee and Schmucke's four bills, which the countess recognized, and threw into the fire.

"What would have become of you, poor Marie, in three months from now? You would have been dragged into Court by bailiffs. Don't hang your head, don't be ashamed; you have been betrayed by the noblest of feelings; you have trifled, not with a man, but with your own imagination. There is not a woman—not one, do you hear, Marie?—who would not have been fascinated in your place. It would be absurd that men, who, in the course of twenty years, have committed a thousand acts of folly, should insist that a woman is not to lose her head once in a lifetime. Pray heaven I may never triumph over you or burden you with a pity such as you repudiated with scorn the other day! Possibly this wretched man was sincere when he wrote you, sincere in trying to put an end to himself, and sincere in returning that very evening to Florine. A man is a poor creature compared to a woman. I am speaking now for you, not for myself. I am tolerant, but society is not; it shuns the woman who makes a scandal; it will allow none to be rich at once in its regard and in the indulgence of passion. Whether this is just or not, I cannot say. Enough that the world is cruel. It may be that, taken in the mass, it is harsher than are the individuals separately. A thief, sitting in the pit, will applaud the triumph of innocence, and filch its jewels as he goes out. Society has no balm for the ills it creates; it honors clever roguery, and leaves unrewarded silent devotion. All this I see and know; but if I cannot reform the world, at least I can protect you from yourself. We have here to do with a man who brings you nothing but trouble, not with a saintly and pious love, such as sometimes commands self-effacement and brings its own excuse with it. Perhaps I have been to blame in not bring-

ing more variety into your peaceful life; I ought to have enlivened our calm routine with the stir and excitement of
travel and change.　I can see also an explanation of the
attraction which drew you to a man of note, in the envy you
aroused in certain women.　Lady Dudley, Madame d'Espard,
Madame de Manerville, and my sister-in-law Émilie count for
something in all this.　These women, whom I warned you
against, have no doubt worked on your curiosity, more with
the object of annoying me than in order to precipitate you
among storms which, I trust, may have only threatened without breaking over you."

The countess, as she listened to these generous words, was
tossed about by a host of conflicting feelings, but lively admiration for Félix dominated the tempest.　A noble and high-
spirited soul quickly responds to gentle handling.　This sensitiveness is the counterpart of physical grace.　Marie appreciated
a magnanimity which sought in self-depreciation a screen for
the blushes of an erring woman.　She made a frantic motion
to leave the room, then turned back, fearing lest her husband
should misunderstand and take alarm.

"Wait!" she said, as she vanished.

Félix had artfully prepared her defense, and he was soon
recompensed for his adroitness; for his wife returned with the
whole of Nathan's letters in her hand, and held them out to
him.

"Be my judge," she said, kneeling before him.

"How can a man judge where he loves?" he replied.

He took the letters and threw them on the fire; later, the
thought that he had read them might have stood between him
and his wife.　Marie, her head upon his knees, burst into
tears.

"My child, where are yours?" he said, raising her head.

At this question, the countess no longer felt the intolerable
burning of her cheeks, a cold chill went through her.

"That you may not suspect your husband of slandering the

man whom you have thought worthy of you, I will have those letters restored to you by Florine herself."

"Oh! surely he would give them back if I asked him," she returned.

"And supposing he refused?"

The countess hung her head.

"The world is horrid," she said; "I will not go into it any more; I will live alone with you, if you forgive me."

"You might weary again. Beside, what would the world say if you left it abruptly? When spring comes, we will travel, we will go to Italy, we will wander about Europe, until another child comes to need your care. We must not give up the ball to morrow, for it is the only way to get hold of your letters without compromising ourselves; and when Florine brings them to you, will not that be the measure of her power?"

"And I must see that?" said the terrified countess.

"To-morrow night."

Toward midnight next evening Nathan was pacing the promenade at the masked ball, giving his arm to a domino with a very fair imitation of the conjugal manner. After two or three turns two masked women came up to them.

"Fool! you have done for yourself; Marie is here and sees you," said Vandenesse, in the disguise of a woman, to Nathan, while the countess, all trembling, addressed Florine—

"If you will listen, I will tell you secrets which Nathan has kept from you, and which will show you the dangers that threaten your love for him."

Nathan had abruptly dropped Florine's arm in order to follow the count, who escaped him in the crowd. Florine went to take a seat beside the countess, who had drawn her away to a form by the side of Vandenesse, now returned to look after his wife.

"Speak out, my dear," said Florine, "and don't suppose you can keep me long on the tenter-hooks. Not a creature

in the world can get Raoul from me, I can tell you. He is
bound to me by habit, which is better than love any day.''

"In the first place, are you Florine?" said Félix, resuming
his natural voice.

"A pretty question indeed! If you don't know who I am,
why should I believe you, pray?"

"Go and ask Nathan, who is hunting now for the mistress
of whom I speak, where he spent the night three days ago!
He tried to stifle himself with charcoal, my dear, unknown to
you, because he was ruined. That's all you know about the
affairs of the man whom you profess to love; you leave him
penniless, and he kills himself, or rather he doesn't, he tries
to and fails. Suicide when it doesn't come off is much on a
par with a bloodless duel.''

"It is a lie," said Florine. "He dined with me that day,
but not till after sunset. The bailiffs were after him, poor
boy. He was in hiding, that's all.''

"Well, you can go and ask at the Hôtel du Mail, Rue du
Mail, whether he was not brought there at the point of death
by a beautiful lady, with whom he has had clandestine relations for a year; the letters of your rival are hidden in your
house, under your very nose. If you care to catch Nathan
out, we can go all three to your house; there I shall give you
ocular proof that you can get him clear of his difficulties very
shortly if you like to be good-natured.''

"That's not good enough for Florine, thank you, my
friend. I know very well that Nathan can't have a love
affair.''

"Because, I suppose, he has redoubled his attentions to
you of late, as if that were not the very proof that he is
tremendously in love——''

"With a society woman?—Nathan?" said Florine. "Oh!
I don't trouble about a trifle like that.''

"Very well, would you like him to come and tell you himself that he won't take you home this evening?''

"If you get him to say that," answered Florine, "I will let you come with me, and we can hunt together for those letters, which I shall believe in when I see them."

"Stay here," said Félix, "and watch."

He took his wife's arm and waited within a few steps of Florine. Before long Nathan, who was walking up and down the promenade, searching in all directions for his mask like a dog who has lost its master, returned to the spot where the mysterious warning had been spoken. Seeing evident marks of disturbance on Raoul's brow, Florine planted herself firmly in front of him and said in a commanding voice:

"You must not leave me; I have a reason for wanting you."

"Marie!" whispered the countess, by her husband's instructions, in Raoul's ear. Then she added: "Who is that woman? Leave her immediately, go outside, and wait for me at the foot of the staircase."

In this terrible strait, Raoul shook off roughly the arm of Florine, who was quite unprepared for such violence, and, though clinging to him forcibly, was obliged to let go. Nathan at once lost himself in the crowd.

"What did I tell you?" cried Félix in the ear of the stupefied Florine, to whom he offered his arm.

"Come," she said, "let us go, whoever you are. Have you a carriage?"

Vandenesse's only reply was to hurry Florine out and hasten to rejoin his wife at a spot agreed upon under the colonnade. In a few minutes the three dominoes, briskly conveyed by Vandenesse's coachman, arrived at the house of the actress, who took off her mask. Mme. de Vandenesse could not repress a thrill of surprise at the sight of the actress, boiling with rage, magnificent in her wrath and jealousy.

"There is," said Vandenesse, "a certain writing-case, the key of which has never been in your hands; the letters must be in it."

"You have me there; you know something, at any rate, which has been bothering me for some days," said Florine, dashing into the study to fetch the writing-case.

Vandenesse saw his wife grow pale under her mask. Florine's room told more of Nathan's intimacy with the actress than was altogether pleasant for a romantic lady-love. A woman's eye is quick to see the truth in such matters, and the countess read in the promiscuous household arrangements a confirmation of what Vandenesse had told her.

Florine returned with the case.

"How shall we open it?" she said,

Then she sent for a large kitchen knife, and when her maid brought it, brandished it with a mocking air, exclaiming—

"This is the way to cut off the pretty dears' heads!"*

The countess shuddered. She realized now, even more than her husband's words had enabled her to do the evening before, the depths from which she had so narrowly escaped.

"What a fool I am!" cried Florine. "His razor would be better."

She went to fetch the razor, which had just served Nathan for shaving, and cut the edges of the morocco. They fell apart, and Marie's letters appeared. Florine took up one at random.

"Sure enough, this is some fine lady's work! Only see how she can spell!"

Vandenesse took the letters and handed them to his wife, who carried them to a table in order to see if they were all there.

"Will you give them up for this?" said Vandenesse, holding out to Florine the bill for forty thousand francs.

"What a donkey he is to sign such things! 'Bond for bills,'" cried Florine, reading the document. "Ah! yes, you shall have your fill of countesses! And I, who worked

---

* In the French, "*poulets*," which means "love-letters" as well as "chickens."

myself to death, body and soul, raising money in the provinces for him—I, who slaved like a broker to save him! That's a man all over; go to the devil for him, and he'll trample you under foot! I shall have it out with him for this."

Mme. de Vandenesse had fled with the letters.

" Hi, there! pretty domino! leave me one, if you please, just to throw in his face."

" That is impossible now," said Vandenesse.

" And why, pray? "

" The other domino is your late rival."

"You don't say so! Well, she might have said ' Thank you!' " cried Florine.

" And what then do you call the forty thousand francs? " said Vandenesse, with a polite bow.

It very seldom happens that a young fellow who has once attempted suicide cares to taste for a second time its discomforts. When suicide does not cure a man of life altogether, it cures him of a self-sought death. Thus Raoul no longer thought of making away with himself even after Florine's possession of Schmucke's guarantee—plainly through the intervention of Vandenesse—had reduced him to a still worse plight than that from which he had tried to escape. He made an attempt to see the countess again in order to explain to her the nature of the love which burned brighter than ever in his breast. But the first time they met in society, the countess fixed Raoul with that stony, scornful glance which makes an impassable barrier between a man and a woman. With all his audacity, Nathan made no further attempt during the winter to approach or address the countess.

He unburdened his soul, however, to Blondet, discoursing to him of Laura and Beatrice, whenever the name of Mme. de Vandenesse occurred. He paraphrased that beautiful passage of one of the greatest poets of his day—" Dream of the soul, blue flower with golden heart, whose spreading roots, finer a thousandfold than fairies' silken tresses, pierce to the inmost being and draw their life from all that is purest there : flower sweet and bitter ! To uproot thee is to draw the heart's blood, oozing in ruddy drops from thy broken stem ! Ah ! cursed flower, how thou hast thriven on my soul ! "

"You're driveling, old boy," said Blondet. "I grant you there was a pretty enough flower, only it has nothing to do with the soul ; and instead of crooning like a blind man before an empty shrine, you had better be thinking how to get out of this scrape, so as to put yourself straight with the authorities and settle down. You are too much of the artist to make a politician. You have been played on by men who are your inferiors. Go and get yourself played on some other stage."

"Marie can't prevent my loving her," said Nathan. "She shall be my Beatrice."

"My dear fellow, Beatrice was a child of twelve, whom Dante never saw again ; otherwise, would she have been Beatrice? If we are to make a divinity of a woman, we must not see her to-day in a mantle, to-morrow in a low-necked dress, the day after on the boulevards, cheapening toys for her last baby. While there is Florine handy to play by turns a comedy duchess, a tragedy middle-class wife, a negress, a marchioness, a colonel, a Swiss peasant-girl, a Peruvian virgin of the sun (the only virginity she knows much about), I don't know why one should bother about society women."

Du Tillet, by means of a forced sale, compelled the penniless Nathan to surrender his share in the paper. The great man received only five votes in the constituency which elected du Tillet.

When the Comtesse de Vandenesse, after a long and delightful time of travel in Italy, returned in the following winter to Paris, Nathan had exactly carried out the forecast of Félix. Following Blondet's advice, he was negotiating with the party in power. His personal affairs were so embarrassed that, one day in the Champs-Élysées, the Comtesse Marie saw her ancient adorer walking in the sorriest plight, with Florine on his arm. In the eyes of a woman, the man to whom she is indifferent is always more or less ugly; but the man whom she has ceased to love is a monster, especially if he is of the type to which Nathan belonged. Mme. de Vandenesse felt a pang of shame as she remembered her fancy for Raoul. Had she not been cured before of any unlawful passion, the contrast which this man, already declining in popular estimation, then offered to her husband, would have sufficed to give the latter precedence over an angel.

At the present day this ambitious author, of ready pen but halting character, has at last capitulated and installed himself in a sinecure like any ordinary being. Having supported every scheme of disintegration, he now lives in peace beneath the shade of a ministerial broad-sheet. The cross of the Legion of Honor, fruitful text of his mockery, adorns his button-hole. PEACE AT ANY PRICE, the stock-in-trade of his denunciation as editor of a revolutionary organ, has now become the theme of his laudatory articles. The hereditary principle, butt of his Saint-Simonian oratory, is defended by him to-day in weighty arguments. This inconsistency has its origin and explanation in the change of front of certain men who, in the course of our latest political developments, have acted as Raoul did.

JARDIES, *December*, 1838.

LETTERS OF TWO BRIDES.

To George Sand.

Your name, dear George, while casting a reflected radiance on my book, can gain no new glory from this page.   And yet it is neither self-interest nor diffidence which has led me to place it there, but only the wish that it should bear witness to the solid friendship between us, which has survived our wanderings and separations, and triumphed over the busy malice of the world.   This feeling is hardly likely now to change. The goodly company of friendly names, which will remain attached to my works, forms an element of pleasure in the midst of the vexation caused by their increasing number.   Each fresh book, in fact, gives rise to fresh annoyance, were it only in the reproaches aimed at my too prolific pen, as though it could rival in fertility the world from which I draw my models ! Would it not be a fine thing, George, if the future antiquarian of dead literatures were to find in this company none but great names and generous hearts, friends bound by pure and holy ties, the illustrious figures of the century ?   May I not justly pride myself on this assured possession, rather than on a popularity necessarily unstable ?   For him who knows you well, it is happiness to be able to sign himself, as I do here,

Your friend,

DE BALZAC.

PARIS, *June,* 1840.

(136)

FIRST PART.

I.

LOUISE DE CHAULIEU TO RENÉE DE MAUCOMBE.

PARIS, *September.*

SWEETHEART, I too am free of school! And I am the first too, unless you have written to Blois, at our sweet tryst of letter-writing. Raise those great, sparkling black eyes of yours, fixed on my opening sentence, and keep this excitement for the letter which shall tell you of my first love. By the way, why always "first?" Is there, I wonder, a second love?

"Don't go running on like this," you will say, "but tell me rather how you made your escape from the convent where you were to take your vows." Well, dear, I don't know about the Carmelites, but the miracle of my own deliverance was, I can assure you, most humdrum. The cries of an alarmed conscience triumphed over the dictates of a stern policy—there's the whole mystery. The sombre melancholy which seized me after you left hastened the happy climax, my aunt did not want to see me die of a decline, and my mother, whose one unfailing cure for my malady was a novitiate, gave way before her.

So, here I am in Paris, thanks to you too, my love! Dear Renée, could you have seen me the day I found myself parted from you, well might you have gloried in the deep impression you had made on so youthful a bosom. We had lived so constantly together, sharing our dreams and letting our fancy roam together, that I verily believe our souls had become welded together, like those two Hungarian girls, whose death

we heard about from M. Beauvisage*—poor misnamed being!
Never surely was man better cut out by nature for the post of
convent physician!

Tell me, did you not droop and sicken with your darling?

In my gloomy depression, I could do nothing but count
over the ties which bind us. But it seemed as though distance
had loosened them; I wearied of life, like a turtle-dove
widowed of her mate. Death smiled sweetly on me, and I
was proceeding quietly to die. To be at Blois, at the Carmelites, consumed by dread of having to take my vows there,
a Mlle. de la Vallière, but without her prelude, and without
my Renée! Why should I not be sick—sick unto death?

How different it used to be! That monotonous existence,
where every hour brings its duty, its prayer, its task, with
such desperate regularity that you can tell what a Carmelite
sister is doing in any place, at any hour of the night or day;
that deadly dull routine, which crushes out all interest in one's
surroundings, had become for us two a world of life and
movement. Imagination had thrown open her fairy realms,
and in these our spirits ranged at will, each in turn serving
as magic steed to the other, the more alert quickening the
drowsy; the world from which our bodies were shut out became the playground of our fancy, which reveled there in
frolicsome adventure. The very "Lives of the Saints,"
dreary as it is, helped us to understand what was so carefully
left unsaid! But the day when I was reft of your sweet company, I became a true Carmelite, such as they appeared to us,
a modern Danaïd, who, instead of trying to fill a bottomless
barrel, draws every day, from heaven knows what deep, an
empty pitcher, thinking to find it full.

My aunt knew nothing of this inner life. How should
she, who has made a paradise for herself within the two
acres of her convent, understand my revolt against life? A
religious life, if embraced by girls of our age, demands either

* Handsome face.

an extreme simplicity of soul, such as we, sweetheart, do not possess, or else an ardor for self-sacrifice like that which makes my aunt so noble a character. But she sacrificed herself for a brother to whom she was devoted ; to do the same for an unknown person or an idea is surely more than can be asked of mortals.

For the last two weeks I have been gulping down so many reckless words, burying so many reflections in my bosom, and accumulating such a store of things to tell, fit for your ear alone, that I should certainly have been suffocated but for the resource of letter-writing as a sorry substitute for our beloved talks. How hungry one's heart gets! I am beginning my journal this morning, and I picture to myself that yours is already started, and that, in a few days, I shall be at home in your beautiful Gémenos valley, which I know only through your descriptions, just as you will live that Paris life, revealed to you hitherto only in our dreams.

Well, then, sweet child, know that on a certain morning— a red-letter day in my life—there arrived from Paris a lady companion and Philippe, the last remaining of my grandmother's valets, charged to carry me off. When my aunt summoned me to her room and told me the news, I could not speak for joy, and only gazed at her stupidly.

"My child," she said, in her guttural voice, "I can see that you leave me without regret, but this farewell is not the last ; we shall see you here again. God has placed on your forehead the sign of the elect. You have the pride which leads to heaven or to hell, but your nature is too noble to choose the downward path. I know you better than you know yourself; with you, passion, I can see, will be very different from what it is with most women."

She drew me gently to her and kissed my forehead. The kiss made my flesh creep, for it burned with that consuming fire which eats away her life, which has turned to black the azure of her eyes, and softened the lines about them, has furrowed the warm ivory of her temples, and cast a sallow tinge over the beautiful face.

Before replying, I kissed her hands.

"Dear aunt," I said, "I shall never forget your kindness; and if it has not made your nunnery all that it ought to be for my health of body and soul, you may be sure nothing short of a broken heart will bring me back again—and that you would not wish for me. You will not see me here again till my royal lover has deserted me, and I warn you that if I catch him, death alone shall tear him from me. I fear no Montespan."

She smiled and said—

"Go, madcap, and take your idle fancies with you. There is certainly more of the bold Montespan in you than of the gentle la Vallière."

I threw my arms round her. The poor lady could not refrain from escorting me to the carriage, where her tender gaze was divided between the armorial bearings and myself.

At Beaugency night overtook me, still sunk in a stupor of the mind produced by these strange parting words. What can be awaiting me in this world for which I have so hungered?

To begin with, I found no one to receive me; my heart had been schooled in vain. My mother was at the Bois de Boulogne, my father at the Council; my brother, the Duc de Rhétoré, never comes in, I am told, till it is time to dress for dinner. Miss Griffith (she is not unlike a griffin) and Philippe took me to my rooms.

The suite is the one which belonged to my beloved grandmother, the Princesse de Vaurémont, to whom I owe some sort of a fortune of which no one has ever said one word to me. As you read this, you will understand the sadness which came over me as I entered a place sacred to so many memories, and found the rooms just as she had left them! I was to sleep in the bed where she died.

Sitting down on the edge of her sofa, I burst into tears, forgetting I was not alone, and remembering only how often I had stood there by her knees, the better to hear her words. There I had gazed upon her face, buried in its brown laces, and worn as much by age as by the pangs of approaching death. The room seemed to me still warm with the heat which she kept up there. How comes it that Armande-Louise-Marie de Chaulieu must be like some peasant-girl, who sleeps in her mother's bed the very morrow of her death? For to me it was as though the princess, who died in 1817, had passed away but yesterday.

I saw many things in the room which ought to have been removed. Their presence showed the carelessness with which people, busy with affairs of State, may treat their own, and also the little thought which had been given since her death to this grand old lady, who will always remain one of the striking figures of the eighteenth century. Philippe seemed to divine something of the cause of my tears. He told me that the furniture of the princess had been left to me in her will and that my father had allowed all the larger suites to remain dismantled, as the Revolution had left them. On hearing this I rose, and Philippe opened the door of the small drawing-room which leads into the reception-rooms.

In these I found all the well-remembered wreckage ; the panels above the doors, which had contained valuable pictures, bare of all but empty frames ; broken marbles, mirrors carried off. In old days I was afraid to go up the state staircase and cross these vast, deserted rooms ; so I used to go to the princess' rooms by a small staircase which runs under the arch of the larger one and leads to the secret door of her dressing-room.

My suite, consisting of a drawing-room, bedroom, and the pretty morning-room in scarlet and gold, of which I have told you, lies in the wing on the side of the Invalides. The house is only separated from the boulevard by a wall, covered

with creepers, and by a splendid avenue of trees, which mingle
their foliage with that of the young elms on the sidewalk of
the boulevard. But for the blue-and-gold dome of the Invalides and its gray stone mass, you might be in a wood.

The style of decoration in these rooms, together with their
situation, indicates that they were the old show suite of the
duchesses, while the dukes must have had theirs in the wing
opposite. The two suites are decorously separated by the two
main blocks, as well as by the central one, which contains
those vast, gloomy, resounding halls shown me by Philippe,
all despoiled of their splendor, as in the days of my childhood.

Philippe grew quite confidential when he saw the surprise
depicted on my countenance. For you must know that in
this home of diplomacy the very servants have a reserved and
mysterious air. He went on to tell me that it was expected a
law would soon be passed restoring to the fugitives of the
Revolution the value of their property, and that my father is
waiting to restore his house till this restitution is made, the
king's architect having estimated the damage at three hundred
thousand francs.

This piece of news flung me back despairing on my drawing-room sofa. Could it be that my father, instead of spending this money in arranging a marriage for me, would have
left me to die in the convent? This was the first thought to
greet me on the threshold of my home.

Ah! Renée, what would I have given then to rest my head
upon your shoulder, or to transport myself to the days when
my grandmother made the life of these rooms? You two in
all the world have been alone in loving me—you away at
Maucombe, and she who survives only in my heart, the dear
old lady, whose still youthful eyes used to open from sleep at
my call. How well we understood each other!

These memories suddenly changed my mood. What at
first had seemed profanation, now breathed of holy associa-

tion. It was sweet to inhale the faint odor of the powder she loved still lingering in the room; sweet to sleep beneath the shelter of those yellow damask curtains with their white pattern, which must have retained something of the spirit emanating from her eyes and breath. I told Philippe to rub up the old furniture and make the rooms look as if they were lived in; I explained to him myself how I wanted everything arranged, and where to put each piece of furniture. In this way I entered into possession, and showed how an air of youth might be given to the dear old things.

The bedroom is white in color, a little dulled with time, just as the gilding of the fanciful arabesques shows here and there a patch of red; but this effect harmonizes well with the faded colors of the Savonnerie tapestry, which was presented to my grandmother by Louis XV. along with his portrait. The timepiece was a gift from the Maréchal de Saxe, and the china ornaments on the mantelpiece came from the Maréchal de Richelieu. My grandmother's portrait, painted at the age of twenty-five, hangs in an oval frame opposite that of the King. The prince, her husband, is conspicuous by his absence. I like this frank negligence, untinged by hypocrisy —a characteristic touch which sums up her charming personality. Once when my grandmother was seriously ill, her confessor was urgent that the prince, who was waiting in the drawing-room, should be admitted.

"He can come in with the doctor and his drugs," was the reply.

The bed has a canopy and well-stuffed back, and the curtains are looped up with fine wide bands. The furniture is of gilded wood, upholstered in the same yellow damask with white flowers which drapes the windows, and which is lined there with a white silk that looks as though it were watered. The panels over the doors have been painted, by what artist I can't say, but they represent one a sunrise, the other a moonlight scene.

The fireplace is a very interesting feature in the room. It is easy to see that life in the last century centred largely round the hearth, where great events were enacted. The copper-gilt grate is a marvel of workmanship, and the mantelpiece is most delicately finished; the andirons are beautifully chased; the bellows are a perfect gem. The tapestry of the screen comes from the Gobelins and is exquisitely mounted; charming fantastic figures run all over the frame, on the feet, the supporting bar, and the wings; the whole thing is wrought like a fan.

Dearly should I like to know who was the giver of this dainty work of art, which was such a favorite with her. How often have I seen the old lady, her feet upon the bar, reclining in the easy-chair, with her dress half raised in front, toying with the snuff-box, which lay upon the ledge between her box of pastilles and her silk mits. What a coquette she was! To the day of her death she took as much pains with her appearance as though the beautiful portrait had been painted only yesterday, and she were waiting to receive the throng of exquisites from the Court! How the armchair recalls to me the inimitable sweep of her skirts as she sank back in it!

These women of a past generation have carried off with them secrets which are very typical of their age. The princess had a certain turn of the head, a way of dropping her glances and her remarks, a choice of words, which I look for in vain, even in my mother. There was subtlety in it all, and there was good-nature; the points were made without any affecta-tion. Her talk was at once lengthy and concise; she told a good story, and could put her meaning in three words. Above all, she was extremely free-thinking, and this has undoubtedly had its effect on my way of looking at things.

From seven years old till I was ten, I never left her side; it pleased her to attract me as much as it pleased me to go. This preference was the cause of more than one passage at arms between her and my mother, and nothing intensifies feeling like the icy breath of persecution. How charming was her greeting: "Here you are, little rogue!" when curiosity had taught me how to glide with stealthy snake-like movements to her room. She felt that I loved her, and this childish affection was welcome as a ray of sunshine in the winter of her life.

I don't know what went on in her rooms at night, but she had many visitors; and when I came on tiptoe in the morning to see if she were awake, I would find the drawing-room furniture disarranged, the card-tables set out, and patches of snuff scattered about.

This drawing-room is furnished in the same style as the bedroom. The chairs and tables are oddly shaped, with claw feet and hollow mouldings. Rich garlands of flowers, beautifully designed and carved, wind over the mirrors and hang down in festoons. On the consoles are fine china vases. The ground colors are scarlet and white. My grandmother was a high-spirited, striking brunette, as might be inferred from her choice of colors. I have found in the drawing-room a writing-table I remember well; the figures on it used to fascinate me; it is plaited in graven silver, and was a present from one of the Genoese Lomellini. Each side of the table represents the occupations of a different season; there are hundreds of figures in each picture, and all in relief.

I remained alone for two hours, while old memories rose before me, one after another, on this spot, hallowed by the death of a woman most remarkable even among the witty and beautiful Court ladies of Louis XV.'s day.

You know how abruptly I was parted from her, at a day's notice, in 1816.

"Go and bid good-by to your grandmother," said my mother.

The princess received me as usual, without any display of feeling, and expressed no surprise at my departure.

10

"You are going to the convent, dear," she said, "and will see your aunt there, who is an excellent woman. I shall take care, though, that they don't make a victim of you; you shall be independent, and able to marry whom you please."

Six months later she died. Her will had been given into the keeping of the Prince de Talleyrand, the most devoted of all her old friends. He contrived, while paying a visit to Mlle. de Chargebœuf, to intimate to me, through her, that my grandmother forbade me to take the vows. I hope, sooner or later, to meet the prince, and then I shall doubtless learn more from him.

Thus, sweetheart, if I have found no one in flesh and blood to meet me, I have comforted myself with the shade of the dear princess, and have prepared myself for carrying out one of our pledges, which was, as you know, to keep each other informed of the smallest details in our homes and occupations. It makes such a difference to know where and how the life of one we loved is passed! Send me a faithful picture of the veriest trifles around you, omitting nothing, not even the sunset lights among the tall trees.

October 10th.

It was three in the afternoon when I arrived. About halfpast five, Rose came and told me that my mother had returned, so I went downstairs to pay my respects to her.

My mother lives in a suite on the first floor, exactly corresponding to mine, and in the same block. I am just over her head, and the same secret staircase serves for both. My father's rooms are in the block opposite, but are larger by the whole of the space occupied by the grand staircase on our side of the building. These ancestral mansions are so spacious that my father and mother continue to occupy the first-floor rooms, in spite of the social duties which have once more devolved on them with the return of the Bourbons, and are even able to receive in them.

I found my mother, dressed for the evening, in her drawing-room, where nothing is changed. I came slowly down the stairs, speculating with every step how I should be met by this mother who had shown herself so little of a mother to me, and from whom, during eight years, I had heard nothing beyond the two letters of which you know. Judging it unworthy to simulate an affection I could not possibly feel, I put on the air of a pious imbecile, and entered the room with many inward qualms, which however soon disappeared. My mother's tact was equal to the occasion. She made no pretense of emotion; she neither held me at arm's-length nor hugged me to her bosom like a beloved daughter, but greeted me as though we had parted the evening before. Her manner was that of the kindliest and most sincere friend, as she addressed me like a grown person, first kissing me on the forehead.

" My dear little one," she said, " if you were really dying at the convent, it is much better to live here with your family. You frustrate your father's plans and mine; but the age of blind obedience to parents is past. M. de Chaulieu's intention, and in this I am quite at one with him, is to lose no opportunity of making your life pleasant and of letting you see the world. At your age I should have thought as you do, therefore I am not vexed with you; it is impossible you should understand what we expected from you. You will not find any absurd severity in me; and if you have ever thought me heartless, you will soon find out your mistake. Still, though I wish you to feel perfectly free, I think that, to begin with, you would do well to follow the counsels of a mother, who wishes to be a sister to you."

I was quite charmed by the duchess, who talked in a gentle voice, straightening my convent tippet as she spoke. At the age of thirty-eight she is still beautiful as an angel. She has dark-blue eyes, with silken lashes, a smooth forehead, and a complexion so pink and white that you might think she paints. Her bust and shoulders are marvelous, and her waist is as slender as yours. Her hand is milk-white and extraordinarily beautiful; the nails catch the light in their perfect polish, the thumb is like ivory, the little finger stands just a little apart from the rest. Her foot matches the hand; it is the Spanish foot of Mlle. de Vandenesse. If she is like this at forty, at sixty she will still be a beautiful woman.

I replied, sweetheart, like a good little girl. I was as nice to her as she to me, nay, nicer. Her beauty completely vanquished me; it seemed only natural that such a woman should be absorbed in her regal part. I told her this as simply as though I had been talking to you. I daresay it was a surprise to her to hear words of affection from her daughter's mouth, and the unfeigned homage of my admiration evidently touched her deeply. Her manner changed and became even more engaging; she dropped all formality as she said—

"I am much pleased with you, and I hope we shall remain good friends."

The words struck me as charmingly naïve, but I did not let this appear, for I saw at once that the prudent course was to allow her to believe herself much deeper and cleverer than her daughter. So I only stared vacantly and she was delighted. I kissed her hands repeatedly, telling her how happy it made me to be so treated and to feel at my ease with her. I even confided to her my previous tremors. She smiled, put her arm round my neck, and drawing me toward her, kissed me on the forehead most affectionately.

"Dear child," she said, "we have people coming to dinner to-day. Perhaps you will agree with me that it is better for you not to make your first appearance in society till you have been in the dressmaker's hands; so, after you have seen your father and brother, you can go upstairs again."

I assented most heartily. My mother's exquisite dress was the first revelation to me of the world which our dreams had pictured; but I did not feel the slightest desire to rival her.

My father now entered, and the duchess presented me to him.

He became all at once most affectionate, and played the father's part so well, that I could not but believe his heart to be in it. Taking my two hands in his, and kissing them, with more of the lover than the father in his manner, he said—

"So this is my rebel daughter!"

And he drew me toward him, with his arm passed tenderly round my waist, while he kissed me on the cheeks and forehead.

"The pleasure with which we shall watch your success in society will atone for the disappointment we felt at your change of vocation," he said. Then, turning to my mother: "Do you know that she is going to turn out very pretty, and you will be proud of her some day? Here is your brother, Rhétoré. Alphonse," he said to a fine young man who came in, "here is your convent-bred sister who threatens to send her nun's frock to the deuce."

My brother came up in a leisurely way and took my hand, which he pressed.

"Come, come, you may kiss her," said my father.

And he kissed me on both cheeks.

"I am delighted to see you," he said, "and I take your side against my father."

I thanked him, but could not help thinking he might have come to Blois when he was at Orleans visiting our marquis brother in his quarters.

Fearing the arrival of strangers, I now withdrew. I tidied up my rooms, and laid out on the scarlet velvet of my lovely table all the materials necessary for writing you, meditating all the while on my new situation.

This, my fair sweetheart, is a true and veracious account of the return of a girl of eighteen, after an absence of nine years, to the bosom of one of the noblest families in the kingdom. I was tired by the journey as well as by all the emotions I had been through, so I went to bed in convent fashion, at eight o'clock, after supper. They have preserved even a little Saxe service which the dear princess used when she had a fancy for taking her meals alone.

II.

THE SAME TO THE SAME.

November 25th.

Next morning I found my rooms put in order and dusted, and even flowers put in the vases, by old Philippe. I began to feel at home. Only it didn't occur to anybody that a Carmelite schoolgirl has an early appetite, and Rose had no end of trouble in getting breakfast for me.

" Mlle. goes to bed at dinner-time," she said to me, " and gets up when the duke is just returning home."

I began to write. About one o'clock my father knocked at the door of the small drawing-room and asked if he might come in. I opened the door; he came in, and found me writing you.

" My dear," he began, " you will have to get yourself clothes, and to make these rooms comfortable. In this purse you will find twelve thousand francs, which is the yearly income I propose allowing you for your expenses. You will make arrangements with your mother as to some governess whom you may like, in case Miss Griffith doesn't please you, for Mme. de Chaulieu will not have time to go out with you in the mornings. A carriage and manservant shall be at your disposal."

" Let me keep Philippe," I said.

" So be it," he replied. " But don't be uneasy; you have money enough of your own to be no burden either to your mother or me."

" May I ask how much I have ?"

A FAMOUS DRESSMAKER, BY NAME VICTORINE, HAS COME.

"Certainly, my child," he said. "Your grandmother left you five hundred thousand francs; this was the amount of her savings, for she would not alienate a foot of land from the family. This sum has been placed in Government stock, and, with the accumulated interest, now brings in about forty thousand francs a year. With this I had purposed making an independence for your second brother, and it is here that you have upset my plans. Later, however, it is possible that you may fall in with them. It shall rest with yourself, for I have confidence in your good sense far more than I had expected.

"I do not need to tell you how a daughter of the Chaulieus ought to behave. The pride so plainly written in your features is my best guarantee. Safeguards, such as common people surround their daughters with, would be an insult in our family. A slander reflecting on your name might cost the life of the man bold enough to utter it, or the life of one of your brothers, if by chance the right should not prevail. No more on this subject. Good-by, little one."

He kissed me on the forehead and went out. I cannot understand the relinquishment of this plan after nine years' persistence in it, My father's frankness is what I like. There is no ambiguity about his words. My money ought to belong to his marquis son. Who, then, has had bowels of mercy? My mother? My father? Or could it be my brother?

I remained sitting on my grandmother's sofa, staring at the purse which my father had left on the mantel, at once pleased and vexed that I could not withdraw my mind from the money. It is true, further speculation was useless. My doubts had been cleared up and there was something fine in the way my pride was spared.

Philippe has spent the morning rushing about among the various stores and workpeople who are to undertake the task of my metamorphosis. A famous dressmaker, by name Victorine, has come, as well as a woman for underclothing, and a shoemaker. I am as impatient as a child to know what I shall be like when I emerge from the sack which constituted the conventual uniform; but all these tradespeople take a long time; the corsetmaker requires a whole week if my figure is not to be spoilt. You see, I have a figure, dear; this becomes serious. Janssen, the operatic shoemaker, solemnly assures me that I have my mother's foot. The whole morning has gone in these weighty occupations. Even a glovemaker has come to take the measure of my hand. The underclothing woman has received my orders.

At the meal which I call dinner, and the others lunch, my mother told me that we were going together to the milliner's to see some hats, so that my taste should be formed, and I might be in a position to order my own.

This burst of independence dazzles me. I am like a blind man who has just recovered his sight. Now I begin to understand the vast interval which separates a Carmelite sister from a girl in society. Of ourselves we could never have conceived it.

During this lunch my father seemed absent-minded, and we left him to his thoughts; he is deep in the King's confidence. I was entirely forgotten; but, from what I have seen, I have no doubt he will remember me when he has need of me. He is a very attractive man in spite of his fifty years. His figure is youthful; he is well made, fair, and extremely graceful in his movements. He has the diplomatic face, at once dumb and expressive; his nose is long and slender, and he has brown eyes.

What a handsome pair! Strange thoughts assail me as it becomes plain to me that these two, so perfectly matched in birth, wealth, and mental superiority, live entirely apart, and have nothing in common but their name. The show of unity is only for the world.

The cream of the Court and diplomatic circles were here last night. Very soon I am going to a ball given by the Duchesse de Maufrigneuse, and I shall be presented to the society I am so eager to know. A dancing-master is coming every morning to give me lessons, for I must be able to dance in a month, or I can't go to the ball.

Before dinner, my mother came to talk about the governess with me. I have decided to keep Miss Griffith, who was recommended by the English ambassador. Miss Griffith is the daughter of a clergyman; her mother was of good family, and she is perfectly well bred. She is thirty-six, and will teach me English. The good soul is quite handsome enough to have ambitions; she is Scotch—poor and proud—and will act as my chaperon. She is to sleep in Rose's room. Rose will be under her orders. I saw at a glance that my governess would be governed by me. In the six days we have been together, she has made very sure that I am the only person likely to take an interest in her; while, for my part, I have ascertained that, for all her statuesque features, she will prove accommodating. She seems to me a kindly soul, but cautious. I have not been able to extract a word of what passed between her and my mother.

Another trifling piece of news! My father has this morning refused the appointment as Minister of State which was offered him. This accounts for his preoccupied manner last night. He says he would prefer an embassy to the worries of public debate. Spain in especial attracts him.

This news was told me at lunch, the one moment of the day when my father, mother, and brother see each other in an easy way. The servants then only come when they are rung for. The rest of the day my brother, as well as my father, spends out of the house. My mother has her toilet to make; between two and four she is never visible; at four o'clock she goes out for an hour's drive; when she is not dining out, she receives from six to seven, and the evening is given to entertainments of various kinds—theatres, balls, concerts, at homes. In short, her life is so full, that I don't believe she ever has a quarter of an hour to herself. She must spend a considerable time dressing in the morning; for at lunch, which takes place between eleven and twelve, she is exquisite. The meaning of the things that are said about her is dawning on me. She begins the day with a bath barely warmed, and a cup of cold coffee with cream; then she dresses. She is never, except on some great emergency, called before nine o'clock. In summer there are morning rides, and at two o'clock she receives a young man whom I have never yet contrived to see.

Behold our family life! We meet at lunch and dinner, though often I am alone with my mother at this latter meal, and I foresee that still oftener I shall take it in my own rooms (following the example of my grandmother) with only Miss Griffith for company, for my mother frequently dines out. I have ceased to wonder at the indifference my family have shown to me. In Paris, my dear, it is a miracle of virtue to love the people who live with you, for you see little enough of them; as for the absent—they do not exist!

Knowing as this may sound, I have not yet set foot in the streets, and am deplorably ignorant. I must wait till I am less of the country cousin and have brought my dress and deportment into keeping with the society I am about to enter, the whirl of which amazes me even here, where only distant murmurs reach my ear. So far I have not gone beyond the garden; but the Italian opera opens in a few days, and my mother has a box there. I am crazy with delight at the thought of hearing Italian music and seeing French acting.

Already I begin to drop convent habits for those of society. I spend the evening writing to you till the moment for going to bed arrives. This has been postponed to ten o'clock, the hour at which my mother goes out, if she is not at the theatre. There are twelve theatres in Paris.

I am grossly ignorant and I read a lot, but quite indiscriminately, one book leading to another. I find the names of fresh books on the cover of the one I am reading; but as I have no one to direct me, I light on some which are fearfully dull. What modern literature I have read all turns upon love, the subject which used to bulk so largely in our thoughts, because it seemed that our fate was determined by man and for man. But how inferior are these authors to two little girls, known as Sweetheart and Darling—otherwise Renée and Louise. Ah! my love, what wretched plots, what ridiculous situations, and what poverty of sentiment! Two books, however, have given me wonderful pleasure—"Corinne" and "Adolphe." Apropos of this, I asked my father one day whether it would be possible for me to see Mme. de Staël. My father, mother, and Alphonse all burst out laughing, and Alphonse said:

"Where in the world has she sprung from?"

To which my father replied:

"What fools we are! She springs from the Carmelites."

"My child, Mme. de Staël is dead," said my mother gently.

When I had finished "Adolphe," I asked Miss Griffith how a woman could be betrayed.

"Why, of course, when she loves," was her reply.

Renée, tell me, do you think we could be betrayed by a man?

Miss Griffith has at last discerned that I am not an utter ignoramus, that I have somewhere a hidden vein of knowledge, the knowledge we learned from each other in our random arguments. She sees that it is only superficial facts of which I am ignorant. The poor thing has opened her heart to me. Her curt reply to my question, when I compare it with all the sorrows I can imagine, makes me feel quite creepy. Once more she urged me not to be dazzled by the glitter of society, to be always on my guard, especially against what most attracted me. This is the sum-total of her wisdom, and I can get nothing more out of her. Her lectures, therefore, become a trifle monotonous, and she might be compared in this respect to the bird which has only one cry.

III.

THE SAME TO THE SAME.

December.

My Darling:—Here I am ready to make my bow to the world. By way of preparation I have been trying to commit all the follies I could think of before sobering down for my entry. This morning, I have seen myself, after many rehearsals, well and duly equipped—stays, shoes, curls, dress, ornaments—all in order. Following the example of duelists before a meeting, I tried my arms in the privacy of my chamber. I wanted to see how I would look, and had no difficulty in discovering a certain air of victory and triumph, bound to carry all before it. I mustered all my forces, in accordance with that splendid maxim of antiquity: "Know thyself!" and boundless was my delight in thus making my own acquaintance. Griffith was the sole spectator of this doll's play, in which I was at once doll and child. You think you know me? You are hugely mistaken!

Here is a portrait, then, Renée, of your sister, formerly disguised as a Carmelite, now brought to life again as a frivolous society girl. She is one of the greatest beauties in France —Provence, of course, excepted. I don't see that I can give a more accurate summary of this interesting topic.

True, I have my weak points; but were I a man, I should adore them. They arise from what is most promising in me. When you have spent a fortnight admiring the exquisite curves of your mother's arms, and that mother, the Duchesse de Chaulieu, it is impossible, my dear, not to deplore your own angular elbows. Yet there is consolation in observing the fineness of the wrist, and a certain grace of line in those hollows, which will yet fill out and show plump, round, and well modeled, under the satiny skin. The somewhat crude outline of the arms is seen again in the shoulders. Strictly speaking, indeed, I have no shoulders, but only two bony blades, standing out in harsh relief. My figure also lacks pliancy ; there is a stiffness about the side-lines.

Poof! There's the worst out. But then the contours are bold and delicate, the bright, pure flame of health bites into the vigorous lines, a flood of life and of blue blood pulses under the transparent skin, and the fairest daughter of Eve would seem a negress beside me! I have the foot of a gazelle! My joints are finely turned, my features of a Greek correctness. It is true, madame, that the flesh tints do not melt into each other ; but, at least, they stand out clear and bright. In short, I am a very pretty green fruit, with all the charm of unripeness. I see a great likeness to the face in my aunt's old missal, which rises out of a violet lily.

There is no silly weakness in the blue of my insolent eyes ; the white is pure mother-of-pearl, prettily marked with tiny veins, and the thick, long lashes fall like a silken fringe. My forehead sparkles, and the hair grows deliciously ; it ripples into waves of pale gold, growing browner toward the centre, whence escape little rebel locks, which alone would tell that my fairness is not of the insipid and hysterical type. I am a tropical blonde, with plenty of blood in my veins, a blonde more apt to strike than to turn the cheek. What do you think the hairdresser proposed? He wanted, if you please, to smooth my hair into two bands and place over my forehead a pearl, kept in place by a gold chain! He said it would recall the Middle Ages.

I told him I was not aged enough to have reached the middle, or to be of any age but what I am!

The nose is slender, and the well-cut nostrils are separated by a sweet little pink partition—an imperious, mocking nose, with a tip too sensitive ever to grow coarse or red. Sweetheart, if this won't find a husband for even a dowerless maiden, I'm a donkey. The ears are daintily curled, a pearl hanging from either lobe would show yellow. The neck is long, and has an undulating motion full of dignity. In the shade the white ripens to a golden tinge. Perhaps the mouth is a little large. But how expressive! what a color on the lips! how prettily the teeth laugh!

Then, dear, there is a harmony running through all. What a gait! what a voice! We have not forgotten how our grandmother's skirts fell into place without a touch. In a word, I am lovely and charming. When the mood comes, I can laugh one of our good old laughs, and no one will think the less of me; the dimples, impressed by Comedy's light fingers on my fair cheeks, will command respect. Or I can let my eyes fall and my heart freeze under my snowy brow. I can pose as a Madonna with melancholy, swan-like neck, and the painters' virgins will be nowhere; my place in heaven would be far above them. A man would be forced to chant when he spoke to me.

So, you see, my panoply is complete, and I can run the whole gamut of coquetry from deepest bass to shrillest treble. It is a huge advantage not to be all of one piece. Now, my mother is neither playful nor virginal. Her only attitude is an imposing one; when she ceases to be majestic, she is ferocious. It is difficult for her to heal the wounds she makes, whereas I can wound and heal together. We are absolutely unlike, and therefore there could not possibly be rivalry between us, unless indeed we quarreled over the greater or less perfection of our extremities, which are similar. I take after my father, who is shrewd and subtle. I have the manner of my grandmother and her charming voice, which becomes falsetto when forced, but is a sweet-toned chest voice at the ordinary pitch of a quiet talk.

I feel as if I had left the convent to-day for the first time. For society I do not yet exist; I am unknown to it. What a ravishing moment! I still belong only to myself, like a flower just blown, unseen yet of mortal eye.

In spite of this, my sweet, as I paced the drawing-room during my self-inspection, and saw the poor cast-off school-clothes, a queer feeling came over me. Regret for the past, anxiety about the future, fear of society, a long farewell to the pale daisies which we used to pick and strip of their petals in light-hearted innocence, there was something of all that; but strange, fantastic visions also rose, which I crushed back into the inner depths, whence they had sprung, and whither I dared not follow them.

My Renée, I have a regular trousseau! It is all beautifully laid away and perfumed in the cedar-wood drawers with lac-quered front of my charming dressing-table. There are rib-bons, shoes, gloves, all in lavish abundance. My father has kindly presented me with the pretty gewgaws a girl loves—a dressing-case, toilet service, scent-box, fan, sunshade, prayer-book, gold chain, cashmere shawl. He has also promised to give me riding lessons. And I can dance! To-morrow, yes, to-morrow evening, I come out!

My dress is white lawn, and on my head I wear a garland of white roses in Greek style. I shall put on my Madonna face; I mean to play the simpleton, and have all the women on my side. My mother is miles away from any idea of what I write to you. She believes me quite destitute of mind, and would be dumfounded if she read my letter. My brother honors me with a profound contempt, and is uniformly and politely indifferent.

He is a handsome young fellow, but melancholy, and given to moods. I have divined his secret, though neither the duke nor duchess has an inkling of it. In spite of his youth and his title, he is jealous of his father. He has no position in the State, no post at Court, he never has to say: "I am going to the Chamber." I alone in the house have sixteen hours for meditation. My father is absorbed in public business and his own amusements; my mother, too, is never at leisure; no member of the household by any chance practices self-examination, they are constantly in company, and have hardly time to breathe.

I should immensely like to know what is the potent charm wielded by society to keep people prisoner from nine every evening till two or three in the morning, and force them to be so lavish alike of strength and money. When I longed for it, I had no idea of the separations it brought about, or its overmastering spell. But, then, I forget, it is Paris which does it all.

It is possible, it seems, for members of one family to live side by side and know absolutely nothing of each other. A half-fledged nun arrives, and in a couple of weeks has grasped domestic details, of which the master diplomatist at the head of the house is quite ignorant. Or perhaps he *does* see, and shuts his eyes deliberately, as part of the father's role. There is a mystery here which I must plumb.

IV.

THE SAME TO THE SAME.

December 15th.

Yesterday, at two o'clock, I went to drive in the Champs-Élysées and the Bois de Boulogne. It was one of those autumn days which we used to find so beautiful on the banks of the Loire. So I have seen Paris at last! The Place Louis XV. is certainly very fine, but the beauty is that of man's handiwork.

I was dressed to perfection, pensive, with set face (though inwardly much tempted to laugh), under a lovely hat, my hands folded. Would you believe it? Not a single smile was thrown at me, not one poor youth was struck motionless as I passed, not a soul turned to look again ; and yet the carriage proceeded with a deliberation worthy of my pose.

No, I am wrong, there was one—a duke, and a charming man—who suddenly reined in as he went by. The individual who thus saved appearances for me was my father, and he proclaimed himself highly gratified by what he saw. I met my mother also, who sent me a butterfly kiss from the tips of her fingers. The Griffith, who fears no man, cast her glances hither and thither without discrimination. In my judgment, a young woman should always know exactly what her eye is resting on.

I was mad with rage. One man actually inspected my carriage without noticing me. This flattering homage probably came from a carriage-maker. I have been quite out in the reckoning of my forces. Plainly, beauty, that rare gift which comes from heaven, is commoner in Paris than I thought. I saw hats doffed with deference to simpering fools; a purple face called forth murmurs of: "It is she!" My mother received an immense amount of admiration. There is an answer to this problem, and I mean to find it.

The men, my dear, seemed to me generally very ugly. The few exceptions are bad copies of us. Heaven knows what evil genius has inspired their costume; it is amazingly inelegant compared with those of former generations. It has no distinction, no beauty of color or romance; it appeals neither to the senses, nor the mind, nor the eye, and it must be very uncomfortable. It is meagre and stunted. The hat, above all, struck me; it is a sort of truncated column, and does not adapt itself in the least to the shape of the head; but I am told it is easier to bring about a revolution than to invent a graceful hat. Courage in Paris recoils before the thought of appearing in a round felt; and, for lack of one day's daring, men stick all their lives to this ridiculous headpiece. And yet Frenchmen are said to be fickle!

The men are hideous any way, whatever they put on their heads. I have seen nothing but worn, hard faces, with neither calm nor peace in the expression; the harsh lines and

11

furrows speak of foiled ambition and smarting vanity.   A fine forehead is rarely seen.

"And these are the product of Paris!" I said to Miss Griffith.

"Most cultivated and pleasant men," she replied.

I was silent.   The heart of a spinster of thirty-six is a well of tolerance.

In the evening I went to the ball, where I kept close to my mother's side.   She gave me her arm with a devotion which did not miss its reward.   All the honors were for her; I was made the pretext for charming compliments.   She was clever enough to find me fools for my partners, who one and all expatiated on the heat and the beauty of the ball, till you might suppose I was freezing and blind.   Not one failed to enlarge on the strange, unheard-of, extraordinary, odd, remarkable fact—that he saw me for the first time.

My dress, which dazzled me as I paraded alone in my white-and-gold drawing-room, was barely noticeable amidst the gorgeous finery of most of the married women.   Each had her band of faithful followers, and they all watched each other askance.   A few were radiant in triumphant beauty, and amongst these was my mother.   A girl at a ball is a mere dancing machine—a thing of no consequence whatever.

The men, with rare exceptions, did not impress me more favorably here than at the Champs-Élysées.   They have a used-up look; their features are meaningless, or rather they have all the same meaning.   The proud, stalwart bearing which we find in the portraits of our ancestors—men who joined moral to physical vigor—has disappeared.   Yet in this gathering there was one man of remarkable ability, who stood out from the rest by the beauty of his face.   But even he did not rouse in me the feeling which I should have expected.   I do not know his works, and he is a man of no family   Whatever the genius and the merits of a plebeian or a commoner, he could never stir my blood.   Beside, this man was obviously so much more taken up with himself than with anybody else, that I could not but think these great brain-workers must look on us as things rather than persons. When men of intellectual power love, they ought to give up writing, otherwise their love is not the real thing. The lady of their heart does not come first in all their thoughts. I seemed to read all this in the bearing of the man I speak of. I am told he is a professor, orator, and author, whose ambition makes him the slave of every bigwig.

My mind was made up on the spot. It was unworthy of me, I determined, to quarrel with society for not being impressed by my merits, and I gave myself up to the simple pleasure of dancing, which I thoroughly enjoyed. I heard a great deal of inept gossip about people of whom I knew nothing; but perhaps it is my ignorance on many subjects which prevents me from appreciating it, as I saw that most men and women took a lively pleasure in certain remarks, whether falling from their own lips or those of others. Society bristles with enigmas which look hard to solve. It is a perfect maze of intrigue. Yet I am fairly quick of sight and hearing, and as to my wits, Mlle. de Maucombe does not need to be told!

I returned home tired with a pleasant sort of tiredness, and in all innocence began describing my sensations to my mother, who was with me. She checked me with the warning that I must never say such things to any one but her.

"My dear child," she added, "it needs as much tact to know when to be silent as when to speak."

This advice brought home to me the nature of the sensations which ought to be concealed from every one, not excepting perhaps even a mother. At a glance I measured the vast field of feminine duplicity. I can assure you, sweetheart, that we, in our unabashed simplicity, would pass for two very wide-awake little scandal-mongers. What lessons may be conveyed in a finger on the lips, in a word, a look! All in a moment I was seized with excessive shyness. What! may I never again speak of the natural pleasure I feel in the exercise of dancing? "How then," I said to myself, "about the deeper feelings?"

I went to bed sorrowful, and I still suffer from the shock produced by this first collision of my frank, joyous nature with the harsh laws of society. Already the highway hedges are flecked with my white wool! Farewell, beloved.

V.

RENÉE DE MAUCOMBE TO LOUISE DE CHAULIEU.

October.

How deeply your letter moved me; above all, when I compare our widely different destinies! How brilliant is the world you are entering, how peaceful the retreat where I shall end my modest career!

In the Castle of Maucombe, which is so well known to you by description that I shall say no more of it, I found my room almost exactly as I left it; only now I can enjoy the splendid view it gives of the Gémenos valley, which my childish eyes used to see without comprehending. Two weeks after my arrival, my father and mother took me, along with my two brothers, to dine with one of our neighbors, M. de l'Estorade, an old gentleman of good family, who has made himself rich, after the provincial fashion, by scraping and paring.

M. de l'Estorade was unable to save his only son from the clutches of Bonaparte; after successfully eluding the conscription, he was forced to send him to the army in 1813, to join the Emperor's bodyguard. After Leipsic no more was heard of him. M. de Montriveau, whom the father interviewed in 1814, declared that he had seen him taken by the Russians. Mme. de l'Estorade died of grief whilst a vain search was being made in Russia. The baron, a very pious old man, practiced that fine theological virtue which we used to cultivate at Blois—Hope! Hope made him see his son in dreams. He hoarded his income for him, and guarded carefully the portion of inheritance which fell to him from the family of the late Mme. de l'Estorade, no one venturing to ridicule the old man.

At last it dawned upon me that the unexpected return of this son was the cause of my own. Who could have imagined, whilst fancy was leading us a giddy dance, that my destined husband was slowly traveling on foot through Russia, Poland, and Germany? His bad luck only forsook him at Berlin, where the French Minister helped his return to his native country. M. de l'Estorade, the father, who is a small landed proprietor in Provence, with an income of about ten thousand livres, has not sufficient European fame to interest the world in the wandering Knight de l'Estorade, whose name smacks of his adventures.

The accumulated income of twelve thousand livres from the property of Mme. de l'Estorade, with the addition of the father's savings, provides the poor guard of honor with something like two hundred and fifty thousand livres, not counting house and lands—quite a considerable fortune in Provence. His worthy father had bought, on the very eve of the chevalier's return, a fine but badly-managed estate, where he designs to plant ten thousand mulberry-trees, raised in his nursery with a special view to this acquisition. The baron, having found his long-lost son, has now but one thought, to marry him, and marry him to a girl of good family.

My father and mother entered into their neighbor's idea with an eye to my interests so soon as they discovered that Renée de Maucombe would be acceptable without a dowry, and that the money the said Renée ought to inherit from her parents would be duly acknowledged as hers in the contract. In a similar way, my younger brother, Jean de Maucombe, as soon as he came of age, signed a document stating that he had received from his parents an advance upon the estate equal in amount to one-third of the whole. This is the device by which the nobles of Provence elude the infamous Civil Code of M. de Bonaparte, a code which will drive as many girls of good family into convents as it will find husbands for. The French nobility, from the little I have been able to gather, seem to be much divided on these matters.

The dinner, darling, was a first meeting between your sweetheart and the exile. The Comte de Maucombe's servants donned their old laced liveries and hats, the coachman his great top-boots; we sat five in the antiquated carriage, and arrived in state about two o'clock—the dinner was for three—at the grange, which is the dwelling of the Baron de l'Estorade.

My father-in-law to be has, you see, no castle, only a simple country house, standing beneath one of our hills, at the entrance of that noble valley, the pride of which is undoubtedly the Castle of Maucombe. The building is quite unpretentious: four pebble walls covered with a yellowish wash, and roofed with hollow tiles of a good red, constitute the grange. The rafters bend under the weight of this brick-kiln. The windows, inserted casually, without any attempt at symmetry, have enormous shutters, painted yellow. The garden in which it stands is a Provençal garden, inclosed by low walls, built of big round pebbles set in layers, alternately sloping or upright, according to the artistic taste of the mason, which finds here its only outlet. The mud in which they are set is falling away in places.

Thanks to an iron railing at the entrance facing the road, this simple farm has a certain air of being a country-seat. The railing, long sought with tears, is so emaciated that it recalled Sister Angélique to me. A flight of stone steps leads to the door, which is protected by a pent-house roof, such as no peasant on the Loire would tolerate for his coquettish white stone house, with its blue roof, glittering in the sun. The garden and surrounding walks are horribly dusty, and the trees seem burnt up. It is easy to see that for years the baron's life has been a mere rising up and going to bed again, day after day, without a thought beyond that of piling up coppers. He eats the same food as his two servants, a Provençal lad and the old woman who used to wait on his wife. The rooms are scantily furnished.

Nevertheless, the house of l'Estorade had done its best; the cupboards had been ransacked, and its last man beaten up for the dinner, which was served to us on old silver dishes, blackened and battered. The exile, my darling pet, is like the railing, emaciated! He is pale and silent, and bears traces of suffering. At thirty-seven he might be fifty. The once beautiful ebon locks of youth are streaked with white like a lark's wing. His fine blue eyes are cavernous; he is a little deaf, which suggests the Knight of the Sorrowful Countenance.

Spite of all this, I have graciously consented to become Mme. de l'Estorade and to receive a dowry of two hundred and fifty thousand francs, but only on the express condition of being allowed to work my will upon the grange and make a park around it. I have demanded from my father, in set terms, a grant of a water-course, which can be brought thither from Maucombe. In a month I shall be Mme. de l'Estorade; for, dear, I have made a good impression. After the snows of Siberia a man is ready enough to see merit in those black eyes, which, according to you, used to ripen fruit with a look. Louis de l'Estorade seems well content to marry the "fair Renée de Maucombe"—such is your friend's splendid title.

Whilst you are preparing to reap the joys of that many-sided existence which awaits a young lady of the Chaulieu family, and to queen it in Paris, your poor little loved one, Renée, that child of the desert, has fallen from the empyrean, whither together we had soared, into the vulgar realities of a life as homely as a daisy's. I have vowed to myself to comfort this young man, who has never known youth, but passed straight from his mother's arms to the embrace of war, and

from the joys of his country home to the frosts and forced
labor of Siberia.

Humble country pleasures will enliven the monotony of
my future. It shall be my ambition to enlarge the oasis
round my house, and to give it the lordly shade of fine trees.
My turf, though Provençal, shall be always green. I shall
carry my park up the hillside and plant on the highest point
some pretty kiosk, whence, perhaps, my eyes may catch the
shimmer of the Mediterranean. Orange and lemon trees, and
all choicest things that grow, shall embellish my retreat ; and
there will I be a mother among my children. The poetry of
Nature, which nothing can destroy, shall hedge us round ;
and standing loyally at the post of duty, we need fear no
danger. My religious feelings are shared by my father-in-law
and by the chevalier.

Ah ! darling, my life unrolls itself before my eyes like one
of the great highways of France, level and easy, shaded with
evergreen trees. This century will not see another Bonaparte ;
and my children, if I have any, will not be rent from me.
They will be mine to train and make men of—the joy of my
life. If you also are true to your destiny, you who ought to
find your mate amongst the great ones of the earth, the children of your Renée will not lack a zealous protectress.

Farewell, then, for me at least, to the romances and thrilling adventures in which we used ourselves to play the part
of heroine. The whole story of my life lies before me now ;
its great crisis will be the teething and nutrition of the young
Masters de l'Estorade, and the mischief they do to my shrubs
and me. To embroider their caps, to be loved and admired
by a sickly man at the mouth of the Gémenos valley—there
are my pleasures. Perhaps some day the country dame may
go and spend a winter in Marseilles ; but danger does not
haunt the purlieus of a narrow provincial stage. There will
be nothing to fear, not even an admiration such as could only
make a woman proud. We shall take a great deal of interest

in the silkworms for whose benefit our mulberry-leaves will be sold! We shall know the strange vicissitudes of life in Provence, and the storms that may attack even a peaceful household. Quarrels will be impossible, for M. de l'Estorade has formally announced that he will leave the reins in his wife's hands; and as I shall do nothing to remind him of this wise resolve, it is likely he may persevere in it.

You, my dear Louise, will supply the romance of my life. So you must narrate to me in full all your adventures, describe your balls and parties, tell me what you wear, what flowers crown your lovely golden locks, and what are the words and manners of the men you meet. Your other self will be always there—listening, dancing, feeling her finger-tips pressed—with you. If only I could have some fun in Paris now and then, while you played the house-mother at La Crampade! such is the name of our grange. Poor M. de l'Estorade, who fancies he is marrying one woman! Will he find out there are two?

I am writing nonsense now, and as henceforth I can only be foolish by proxy, I had better stop. One kiss, then, on each cheek—my lips are still virginal, he has only dared to take my hand. Oh! our deference and propriety are quite disquieting, I assure you. There, I am off again. Good-by, dear.

P.S.—I have just opened your third letter. My dear, I have about one thousand livres with which to do what I wish; spend them for me on pretty things, such as we can't find here nor even at Marseilles. While speeding on your own business, give a thought to the recluse of La Crampade. Remember that on neither side have the heads of the family any people of taste in Paris to make their purchases. I shall reply to your letter later.

VI.

DON FÉLIPE HÉNAREZ TO DON FERNAND.

PARIS, *September.*

The address of this letter, my brother, will show you that the head of your house is out of reach of danger. If the massacre of our ancestors in the Court of Lions made Spaniards and Christians of us against our will, it left us a legacy of Arab cunning; and it may be that I owe my safety to the blood of the Abencerrages still flowing in my veins.

Fear made Ferdinand's acting so good, that Valdez actually believed in his protestations. But for me the poor admiral would have been done for. Nothing, it seems, will teach the Liberals what a king is. This particular Bourbon has been long known to me; and the more his majesty assured me of his protection, the stronger grew my suspicions. A true Spaniard has no need to repeat a promise. A flow of words is a sure sign of duplicity.

Valdez took ship on an English vessel. For myself, no sooner did I see the cause of my beloved Spain wrecked in Andalusia, than I wrote to the steward of my Sardinian estate to make arrangements for my escape. Some hardy coral fishers were dispatched to wait for me at a point on the coast; and when Ferdinand urged the French to secure my person, I was already in my barony of Macumer, amidst brigands who defy all law and all avengers.

The last Hispano-Moorish family of Granada has found once more the shelter of an African desert, and even a Saracen horse, in an estate which comes to it from Saracens. How the eyes of these brigands—who but yesterday had dreaded my authority—sparkled with savage joy and pride when they found they were protecting against the King of Spain's vendetta the Duc de Soria, their master and a Hénarez—the first who had come to visit them since the time when the island belonged to the Moors. More than a score of rifles were ready to point at Ferdinand of Bourbon, son of a race which was still unknown when the Abencerrages arrived as conquerors on the banks of the Loire.

My idea had been to live on the income of these huge estates, which, unfortunately, we have so greatly neglected; but my stay there convinced me that this was impossible, and that Queverdo's reports were only too correct. The poor man had twenty-two lives at my disposal, but not a single réal; prairies of twenty thousand acres, and not a house; virgin forests, and not a stick of furniture! A million piastres and a resident master for half a century would be necessary to make these magnificent lands pay. I must see to this.

The conquered have time during their flight to ponder their own case and that of their vanquished party. At the spectacle of my noble country, a corpse for monks to prey on, my eyes filled with tears; I read in it the presage of Spain's gloomy future.

At Marseilles I heard of Riego's end. Painfully did it come home to me that my life also would henceforth be a martyrdom, but a martyrdom protracted and unnoticed. Is existence worthy the name, when a man can no longer die for his country or live for a woman? To love, to conquer, this twofold form of the same thought, is the law graven on our sabres, emblazoned on the vaulted roofs of our palaces, ceaselessly whispered by the water, which rises and falls in our marble fountains. But in vain does it nerve my heart; the sabre is broken, the palace in ashes, the living spring sucked up by the barren sand.

Here, then, is my last will and testament.

Don Fernand, you will understand now why I put a check upon your ardor and ordered you to remain faithful to the reigning king. As your brother and friend, I implore you to obey me ; as your master, I command. You will go to the King and will ask from him the grant of my dignities and property, my office and titles. He will perhaps hesitate, and may treat you to some regal scowls; but you must tell him that you are loved by Marie Hérédia, and that Marie can marry none but a Duc de Soria. This will make the King radiant. It is the immense fortune of the Hérédia family which alone has stood between him and the accomplishment of my ruin. Your proposal will seem to him, therefore, to deprive me of a last resource, and he will gladly hand over to you my spoils.

You will then marry Marie. The secret of the mutual love against which you fought was no secret to me, and I have prepared the old count to see you take my place. Marie and I were merely doing what was expected of us in our position and carrying out the wishes of our fathers ; everything else is in your favor. You are beautiful as a child of love, and are possessed of Marie's heart. I am an ill-favored Spanish grandee, for whom she feels an aversion to which she will not confess. Some slight reluctance there may be on the part of the noble Spanish girl on account of my misfortunes, but this you will soon overcome.

Duc de Soria, your predecessor would neither cost you a regret nor rob you of a maravedi. My mother's diamonds, which will suffice to make me independent, I will keep, because the gap caused by them in the family estate can be filled by Marie's jewels. You can send them, therefore, by my nurse, old Urraca, the only one of my servants whom I wish to retain. No one can prepare my chocolate as she does.

During our brief revolution, my life of unremitting toil was reduced to the barest necessaries, and these my salary was sufficient to provide. You will therefore find the income of the two last years in the hands of your steward. This sum is mine ; but a Duc de Soria cannot marry without a large expenditure of money, therefore we will divide it. You will

not refuse this wedding present from your brother, the brigand.
Beside, I mean to have it so.

The barony of Macumer, not being Spanish territory, but
in Sardinia, remains to me.   Thus I have still a country and a
name, should I wish to take up a position in the world again.

Thank heaven, this finishes our business, and the house of
Soria is saved !

At the very moment when I drop into simple Baron de
Macumer, the French cannon announce the arrival of the
Duc d'Angoulême.   You will understand why I break off.

October.

When I arrived here I had not ten doubloons in my pocket.
He would indeed be a poor sort of leader who, in the midst
of calamities he has not been able to avert, has found means
to feather his own nest.   For the vanquished Moor there
remains a horse and the desert ; for the Christian foiled of his
hopes, the cloister and a few gold-pieces.

But my present resignation is mere weariness.   I am not
yet so near the monastery as to have abandoned all thoughts
of life.   Ozalga had given me several letters of introduction
to meet all emergencies, amongst these one to a bookseller,
who takes with our fellow-countrymen the place which Galig-
nani holds with the English in Paris.   This man has found
eight pupils for me at three francs a lesson.   I go to my
pupils every alternate day, so that I have four lessons a day
and earn twelve francs, which is much more than I require.
When Urraca comes I shall make some Spanish exile happy
by passing on to him my connection.

I lodge in the Rue Hillerin-Bertion with a poor widow,
who takes boarders.   My room faces south and looks out on
a little garden.   It is perfectly quiet ; I have green trees to
look upon, and spend the sum of one piastre a day.   I am
amazed at the amount of calm, pure pleasure which I enjoy
in this life, after the fashion of Dionysius at Corinth.   From

sunrise until ten o'clock I smoke and take my chocolate, sitting at my window and contemplating two Spanish plants, a broom which rises out of a clump of jessamine—gold on a white ground, colors which must send a thrill through any scion of the Moors. At ten o'clock I start for my lessons, which last till four, when I return for dinner. Afterward I read and smoke till I go to bed.

I can put up for a long time with a life like this, compounded of work and meditation, of solitude and society. Be happy, therefore, Fernand; my abdication has brought no afterthoughts; I have no regrets like Charles V., no longing to try the game again like Napoleon. Five days and nights have passed since I wrote my will; to my mind they might have been five centuries. Honor, titles, wealth, are for me as though they had never existed.

Now that the conventional barrier of respect which hedged me round has fallen, I can open my heart to you, dear boy. Though cased in the armor of gravity, this heart is full of tenderness and devotion, which have found no object, and which no woman has divined, not even she who, from her cradle, has been my destined bride. In this lies the secret of my political enthusiasm. Spain has taken the place of a mistress and received the homage of my heart. And now Spain, too, is gone! Beggared of all, I can gaze upon the ruin of what once was me and speculate over the mysteries of my being.

Why did life animate this carcase, and when will it depart? Why has that race, preëminent in chivalry, breathed all its primitive virtues—its tropical love, its fiery poetry—into this its last offshoot, if the seed was never to burst its rugged shell, if no stem was to spring forth, no radiant flower scatter aloft its Eastern perfumes? Of what crime have I been guilty before my birth that I can inspire no love? Did fate from my very infancy decree that I should be stranded, a useless hulk, on some barren shore? I find in my soul the image

I SMOKE AND TAKE MY CHOCOLATE, SITTING AT MY
WINDOW.

I SMOKE AND TAKE MY CHOCOLATE, SITTING AT MY
WINDOW.

of the deserts where my fathers ranged, illumined by a scorching sun which shrivels up all life. Proud remnant of a fallen
race, vain force, love run to waste, an old man in the prime
of youth, here better than elsewhere shall I await the last
grace of death. Alas! under this murky sky no spark will
kindle these ashes again to flame. Thus my last words may
be those of Christ: "My God, why hast Thou forsaken
me?" Cry of agony and terror, to the core of which no
mortal has ventured yet to penetrate!

You can realize now, Fernand, what a joy it is to me to
live afresh in you and Marie. I shall watch you henceforth
with the pride of a creator satisfied in his work. Love each
other well and go on loving if you would not give me pain;
any discord between you would hurt me more than it would
yourselves.

Our mother had a presentiment that events would one day
serve her wishes. It may be that the longing of a mother
constitutes a pact between herself and God. Was she not,
moreover, one of those mysterious beings who can hold con-
verse with heaven and bring back thence a vision of the
future? How often have I not read in the lines of her forehead that she was coveting for Fernand the honors and the
wealth of Félipe! When I said so to her, she would reply
with tears, laying bare the wounds of a heart, which of right
was the undivided property of both her sons, but which an
irresistible passion gave to you alone.

Her spirit, therefore, will hover joyfully above your heads
as you bow them at the altar. My mother, have you not a
caress for your Félipe now that he has yielded to your favorite
even the girl whom you regretfully thrust into his arms?
What I have done is pleasing to our womankind, to the dead,
and to the King; it is the will of God. Make no difficulty
then, Fernand; obey, and be silent.

P.S.—Tell Urraca to be sure and call me nothing but M.

Hénarez. Don't say a word about me to Marie. You must
be the one living soul to know the secrets of the last Christian-
ized Moor, in whose veins runs the blood of a great family,
which took its rise in the desert and is now about to die out
in the person of a solitary exile. Farewell.

VII.

LOUISE DE CHAULIEU TO RENÉE DE MAUCOMBE.

What! To be married so soon! But this is unheard of.
At the end of a month you become engaged to a man who is
a stranger to you, and about whom you know nothing. The
man may be deaf—there are so many kinds of deafness!—he
may be sickly, tiresome, insufferable!

Don't you see, Renée, what they want with you? You are
needful for carrying on the glorious stock of the l'Estorades,
that is all. You will be buried in the provinces. Are these
the promises we made each other? Were I you, I would
sooner set off to the Hyères islands in a boat, on the chance
of being captured by an Algerian corsair and sold to the
Grand Turk. Then I should be a Sultana some day, and
wouldn't I make a stir in the harem while I was young—yes,
and afterward too!

You are leaving one convent to enter another. I know
you; you are a coward, and you will submit to the yoke of
family life with a lamb-like docility. But I am here to direct
you; you must come to Paris. There we shall drive the men
wild and hold a court like queens. Your husband, sweet
love, in three years from now may become a member of the
Chamber. I know all about members now, and I will explain
it to you. You will work that machine very well; you can
live in Paris, and become there what my mother calls a woman
of fashion. Oh! you needn't suppose I will leave you in
your grange!

For a whole fortnight now, my dear, I have been living the life of society: one evening at the Italiens, another at the grand opera, and always a ball afterward. Ah! society is a witching world. The music of the opera enchants me; and whilst my soul is plunged in divine pleasure, I am the centre of admiration and the focus of all the opera-glasses. But a single glance will make the boldest youth drop his eyes.

I have seen some charming young men there; all the same, I don't care for any of them; not one has roused in me the emotion which I feel when I listen to Garcia in his splendid duet with Pellegrini in "Otello." Heavens! how jealous Rossini must have been to express jealousy so well! What a cry in "Il mio cor si divide!" I'm speaking Greek to you, for you never heard Garcia, but then you know how jealous I am!

What a wretched dramatist Shakespeare is! Othello is in love with glory; he wins battles, he gives orders, he struts about and is all over the place while Desdemona sits at home; and Desdemona, who sees herself neglected for the silly fuss of public life, is quite meek all the time. Such a sheep deserves to be slaughtered. Let the man whom I deign to love beware how he thinks of anything but loving me!

For my part, I like those long trials of the old-fashioned chivalry. That lout of a young lord, who took offense because his sovereign lady sent him down among the lions to fetch her glove, was, in my opinion, very impertinent, and a fool too. Doubtless the lady had in reserve for him some exquisite flower of love, which he lost, as he well deserved— the puppy!

But here am I running on as though I had not a great piece of news to tell you! My father is certainly going to represent our master the King at Madrid. I say *our* master, for I shall make part of the embassy. My mother wishes to remain

12

here, and my father will take me so as to have some woman about him.

My dear, this seems to you, no doubt, very simple, but there are horrors behind it, all the same: in a fortnight I have probed the secrets of the house. My mother would accompany my father to Madrid if he would take M. de Canalis as a secretary to the embassy. But the King appoints the secretaries; the duke dare neither annoy the King, who hates to be opposed, nor vex my mother; and the wily diplomat believes he has cut the knot by leaving the duchess here. M. de Canalis, who is the great poet of the day, is the young man who cultivates my mother's society, and who no doubt studies diplomacy with her from three o'clock to five. Diplomacy must be an interesting subject, for he is as regular as a gambler on the Stock Exchange.

The Duc de Rhétoré, our elder brother, solemn, cold, and whimsical, would be extinguished by his father at Madrid, therefore he remains in Paris. Miss Griffith has found out, also, that Alphonse is in love with a ballet-girl at the opera. How is it possible to fall in love with legs and pirouettes? We have noticed that my brother comes to the theatre only when Tullia dances there; he applauds the steps of this creature, and then goes out. Two ballet-girls in a family are, I fancy, more destructive than the plague. My second brother is with his regiment, and I have not yet seen him. Thus it comes about that I have to act as the Antigone of his majesty's ambassador. Perhaps I may get married in Spain, and perhaps my father's idea is a marriage there without dowry, after the pattern of yours with this broken-down guard of honor. My father asked if I would go with him, and offered me the use of his Spanish teacher.

"Spain, the country for castles in the air!" I cried. "Perhaps you hope it may mean marriages for me!"

For sole reply he honored me with a meaning look. For some days he has amused himself with teasing me at lunch;

he watches me, and I dissemble. In this way I have played
with him cruelly as father and ambassador *in petto*. Hadn't
he taken me for a fool? He asked what I thought of this
and that young man, and of some girls whom I had met in
several houses. I replied with quite inane remarks on the
color of their hair, their faces, and the difference in their
figures. My father seemed disappointed at my crassness, and
inwardly blamed himself for having asked me.

"Still, father," I added, "don't suppose I am saying what
I really think: mother made me afraid the other day that I
had spoken more frankly than I ought of my impressions."

"With your family you may speak quite freely," my mother
replied.

"Very well, then," I went on. "The young men I have
met so far strike me as too self-interested to excite interest in
others; they are much more taken up with themselves than
with their company. They can't be accused of lack of candor
at any rate. They put on a certain expression to talk to us,
and drop it again in a moment, apparently satisfied that we
don't use our eyes. The man as he converses is the lover;
silent, he is the husband. The girls, again, are so artificial that
it is impossible to know what they really are, except from the
way they dance; their figures and movements alone are not a
sham. But what has alarmed me most in this fashionable
society is its brutality. The little incidents which take place
when supper is announced give one some idea—to compare
small things with great—of what a popular rising might be.
Courtesy is only a thin veneer on the general selfishness. I
imagined society very different. Women count for little in
it; that may, perhaps, be a survival of Bonapartist ideas."

"Armande is coming on extraordinarily," said my mother.

"Mother, did you think I should never get beyond asking
to see Mme. de Staël?"

My father smiled, and rose from the table.

Saturday.

My dear, I have left one thing out. Here is the titbit I have reserved for you. The love which we pictured must be extremely well hidden ; I have not seen a trace of it. True, I have caught in drawing-rooms now and again a quick exchange of glances, but how colorless it all is ! Love, as we imagined it, a world of wonders, of glorious dreams, of charming realities, of sorrows that waken sympathy, and smiles that make sunshine, does not exist. The bewitching words, the constant interchange of happiness, the misery of absence, the flood of joy at the presence of the beloved one—where are they? What soil produces these radiant flowers of the soul ? Which is wrong? Who has lied to us? Ourselves or the world ?

I have already seen hundreds of men, young and middle-aged ; not one has stirred the least feeling in me. No proof of admiration and devotion on their part, not even a sword drawn in my behalf, would have moved me. Love, dear, is the product of such rare conditions that it is quite possible to live a lifetime without coming across the being on whom nature has bestowed the power of making one's happiness. The thought is enough to make one shudder ; for if this being is found too late, what then ?

For some days I have begun to tremble when I think of the destiny of women, and to understand why so many wear a sad face beneath the flush brought by the unnatural excitement of social dissipation. Marriage is a mere matter of chance. Look at yours. A storm of wild thoughts has passed over my mind. To be loved every day the same, yet with a difference, to be loved as much after ten years of happiness as on the first day ! such a love demands years. The lover must be allowed to languish, curiosity must be piqued and satisfied, feeling aroused and responded to.

Is there, then, a law for the inner fruits of the heart, as there is for the visible fruits of nature ? Can joy be made lasting? In what proportion should love mingle tears with its pleasures? The cold policy of the funereal, monotonous, persistent routine of the convent seemed to me at these moments the only real life; while the wealth, the splendor, the tears, the delights, the triumph, the joy, the satisfaction, of a love equal, shared, and sanctioned, appeared a mere idle vision.

I see no room in this city for the gentle ways of love, for precious walks in shady alleys, the full moon sparkling on the water, while the suppliant pleads in vain. Rich, young, and beautiful, I have only to love, and love would become my sole occupation, my life; yet in the three months during which I have come and gone, eager and curious, nothing has appealed to me in the bright, covetous, keen eyes around me. No voice has thrilled me, no glance has made the world seem brighter.

Music alone has filled my soul, music alone has at all taken the place of our friendship. Sometimes, at night, I will linger for an hour by my window, gazing into the garden, summoning the future, with all it brings, out of the mystery which shrouds it. There are days too when, having started for a drive, I get out and walk in the Champs-Élysées, and picture to myself that the man who is to waken my slumbering soul is at hand, that he will follow and look at me. Then I meet only mountebanks, vendors of gingerbread, jugglers, passers-by hurrying to their business, or lovers who try to escape notice. These I am tempted to stop, asking them, "You who are happy, tell me, what is love?"

But the impulse is repressed, and I return to my carriage, swearing to die an old maid. Love is undoubtedly an incarnation, and how many conditions are needful before it can take place! We are not certain of never quarreling with ourselves, how much less so when there are two? This is a problem which God alone can solve.

I begin to think that I shall return to the convent. If I

remain in society, I shall do things which will look like follies, for I cannot possibly reconcile myself to what I see. I am perpetually wounded either in my sense of delicacy, my inner principles, or my secret thoughts.

Ah! my mother is the happiest of women, adored as she is by Canalis, her great little man. My love, do you know I am seized sometimes with a horrible craving to know what goes on between my mother and that young man? Griffith tells me she has gone through all these moods; she has longed to fly at women whose happiness was written on their faces; she has blackened their character, torn them to pieces. According to her, virtue consists in burying all these savage instincts in one's innermost heart. But what then of the heart? It becomes the sink of all that is worst in us.

It is very humiliating that no adorer has yet turned up for me. I am a marriageable girl, but I have brothers, a family, relations, who are sensitive on the point of honor. Ah! if that is what keeps men back, they are poltroons.

The part of Chimène in the "Cid" and that of the Cid captivate me. What a marvelous play! Well, good-by.

VIII.

THE SAME TO THE SAME.

January.

Our teacher is a poor refugee, forced to keep in hiding on account of the part he played in the revolution which the Duc d'Angoulême has just quelled—a triumph to which we owe some splendid fêtes. Though a Liberal, and doubtless a man of the people, he has awakened my interest: I fancy that he must have been condemned to death. I make him talk for the purpose of getting at his secret; but he is of a truly Castilian taciturnity, proud as though he were Gonsalvo di Cordova, and nevertheless angelic in his patience and gentleness. His pride is not irritable like Miss Griffith's, it belongs to his inner nature; he forces us to civility because his own manners are so perfect, and holds us at a distance by the respect he shows us. My father declares that there is a great deal of the nobleman in Señor Hénarez, whom, among ourselves, he calls in fun Don Hénarez.

A few days ago I took the liberty of addressing him thus. He raised his eyes, which are generally bent on the ground, and flashed a look from them that quite abashed me; my dear, he certainly has the most beautiful eyes imaginable. I asked him if I had offended him in any way, and he said to me in his grand, rolling Spanish—

"Mademoiselle, I am here only to teach you Spanish."

I blushed, and felt quite snubbed. I was on the point of making some pert answer, when I remembered what our dear mother in God used to say to us, and I replied instead—

"It would be a kindness to tell me if you have anything to complain of."

A tremor passed through him, the blood rose in his olive cheeks; he replied in a voice of some emotion—

"Religion must have taught you, better than I can, to respect the unhappy. Had I been a *don* in Spain, and lost everything in the triumph of Ferdinand VII., your witticism would be unkind; but if I am only a poor teacher of languages, is it not a heartless satire? Neither is worthy of a young lady of rank."

I took his hand, saying—

"In the name of religion also, I beg you to pardon me."

He bowed, opened my "Don Quixote," and sat down.

This little incident disturbed me more than the harvest of compliments, gazing, and pretty speeches on my most successful evening. During the lesson I watched him attentively, which I could do the more safely, as he never looks at me.

As the result of my observations, I made out that the tutor, whom we took to be forty, is a young man, some years under thirty. My governess, to whom I had handed him over, remarked on the beauty of his black hair and of his pearly teeth. As to his eyes, they are velvet and fire; but here ends the catalogue of his good points. Apart from this, he is plain and insignificant. Though the Spaniards have been described as not a cleanly people, this man is most carefully rigged up, and his hands are whiter than his face. He stoops a little, and has an extremely large, oddly-shaped head. His ugliness, which, however, has a dash of piquancy, is aggravated by smallpox marks, which seam his face. His forehead is very prominent, and the shaggy eyebrows meet, giving a repellent air of harshness. There is a frowning, plaintive look on his face, reminding one of a sickly child, which owes its life to superhuman care, as Sister Marthé did. As my father observed, his features are a shrunken reproduction of those of Cardinal Ximenes. The natural dignity of our tutor's manners seems to disconcert the dear duke, who doesn't like him, and is never at ease with him: he can't bear to come in contact with superiority of any kind.

As soon as we both know enough Spanish, we start for Madrid. When Hénarez returned, two days after the reproof he had given me, I remarked by way of showing my gratitude—

"I have no doubt that you left Spain in consequence of political events. If my father is sent there, as seems to be expected, we shall be in a position to help you, and might be able to obtain your pardon, in case you are under sentence."

"It is impossible for any one to help me," he replied.

"But," I said, "is that because you refuse to accept any help, or because the thing itself is impossible?"

"Both," he said, with a bow, and in a tone which forbade continuing the subject.

My father's blood chafed in my veins. I was offended by this haughty demeanor, and promptly dropped Señor Hénarez.

All the same, my dear, there is something fine in this rejection of any aid. "He would not accept even our friendship," I reflected, whilst conjugating a verb. Suddenly I stopped short and told him what was in my mind, but in Spanish. Hénarez replied very politely that equality of sentiment was necessary between friends, which did not exist in this case, and therefore it was useless to consider the question.

"Do you mean equality in the amount of feeling on either side, or equality in rank?" I persisted, determined to shake him out of his provoking gravity.

He raised once more those awe-inspiring eyes, and mine fell before them. Dear, this man is a hopeless enigma. He seemed to ask whether my words meant love; and the mixture of joy, pride, and agonized doubt in his glance went to my heart. It was plain that advances, which would be taken for what they were worth in France, might land me in difficulties with a Spaniard, and I drew back into my shell, feeling not a little foolish.

The lesson over, he bowed, and his eyes were eloquent of the humble prayer: "Don't trifle with a poor wretch."

This sudden contrast to his usual grave and dignified manner made a great impression on me. It seems horrible to think and to say, but I can't help believing that there are treasures of affection in that man.

IX.

December.

All is over, my dear child, and it is Mme. de l'Estorade who writes you. But between us there can be no change; it is only a girl the less.

Don't be troubled; I did not give my consent recklessly or without much thought. My life is henceforth mapped out for me, and the freedom from all uncertainty as to the road to follow suits my mind and disposition. A great moral power has stepped in, and once for all swept what we call chance out of my life. We have the property to develop, our home to beautify and adorn; for me there is also a household to direct and sweeten and a husband to reconcile to life. In all probability I shall have a family to look after, children to educate.

What would you have? Every-day life cannot be cast in heroic mould. No doubt there seems, at any rate at first sight, no room left in this scheme of life for that longing after the infinite which expands the mind and soul. But what is there to prevent me from launching on that boundless sea our familiar craft? Nor must you suppose that the humble duties to which I dedicate my life give no scope for passion. To restore faith in happiness to an unfortunate, who has been the sport of adverse circumstances, is a noble work, and one which alone may suffice to relieve the monotony of my existence. I can see no opening left for suffering, and I see a great deal of good to be done. I need not hide from you that the love I have for Louis de l'Estorade is not of the kind which makes the heart throb at the sound of a step, and thrills us at the lightest tones of a voice, or the caress of a burning glance; but, on the other hand, there is nothing in him which offends me.

What am I to do, you will ask, with that instinct for all which is great and noble, with those mental energies, which have made the link between us and which we still possess? I admit that this thought has troubled me. But are these faculties less ours because we keep them concealed, using them only in secret for the welfare of the family, as instruments to produce the happiness of those confided to our care, to whom we are bound to give ourselves without reserve? The time during which a woman can look for admiration is short, it will soon be past; and if my life has not been a great one, it will at least have been calm, tranquil, free from shocks.

Nature has favored our sex in giving us a choice between

love and motherhood. I have made mine. My children shall
be my gods, and this spot of earth my Eldorado.

I can say no more to-day. Thank you much for all the
things you have sent me. Give a glance at my needs on the
inclosed list. I am determined to live in an atmosphere of
refinement and luxury, and to take from provincial life only
what makes its charms. In solitude a woman can never be
vulgarized—she remains herself. I count greatly on your
kindness for keeping me up to the fashion. My father-in-law
is so delighted that he can refuse me nothing, and turns his
house upside down. We are getting workpeople from Paris
and renovating everything.

X.

MLLE. DE CHAULIEU TO MME. DE L'ESTORADE.

January.

Oh! Renée, you have made me miserable for days! So
that bewitching body, those beautiful proud features, that
natural grace of manner, that soul full of priceless gifts, those
eyes, where the soul can slake its thirst as at a fountain of
love, that heart with its exquisite delicacy, that breadth of
mind, those rare powers—fruit of nature and of our interchange of thought—treasures whence should issue a unique
satisfaction of passion and desire, hours of poetry to outweigh years, joys to make a man serve a lifetime for one
gracious gesture—all this is to be buried in the tedium of a
tame, commonplace marriage, to vanish in the emptiness of
an existence which you will come to loathe! I hate your
children before they are born. They will be monsters!

So you know all that lies before you; you have nothing
left to hope, or fear, or suffer? And supposing the glorious
morning rises which will bring you face to face with the man
destined to rouse you from the sleep into which you are plunging! Ah! a cold shiver goes through me at the thought.

Well, at least you have a friend. You, it is understood, are to be the guardian angel of your valley. You will grow familiar with its beauties, will live with it in all its aspects, till the grandeur of nature, the slow growth of vegetation, compared with the lightning rapidity of thought, become like a part of yourself; and as your eye rests on the laughing flowers, you will question your own heart. When you walk between your husband, silent and contented, in front, and your children screaming and romping behind, I can tell you beforehand what you will write to me. Your misty valley, your hills, bare or shaded with magnificent trees, your meadow, the wonder of Provence, with its fresh water dispersed in little runlets, the different effects of the atmosphere, this whole world of infinity which laps you round, and which God has made so various, will recall to you the infinite sameness of your soul's life. But at least I shall be there, my Renée, and in me you will find a heart which no social pettiness shall ever corrupt, a heart all your own.

Monday.

My dear, my Spaniard is quite adorably melancholy; there is something calm, severe, manly, and mysterious about him which interests me profoundly. His unvarying solemnity and the silence which envelops him act like an irritant on the mind. His mute dignity is worthy of a fallen king. Griffith and I spend our time over him as though he were a riddle.

How odd it is! A language-master captures my fancy as no other man has done. Yet by this time I have passed in review all the young men of family, the attachés to embassies, and the ambassadors, generals, and inferior officers, the peers of France, their sons and nephews, the Court, and the town.

The coldness of the man provokes me. The sandy waste which he tries to place, and does place, between us is covered by his deep-rooted pride; he wraps himself in mystery. The hanging back is on his side, the boldness on mine. This odd situation affords me the more amusement because the whole thing is mere trifling. What is a man, a Spaniard, and a teacher of languages to me? I make no account of any man whatever, were he a king. We are worth far more, I am sure, than the greatest of them. What a slave I would have made of Napoleon! If he had loved me, shouldn't he have felt the whip!

Yesterday I aimed a satirical shaft at M. Hénarez which must have touched him to the quick. He made no reply; the lesson was over, he took his hat, and bowed with a glance at me, in which I read that he would never return. This suits me capitally; there would be something ominous in starting an imitation "Nouvelle Héloïse." I have just been reading Rousseau's, and it has left me with a strong distaste for love. Passion which can argue and moralize seems to me detestable. Clarissa also is much too pleased with herself and her long, little letter; but Richardson's work is an admirable picture, my father tells me, of Englishwomen. Rousseau's seems to me a sort of philosophical sermon, cast in the form of letters.

Love, as I conceive it, is a purely personal poem. In all that books tell us about it, there is nothing which is not at once false and true. And so, my pretty one, as you will henceforth be an authority only on conjugal love, it seems to me my duty—in the interest, of course, of our common life —to remain unmarried and have a grand passion, so that we may enlarge our experience.

Tell me every detail of what happens to you, especially in the first few days, with that strange animal called a husband. I promise to do the same for you if ever I am loved.

Farewell, poor, dear, gobbled-up, martyred darling.

XI.

MME. DE L'ESTORADE TO MLLE. DE CHAULIEU.

LA CRAMPADE.

You and your Spaniard make me shudder, my darling. I write this line to beg of you to dismiss him. All that you say of him corresponds with the character of those dangerous adventurers who, having nothing to lose, will take any risk. This man cannot be your husband, and must not be your lover. I will write to you more fully about the inner history of my married life when my heart is free from the anxiety your last letter has caused me.

XII.

MLLE. DE CHAULIEU TO MME. DE L'ESTORADE.

February.

At nine o'clock this morning, sweetheart, my father was announced in my rooms. I was up and dressed. I found him solemnly seated beside the fire in the drawing-room, looking more thoughtful than usual. He pointed to the armchair opposite him. Divining his meaning, I sank into it with a gravity, which so well aped his, that he could not refrain from smiling, though the smile was dashed with melancholy.

"You are quite a match for your grandmother in quick-wittedness," he said.

"Come, father, don't play the courtier here," I replied; "you want something from me."

He rose, visibly agitated, and talked to me for half an hour. This conversation, dear, really ought to be preserved. As soon as he had gone, I sat down to my table and tried to recall his words. This is the first time that I have seen my father revealing his inner thoughts.

He began by flattering me, and he did not do it badly. I was bound to be grateful to him for having understood and appreciated me.

"Armande," he said, "I was much mistaken in you, and you have agreeably surprised me. When you arrived from the convent, I took you for an average young girl, ignorant and not particularly intelligent, easily to be bought off with trinkets and ornaments, and with little turn for reflection."

"You are complimentary to young girls, father."

"Oh! there is no such thing as youth nowadays," he said, with an air of the diplomat. "Your mind is amazingly open. You take everything at its proper worth; your clear-sightedness is extraordinary, there is no hoodwinking you. You pass for being blind, and all the time you have laid your hand on causes, while other people are still puzzling over effects. In short, you are a minister in petticoats, the only person here capable of understanding me. It follows, then, that if I have any sacrifice to ask from you, it is only to yourself I can turn for help in persuading you.

"I am therefore going to explain to you, quite frankly, my former plans, to which I still adhere. In order to recommend them to you, I must show that they are connected with feelings of a very high order, and I shall thus be obliged to enter into political questions of the greatest importance to the kingdom, which might be wearisome to any one less intelligent than you are. When you have heard me, I hope you will take time for consideration, six months if necessary. You are entirely your own mistress; and if you decline to make the sacrifice I ask, I shall bow to your decision and trouble you no further."

This preface, my sweet dear, made me really serious, and I said—

"Speak, father."

Here, then, is the deliverance of the statesman:

"My child, France is in a very critical position, which is

understood only by the King and by a few superior minds. But the King is a head without arms; the great nobles, who are in the secret of the danger, have no authority over the men whose coöperation is needful in order to bring about a happy result. These men, cast up by popular election, refuse to lend themselves as instruments. Even the able men among them carry on the work of pulling down society, instead of helping us to strengthen the edifice.

"In a word, there are only two parties—the party of Marius and the party of Sulla. I am for Sulla against Marius. This, roughly speaking, is our position. To go more into details: the Revolution is still active; it is imbedded in the law and written on the soil; it fills people's minds. The danger is all the greater because the larger number of the King's counselors, seeing it destitute of armed forces and of money, believe it completely vanquished. The King is an able man and not easily blinded; but from day to day he is won over by his brother's partisans, who want to hurry things on. He has not two years to live, and thinks more of a peaceful death-bed than of anything else.

"Shall I tell you, my child, which is the most destructive of all the consequences entailed by the Revolution? You would never guess. In guillotining Louis XVI. the Revolution decapitated every head of a family. The Family has ceased to exist; we have only individuals. In their desire to become a nation, Frenchmen have abandoned the idea of empire; in proclaiming the equal rights of all children to their father's inheritance, they have killed Family spirit and have created the State treasury. But all this has paved the way for weakened authority, for the blind force of the masses, for the decay of art and the supremacy of individual interests, and has left the road open to the foreign invader.

"We stand between two policies—either to found the State on the basis of the Family, or to rest it on individual interest —in other words, between democracy and aristocracy, between free discussion and obedience, between Catholicism and religious indifference. I am among the few who are resolved to oppose what is called the people, and that in the people's true interest. It is not now a question of feudal rights, as fools are told, nor of rank ; it is a question of the State and of the existence of France. The country which does not rest on the foundation of paternal authority cannot be stable. That is the foot of the ladder of responsibility and subordination, which has for its summit the King.

" The King stands for us all. To die for the King is to die for one's self, for one's family, which, like the kingdom, cannot die. All animals have certain instincts; the instinct of man is for family life. A country is strong which consists of wealthy families, every member of whom is interested in defending a common treasure ; it is weak when composed of scattered individuals, to whom it matters little whether they obey seven or one, a Russian or a Corsican, so long as each keeps his own plot of land, blind, in their wretched egotism, to the fact that the day is coming when this, too, will be torn from them.

" Terrible calamities are in store for us, in case our party fails. Nothing will be left but penal or fiscal laws—your money or your life. The most generous nation on the earth will have ceased to obey the call of noble instincts. Wounds past curing will have been fostered and aggravated, an all-pervading jealousy being the first. Then the upper classes will be submerged ; equality of desire will be taken for equality of strength ; true distinction, even when proved and recognized, will be threatened by the advancing tide of middle-class prejudice. It was possible to choose one man out of a thousand, but, amongst three millions, discrimination becomes impossible, when all are moved by the same ambitions and attired in the same livery of mediocrity. No foresight will warn this victorious horde of that other terrible horde, soon to be arrayed against them in the peasant propri-

13

etors; in other words, twenty million acres of land, alive, stirring, arguing, deaf to reason, insatiable of appetite, obstructing progress, masters in their brute force——"

"But," said I, interrupting my father, "what can I do to help the State? I feel no vocation for playing Joan of Arc in the interests of the Family or for finding a martyr's stake in a convent."

"You are a little hussy," cried my father. "If I speak sensibly to you, you are full of jokes; when I jest, you talk like an ambassadress."

"Love lives on contradictions," was my reply.

And he laughed till the tears stood in his eyes.

"You will reflect on what I have told you; you will do justice to the large and confiding spirit in which I have broached the matter, and possibly events may assist my plans. I know that, so far as you are concerned, they are injurious and unfair, and this is the reason why I appeal for your sanction of them less to your heart and your imagination than to your reason. I have found more judgment and commonsense in you than in any one I know——"

"You flatter yourself," I said, with a smile, "for I am every inch your child!"

"In short," he went on, "one must be logical. You can't have the end without the means, and it is our duty to set an example to others. From all this I deduce that you ought not to have money of your own till your younger brother is provided for, and I want to employ the whole of your inheritance in purchasing an estate for him to go with the title."

"But," I said, "you won't interfere with my living in my own fashion and enjoying life if I resign you my fortune?"

"Provided," he replied, "that your view of life does not conflict with the family honor, reputation, and, I may add, glory."

"Come, come," I cried, "what has become of my excellent judgment?"

"There is not in all France," he said, with bitterness, "a man who would take for wife a daughter of one of our noblest families without a dowry and bestow one on her. If such a husband could be found, it would be among the class of rich parvenus; on this point I belong to the eleventh century."

"And I also," I said. "But why despair? Are there no aged peers?"

"Louise!" he exclaimed, "you know too much."

Then he left me, smiling and kissing my hand.

I received your letter this very morning, and it led me to contemplate that abyss into which you say that I may fall. A voice within seemed to utter the same warning. So I took my precautions. Hénarez, my dear, dares to look at me, and his eyes are disquieting. They inspire me with what I can only call an unreasoning dread. Such a man ought no more to be looked at than a frog; he is ugly—and fascinating.

For two days I have been hesitating whether to tell my father point-blank that I want no more Spanish lessons and have Hénarez sent about his business. But in spite of all my brave resolutions, I feel that the horrible sensation which comes over me when I see that man has become necessary to me. I say to myself: "Once more, and then I will speak."

His voice, my dear, is sweetly thrilling; his speaking is just like la Fodor's singing. His manners are simple, entirely free from affectation. And what teeth!

Just now, as he was leaving, he seemed to divine the interest I take in him, and made a gesture—oh! most respectfully— as though to take my hand and kiss it; then checked himself, apparently terrified at his own boldness and the chasm he had been on the point of bridging. There was the merest suggestion of all this, but I understood it and smiled, for nothing is more pathetic than to see the frank impulse of an inferior checking itself abashed. The love of a plebeian for a girl of noble birth implies such courage!

My smile emboldened him. The poor fellow looked blindly

about for his hat; he seemed determined not to find it, and I handed it to him with prefect gravity. His eyes were wet with unshed tears. It was a mere passing moment, yet a world of facts and ideas were contained in it. We understood each other so well that, on a sudden, I held out my hand for him to kiss.

Possibly this was equivalent to telling him that love might bridge the interval between us. Well, I cannot tell what moved me to do it. Griffith had her back turned as I proudly extended my little white paw. I felt the fire of his lips, tempered by two big tears. Oh! my love, I lay in my armchair, nerveless, dreamy. I was happy, and I cannot explain to you how or why. What I felt only a poet could express. My condescension, which fills me with shame now, seemed to me then something to be proud of; he had fascinated me, that is my one excuse.

Friday.

This man is really very handsome. He talks admirably, and has remarkable intellectual power. My dear, he is a very Bossuet in force and persuasiveness when he explains the mechanism, not only of the Spanish tongue, but also of human thought and of all language. His mother tongue seems to be French. When I expressed surprise at this, he replied that he came to France when quite a boy, following the King of Spain to Valençay.

What has passed within this enigmatic being? He is no longer the same man. He came, dressed quite simply, but just as any gentleman would be for a morning walk. He put forth all his eloquence, and flashed wit, like rays from a beacon, all through the lesson. Like a man roused from lethargy, he revealed to me a new world of thoughts. He told me the story of some poor devil of a valet who gave up his life for a single glance from a queen of Spain.

"What could he do but die?" I exclaimed.

This delighted him, and he looked at me in a way which was truly alarming.

In the evening I went to a ball at the Duchesse de Lenoncourt's. The Prince de Talleyrand happened to be there; and I got M. de Vandenesse, a charming young man, to ask him whether, among the guests at his country-place in 1809, he remembered any one of the name of Hénarez. Vandenesse reported the Prince's reply, word for word, as follows:

"Hénarez is the Moorish name of the Soria family, who are, they say, descendants of the Abencerrages, converted to Christianity. The old duke and his two sons were with the King. The eldest, the present Duc de Soria, has just had all his property, titles, and dignities confiscated by King Ferdinand, who in this way avenges a long-standing feud. The duke made a huge mistake in consenting to form a constitutional ministry with Valdez. Happily, he escaped from Cadiz before the arrival of the Duc d'Angoulême, who, with the best will in the world, could not have saved him from the King's wrath."

This information gave me much food for reflection. I cannot describe to you the suspense in which I passed the time till my next lesson, which took place this morning.

During the first quarter of an hour I examined him closely, debating inwardly whether he were duke or commoner, without being able to come to any conclusion. He seemed to read my fancies as they arose and to take pleasure in thwarting them. At last I could endure it no longer. Putting down my book suddenly, I broke off the translation I was making of it aloud, and said to him in Spanish:

"You are deceiving us. You are no poor middle-class Liberal. You are the Duc de Soria!"

"Mademoiselle," he replied, with a gesture of sorrow, "unhappily, I am not the Duc de Soria."

I felt all the despair with which he uttered the word "unhappily." Ah! my dear, never should I have conceived it possible to throw so much meaning and passion into a single word. His eyes had dropped, and he dared no longer look at me.

"M. de Talleyrand," I said, "in whose house you spent your years of exile, declares that any one bearing the name of Hénarez must be either the late Duc de Soria or a lackey."

He looked at me with eyes like two black burning coals, at once blazing and ashamed. The man might have been in the torture-chamber. All he said was:

"My father was in truth a servant of the King of Spain."

Griffith could make nothing of this sort of lesson. An awkward silence followed each question and answer.

"In one word," I said, "tell me, are you a noble or bourgeoise?"

"You know, mademoiselle, that in Spain even beggars are noble."

This reticence provoked me. Since the last lesson I had given play to my imagination in a little practical joke. I had drawn an ideal portrait of the man whom I should wish for my lover in a letter which I designed giving him to translate. So far, I had only put Spanish into French, not French into Spanish; I pointed this out to him, and begged Griffith to bring me the last letter I had received from a friend of mine.

"I shall find out," I thought, "from the effect my sketch has on him, what sort of blood runs in his veins."

I took the paper from Griffith's hands, saying—

"Let me see if I have copied it rightly."

For it was all in my writing. I handed him the paper, or, if you will, the snare, and I watched him while he read as follows—

"He who is to win my heart, my dear, must be harsh and unbending with men, but gentle with women. His eagle eye must have power to quell with a single glance the least approach to ridicule. He will have a pitying smile for those who would jeer at sacred things, above all, at that poetry of the heart, without which life would be but a dreary commonplace. I have the greatest scorn for those who would rob us of the living fountain of religious beliefs, so rich in solace. His faith, therefore, should have the simplicity of a child, though united to the firm conviction of an intelligent man, who has examined the foundations of his creed. His fresh and original way of looking at things must be entirely free from affectation or desire to show off. His words will be few and fit, and his mind so richly stored, that he cannot possibly become a bore to himself any more than to others.

"All his thoughts must have a high and chivalrous character, without alloy of self-seeking; while his actions should be marked by a total absence of interested or sordid motives. Any weak points he may have will arise from the very elevation of his views above those of the common herd, for in every respect I would have him superior to his age. Ever mindful of the delicate attentions due to the weak, he will be gentle to all women, but not prone lightly to fall in love with any; for love will seem to him too serious to turn into a game.

"Thus it might happen that he would spend his life in ignorance of true love, while all the time possessing those qualities most fitted to inspire it. But if ever he find the ideal woman who has haunted his waking dreams, if he meet with a nature capable of understanding his own, one who could fill his soul and pour sunshine over his life, could shine as a star through the mists of this chill and gloomy world, lend fresh charm to existence, and draw music from the hitherto silent chords of his being—needless to say, he would recognize and welcome his good fortune.

"And she, too, would be happy. Never, by word or look, would he wound the tender heart which abandoned itself to him, with the blind trust of a child reposing in its mother's arms. For were the vision shattered, it would be the wreck of her inner life. To the mighty waters of love she would confide her all !

"The man I picture must belong, in expression, in attitude, in gait, in his way of performing alike the smallest and the greatest actions, to that race of the truly great who are always simple and natural. He need not be good-looking, but his hands must be beautiful. His upper lip will curl with a careless, ironical smile for the general public, whilst he reserves for those he loves the heavenly, radiant glance in which he puts his soul."

"Will mademoiselle allow me," he said in Spanish, in a voice full of agitation, "to keep this writing in memory of her ? This is the last lesson I shall have the honor of giving her, and that which I have just received in these words may serve me for an abiding rule of life. I left Spain, a fugitive and penniless, but I have to-day received from my family a sum sufficient for my needs. You will allow me to send some poor Spaniard in my place?"

In other words, he seemed to me to say : "This little game must stop." He rose with an air of marvelous dignity, and left me quite upset by such unheard-of delicacy in a man of his class. He went downstairs and asked to speak with my father.

At dinner my father said to me with a smile—

"Louise, you have been learning Spanish from an ex-minister and a man condemned to death."

"The Duc de Soria," I said.

"Duke !" replied my father. "No, he is not that any longer ; he takes the title now of Baron de Macumer from a property which still remains to him in Sardinia. He is something of an original, I think."

"Don't brand with that word, which with you always implies some mockery and scorn, a man who is your equal, and who, I believe, has a noble nature."

" Baronne de Macumer ? " exclaimed my father, with a laughing glance at me.

Pride kept my eyes fixed on the table.

" But," said my mother, " Hénarez must have met the Spanish ambassador on the steps ? "

" Yes," replied my father, " the ambassador asked me if I was conspiring against the King, his master ; but he greeted the ex-grandee of Spain with much deference, and placed his services at his disposal."

All this, dear Mme. de l'Estorade, happened a fortnight ago, and it is a fortnight now since I have seen the man who loves me, for that he loves me there is not a doubt.   What is he about ?   If only I were a fly, or a mouse, or a sparrow ! I want to see him alone, myself unseen, at his house.   Only think, a man exists, to whom I can say: " Go and die for me ! "   And he is so made that he would go, at least I think so.   Anyhow, there is in Paris a man who occupies my thoughts, and whose glance pours sunshine into my soul.   Is not such a man an enemy, whom I ought to trample under foot ?   What ?   There is a man who has become necessary to me—a man without whom I don't know how to live ?   You married, and I—in love !   Four little months, and those two doves, whose wings erst bore them so high, have fluttered down upon the flat stretches of real life !

Sunday.

Last night, at the Italian opera, I could feel some one was looking at me ; my eyes were drawn, as by a magnet, to two wells of fire, gleaming like carbuncles in a dim corner of the orchestra.   Hénarez never moved his eyes from me.   The wretch had discovered the one spot from which he could see me—and there he was.   I don't know what he may be as a politician, but for love he has a genius: " Behold, my fair

Renée, where our business now stands," as the great Corneille hath said.

XIII.

MME. DE L'ESTORADE TO MLLE. DE CHAULIEU.

LA CRAMPADE, *February.*

MY DEAR LOUISE:—I was bound to wait some time before writing you; but now I know, or rather I have learned, many things which, for the sake of your future happiness, I must tell you. The difference between a girl and a married woman is so vast that the girl can no more comprehend it than the married woman can go back to girlhood again.

I chose to marry Louis de l'Estorade rather than return to the convent; that at least is plain. So soon as I realized that the convent was the only alternative to marrying Louis, I had, as girls say, to "submit," and my submission once made, the next thing was to examine the situation and try to make the best of it.

The serious nature of what I was undertaking filled me at first with terror. Marriage is a matter concerning the whole of life, whilst love aims only at pleasure. On the other hand, marriage will remain when pleasures have vanished, and it is the source of interests far more precious than those of the man and woman entering on the alliance. Might it not, therefore, be that the only requisite for a happy marriage was friendship—a friendship which, for the sake of these advantages, would shut its eyes to many of the imperfections of humanity? Now there was no obstacle to the existence of friendship between myself and Louis de l'Estorade. Having renounced all idea of finding in marriage those transports of love on which our minds used so often, and with such perilous rapture, to dwell, I found a gentle calm settling over me. "If debarred from love, why not seek for happiness?" I said to myself. "Moreover, I am loved, and the love offered me I shall accept. My married life will be no slavery, but rather a perpetual reign. What is there to say against such a situation for a woman who wishes to remain absolute mistress of herself?"

The important point of separating marriage from marital rights was settled in a conversation between Louis and me, in the course of which he gave proof of an excellent temper and a tender heart. Darling, my desire was to prolong that fair season of hope which, never culminating in satisfaction, leaves to the soul its virginity. To grant nothing to duty or the law, to be guided entirely by one's own impulse, retaining perfect independence—what could be more attractive, more honorable?

A contract of this kind, directly opposed to the legal contract, and even to the sacrament itself, could be concluded only between Louis and me. This difficulty, the first which has arisen, is the only one which has delayed the completion of our marriage. Although, at first, I may have made up my mind to accept anything rather than return to the convent, it is only in human nature, having got an inch, to ask for an ell, and you and I, sweet love, are of those who would have the whole.

I watched Louis out of the corner of my eye, and put it to myself, "Has suffering had a softening or a hardening effect on him?" By dint of close study, I arrived at the conclusion that his love amounted to a passion. Once transformed into an idol, whose slightest frown would turn him white and trembling, I realized that I might venture anything. I drew him aside in the most natural manner on solitary walks, during which I discreetly sounded his feelings. I made him talk, and got him to expound to me his ideas and plans for our future. My questions betrayed so many preconceived notions, and went so straight for the weak points in this terrible dual existence, that Louis has since confessed to me the alarm it caused him to find in me so little of the ignorant maiden.

Then I listened to what he had to say in reply. He got mixed up in his arguments, as people do when handicapped by fear; and before long it became clear that chance had given me for adversary one who was the less fitted for the contest because he was conscious of what you magniloquently call my "greatness of soul." Broken by sufferings and misfortune, he looked on himself as a sort of wreck, and three fears in especial haunted him:

First, we are aged respectively thirty-seven and seventeen; and he could not contemplate without quaking the twenty years that divide us. In the next place, he shares our views on the subject of my beauty, and it is cruel for him to see how the hardships of his life have robbed him of youth. Finally, he felt the superiority of my womanhood over his manhood. The consciousness of these three obvious drawbacks made him distrustful of himself; he doubted his power to make me happy, and guessed that he had been chosen as the lesser of two evils—*pis aller.*

One evening he tentatively suggested that I only married him to escape the convent.

"I cannot deny it," was my grave reply.

My dear, it touched me to the heart to see the two great tears which stood in his eyes. Never before had I experienced the shock of emotion which a man can impart to us.

"Louis," I went on, as kindly as I could, "it rests entirely with you whether this marriage of convenience becomes one to which I can give my whole heart. The favor I am about to ask from you will demand self-abnegation on your part, far nobler than the servitude to which a man's love, when sincere, is supposed to reduce him. The question is: Can you rise to the height of friendship such as I understand it?

"Life gives us but one friend, and I wish to be yours. Friendship is the bond between a pair of kindred souls, united in their strength, and yet independent. Let us be friends and comrades to bear jointly the burden of life. Leave me absolutely free. I would put no hindrance in the way of your inspiring me with a love similar to your own; but I am determined to be yours only of my own free gift. Create in me the wish to give up my freedom, and at once I lay it at your feet.

"Infuse with passion, then, if you will, this friendship, and let the voice of love disturb its calm. On my part I will do what I can to bring my feelings into accord with yours. One thing, above all, I would beg of you. Spare me the annoyances to which the strangeness of our mutual position might give rise in our relations with others. I am neither whimsical nor prudish, and should be sorry to get that reputation; but I feel sure that I can trust to your honor when I ask you to keep up the outward appearance of wedded life."

Never, dear, have I seen a man so happy as my proposal made Louis. The blaze of joy which kindled in his eyes dried up the tears.

"Do not fancy," I concluded, "that I ask this from any wish to be eccentric. It is the great desire I have for your respect which prompts my request. If you owe the crown of your love merely to the legal and religious ceremony, what gratitude could you feel to me later for a gift in which my good-will counted for nothing? If during the time that I remained indifferent to you (yielding only a passive obedience, such as my mother has just been urging on me) a child were born to us, do you suppose that I could feel toward it as I would toward one born of our common love? A passionate love may not be necessary in marriage, but, at least, you will admit that there should be no repugnance. Our position will not be without its dangers; in a country life, such as ours will be, ought we not to bear in mind the evanescent nature of passion? Is it not simple prudence to make provision beforehand against the calamities incident to change of feeling?"

He was greatly astonished to find me at once so reasonable and so apt at reasoning ; but he made me a solemn promise, after which I took his hand and pressed it affectionately.

We were married at the end of the week. Secure of my freedom, I was able to throw myself gaily into the petty details which always accompany a ceremony of the kind, and to be my natural self. Perhaps I may have been taken for an " old bird," as they say at Blois. A young girl, delighted with the novel and hopeful situation she had contrived to make for herself, may have passed for a strong-minded woman.

Dear, the difficulties which would beset my life had appeared to me clearly as in a vision, and I was sincerely anxious to make the happiness of the man I had married. Now, in the solitude of a life like ours, marriage soon becomes intolerable unless the woman is the presiding spirit. A woman in such a case needs the charm of a mistress, combined with the solid qualities of a wife. To introduce an element of uncertainty into pleasure is to prolong illusion, and render lasting those selfish satisfactions which all creatures hold, and justly hold, so precious. Conjugal love, in my view of it, should shroud a woman in expectancy, crown her sovereign, and invest her with an exhaustless vital force, a redundancy of life, that makes everything blossom around her. The more she is mistress of herself, the more certainly will the love and happiness she creates be fit to weather the storms of life.

But, above all, I have insisted on the greatest secrecy in regard to our domestic arrangements. A husband who submits to his wife's yoke is justly held an object of ridicule. A woman's influence ought to be entirely concealed. The charm of all we do lies in its unobtrusiveness. If I have made it my task to raise a drooping courage and restore their natural brightness to gifts which I have dimly descried, it must all seem to spring from Louis himself.

Such is the mission to which I dedicate myself, a mission surely not ignoble, and which might well satisfy a woman's ambition. Why, I could glory in this secret which shall fill my life with interest, in this task toward which my every energy shall be bent, while it remains concealed from all but God and you.

I am very nearly happy now, but should I be so without a friendly heart in which to pour this confession? For how make a confidant of him? My happiness would wound him, and has to be concealed. He is sensitive as a woman, like all men who have suffered much.

For three months we remained to each other as we were before marriage. As you may imagine, during this time I made a close study of many small personal matters, which have more to do with love than is generally supposed. In spite of my coldness, Louis grew bolder, and his nature expanded. I saw on his face a new expression, a look of youth. The greater refinement which I introduced into the house was reflected in his person. Insensibly I became accustomed to his presence, and made another self of him. By dint of constant watching I discovered how his mind and countenance harmonize. "The animal that we call a husband," to quote your words, disappeared, and one balmy evening, but I do not well remember which, I discovered in his stead a lover, whose words thrilled me and on whose arm I leant with pleasure beyond words. In short, to be open with you, as I would be with God, before whom concealment is impossible, the perfect loyalty with which he had kept his oath may have piqued me, and I felt a fluttering of curiosity in my heart. Bitterly ashamed, I struggled with myself. Alas! when pride is the only motive for resistance, excuses for capitulation are soon found.

We celebrated our union in secret, and secret it must remain between us. When you are married you will approve this reserve. Enough that nothing was lacking either of satisfaction for the most fastidious sentiment, or of that unexpectedness which brings, in a sense, its own sanction. Every witchery of imagination, of passion, of reluctance overcome, of the ideal passing into reality, played its part.

Yet, spite of all this enchantment, I once more stood out for my complete independence. I can't tell you all my reasons for this. To you alone shall I confide even as much as this. I believe that women, whether passionately loved or not, lose much in their relation with their husbands by not concealing their feelings about marriage and the way they look at it.

My one joy, and it is supreme, springs from the certainty of having brought new life to my husband before I have borne him any children. Louis has regained his youth, strength, and spirits. He is not the same man. With magic touch I have effaced the very memory of his sufferings. It is a complete metamorphosis. Louis is really very attractive now. Feeling sure of my affection, he throws off his reserve and displays unsuspected gifts.

To be the unceasing spring of happiness for a man who knows it and adds gratitude to love, ah! dear one, this is a conviction which fortifies the soul, even more than the most passionate love can do. The force thus developed— at once impetuous and enduring, simple and diversified— brings forth ultimately the family, that noble product of womanhood, which I realize now in all its animating beauty.

The old father has ceased to be a miser. He gives blindly whatever I wish for. The servants are content; it seems as though the bliss of Louis had let a flood of sunshine into the household, where love has made me queen. Even the old man would not be a blot upon my pretty home, and has brought himself into line with all my improvements; to please me he has adopted the dress, and with the dress, the manners of the day.

We have English horses, a coupé, a barouche, and a tilbury. The livery of our servants is simple but in good taste. Of course we are looked on as spendthrifts. I apply all my intellect (I am speaking quite seriously) to managing my household with economy, and obtaining for it the maximum of pleasure with the minimum of cost.

I have already convinced Louis of the necessity of making roads, in order that he may earn the reputation of a man interested in the welfare of his district. I insist too on his studying a great deal. Before long I hope to see him a member of the Council General of the department, through the influence of my family and his mother's. I have told him plainly that I am ambitious, and that I was very well pleased his father should continue to look after the estate and practice economies, because I wished him to devote himself exclusively to politics. If we had children, I should like to see them all prosperous and with good State appointments. Under penalty, therefore, of forfeiting my esteem and affection, he must get himself chosen deputy for the department at the coming elections; my family would support his candidature, and we should then have the delight of spending all our winters in Paris. Ah! my love, by the ardor with which he embraced my plans, I can gauge the depth of his affection.

To conclude, here is a letter he wrote me yesterday from Marseilles, where he had gone to spend a few hours:

"My sweet Renée:—When you gave me permission to love you, I began to believe in happiness; now, I see it unfolding endlessly before me. The past is merely a dim memory, a shadowy background, without which my present bliss would show less radiant. When I am with you, love so transports me that I am powerless to express the depth of my affection; I can but worship and admire. Only at a distance does the power of speech return. You are supremely beautiful, Renée, and your beauty is of the statuesque and regal type, on which time leaves but little impression. No doubt the love of husband and wife depends less on outward beauty than on graces of character, which are yours also in perfection; still, let me

14

say that the certainty of having your unchanging beauty, on which to feast my eyes, gives me a joy that grows with every glance.   There is a grace and dignity in the lines of your face, expressive of the noble soul within, and breathing of purity beneath the vivid coloring.   The brilliance of your dark eyes, the bold sweep of your forehead, declare a spirit of no common elevation, sound and trustworthy in every relation, and well braced to meet the storms of life, should such arise.   The keynote of your character is its freedom from all pettiness. You do not need to be told all this; but I will write it because I would have you know that I appreciate the treasure I possess.   Your favors to me, however slight, will always make my happiness in the far distant future as now ; for I am sensible how much dignity there is in our promise to respect each other's liberty.   Our own impulse shall with us alone dictate the expression of feeling.   We shall be free even in our fetters.   I shall have the more pride in wooing you again now that I know the reward you place on victory.   You cannot speak, breathe, act, or think, without adding to the admiration I feel for your charm both of body and mind.   There is in you a rare combination of the ideal, the practical, and the bewitching which satisfies alike judgment, a husband's pride, desire, and hope, and which extends the boundaries of love beyond those of life itself.   Oh ! my loved one, may the genius of love remain faithful to me, and the future be full of those delights by means of which you have glorified all that surrounds me !   I long for the day which shall make you a mother, that I may see you content with the fullness of your life, may hear you, in the sweet voice I love and with the words that so marvelously express your subtle and original thoughts, bless the love which has refreshed my soul and given new vigor to my powers, the love which is my pride, and whence I have drawn, as from a magic fountain, fresh life.   Yes, I shall be all that you would have me.   I shall take a leading part in the public life of the district, and

on you shall fall the rays of a glory which will owe its existence to the desire of pleasing you."

So much for my pupil, dear! Do you suppose he could
have written like this before? A year hence his style
will have still further improved. Louis is now in his first
transport; what I look forward to is the uniform and continuous sensation of content which ought to be the fruit of a
happy marriage, when a man and woman, in perfect trust and
mutual knowledge, have solved the problem of giving variety
to the infinite. This is the task set before every true wife;
the answer begins to dawn on me, and I shall not rest till I
have made it mine.

You see that he fancies himself—vanity of men!—the chosen
of my heart, just as though he were not my husband. Nevertheless, I have not yet got beyond that external attraction
which gives us strength to put up with a good deal. Yet
Louis is lovable; his temper is wonderfully even, and he per-
forms, as a matter of course, acts on which most men would
plume themselves. In short, if I do not love him, I shall
find no difficulty in being good to him.

So here are my black hair and my black eyes—whose lashes
act, according to you, like Venetian blinds—my commanding
air, and my whole person, raised to the rank of sovereign
power! Ten years hence, dear, why should we not both be
laughing and gay in your Paris, whence I shall carry you off
now and again to my beautiful oasis in Provence?

Oh! Louise, don't spoil the splendid future which awaits
us both! Don't do the mad things with which you threaten
me. My husband is a young man, prematurely old; why
don't you marry some young-hearted graybeard in the
Chamber of Peers? There lies your vocation—but that
Spaniard? oh, no!

XIV.

MADRID.

MY DEAR BROTHER:—You did not make me Duc de Soria in order that my actions should belie the name. How could I tolerate my happiness if I knew you to be a wanderer, deprived of the comforts which wealth everywhere commands? Neither Marie nor I will consent to marry till we hear that you have accepted the money which Urraca will hand over to you. These **two** millions are the fruit **of your** own savings and Marie's.

We have both prayed, kneeling before the same altar—and with what earnestness, God knows!—for your happiness. My dear brother, it cannot be that these prayers will remain unanswered. Heaven will send you the love which you seek, to be the consolation of your exile. Marie read your letter with tears, and is full of admiration for you. As for me, I consent, not for my own sake, but for that of the family. The King justified your expectations. Oh! that I might avenge you by letting him see himself, dwarfed before the scorn with which you flung him his toy, as you might toss a tiger its food.

The only thing I have taken for myself, dear brother, is **my** happiness. I have taken Marie. For this I shall always be beholden to you, as the creature to the Creator. There will be in my life and in Marie's one day not less glorious than our wedding-day—it will **be** the day when we hear that your heart has found its mate, that a woman loves you as you ought to be, and deserve to be, loved. Do not forget that if you live for us, **we** also live for you.

You can write us with perfect confidence under cover to the nuncio, sending your letters *via* Rome. The French ambassador at Rome will, no doubt, undertake to forward them to the Seignor Bemboni, at the State Secretary's office, whom our legate will have advised. No other way should be safe. Farewell, dear exile, dear despoiled one. Be proud at least of the happiness which you have brought to us, if you cannot be happy in it. God will doubtless hear our prayers, which are full of your name. FERNANDO.

XV.

LOUISE DE CHAULIEU TO MME. DE L'ESTORADE.

March.

Ah! my angel, marriage is making a philosopher of you! Your darling face must, indeed, have been jaundiced when you wrote me those terrible views of human life and the duty of women. Do you fancy you will convert me to matrimony by your programme of subterranean labors?

Alas! is this then the outcome for you of our too-instructed dreams! We left Blois all innocent, armed with the pointed shafts of meditation, and, lo! the weapons of that purely ideal experience have turned against your own breast! If I did not know you for the purest and most angelic of created beings, I declare I should say that your calculations actually smack of vice. What, my dear, in the interest of your country home, you submit your pleasures to a periodic thinning, as you do your timber. Oh! rather let me perish in all the violence of the heart's storms than live in the arid atmosphere of your cautious arithmetic!

As girls, we were both unusually enlightened, because of the large amount of study we gave to our chosen subjects; but, my child, philosophy without love, or disguised under a sham love, is the most hideous of conjugal hypocrisies. I should imagine that even the biggest of fools might detect now and again the owl of wisdom squatting in your bower of roses—

a ghastly phantom sufficient to put to flight the most promising of passions. You make your own fate, instead of waiting, a plaything in its hands.

We are each developing in strange ways. A large dose of philosophy to a grain of love is your recipe; a large dose of love to a grain of philosophy is mine. Why, Rousseau's Julie, whom I thought so pedantic, is a mere beginner to you. Woman's virtue, quotha! How you have weighed up life! Alas! I make fun of you, and, after all, perhaps you are right.

In one day you have made a holocaust of your youth and become a miser before your time. Your Louis will be happy, I daresay. If he loves you, of which I make no doubt, he will never find out, that, for the sake of your family, you are acting as a courtesan does for money; and certainly men seem to find happiness with them, judging by the fortunes they thus squander. A keen-sighted husband might no doubt remain in love with you, but what sort of gratitude could he feel in the long run for a woman who had made of duplicity a sort of necessary moral armor, as indispensable as her corsets?

Love, dear, is in my eyes the first principle of all the virtues, conformed to the divine likeness. Like all other first principles, it is not a matter of arithmetic; it is the Infinite in us. I cannot but think you have been trying to justify in your own eyes the frightful position of a girl, married to a man for whom she feels nothing more than esteem. You prate of duty, and make it your rule and measure; but surely to take necessity as the spring of action is the moral theory of atheism? To follow the impulse of love and feeling is the secret law of every woman's heart. You are acting a man's part, and your Louis will have to play the woman!

Oh! my dear, your letter has plunged me into an endless train of thought. I see now that the convent can never take the place of mother to a girl. I beg of you, my grand angel with the black eyes, so pure and proud, so serious and so pretty, do not turn away from these cries, which the first reading of your letter has torn from me! I have taken comfort in the thought that, while I was lamenting, love was doubtless busy knocking down the scaffolding of reason.

It may be that I shall do worse than you without any reasoning or calculations. Passion is an element in life bound to have a logic not less pitiless than yours.

Monday.

Yesterday night I placed myself at the window as I was going to bed, to look at the sky, which was wonderfully clear. The stars were like silver nails, holding up a veil of blue. In the silence of the night I could hear some one breathing, and by the half-light of the stars I saw my Spaniard, perched like a squirrel on the branches of one of the trees lining the boulevard, and doubtless lost in admiration of my windows.

The first effect of this discovery was to make me withdraw into the room, my feet and hands quite limp and nerveless; but, beneath the fear, I was conscious of a delicious undercurrent of joy. I was overpowered but happy. Not one of those clever Frenchmen, who aspire to marry me, has had the brilliant idea of spending the night in an elm-tree at the risk of being carried off by the watch. My Spaniard has, no doubt, been there for some time. Ah! he won't give me any more lessons, he wants to receive them—well, he shall have one. If only he knew what I said to myself about his superficial ugliness! Others can philosophize beside you, Renée! It was horrid, I argued, to fall in love with a handsome man. Is it not practically avowing that the senses count for three parts out of four in a genuine passion which ought to be supersensual?

Having got over my first alarm, I craned my neck behind the window in order to see him again—and well was I rewarded! By means of a hollow cane he blew me in through the window a letter, cunningly rolled round a leaden pellet.

Good heavens! will he suppose I left the window open on purpose?

But what was to be done? To shut it suddenly would be to make one's self an accomplice.

I did better. I returned to my window as though I had seen nothing and heard nothing of the letter, then I said aloud—

"Come and look at the stars, Griffith."

Griffith was sleeping as only old maids can. But the Moor, hearing me, slid down, and vanished with ghostly rapidity.

He must have been dying of fright, and so was I, for I did not hear him go away; apparently he remained at the foot of the elm. After a good quarter of an hour, during which I lost myself in contemplation of the heavens, and battled with the waves of curiosity, I closed my window and sat down on the bed to unfold the delicate bit of paper, with the tender touch of a worker amongst the ancient manuscripts at Naples. It felt redhot to my fingers. "What a horrible power this man has over me!" I said to myself.

All at once I held out the paper to the candle—I would burn it without reading a word. Then a thought stayed me, "What can he have to say that he writes so secretly?" Well, dear, I *did* burn it, reflecting that, though any other girl in the world would have devoured the letter, it was not fitting that I—Armande-Louise-Marie de Chaulieu—should read it.

The next day, at the Italian opera, he was at his post. But I feel sure that, ex-prime minister of a constitutional government though he is, he could not discover the slightest agitation of mind in any movement of mine. I might have seen nothing and received nothing the evening before. This was most satisfactory to me, but he looked very sad. Poor man! in Spain it is so natural for love to come in at the window! During the interval, it seems, he came and walked in the passages. This I learned from the chief secretary of the Spanish embassy, who also told the story of a noble action of his.

As Duc de Soria he was to marry one of the richest heiresses in Spain, the young princess, Marie Hérédia, whose wealth would have mitigated the bitterness of exile. But it seems that Marie, disappointing the wishes of the fathers, who had betrothed them in their earliest childhood, loved the younger son of the house of Soria, to whom my Félipe gave her up, allowing himself to be despoiled for his younger brother by the King of Spain.

"He would perform this piece of heroism quite simply," I said to the young man.

"You know him then?" was his ingenuous reply.

My mother smiled.

"What will become of him, for he is condemned to death?" I asked.

"Though dead to Spain, he can live in Sardinia."

"Ah! then Spain is the country of tombs as well as castles?" I said, trying to carry it off as a joke.

"There is everything in Spain, even Spaniards of the old school," my mother replied.

"The Baron de Macumer obtained a passport, not without difficulty, from the King of Sardinia," the young diplomatist went on. "He has now become a Sardinian subject, and he possesses a magnificent estate in the island with full feudal rights. He has a palace at Sassari. If Ferdinand VII. were to die, Macumer would probably go in for diplomacy, and the Court of Turin would make him ambassador. Though young, he is——"

"Ah! he is young?"

"Certainly, mademoiselle—though young, he is one of the most distinguished men in Spain."

I scanned the house meanwhile through my opera-glass, and seemed to lend an inattentive ear to the secretary; but, between ourselves, I was wretched at having burnt his letter. In what terms would a man like that express his love? For he does love me. To be loved, adored in secret; to know that in this house, where all the great men of Paris were collected, there was one entirely devoted to me, unknown to everybody! Ah! Renée, now I understand the life of Paris, its balls and its gayeties. It all flashed on me in the true light. When we love, we must have society, were it only to sacrifice it to our love. I felt a different creature—and such a happy one! My vanity, pride, self-love—all were flattered. Heaven knows what glances I cast upon the brilliant audience!

"Little rogue!" the duchess whispered in my ear with a smile.

Yes, Renée, my wily mother had deciphered the hidden joy in my bearing, and I could only haul down my flag before such feminine strategy. Those two words taught me more of worldly wisdom than I have been able to pick up in a year—for we are in March now. Alas! no more Italian opera in another month. How will life be possible without that heavenly music, when one's heart is full of love?

When I got home, my dear, with determination worthy of a Chaulieu, I opened my window to watch a shower of rain. Oh! if men knew the magic spell that a heroic action throws over us, they would indeed rise to greatness! a poltroon would turn hero! What I had learned about my Spaniard drove me into a very fever. I felt certain that he was there, ready to aim another letter at me.

I was right, and this time I burnt nothing. Here, then, is the first love-letter I have received, madame logician: each to her kind:

"Louise, it is not for your peerless beauty I love you, nor for your gifted mind, your noble feeling, the wondrous charm of all you say and do, nor yet for your pride, your queenly scorn of baser metals—a pride blended in you with charity, for what angel could be more tender? Louise, I love you because, for the sake of a poor exile, you have unbent this lofty majesty, because by a gesture, a glance, you have brought consolation to a man so far beneath you that the utmost he could hope for was your pity, the pity of a generous heart.

You are the one woman whose eyes have shone with a tenderer light when bent on me.

"And because you let fall this glance—a mere grain of dust, yet a grace surpassing any bestowed on me when I stood at the summit of a subject's ambition—I long to tell you, Louise, how dear you are to me, and that my love is for yourself alone, without a thought beyond, a love that far more than fulfills all the conditions laid down by you for an ideal passion.

"Know then, idol of my highest heaven, that there is in the world an offshoot of the Saracen race, whose life is in your hands, who will receive your orders as a slave, and deem it an honor to execute them. I have given myself to you absolutely and for the mere joy of giving, for a single glance of your eye, for a touch of the hand which one day you offered to your Spanish master. I am but your servitor, Louise; I claim no more.

"No, I dare not think that I could ever be loved; but perchance my devotion may win for me toleration. Since that morning when you smiled upon me with generous girlish impulse, divining the misery of my lonely and rejected heart, you reign there alone. You are the absolute ruler of my life, the queen of my thoughts, the god of my heart; I find you in the sunshine of my home, the fragrance of my flowers, the balm of the air I breathe, the pulsing of my blood, the light that visits me in sleep.

"One thought alone troubled this happiness—your ignorance. All unknown to you was this boundless devotion, the trusty arm, the blind slave, the silent tool, the wealth—for henceforth all I possess is mine only as a trust—which lay at your disposal; unknown to you, the heart waiting to receive your confidence, and yearning to replace all that your life (I know it well) has lacked—the liberal ancestress, so ready to meet your needs, a father to whom you could look for protection in every difficulty, a friend, a brother. The secret of

your isolation is no secret to me! If I am bold, it is because
I long that you should know how much is yours.

"Take all, Louise, and in so doing bestow on me the one
life possible for me in this world—the life of devotion. In
placing the yoke on my neck, you run no risk; I ask nothing
but the joy of knowing myself yours. Needless even to say
that you will never love me; it cannot be otherwise. I must
love from afar, without hope, without reward beyond my own
love.

"In my anxiety to know whether you will accept me as
your servant, I have racked my brain to find some way in
which you may communicate with me without any danger of
compromising yourself. Injury to your self-respect there can
be none in sanctioning a devotion which has been yours for
many days without your knowledge. Let this, then, be the
token. At the opera this evening, if you carry in your hand
a bouquet consisting of one red and one white camellia—emblem of a man's blood at the service of the purity he worships
—that will be my answer. I ask no more; thenceforth, at
any moment, ten years hence or to-morrow, whatever you demand shall be done, so far as it is possible for man to do it,
by your happy servant,

"FÉLIPE HÉNAREZ."

P. S.—You must admit, dear, that great lords know how to
love! See the spring of the African lion! What restrained
fire! What loyalty! What sincerity! How high a soul in
low estate! I felt quite small and dazed as I said to myself:
"What shall I do?"

It is the mark of a great man that he puts to flight all ordinary calculations. He is at once sublime and touching, childlike and of the race of giants. In a single letter Hénarez
has outstripped volumes from Lovelace or Saint-Preux. Here
is true love, no beating about the bush. Love may be or it

may not, but where it is, it ought to reveal itself in its immensity.

Here am I, shorn of all my little arts! To refuse or accept! That is the alternative boldly presented me, without the ghost of an opening for a middle course. No fencing allowed! This is no longer Paris; we are in the heart of Spain or the far East. It is the voice of Abencerrage, and it is the scimitar, the horse, and the head of Abencerrage which he offers, prostrate before a Catholic Eve! Shall I accept this last descendant of the Moors? Read again and again his Hispano-Saracenic letter, Renée dear, and you will see how love makes a clean sweep of all the Judaic bargains of your philosophy.

Renée, your letter lies heavy on my heart; you have vulgarized life for me. What need have I for finessing? Am I not mistress for all time of this lion whose roar dies out in plaintive and adoring sighs? Ah! how he must have raged in his lair of the Rue Hillerin-Bertin! I know where he lives, I have his card: F. BARON DE MACUMER.

He has made it impossible for me to reply. All I can do is to fling two camellias in his face. What fiendish arts does love possess—pure, honest, simple-minded love! Here is the most tremendous crisis of a woman's heart resolved into an easy, simple action. Oh, Asia! I have read the "Arabian Nights," here is their very essence: two flowers, and the question is settled. We clear the fourteen volumes of "Clarissa Harlowe" with a bouquet. I writhe before this letter, like a thread in the fire. To take, or not to take, my two camellias. Yes or No, kill or give life! At last a voice cries to me, "Test him!" Yes, I will test him.

CHAPTER XVI.

THE SAME TO THE SAME.

March.

I am dressed in white—white camellias in my hair, and another in my hand. My mother has red camellias; so it would not be impossible to take one from her—if I wished! I have a strange longing to put off the decision to the last moment, and make him pay for his red camellia by a little suspense.

What a vision of beauty! Griffith begged me to stop for a little and be admired. The solemn crisis of the evening and the drama of my secret reply have given me a color; on each cheek I sport a red camellia laid upon a white!

I A.M.

Everybody admired me, but only one adored. He hung his head as I entered with a white camellia, but turned pale as the flower when, later, I took a red one from my mother's hand. To arrive with the two flowers might possibly have been accidental; but this deliberate action was a reply. My confession, therefore, is fuller than it need have been.

The opera was "Romeo and Juliet." As you don't know the duet of the two lovers, you can't understand the bliss of two neophytes in love, as they listen to this divine outpouring of the heart.

On returning home I went to bed, but only to count the steps which resounded on the sidewalk. My heart and head, darling, are all on fire now. What is he doing? What is he thinking of? Has he a thought, a single thought, that is not of me? Is he, *in very truth,* the devoted slave he painted himself? How to be sure? Or, again, has it ever entered his head that, if I accept him, I lay myself open to the shadow of a reproach or am in any sense rewarding or thanking him? I am harrowed by the hair-splitting casuistry of the heroines in "The Great Cyrus" and "Astræa," by all the subtle arguments of the court of love.

Has he any idea that, in affairs of love, a woman's most trifling actions are but the issue of long brooding and inner conflicts, of victories won only to be lost! What are his thoughts at this moment? How can I give him my orders to write every evening the particulars of the day just gone? He is my slave whom I ought to keep busy. I shall deluge him with work!

Sunday Morning.

Only toward morning did I sleep a little. It is midday now. I have just got Griffith to write the following letter:

"*To the Baron de Macumer.*

"Mademoiselle de Chaulieu begs me, Monsieur le Baron, to ask you to return to her the copy of a letter written to her by a friend, which is in her own handwriting, and which you carried away. Receive, etc.,

"S. GRIFFITH."

My dear, Griffith has gone out; she has gone to the Rue Hillerin-Bertin; she has handed in this little love-letter for my slave, who returned to me in an envelope my ideal portrait, stained with tears. He has obeyed. Oh! my sweet, it must have been dear to him! Another man would have refused to send it in a letter full of flattery; but the Saracen has fulfilled his promises. He has obeyed. It moves me to tears.

XVII.

THE SAME TO THE SAME.

April 2d.

Yesterday the weather was splendid. I dressed myself like a girl who wants to look her best in her sweetheart's eyes. My father, yielding to my entreaties, has given me the prettiest turnout in Paris—two dapple-gray horses and a barouche, which is a masterpiece of elegance. I was making a first trial of this, and peeped out like a flower from under my sunshade lined with white silk.

As I drove up the avenue of the Champs-Élysées, I saw my Abencerrage approaching on an extraordinarily beautiful horse. Almost every man now-a-days is a finished jockey, and they all stopped to admire and inspect it. He bowed to me, and on receiving a friendly sign of encouragement, slackened his horse's pace so that I was able to say to him:

"You are not vexed with me for asking for my letter; it was no use to you?" Then in a lower voice, "You have already transcended the ideal—— Your horse makes you an object of general interest," I went on aloud.

"My steward in Sardinia sent it to me. He is very proud of it; for this horse, which is of Arabian blood, was born in my stables."

This morning, my dear, Hénarez was on an English sorrel, also very fine, but not such as to attract attention. My light, mocking words had done their work. He bowed to me, and I replied with a slight inclination of the head.

The Duc d'Angoulême has bought Macumer's horse. My slave understood that he was deserting the role of simplicity by attracting the notice of the crowd. A man ought to be remarked for what he is, not for his horse, or anything else belonging to him. To have too beautiful a horse seems to me a piece of bad taste, just as much as wearing a huge diamond pin. I was delighted at being able to find fault with him. Perhaps there may have been a touch of vanity in what he did, very excusable in a poor exile, and I like to see this childishness.

Oh! my dear old preacher, do my love affairs amuse you as much as your dismal philosophy gives me the creeps? Dear Philip the Second in petticoats, are you comfortable in my barouche? Do you see those velvet eyes, humble, yet so eloquent, and glorying in their servitude, which flash on me as some one goes by? He is a hero, Renée, and he wears my livery, and always a red camellia in his button-hole, while I have always a white one in my hand.

How clear everything becomes in the light of love! How well I know my Paris now! It is all transfused with meaning. And love here is lovelier, grander, more bewitching than elsewhere.

I am convinced now that I could never torment or flirt with a fool or make any impression on him. It is only men of real distinction who can enter into our feelings and feel our influence. Oh! my poor friend, forgive me. I forgot our l'Estorade. But didn't you tell me you were going to make a genius of him? I know what that means. You will dry nurse him till some day he is able to understand you.

Good-by. I am a little off my head, and must stop.

XVIII.

MME. DE L'ESTORADE TO LOUISE DE CHAULIEU.

April.

My angel—or ought I not rather to say my imp of evil?— you have, without meaning it, grieved me sorely. I would say wounded were we not one soul. And yet it is possible to wound one's self.

15

How plain it is that you have never realized the force of the word *indissoluble* as applied to the contract binding man and woman! I have no wish to controvert what has been laid down by philosophers or legislators—they are quite capable of doing this for themselves—but, dear one, in making marriage irrevocable and imposing on it a relentless formula, which admits of no exceptions, they have rendered each union a thing as distinct as one individual is from another. Each has its own inner laws which differ from those of others. The laws regulating married life in the country, for instance, where husband and wife are never out of each other's sight, cannot be the same as those regulating a household in town, where frequent distractions give variety to life. Or conversely, married life in Paris, where existence is one perpetual whirl, must demand different treatment from the more peaceful home in the provinces.

But if place alters the conditions of marriage, much more does character. The wife of a man born to be a leader need only resign herself to his guidance; whereas the wife of a fool, conscious of superior power, is bound to take the reins in her own hand if she would avert calamity.

You speak of vice; and it is possible that, after all, reason and reflection produce a result not dissimilar from what we call by that name. For what does a woman mean by it but perversion of feeling through calculation? Passion is vicious when it reasons, admirable only when it springs from the heart and spends itself in sublime impulses that set at naught all selfish considerations. Sooner or later, dear one, you too will say, "Yes! dissimulation is the necessary armor of a woman, if by dissimulation be meant courage to bear in silence, prudence to foresee the future."

Every married woman learns to her cost the existence of certain social laws, which, in many respects, conflict with the laws of nature. Marrying at our age, it would be possible to have a dozen children. What is this but another name for a dozen crimes, a dozen misfortunes? It would be handing over to poverty and despair twelve innocent darlings; whereas two children would mean the happiness of both, a double blessing, two lives capable of developing in harmony with the customs and laws of our time. The natural law and the code are in hostility, and we are the battle-ground. Would you give the name of vice to the prudence of the wife who guards her family from destruction through its own acts? One calculation or a thousand, what matter, if the decision no longer rests with the heart?

And of this terrible calculation you will be guilty some day, my noble Baronne de Macumer, when you are the proud and happy wife of the man who adores you; or rather, being a man of sense, he will spare you by making it himself. (You see, dear dreamer, that I have studied the code in its bearings on conjugal relations.) And when at last that day comes, you will understand that we are answerable only to God and to ourselves for the means we employ to keep happiness alight in the heart of our homes. Far better is the calculation which succeeds in this than the reckless passion which introduces trouble, heartburnings, and dissension.

I have reflected painfully on the duties of a wife and mother of a family. Yes, sweet one, it is only by a sublime hypocrisy that we can attain the noblest ideal of a perfect woman. You tax me with insincerity because I dole out to Louis, from day to day, the measure of his intimacy with me; but is it not too close an intimacy which provokes rupture? My aim is to give him, in the very interest of his happiness, many occupations, which will all serve as distractions to his love; and this is not the reasoning of passion. If affection be inexhaustible, it is not so with love: the task, therefore, of a woman—truly no light one—is to spread it out thriftily over a lifetime.

At the risk of exciting your disgust, I must tell you that I persist in the principles I have adopted, and hold myself both heroic and generous in so doing. Virtue, my pet, is an abstract idea, varying in its manifestations with the surroundings. Virtue in Provence, in Constantinople, in London, and in Paris bears very different fruit, but is none the less virtue. Each human life is a substance compacted of widely dissimilar elements, though, viewed from a certain height, the general effect is the same.

If I wished to make Louis unhappy and to bring about a separation, all I need do is to leave the helm in his hands. I have not had your good fortune in meeting with a man of the highest distinction, but I may perhaps have the satisfaction of helping him on the road to it. Five years hence let us meet in Paris and see! I believe we shall succeed in mystifying you. You will tell me then that I was quite mistaken, and that M. de l'Estorade is a man of great natural gifts.

As for this brave love, of which I know only what you tell me, these tremors and night-watches by starlight on the balcony, this idolatrous worship, this deification of woman—I knew it was not for me. You can enlarge the borders of your brilliant life as you please; mine is hemmed in to the boundaries of La Crampade.

And you reproach me for the jealous care which alone can nurse this modest and fragile shoot into a wealth of lasting and mysterious happiness! I believe myself to have found out how to adapt the charm of a mistress to the position of a wife, and you have almost made me blush for my device. Who shall say which of us is right, which wrong? Perhaps we are both right and both wrong. Perhaps this is the heavy price which society exacts for our furbelows, our titles, and our children.

I, too, have my red camellias, but they bloom on my lips in smiles for my double charge—the father and the son—whose slave and mistress I am. But, my dear, your last letters made me feel what I have lost! You have taught me all a woman sacrifices in marrying. One single glance did I take at those beautiful wild plateaus where you range at your sweet will, and I will not tell you the tears that fell as I read. But regret is not remorse, though it may be first cousin to it.

You say, "Marriage has made you a philosopher!" Alas! bitterly did I feel how far this was from the truth, as I wept to think of you swept away on love's torrent. But my father has made me read one of the profoundest thinkers of these parts, the man on whom the mantle of Bossuet has fallen, one of those hard-headed theorists whose words force conviction. While you were reading "Corinne," I conned Bonald; and here is the whole secret of my philosophy. He revealed to me the Family in its strength and holiness. According to Bonald, your father was right in his homily.

Farewell, my dear fancy, my friend, my wild other self.

XIX.

LOUISE DE CHAULIEU TO MME. DE L'ESTORADE.

Well, my Renée, you are a love of a woman, and I quite agree now that we can only be virtuous by cheating. Will that satisfy you? Moreover, the man who loves us is our property; we can make a fool or a genius of him as we please; only, between ourselves, the former happens more commonly. You will make yours a genius, and you won't tell the secret— there are two heroic actions, if you will!

Ah! if there were no future life, how nicely you would be sold, for this is martyrdom into which you are plunging of your own accord. You want to make him ambitious and to keep him in love! Child that you are, surely the last alone is sufficient.

Tell me, to what point is calculation a virtue, or virtue calculation? You won't say? Well, we won't quarrel over that, since we have Bonald to refer to. We are, and intend to remain, virtuous; nevertheless at this moment I believe that you, with all your pretty little knavery, are a better woman than I am.

Yes, I am shockingly deceitful. I love Félipe, and I conceal it from him with an odious hypocrisy. I long to see him leap from his tree to the top of the wall, and from the wall to my balcony—and if he did, how I should wither him with my scorn! You see, I am frank enough with you.

What restrains me? Where is the mysterious power which prevents me from telling Félipe, dear fellow, how supremely happy he has made me by the outpouring of his love—so pure, so absolute, so boundless, so unobtrusive, and so overflowing?

Mme. de Mirbel is painting my portrait, and I intend to give it to him, my dear. What surprises me more and more every day is the animation which love puts into life. How full of interest is every hour, every action, every trifle! and what amazing confusion between the past, the future, and the present! One lives in three tenses at once. Is it still so after the heights of happiness are reached? Oh! tell me, I implore you, what is happiness? Does it soothe, or does it excite? I am horribly restless; I seem to have lost all my bearings; a force in my heart drags me to him, spite of reason and spite of propriety. There is this gain, that I am better able to enter into your feelings.

Félipe's happiness consists in feeling himself mine; the aloofness of his love, his strict obedience, irritate me, just as his attitude of profound respect provoked me when he was only my Spanish master. I am tempted to cry out to him as he passes: "Fool, if you love me so much as a picture, what will it be when you know the real me?"

Oh! Renée, you burn my letters, don't you? I will burn yours. If other eyes than ours were to read these thoughts which pass from heart to heart, I should send Félipe to cut them out, and perhaps to kill the owners, by way of additional security.

Monday.

Oh! Renée, how is it possible to fathom the heart of man? My father ought to introduce me to M. Bonald, since he is so learned; I would ask him. I envy the privilege of God, who can read the undercurrents of the heart.

Does he still worship? That is the whole question.

If ever, in gesture, glance, or tone, I were to detect the slightest falling off in the respect he used to show me in the days when he was my instructor in Spanish, I feel that I should have strength to put the whole thing from me. "Why these fine words, these grand resolutions?" you will say. Dear, I will tell you.

My fascinating father, who treats me with the devotion of an Italian *cavaliere servente* for his lady, had my portrait painted, as I told you, by Mme. de Mirbel. I contrived to get a copy made, good enough to do for the duke, and sent the original to Félipe. I dispatched it yesterday, and these lines with it:

"Don Félipe, your single-hearted devotion is met by a blind confidence. Time will show whether this is not to treat a man as more than human."

It was a big reward. It looked like a promise and—dreadful to say—a challenge; but—which will seem to you still more dreadful—I quite intended that it should suggest both these things, without going so far as actually to commit me. If in his reply there is "Dear Louise!" or even "Louise," he is done for!

Tuesday.

No, he is not done for. The constitutional minister is perfect as a lover. Here is his letter:

"Every moment passed away from your sight has been

filled by me with ideal pictures of you, my eyes closed to the outside world and fixed in meditation on your image, which used to obey the summons too slowly in that dim palace of dreams, glorified by your presence. Henceforth my gaze will rest upon this wondrous ivory—this talisman, might I not say? —since your blue eyes sparkle with life as I look, and paint passes into flesh and blood. If I have delayed writing, it is because I could not tear myself away from your presence, which wrung from me all that I was bound to keep most secret.

"Yes, closeted with you all last night and to-day, I have, for the first time in my life, given myself up to full, complete, and boundless happiness. Could you but see yourself where I have placed you, between the Virgin and God, you might have some idea of the agony in which the night has passed. But I would not offend you by speaking of it; for one glance from your eyes, robbed of the tender sweetness which is my life, would be full of torture for me, and I implore your clemency therefore in advance. Queen of my life and of my soul, oh! that you could grant me but one-thousandth part of the love I bear you!

"This was the burden of my prayer; doubt worked havoc in my soul as I oscillated between belief and despair, between life and death, darkness and light. A criminal whose verdict hangs in the balance is not more racked with suspense than I, as I own to my temerity. The smile imaged on your lips, to which my eyes turned ever and again, was alone able to calm the storm roused by the dread of displeasing you. From my birth no one, not even my mother, has smiled on me. The beautiful young girl who was designed for me rejected my heart and gave hers to my brother. Again, in politics all my efforts have been defeated. In the eyes of my king I have read only thirst for vengeance; from childhood he has been my enemy, and the vote of the Cortes which placed me in power was regarded by him as a personal insult.

"Less than this might breed despondency in the stoutest heart. Beside, I have no illusion ; I know the ill-grace of my person, and am well aware how difficult it is to do justice to the heart within so rugged a shell. To be loved had ceased to be more than a dream to me when I met you. Thus when I bound myself to your service I knew that devotion alone could excuse my passion.

"But, as I look upon this portrait and listen to your smile that whispers of rapture, the rays of a hope which I had sternly banished pierce the gloom, like the light of dawn, again to be obscured by rising mists of doubt and fear of your displeasure, if the morning should break to-day. No, it is impossible you should love me yet—I feel it, but in time, as you make proof of the strength, the constancy, and depth of my affection, you may yield me some foothold in your heart. If my daring offends you, tell me so without anger, and I will return to my former part. But if you consent to try and love me, be merciful and break it gently to one. who has placed the happiness of his life in the single thought of serving you."

My dear, as I read these last words, he seemed to rise before me, pale as the night when the camellias told their story and he knew his offering was accepted. These words, in their humility, were clearly something quite different from the usual flowery rhetoric of lovers, and a wave of feeling broke over me ; I breathed the breath of happiness.

The weather has been atrocious ; impossible to go to the Bois without exciting all sorts of suspicions. Even my mother, who often goes out, regardless of rain, remains at home, and alone.

Wednesday Evening.

I have just seen *him* at the opera, my dear ; he is another man. He came to our box, introduced by the Sardinian ambassador.

Having read in my eyes that this audacity was taken in good part, he seemed awkwardly conscious of his limbs, and addressed the Marquise d'Espard as "Mademoiselle." A light far brighter than the glare of the chandeliers flashed from his eyes. At last he went out with the air of a man who didn't know what he might do next.

"The Baron de Macumer is in love!" exclaimed Mme. de Maufrigneuse.

"Strange, isn't it, for a fallen minister?" replied my mother.

I had sufficient presence of mind myself to regard with curiosity Mmes. de Maufrigneuse and d'Espard and my mother, as though they were talking a foreign language and I wanted to know what it was all about, but inwardly my soul sank in the waves of an intoxicating joy. There is only one word to express what I felt, and that is: rapture. Such love as Félipe's surely makes him worthy of mine. I am the very breath of his life, my hands hold the thread that guides his thoughts. To be quite frank, I have a mad longing to see him clear every obstacle and stand before me, asking boldly for my hand. Then I should know whether this storm of love would sink to placid calm at a glance from me.

Ah! my dear, I stopped here, and I am still all in a tremble. As I wrote, I heard a slight noise outside, and rose to see what it was. From my window I could see him coming along the ridge of the wall at the risk of his life. I went to the bedroom window and made him a sign, it was enough; he leapt from the wall—ten feet—and then ran along the road, so far as I could see him, in order to show me that he was not hurt. That he should think of my fear at the moment when he must have been made giddy by his fall moved me so much that I am still crying; I don't know why. Poor ungainly man! what was he coming for? what had he to say to me?

I dare not write any more of my thoughts, and shall go to

bed joyful, thinking of all that we would say if we were to-gether. Farewell, fair silent one. I have not time to scold you for not writing, but it is more than a month since I have heard from you! Does this mean that you are at last happy! Have you lost the "complete independence" which you were so proud of, and which to-night has so nearly played me false?

XX.

RENÉE DE L'ESTORADE TO LOUISE DE CHAULIEU.

May.

If love be the life of the world, why do austere philosophers count it for nothing in marriage? Why should Society take for its first law that the woman must be sacrificed to the Family, introducing thus a note of discord into the very heart of marriage? And this discord was foreseen, since it was to meet the dangers arising from it that men were armed with new-found powers against us. But for these, we should have been able to bring their whole theory to nothing, whether by the force of love or of a secret, persistent aversion.

I see in marriage, as it at present exists, two opposing forces which it was the task of the lawgiver to reconcile. "When will they be reconciled?" I said to myself, as I read your letter. Oh! my dear, one such letter alone is enough to overthrow the whole fabric constructed by the sage of Aveyron, under whose shelter I had so cheerfully ensconced myself! The laws were made by old men—any woman can see that— and they have been prudent enough to decree that conjugal love, apart from passion, is not degrading, and that a woman in yielding herself may dispense with the sanction of love, provided the man can legally call her his. In their exclusive concern for the Family they have imitated Nature, whose one care is to propagate the species.

Formerly I was a person, now I am a chattel. Not a few tears have I gulped down, alone and far from every one. How gladly would I have exchanged them for a consoling smile! Why are our destinies so unequal? Your soul expands in the atmosphere of a lawful passion. For you, virtue will coincide with pleasure. If you encounter pain, it will be of your own free choice. Your duty, if you marry Félipe, will be one with the sweetest, freest indulgence of feeling. Our future is big with the answer to my question, and I look for it with restless eagerness.

You love and are adored. Oh! my dear, let this noble romance, the old subject of our dreams, take full possession of your soul. Womanly beauty, refined and spiritualized in you, was created by God, for His own purposes, to charm and to delight. Yes, my sweet, guard well the secret of your heart, and submit Félipe to those ingenious devices of ours for testing a lover's metal. Above all, make trial of your own love, for this is even more important. It is so easy to be misled by the deceptive glamour of novelty and passion, and by the vision of happiness.

Alone of the two friends, you remain in your maiden independence; and I beseech you, dearest, do not risk the irrevocable step of marriage without some guarantee. It happens sometimes, when two are talking together, apart from the world, their souls stripped of social disguise, that a gesture, a word, a look lights up, as by a flash, some dark abyss. You have courage and strength to tread boldly in paths where others would be lost.

You have no conception with what anxiety I watch you. Across all this space I see you; my heart beats with yours. Be sure, therefore, to write and tell me everything. Your letters create an inner life of passion within my homely, peaceful household, which reminds me of a level highway on a gray day. The only event here, my sweet, is that I am playing cross-purposes with myself. But I don't want to tell you about it just now ; it must wait for another day.   With dogged obstinacy, I pass from despair to hope, now yielding, now holding back.   It may be that I ask from life more than we have a right to claim.   In youth we are so ready to believe that the ideal and the real will harmonize !

I have been pondering alone, seated beneath a rock in my park, and the fruit of my pondering is that love in marriage is a happy accident on which it is impossible to base a universal law.   My Aveyron philosopher is right in looking on the Family as the only possible unit in society, and in placing woman in subjection to the Family, as she has been in all ages. The solution of this great—for us almost awful—question lies in our first child.   For this reason, I would gladly be 'a mother, were it only to supply food for the consuming energy of my soul.

Louis' temper remains as perfect as ever ; his love is of the active, my tenderness of the passive, type.   He is happy, plucking the flowers which bloom for him, without troubling about the labor of the earth which has produced them.   Blessed self-absorption !   At whatever cost to myself, I fall in with his illusions, as a mother, in my idea of her, should be ready to spend herself to satisfy a fancy of her child.   The intensity of his joy blinds him, and even throws its reflection upon me. The smile or look of satisfaction which the knowledge of his content brings to my face is enough to satisfy him.   And so, "my child" is the pet name which I give him when we are alone.

And I wait for the fruit of all these sacrifices which remain a secret between God, myself, and you.   On motherhood I have staked enormously ; my credit account is now too large, I fear I shall never receive full payment.   To it I look for employment of my energy, expansion of my heart, and the compensation of a world of joys.   Pray heaven I be not deceived !   It is a question of all my future and, horrible thought, of my virtue.

XXI.

LOUISE DE CHAULIEU TO RENÉE DE L'ESTORADE.

June.

DEAR WEDDED SWEETHEART:—Your letter has arrived at the very moment to hearten me for a bold step which I have been meditating night and day. I feel within me a strange craving for the unknown, or, if you will, the forbidden, which makes me uneasy and reveals a conflict in progress in my soul between the laws of society and of nature. I cannot tell whether nature in me is the stronger of the two, but I surprise myself in the act of mediating between the hostile powers.

In plain words, what I wanted was to speak with Félipe, alone, at night, under the lime-trees at the bottom of our garden. There is no denying that this desire beseems the girl who has earned the epithet of an "up-to-date young lady," bestowed on me by the duchess in jest, and which my father has approved.

Yet to me there seems a method in this madness. I should recompense Félipe for the long nights he has passed under my window, at the same time that I should test him, by seeing what he thinks of my escapade and how he comports himself at a critical moment. Let him cast a halo round my folly— behold in him my husband; let him show one iota less of the tremulous respect with which he bows to me in the Champs-Élysées—farewell, Don Félipe.

As for society, I run less risk in meeting my lover thus than when I smile to him in the drawing-rooms of Mme. de Maufrigneuse and the old Marquise de Beauséant, where spies now surround us on every side; and heaven only knows how people stare at the girl, suspected of a weakness for a grotesque, like Macumer.

I cannot tell you to what a state of agitation I am reduced

by dreaming of this idea, and the time I have given to planning its execution. I wanted you badly. What happy hours we should have chattered away, lost in the mazes of uncertainty, enjoying in anticipation all the delights and horrors of a first meeting in the silence of night, under the noble lime-trees of the Chaulieu mansion, with the moonlight dancing through the leaves! As I sat alone, every nerve tingling, I cried, "Oh! Renée, where are you?" Then your letter came, like a match to gunpowder, and my last scruples went by the board.

Through the window I tossed to my bewildered adorer an exact tracing of the key of the little gate at the end of the garden, together with this note—

"Your madness must really be put a stop to. If you broke your neck you would ruin the reputation of the woman you profess to love. Are you worthy of a new proof of regard, and do you deserve that I should talk with you under the limes at the foot of the garden at the hour when the moon throws them into shadow?"

Yesterday, at one o'clock, when Griffith was going to bed, I said to her—

"Take your shawl, dear, and come out with me. I want to go to the bottom of the garden without any one of the household knowing."

Without a word, she followed me. Oh! my Renée, what an awful moment when, after a little pause full of delicious thrills of agony, I saw him gliding along like a shadow. When he had reached the garden safely, I said to Griffith—

"Don't be astonished, but the Baron de Macumer is here, and, indeed, it is on that account I brought you with me."

No reply from Griffith.

"What would you have with me?" said Félipe, in a tone of such agitation that it was easy to see he was driven beside himself by the noise, slight as it was, of our dresses in the silence of the night and of our steps upon the gravel.

"I want to say to you what I could not write," I replied.

Griffith withdrew a few steps. It was one of those mild nights when the air is heavy with the scent of flowers. My head swam with the intoxicating delight of finding myself all but alone with him in the friendly shade of the lime-trees, beyond which lay the garden, shining all the more brightly because the white facade of the house reflected the moonlight. The contrast seemed, as it were, an emblem of our clandestine love leading up to the glaring publicity of a wedding. Neither of us could do more at first than drink in silently the ecstasy of a moment, as new and marvelous for him as for me. At last I found tongue to say, pointing to the elm-tree—

"Although I am not afraid of scandal, you shall not climb that tree again. We have long enough played schoolboy and schoolgirl, let us rise now to the height of our destiny. Had the fall killed you, I should have died disgraced——"

I looked at him. Every scrap of color had left his face.

"And if you had been found there, suspicion would have attached either to my mother or myself."

"Forgive me," he murmured.

"If you walk along the boulevard, I shall hear your step; and when I want to see you, I will open my window. But I would not run such a risk unless some emergency arose. Why have you forced me by your rash act to commit another, and one which may lower me in your eyes?"

The tears which I saw in his eyes were to me the most eloquent of answers.

"What I have done to-night," I went on with a smile, "must seem to you the height of madness."

After we had walked up and down in silence more than once, he recovered composure enough to say—

"You must think me a fool; and, indeed, the delirium of my joy has robbed me of both nerve and wits. But of this at least be assured, whatever you do is sacred in my eyes from the very fact that it seemed right to you. I honor you as I honor my God beside. And then, Miss Griffith is here."

"She is here for the sake of others, not for us," I put in hastily.

My dear, he understood me at once.

"I know very well," he said, with the humblest glance at me, "that whether she is there or not makes no difference. Unseen of men, we are still in the presence of God, and our own esteem is not less important to us than that of the world."

"Thank you, Félipe," I said, holding out my hand to him with a gesture which you ought to see. "A woman, and I am nothing if not a woman, is on the road to loving the man who understands her. Oh! only on the road," I went on, with a finger on my lips. "Don't let your hopes carry you beyond what I say. My heart will belong only to the man who can read it and know its every turn. Our views, without being absolutely identical, must be the same in their breadth and elevation. I have no wish to exaggerate my own merits; doubtless what seem virtues in my eyes have their corresponding defects. All I can say is, I should be heartbroken without them."

"Having first accepted me as your servant, you now permit me to love you," he said, trembling and looking in my face at each word. "My first prayer has been more than answered."

"But," I hastened to reply, "your position seems to me a better one than mine. I should not object to change places, and this change it lies with you to bring about."

"In my turn, I thank you," he replied. "I know the duties of a faithful lover. It is mine to prove that I am worthy of you; the trials shall be as long as you choose to make them. If I belie your hopes, you have only—God! that I should say it—to reject me."

"I know that you love me," I replied. "*So far,*" with a

16

cruel emphasis on the words, "you stand first in my regard. Otherwise you would not be here."

Then we began again to walk up and down as we talked, and I must say that so soon as my Spaniard had recovered himself he put forth the genuine eloquence of the heart. It was not passion it breathed, but a marvelous tenderness of feeling, which he beautifully compared to the divine love. His thrilling voice, which lent an added charm to thoughts, in themselves so exquisite, reminded me of the nightingale's note. He spoke low, using only the middle tones of a fine instrument, and words flowed upon words with the rush of a torrent. It was the overflow of the heart.

"No more," I said, "or I shall not be able to tear myself away."

And with a gesture I dismissed him.

"You have committed yourself now, mademoiselle," said Griffith.

"In England that might be so, but not in France," I replied with nonchalance. "I intend to make a love match, and am feeling my way—that is all."

You see, dear, as love did not come to me, I had to do as Mahomet did with the mountain.

Friday.

Once more I have seen my slave. He has become very timid, and puts on an air of pious devotion, which I like, for it seems to say that he feels my power and fascination in every fibre. But nothing in his look or manner can rouse in these society sibyls any suspicion of the boundless love which I see. Don't suppose though, dear, that I am carried away, mastered, tamed ; on the contrary, the taming, mastering, and carrying away are on my side. In short, I am quite capable of reason. Oh ! to feel again the terror of that fascination in which I was held by the schoolmaster, the plebeian, the man I kept at a distance !

The fact is that love is of two kinds—one which commands, and one which obeys. The two are quite distinct, and the passion to which the one gives rise is not the passion of the other. To get her full of life, perhaps, a woman ought to have experience of both. Can the two passions ever coexist? Can the man in whom we inspire love inspire it in us? Will the day ever come when Félipe is my master? Shall I tremble then, as he does now? These are questions which make me shudder.

He is very blind! In his place I should have thought Mlle. de Chaulieu, meeting me under the limes, a cold, calculating coquette, with starched manners. No, that is not love, it is playing with fire. I am still fond of Félipe, but I am calm and at my ease with him now. No more obstacles! What a terrible thought! It is all ebb-tide within, and I fear to question my heart. His mistake was in concealing the ardor of his love; he ought to have forced my self-control.

In a word, I was naughty, and I have not got the reward such naughtiness brings. No, dear one, however sweet the memory of that half-hour beneath the trees, it is nothing like the excitement of the old time with its: "Shall I go? Shall I not go? Shall I write to him? Shall I not write?"

Is it thus with all our pleasures? Is suspense better than enjoyment? Hope than fruition? Is it the rich who in very truth are the poor? Have we not both perhaps exaggerated feeling by giving to imagination too free a rein? There are times when this thought freezes me. Shall I tell you why? Because I am meditating another visit to the bottom of the garden—without Griffith. Where should I get to then? How far could I go in this direction? Imagination knows no limit, but it is not so with pleasure. Tell me, dear be-corseted philosopher, how can one reconcile the two goals of a woman's existence? One thing is certain, things are most unsatisfactory as they are.

XXII.

LOUISE TO FÉLIPE.

I am not pleased with you. If you did not cry over Racine's "Bérénice," and feel it to be the most terrible of tragedies, there is no kinship in our souls; we shall never get on together, and had better break off at once. Let us meet no more. Forget me; for if I do not have a satisfactory reply, I shall forget you. You will become M. le Baron de Macumer for me, or rather you will cease to be at all.

Yesterday at Mme. d'Espard's you had a self-satisfied air which disgusted me. No doubt, apparently, about your conquest! In sober earnest, your self-possession alarms me. Not a trace in you of the humble slave of your first letter. Far from betraying the absent-mindedness of a lover, you polished epigrams! This is not the attitude of a true believer, always prostrate before his divinity.

If you do not feel me to be the very breath of your life, a being nobler than other women, and to be judged by other standards, then I must be less than a woman in your sight. You have roused in me a spirit of mistrust, Félipe, and its angry mutterings have drowned the accents of tenderness. When I look back upon what has passed between us, I feel in truth that I have a right to be suspicious. For know, Prime Minister of all the Spains, that I have reflected much on the defenseless condition of our sex. My innocence has held a torch, and my fingers are not burnt.

Let me repeat to you, then, what my youthful experience taught me.

In all other matters, duplicity, faithlessness, and broken pledges are brought to book and punished; but not so with love, which is at once the victim, the accuser, the counsel, judge, and executioner. The cruelest treachery, the most heartless crimes, are those which remain for ever concealed, with two hearts alone for witness. How indeed should the victim proclaim them without injury to herself? Love, therefore, has its own code, its own penal system, with which the world has no concern.

Now, for my part, I have resolved never to pardon a serious misdemeanor, and in love, pray, what is not serious? Yesterday you had all the air of a man successful in his suit. You would be wrong to doubt it; and yet, if this assurance robbed you of the charming simplicity which sprang from uncertainty, I should blame you severely. I would have you neither bashful nor self-complacent; I would not have you in terror of losing my affection—that would be an insult—but neither would I have you wear your love lightly as a thing of course. Never should your heart be freer than mine. If you know nothing of the torture that a single stab of doubt brings to the soul, tremble lest I give you a lesson!

In a single glance I confided my heart to you, and you read the meaning. The purest feelings that ever took root in a young girl's breast are yours. The thought and meditation of which I have told you served indeed only to enrich the mind; but if ever the wounded heart turns to the brain for counsel, be sure the young girl would show some kinship with the demon of knowledge and of daring.

I swear to you, Félipe, if you love me, as I believe you do, and if I have reason to suspect the least falling off in the fear, obedience, and respect which you have hitherto professed, if the pure flame of passion which first kindled the fire of my heart should seem to me any day to burn less vividly, you need fear no reproaches. I would not weary you with letters bearing any trace of weakness, pride, or anger, nor even with one of warning like this. But if I spoke no words, Félipe, my face would tell you that death was near. And yet I should not die till I had branded you with infamy, and sown eternal sorrow in your heart; you would see the girl you loved dishonored and lost in this world, and know her doomed to everlasting suffering in the next.

Do not therefore, I implore you, give me cause to envy the old, happy Louise, the object of your pure worship, whose heart expanded in the sunshine of happiness. since, in the words of Dante, she possessed: "Senza brama, sicura ricchezza!" I have searched the "Inferno" through to find the most terrible punishment, some torture of the mind to which I might link the vengeance of God.

Yesterday, as I watched you, doubt went through me like a sharp, cold dagger's point. Do you know what that means? I mistrusted you, and the pang was so terrible, I could not endure it longer. If my service be too hard, leave it, I would not keep you. Do I need any proof of your cleverness? Keep for me the flowers of your wit. Show to others no fine surface to call forth flattery, compliments, or praise. Come to me, laden with hatred or scorn, the butt of calumny, come to me with the news that women flout you and ignore you, and not one loves you; then, ah! then you will know the treasures of Louise's heart and love.

We are only rich when our wealth is buried so deep that all the world might trample it under foot, unknowing. If you were handsome, I don't suppose I should have looked at you twice, or discovered one of the thousand reasons out of which my love sprang. True, we know no more of these reasons than we know why it is the sun makes the flowers to bloom, and ripens the fruit. Yet I could tell you of one reason very dear to me.

The character, expression, and individuality that ennoble your face are a sealed book to all but me. Mine is the power which transforms you into the most lovable of men, and that is why I would keep your mental gifts also for myself. To others they should be as meaningless as your eyes, the charm of your mouth and features. Let it be mine alone to kindle the beacon of your intelligence, as I bring the love-light into your eyes. I would have you the Spanish grandee of old days, cold, ungracious, haughty, a monument to be gazed at from afar, like the ruins of some barbaric power, which no one ventures to explore. Now, you have nothing better to do than to open up pleasant promenades for the public, and show yourself off a Parisian affability!

Is my ideal portrait, then, forgotten? Your excessive cheerfulness was redolent of your love. Had it not been for a restraining glance from me, you would have proclaimed to the most sharp-sighted, keen-witted, and unsparing of Paris salons, that your inspiration was drawn from Armande-Louise-Marie de Chaulieu.

I believe in your greatness too much to think for a moment that your love is ruled by policy; but if you did not show a childlike simplicity when with me, I could only pity you. Despite this first fault, you are still deeply admired by

LOUISE DE CHAULIEU.

XXIII.

FÉLIPE TO LOUISE.

When God beholds our faults, He sees also our repentance. Yes, my beloved mistress, you are right. I felt that I had displeased you, but knew not how. Now that you have explained the cause of your trouble, I find in it fresh motive to adore you. Like the God of Israel, you are a jealous deity, and I rejoice to see it. For what is holier and more precious than jealousy? My fair guardian angel, jealousy is an ever-wakeful sentinel; it is to love what pain is to the body, the faithful herald of evil. Be jealous of your servant, Louise, I beg of you; the harder you strike, the more contrite will he be and kiss the rod, in all submission, which proves that he is not indifferent to you.

But, alas! dear, if the pains it cost me to vanquish my

timidity and master feelings you thought so feeble were invisible to you, will heaven, think you, reward them?   I assure you, it needed no slight effort to show myself to you as I was in the days before I loved.   At Madrid I was considered a good talker, and I wanted you to see for yourself the few gifts I may possess.   If this were vanity, it has been well punished.

Your last glance utterly unnerved me.   Never had I so quailed, even when the army of France was at the gates of Cadiz and I read peril for my life in the dissembling words of my royal master.   Vainly I tried to discover the cause of your displeasure, and the lack of sympathy between us which this fact disclosed was terrible to me.   For in truth I have no wish but to act by your will, think your thoughts, see with your eyes, respond to your joy and suffering, as my body responds to heat and cold.   The crime and the anguish lay for me in the breach of unison in that common life of feeling which you have made so fair.

"I have vexed her!" I exclaimed over and over again, like one distraught.   My noble, my beautiful Louise, if anything could increase the fervor of my devotion or confirm my belief in your delicate moral intuitions, it would be the new light which your words have thrown upon my own feelings. Much in them, of which my mind was formerly but dimly conscious, you have now made clear.   If this be designed as chastisement, what can be the sweetness of your dearly anticipated rewards?

Louise, for me it was happiness enough to be accepted as your servant.   You have given me the life of which I despaired. No longer do I draw a useless breath, I have something to spend myself for; my force has an outlet, if only in suffering for you.   Once more I say, as I have said before, that you will never find me other than I was when first I offered myself as your lowly bondman.   Yes, were you dishonored and lost, to use your own words, my heart would only cling the more closely to you for your self-sought misery. It would be my care to stanch your wounds, and my prayers should importune God with the story of your innocence and your wrongs.

Did I not tell you that the feelings of my heart for you are not a lover's only, that I will be to you father, mother, sister, brother—ay, a whole family—anything or nothing, as you may decree? And is it not your own wish which has confined within the compass of a lover's feeling so many varying forms of devotion? Pardon me, then, if at times the father and brother disappear behind the lover, since you know they are none the less there, though screened from view. Would that you could read the feelings of my heart when you appear before me, radiant in your beauty, the centre of admiring eyes, reclining calmly in your carriage in the Champs-Élysées, or seated in your box at the opera! Then would you know how absolutely free from selfish taint is the pride with which I hear the praises of your loveliness and grace, praises which warm my heart even to the strangers who utter them! When by chance you have raised me to elysium by a friendly greeting, my pride is mingled with humility, and I depart as though God's blessing rested on me. Nor does the joy vanish without leaving a long track of light behind. It breaks on me through the clouds of my cigarette smoke. More than ever do I feel how every drop of this surging blood throbs for you.

Can you be ignorant how you are loved? After seeing you, I return to my study, and the glitter of its Saracenic ornaments sinks to nothing before the brightness of your portrait, when I open the spring that keeps it locked up from every eye and lose myself in endless musings or link my happiness to verse. From the heights of heaven I look down upon the course of a life such as my hopes dare to picture it! Have you never, in the silence of the night, or through the roar of the town, heard the whisper of a voice in your sweet, dainty ear? Does no one of the thousand prayers that I speed to you reach home?

By dint of silent contemplation of your pictured face, I have succeeded in deciphering the expression of every feature and tracing its connection with some grace of the spirit, and then I pen a sonnet to you in Spanish on the harmony of the twofold beauty in which nature has clothed you. These sonnets you will never see, for my poetry is too unworthy of its theme, I dare not send it to you. Not a moment passes without thoughts of you, for my whole being is bound up in you, and if you ceased to be its animating principle, every part would ache.

Now, Louise, can you realize the torture to me of knowing that I had displeased you, while entirely ignorant of the cause? The ideal double life which seemed so fair was cut short. My heart turned to ice within me as, hopeless of any other explanation, I concluded that you had ceased to love me. With heavy heart, and yet not wholly without comfort, I was falling back upon my old post as servant; then your letter came and turned all to joy. Oh! might I but listen for ever to such chiding!

Once a child, picking himself up from a tumble, turned to his mother with the words "Forgive me." Hiding his own hurt, he sought pardon for the pain he had caused her. Louise, I was that child, and such as I was then, I am now. Here is the key to my character, which your slave in all humility places in your hands.

But do not fear, there will be no more stumbling. Keep taut the chain which binds me to you, so that a touch may communicate your slightest wish to him who will ever remain your slave,   FÉLIPE.

XXIV.

October, 1825.

MY DEAR FRIEND:—How is it possible that you, who brought yourself in two months to marry a broken-down invalid in order to mother him, should know anything of that terrible shifting drama, enacted in the recesses of the heart, which we call love—a drama where death lies in a glance or a light reply?

I had reserved for Félipe one last supreme test which was to be decisive. I wanted to know whether his love was the love of a Royalist for his King, who can do no wrong. Why should the loyalty of a Catholic be less supreme?

He walked with me a whole night under the limes at the bottom of the garden, and not a shadow of suspicion crossed his soul. Next day he loved me better, but the feeling was as reverent, as humble, as respectful as ever; he had not presumed an iota. Oh! he is a very Spaniard, a very Abencerrage. He scaled my wall to come and kiss the hand which in the darkness I reached down to him from my balcony. He might have broken his neck; how many of our young men would do the like?

But all this is nothing; Christians suffer the horrible pangs of martyrdom in the hope of heaven. The day before yesterday I took aside the royal ambassador-to-be at the Court of Spain, my much respected father, and said to him with a . smile—

"Sir, some of your friends will have it that you are marrying your dear Armande to the nephew of an ambassador who has been very anxious for this connection, and has long begged for it. Also, that the marriage-contract arranges for his nephew to succeed on his death to his enormous fortune and his title, and bestows on the young couple in the meantime an income of a hundred thousand livres, on the bride a dowry of eight hundred thousand francs. Your daughter weeps, but bows to the unquestioned authority of her honored parent. Some people are unkind enough to say that, behind her tears, she conceals a worldly and ambitious soul.

"Now, we are going to the gentleman's box at the opera to-night, and M. le Baron de Macumer will visit us there."

"Macumer needs a touch of the spur then," said my father, smiling at me, as though I were a female ambassador.

"You mistake Clarissa Harlowe for Figaro!" I cried, with a glance of scorn and mockery. "When you see me with my right hand ungloved, you will give the lie to this impertinent gossip, and will mark your displeasure at it."

"I may make my mind easy about your future. You have no more got a girl's headpiece than Jeanne d'Arc had a woman's heart. You will be happy, you will love nobody, and will allow yourself to be loved."

This was too much. I burst into laughter.

"What is it, little flirt?" he said.

"I tremble for my country's interests——"

And seeing him look quite blank, I added—

"At Madrid!"

"You have no idea how this little nun has learned, in a year's time, to make fun of her father," he said to the duchess.

"Armande makes light of everything," my mother replied, looking me in the face.

"What do you mean?" I asked.

"Why, you are not even afraid of rheumatism on these damp nights," she said, with another meaning glance at me.

"Oh!" I answered, "the mornings are so hot!"

The duchess looked down.

"It's high time she were married," said my father, "and it had better be before I go."

"If you wish it," I replied demurely.

Two hours later, my mother and I, the Duchesse de Maufrigneuse and Mme. d'Espard, were all four blooming like
roses in the front of the box. I had seated myself sideways,
giving only a shoulder to the house, so that I could see everything, myself unseen, in that spacious box which fills one of
the two angles at the back of the hall, between the columns.

Macumer came, stood up, and put his opera-glasses before
his eyes so that he might be able to look at me comfortably.

In the first interval entered the young man whom I call
"king of the profligates." The Comte Henri de Marsay,
who has great beauty of an effeminate kind, entered the box
with an epigram in his eyes, a smile upon his lips, and an air
of satisfaction over his whole countenance. He first greeted
my mother, Mme. d'Espard, and the Duchesse de Maufrigneuse, the Comte d'Esgrignon, and M. de Canalis; then
turning to me, he said—

"I do not know whether I shall be the first to congratulate
you on an event which will make you the object of envy to
many."

"Ah! a marriage!" I cried. "Is it left for me, a girl
fresh from the convent, to tell you that predicted marriages
never come off."

M. de Marsay bent down, whispering to Macumer, and I
was convinced, from the movement of his lips, that what he
said was this—

"Baron, you are perhaps in love with that little coquette,
who has used you for her own ends; but as the question is
one not of love, but of marriage, it is as well for you to know
what is going on."

Macumer treated this officious scandalmonger to one of
those glances of his which seemed to me so eloquent of noble
scorn, and replied to the effect that he was "not in love with
any little coquette." His whole bearing so delighted me,
that directly I caught sight of my father, the glove was off.

Félipe had not a shadow of fear or doubt. How well did

he bear out my expectations! His faith is only in me, society cannot hurt him with its lies. Not a muscle of the Arab's face stirred, not a drop of the blue blood flushed his olive cheek.

The two young counts went out, and I said, laughing, to Macumer—

"M. de Marsay has been treating you to an epigram on me."

"He did more," he replied. "It was an epithalamium."

"You speak Greek to me," I said, rewarding him with a smile and a certain look which always embarrasses him.

My father meantime was talking to Mme. de Maufrigneuse.

"I should think so!" he exclaimed. "The gossip which gets about is scandalous. No sooner has a girl come out than every one is keen to marry her, and the ridiculous stories that are invented! I shall never force Armande to marry against her will. I am going to take a turn in the promenade, otherwise people will be saying that I allowed the rumor to spread in order to suggest the marriage to the ambassador; and Cæsar's daughter ought to be above suspicion, even more than his wife—if that were possible."

The Duchesse de Maufrigneuse and Mme. d'Espard shot glances first at my mother, then at the baron, brimming over with sly intelligence and repressed curiosity. With their serpent's cunning they had at last got an inkling of something going on. Of all mysteries in life, love is the least mysterious! It exhales from women, I believe, like a perfume, and she who can conceal it is a very monster! Our eyes prattle even more than our tongues.

Having enjoyed the delightful sensation of finding Félipe rise to the occasion, as I had wished, it was only in nature I should hunger for more. So I made the signal agreed on for telling him that he might come to my window by the dangerous road you know of. A few hours later I found him, upright as a statue, glued to the wall, his hand resting on the balcony of my window, studying the reflections of the light in my room.

"My dear Félipe," I said, "you have acquitted yourself well to-night; you behaved exactly as I should have done had I been told that you were on the point of marrying."

"I thought," he replied, "that you would hardly have told others before me."

"And what right have you to this privilege?"

"The right of one who is your devoted slave."

"In very truth?"

"I am, and shall ever remain so."

"But suppose this marriage were inevitable; suppose that I had agreed——"

Two flashing glances lit up the moonlight—one directed to me, the other to the precipice which the wall made for us. He seemed to calculate whether a fall together would mean death; but the thought merely passed like lightning over his face and sparkled in his eyes. A power, stronger than passion, checked the impulse.

"An Arab cannot take back his word," he said in a husky voice. "I am your slave to do with as you will; my life is not mine to destroy."

The hand on the balcony seemed as though its hold were relaxing. I placed mine on it as I said—

"Félipe, my beloved, from this moment I am your wife in thought and will. Go in the morning to ask my father for my hand. He wishes to retain my fortune; but if you promise to acknowledge receipt of it in the contract, his consent will no doubt be given. I am no longer Armande de Chaulieu. Leave me at once; no breath of scandal must touch Louise de Macumer."

He listened with blanched face and trembling limbs, then, like a flash, had cleared the ten feet to the ground in safety. It was a moment of agony, but he waved his hand to me and disappeared.

"I am loved then," I said to myself, "as never woman was before." And I fell asleep in the calm content of a child, my destiny for ever fixed.

About two o'clock next day my father summoned me to his private room, where I found the duchess and Macumer. There was an interchange of civilities. I replied quite simply that if my father and M. Hénarez were of one mind, I had no reason to oppose their wishes. Thereupon my mother invited the baron to dinner; and, after dinner, we all four went for a drive in the Bois de Boulogne, where I had the pleasure of smiling ironically to M. de Marsay as he passed on horseback and caught sight of de Macumer sitting opposite us beside my father.

My bewitching Félipe has had his cards reprinted as follows:

HÉNAREZ

(Baron de Macumer, formerly Duc de Soria).

Every morning he brings me with his own hands a splendid bouquet, in which I never fail to find a letter, containing a Spanish sonnet in my honor, which he has composed during the night.

Not to make this letter inordinately large, I send you as specimens only the first and last of these sonnets, which I have translated for your benefit, word for word, and line for line:

FIRST SONNET.

Many a time I've stood, clad in thin silken vest,
Drawn sword in hand, with steady pulse,
Waiting the charge of a raging bull,
And the thrust of his horn, sharper-pointed than Phœbe's crescent.

I've scaled, on my lips the lilt of an Andalusian dance,
The steep redoubt under a rain of fire;
I've staked my life upon a hazard of the dice,
Careless, as though it were a gold doubloon.

My hand would seek the ball out of the cannon's mouth,
But now meseems I grow more timid than a crouching hare,
Or a child spying some ghost in the curtain's folds.

For when your sweet eye rests on me,
An icy sweat covers my brow, my knees give **way,**
I tremble, shrink, my courage gone.

SECOND SONNET.

Last night I fain would sleep to dream of **thee,**
But jealous sleep fled my eyelids,
I sought the balcony and looked toward heaven,
Always my glance flies upward when I think of **thee.**

Strange sight! whose meaning love alone can tell,
The sky had lost its sapphire hue,
The stars, dulled diamonds in their golden mount,
Twinkled no more nor shed their warmth.

The moon, washed of her silver radiance lily-white,
Hung mourning over the gloomy plain, for thou hast robbed
The heavens of all that made them bright.

The snowy sparkle of the moon is on thy lovely brow,
Heaven's azure centres in thine eyes,
Thy lashes fall like starry rays.

What more gracious way of saying to a young girl that
she fills your life? Tell me what you think of this love,
which expends itself in lavishing the treasures alike of the
heart and of the soul. Only within the last ten days have I
grasped the meaning of that Spanish gallantry, so famous in
old days.

Ah me! dear, what is going on now at La Crampade?
How often do I take a stroll there, inspecting the growth of
our crops! Have you no news to give of our mulberry trees,
our last winter's plantations? Does everything prosper as

17

you wish? And while the buds are opening on our shrubs—
I will not venture to speak of the bedding-out plants—have
they also blossomed in the bosom of the wife? Does Louis
continue his policy of madrigals? Do you enter into each
other's thoughts? I wonder whether your little runlet of
wedded peace is better than the raging torrent of my love!
Has my sweet lady professor taken offense? I cannot believe
it; and if it were so, I should send Félipe off at once, post-
haste, to fling himself at her knees and bring back to me my
pardon on her head. Sweet love, my life here is a splendid
success, and I want to know how it fares with life in Provence.
We have just increased our family by the addition of a Spaniard
with the complexion of a Havana cigar, and your congratu-
lations still tarry.

Seriously, my sweet Renée, I am anxious. I am afraid lest
you should be eating your heart out in silence, for fear of
casting a gloom over my sunshine. Write to me at once,
naughty child! and tell me your life in its every minutest
detail; tell me whether you still hold back, whether your
"independence" still stands erect, or has fallen on its knees,
or is sitting down comfortably, which would indeed be serious.
Can you suppose that the incidents of your married life are
without interest for me? I muse at times over all that you
have said to me. Often when, at the opera, I seem absorbed
in watching the pirouetting dancers, I am saying to myself,
"It is half-past nine, perhaps she is in bed. What is she
about? Is she happy? Is she alone with her independence?
or has her independence gone the way of other dead and cast-
off independences?"

A thousand loves.

XXV.

RENÉE DE L'ESTORADE TO LOUISE DE CHAULIEU.

Saucy girl! Why should I write? What can I say? Whilst your life is varied by social festivities, as well as by the anguish, the quarrels, and the flowers of love—all of which you describe so graphically, that I might be watching some first-rate acting at the theatre—mine is as monotonous and regular as though it were passed in a convent.

We always go to bed at nine and get up with daybreak. Our meals are served with a maddening punctuality. Nothing ever happens. I have accustomed myself without much difficulty to this mapping out of the day, which perhaps is, after all, in the nature of things. Where would the life of the universe be but for that subjection to fixed laws which, according to the astronomers, so Louis tells me, rule the spheres! It is not order of which we weary.

Then I have laid upon myself certain rules of dress, and these occupy my time in the mornings. I hold it part of my duty as a wife to look as charming as possible. I feel a certain satisfaction in it, and it causes lively pleasure to the good old man and to Louis. After lunch, we walk. When the newspapers arrive, I disappear to look after my household affairs or to read—for I read a great deal—or to write you. I come back to the others an hour before dinner; and after dinner we play cards, or receive visits, or pay them. Thus my days pass between a contented old man, who has done with passions, and the man who owes his happiness to me. Louis' happiness is so radiant that it has at last warmed my heart.

For women, happiness, no doubt, cannot consist in the mere satisfaction of desire. Sometimes, in the evening, when I am not required to take a hand in the game, and can sink back

in my armchair, imagination bears me on its strong wings
into the very heart of your life. Then, its riches, its changeful tints, its surging passions become my own, and I ask myself to what end such a stormy preface can lead. May it not
swallow up the book itself? For you, my darling, the illusions
of love are possible; for me, only the facts of homely life remain. Yes, your love seems to me a dream!

Therefore I find it hard to understand why you are determined to throw so much romance over it. Your ideal man
must have more soul than fire, more nobility and self-command
than passion. You persist in trying to clothe in living form
the dream of a girl on the threshold of life; you demand
sacrifices for the pleasure of rewarding them; you submit
your Félipe to tests in order to ascertain whether desire, hope,
and curiosity are enduring in their nature. But, child, behind all your fantastic stage scenery rises the altar, where
everlasting bonds are forged. The very morrow of your
marriage the graceful structure raised by your subtle strategy
may fall before that terrible reality which makes of a girl a
woman, of a gallant a husband. Remember that there is no
exemption for lovers. For them, as for ordinary folk like
Louis and me, there lurks beneath the wedding rejoicings the
great "Perhaps" of Rabelais.

I do not blame you, though, of course, it was rash, for talking with Félipe in the garden, or for spending a night with
him, you on your balcony, he on his wall; but you make a
plaything of life, and I am afraid that life may some day turn
the tables. I dare not give you the counsel which my own
experience would suggest; but let me repeat once more from
the seclusion of my valley that the viaticum of married life
lies in these words—resignation and self-sacrifice. For, spite
of all your tests, your coyness, and your vigilance, I can see
that marriage will mean to you what it has been to me. The
greater the passion, the steeper the precipice we have hewn
for our fall—that is the only difference.

Oh! what I would give to see the Baron de Macumer and talk with him for an hour or two! Your happiness lies so near my heart.

XXVI.

LOUISE DE MACUMER TO RENÉE DE L'ESTORADE.

March, 1825.

As Félipe has carried out, with a true Saracenic generosity, the wishes of my father and mother in acknowledging the fortune he has not received from me, the duchess has become even more friendly to me than before. She calls me little sly-boots, little woman of the world, and says I know how to use my tongue.

" But, dear mamma," I said to her the evening before the contract was signed, " you attribute to cunning and smartness on my part what is really the outcome of the truest, simplest, most unselfish, most devoted love that ever was! I assure you that I am not at all the 'woman of the world' you do me the honor of believing me to be."

"Come, come, Armande," she said, putting her arm on my neck and drawing me to her, in order to kiss my forehead, "you did not want to go back to the convent, you did not want to die an old maid, and, like a fine, noble-hearted Chaulieu, as you are, you recognized the necessity of building up your father's family." (The duke was listening. If you knew, Renée, what flattery lies for him in these words.) "I have watched you during a whole winter, poking your little nose into all that goes on, forming very sensible opinions about men and the present state of society in France. And you have picked out the one Spaniard capable of giving you the splendid position of a woman who reigns supreme in her own house. My dear little girl, you treated him exactly as Tullia treats your brother."

"What lessons they give in my sister's convent!" exclaimed my father.

A glance at my father cut him short at once; then, turning to the duchess, I said—

"Madame, I love my future husband, Félipe de Soria, with all the strength of my soul. Although this love sprang up without my knowledge, and though I fought it stoutly when it first made itself felt, I swear to you that I never gave way to it till I had recognized in the Baron de Macumer a character worthy of mine, a heart of which the delicacy, the generosity, the devotion, and the temper are suited to my own."

"But, my dear," she began, interrupting me, "he is as ugly as——"

"As anything you like," I retorted quickly, "but I love his ugliness."

"If you love him, Armande," said my father, "and have the strength to master your love, you must not risk your happiness. Now, happiness in marriage depends largely on the first days——"

"Days only?" interrupted my mother. Then, with a glance at my father, she continued: "You had better leave us, my dear, to have our talk together."

"You are to be married, dear child," the duchess then began in a low voice, "in three days. It becomes my duty, therefore, without silly whimpering, which would be unfitting our rank in life, to give you the serious advice which every mother owes to her daughter. You are marrying a man whom you love, and there is no reason why I should pity you or myself. I have only known you for a year; and if this period has been long enough for me to learn to love you, it is hardly sufficient to justify floods of tears at the idea of losing you. Your mental gifts are even more remarkable than those of your person; you have gratified maternal pride, and have shown yourself a sweet and loving daughter. I, in my turn, can promise you that you will always find a stanch friend in your mother. You smile? Alas! it too often happens that a mother who has lived on excellent terms with her daughter, so long as the daughter is a mere girl, comes to cross-purposes with her when they are both women together.

"It is your happiness which I want, so listen to my words. The love which you now feel is that of a young girl, and is natural to us all, for it is woman's destiny to cling to a man. Unhappily, pretty one, there is but one man in the world for a woman! And sometimes this man, whom fate has marked out for us, is not the one whom we, mistaking a passing fancy for love, choose as husband. Strange as what I say may appear to you, it is worth noting. If we cannot love the man we have chosen, the fault is not exclusively ours, it lies with both, or sometimes with circumstances over which we have no control. Yet there is no reason why the man chosen for us by our family, the man to whom our fancy has gone out, should not be the man whom we can love. The barrier which may arise later between husband and wife is often due to lack of perseverance on both sides. The task of transforming a husband into a lover is not less delicate than that other task of making a husband of the lover, in which you have just proved yourself marvelously successful.

"I repeat it, your happiness is my object. Never allow yourself, then, to forget that the first three months of your married life may work your misery if you do not submit to the yoke with the same forbearance, tenderness, and intelligence that you have shown during the days of courtship. For, my little rogue, you know very well that you have indulged in all the innocent pleasures of a clandestine love affair. If the culmination of your love begins with disappointment, dislike, nay, even with pain, well, come and tell me about it. Don't hope for too much from marriage at first; it will perhaps give you more discomfort than joy. The happiness of married life requires at least as patient cherishing as the early shoots of love.

"To conclude, if by chance you should lose the lover in the husband, you may find in his place the father of your children. In this, my dear child, lies the whole secret of social life. Sacrifice everything to the man whose name you bear, the man whose honor and reputation cannot suffer in the least degree without involving you in frightful consequences. Such sacrifice is thus not only an absolute duty for women of our rank, it is also their wisest policy. This, indeed, is the distinctive mark of great moral principles, that they hold good and are expedient from whatever aspect they are viewed. But I need say no more to you on this point.

"I fancy you are of a jealous disposition, and, my dear, if you knew how jealous I am! But you must not be stupid over it. To publish your jealousy to the world is like playing at politics with your cards upon the table, and those who let their own game be seen learn nothing of their opponents'. Whatever happens, we must know how to endure and suffer in silence."

She added that she intended having some plain talk about me with Macumer the evening before the wedding.

Raising my mother's beautiful arm, I kissed her hand and dropped on it a tear, which the tone of real feeling in her voice had brought to my eyes. In the advice she had given me, I read high principle worthy of herself and of me, true wisdom, and a tenderness of heart unspoilt by the narrow code of society. Above all, I saw that she understood my character. These few simple words summed up the lessons which life and experience had brought her, perhaps at a heavy price. She was moved, and said, as she looked at me—

"Dear little girl, you've got a nasty crossing before you. And most women, in their ignorance or their disenchantment, are as wise as the Earl of Westmoreland!"

We both laughed; but I must explain the joke. The evening before, a Russian princess had told us an anecdote of this gentleman. He had suffered frightfully from sea-sickness in crossing the Channel, and turned tail when he got near Italy, because he heard some one speak of "crossing" the Alps. "Thank you; I've had quite enough crossings already," he said.

You will understand, Renée, that your gloomy philosophy and my mother's lecture were calculated to revive the fears which used to disturb us at Blois. The nearer marriage approached, the more did I need to summon all my strength, my resolution, and my affection to face this terrible passage from maidenhood to womanhood. All our conversations came back to my mind, I re-read your letters and discerned in them a vague undertone of sadness.

This anxiety had one advantage at least; it helped me to the regulation expression for a bride—pale and shrinking- · as commonly depicted. The consequence was that on the day of signing the contract everybody said I looked quite charming and interesting. This morning, at the Mairie, it was an informal business, and only the witnesses were present.

I am writing this tail to my letter while they are putting out my dress for dinner. We shall be married at midnight at the church of Sainte-Valère, after a brilliant reception. I confess that my fears give me a martyr-like and modest air to which I have no right, but which will be admired—why, I cannot conceive. I am delighted to see that poor Félipe is every whit as timorous as I am; society grates on him, he is like a bat in a glass store.

"Thank heaven, the day won't last for ever!" he whispered to me in all innocence. In his bashfulness and timidity he would have liked to have no one there.

The Sardinian ambassador, when he came to sign the contract, took me aside in order to present me with a pearl necklace linked together by six splendid diamonds—a gift from my sister-in-law, the Duchesse de Soria. Along with the necklace was a sapphire bracelet, on the under side of which were engraved the words: "THOUGH UNKNOWN, BELOVED."

Two charming letters came with these presents, which, however, I would not accept without consulting Félipe.

"For," I said, "I should not like to see you wearing ornaments that came from any one but me."

He kissed my hand, quite moved, and replied—

"Wear them for the sake of the inscription, and also that
the love thus offered is sincere."

Saturday Evening.

Here, then, my Renée, are the last words of your girl
friend. After the midnight mass, we set off for an estate
which Félipe, with kind thought for me, has bought in
Nivernais, on the way to Provence. Already my name is
Louise de Macumer, but I leave Paris in a few hours as Louise
de Chaulieu. However I am called, there will never be for
you but one Louise.

XXVII.

THE SAME TO THE SAME.

October, 1825.

I have not written to you, dear, since our marriage, nearly
eight months ago. And not a line from you! Madame, you
are inexcusable.

To begin with, we set off in a post-chaise for the Castle of
Chantepleurs, the property which Macumer has bought in
Nivernais. It stands on the banks of the Loire, sixty leagues
from Paris. Our servants, with the exception of my maid,
were there before us, and we arrived, after a very rapid journey,
the next evening. I slept all the way from Paris to beyond
Montargis. My lord and master put his arm round me and
pillowed my head on his shoulder, upon an arrangement of
handkerchiefs. This was the one liberty he took; and the
almost motherly tenderness which got the better of his drowsi-
ness touched me strangely. I fell asleep then under the fire
of his eyes, and awoke to find them still blazing; the passionate gaze remained unchanged, but what thoughts had come

and gone meanwhile! Twice he had kissed me on the forehead.

At Briare we had breakfast in the carriage. Then followed a talk like our old talks at Blois, while the same Loire we used to admire called forth our praises, and at half-past seven we entered the noble long avenue of lime-trees, acacias, sycamores, and larches which leads to Chantepleurs. At eight we dined; at ten we were in our bedroom, a charming Gothic room, made comfortable with every modern luxury. Félipe, who is thought so ugly, seemed to me quite beautiful in his graceful kindness and the exquisite delicacy of his affection. Of passion, not a trace. All through the journey he might have been an old friend of fifteen years' standing. Later, he has described to me, with all the vivid touches of his first letter, the furious storms that raged within and were not allowed to ruffle the outer surface.

"So far, I have found nothing very terrible in marriage," I said, as I walked to the window and looked out on the glorious moon which lit up a charming park, breathing of heavy scents.

He drew near, put his arm again round me, and said—

"Why fear it? Have I ever yet proved false to my promise in gesture or look? Why should I be false in the future?"

Yet never were words or glances more full of mastery; his voice thrilled every fibre of my heart and roused a sleeping force; his eyes were like the sun in power.

"Oh!" I exclaimed, "what a world of Moorish perfidy in this attitude of perpetual prostration!"

He understood, my dear.

So, my fair sweet one, if I have let months slip by without writing, you can now divine the cause. I have to recall the girl's strange past in order to explain the woman to myself. Renée, I understand you now. Not to her dearest friend, not to her mother, not, perhaps, even to herself, can a happy bride speak of her happiness. This memory ought to remain absolutely our own, an added rapture—a thing beyond words, too sacred for disclosure!

Is it possible that the name of duty has been given to the delicious frenzy of the heart, to the overwhelming rush of passion? And for what purpose? What malevolent power conceived the idea of crushing a woman's sensitive delicacy and all the thousand wiles of her modesty under the fetters of constraint? What sense of duty can force from her these flowers of the heart, the roses of life, the passionate poetry of her nature, apart from love? To claim feeling as a right! Why, it blooms of itself under the sun of love, and shrivels to death under the cold blast of distaste and aversion! Let love guard his own rights!

Oh! my noble Renée! I understand you now. I bow to your greatness, amazed at the depth and clearness of your insight. Yes, the woman who has not used the marriage ceremony, as I have done, merely to legalize and publish the secret election of her heart, has nothing left but to fly to motherhood. When earth fails, the soul makes for heaven!

One hard truth emerges from all that you have said. Only men who are really great know how to love, and now I understand the reason of this. Man obeys two forces—one sensual, one spiritual. Weak or inferior men mistake the first for the last, whilst great souls know how to clothe the merely natural instinct in all the graces of the spirit. The very strength of this spiritual passion imposes severe self-restraint and inspires them with reverence for women. Clearly, feeling is sensitive in proportion to the calibre of the mental powers generally, and this is why the man of genius alone has something of a woman's delicacy. He understands and divines woman, and the wings of passion on which he raises her are restrained by the timidity of the sensitive spirit. But when the mind, the heart, and the senses all have their share in the rapture which transports us—ah! then there is no falling to earth, rather it is to heaven we soar, alas! for only too brief a visit.

Such, dear soul, is the philosophy of the first three months of my married life. Félipe is angelic. Without figure of speech, he is another self, and I can think aloud with him. His greatness of soul passes my comprehension. Possession only attaches him more closely to me, and he discovers in his happiness new motives for loving me. For him, I am the nobler part of himself. I can foresee that years of wedded life, far from impairing his affection, will only make it more assured, develop fresh possibilities of enjoyment, and bind us in more perfect sympathy. What a delirium of joy!

It is part of my nature that pleasure has an exhilarating effect on me; it leaves sunshine behind, and becomes a part of my inner being. The interval which parts one ecstasy from another is like the short night which marks off our long summer days. The sun which flushed the mountain tops with warmth in setting finds them hardly cold when it rises. What happy chance has given me such a destiny? My mother had roused a host of fears in me; her forecast, which, though free from the alloy of vulgar pettiness, seemed to me redolent of jealousy, has been falsified by the event. Your fears and hers, my own—all have vanished in thin air!

We remained at Chantepleurs seven months and a half, for all the world like a couple of runaway lovers fleeing the parental wrath, while the roses of pleasure crowned our love and embellished our dual solitude. One morning, when I was even happier than usual, I began to muse over my lot, and suddenly Renée and her prosaic marriage flashed into my mind. It seemed to me that now I could grasp the inner meaning of your life. Oh! my sweet, why do we speak a different tongue? Your marriage of convenience and my love match are two worlds, as widely separated as the finite from infinity. You still walk the earth, whilst I range the heavens! Your sphere is human, mine divine! Love crowned me queen, you reign by reason and duty. So lofty are the regions where I soar, that a fall would shiver me to atoms.

But no more of this. I shrink from painting to you the rainbow brightness, the profusion, the exuberant joy of love's springtime, as we know it.

For ten days we have been in Paris, staying in a charming house in the Rue du Bac, prepared for us by the architect to whom Félipe intrusted the decoration of Chantepleurs. I have been listening, in all the full content of an assured and sanctioned love, to that divine music of Rossini's, which used to soothe me when, as a restless girl, I hungered vaguely after experience. They say I am more beautiful, and I have a childish pleasure in hearing myself called " Madame."

Friday Morning.

Renée, my fair saint, the happiness of my own life pulls me for ever back to you. I feel that I can be more to you than ever before, you are so dear to me! I have studied your wedded life closely in the light of my own opening chapters; and you seem to me to come out of the scrutiny so great, so noble, so splendid in your goodness, that I here declare myself your inferior and humble admirer, as well as your friend. When I think what marriage has been to me, it seems to me that I should have died, had it turned out otherwise. And *you live!* Tell me what your heart feeds on! Never again shall I make fun of you. Mockery, my sweet, is the child of ignorance; we jest at what we know nothing of. " Recruits will laugh where the veteran soldier looks grave," was a remark made to me by the Comte de Chaulieu, that poor cavalry officer whose campaigning so far has consisted in marches from Paris to Fontainebleau and back again.

I surmise, too, my dear love, that you have not told me all! There are wounds which you have hidden. You suffer! I am convinced of it. In trying to make out at this distance and from the scraps you tell me the reasons of your conduct, I have weaved together all sorts of romantic theories about you. " She has made a mere experiment in marriage," I thought one evening, "and what is happiness for me has proved only suffering to her. Her sacrifice is barren of reward, and she would not make it greater than need be. The unctuous axioms of social morality are only used to cloak her disappointment." Ah! Renée, the best of happiness is that it needs no dogma and no fine words to pave the way; it speaks for itself, while theory has been piled upon theory to justify the system of women's vassalage and thralldom. If self-denial be so noble, so sublime, what, pray, of my joy, sheltered by the gold-and-white canopy of the church, and witnessed by the hand and seal of the most sour-faced of mayors? Is it a thing out of nature?

For the honor of the law, for her own sake, but most of all to make my happiness complete, I long to see my Renée happy. Oh! tell me that you see a dawn of love for this Louis who adores you! Tell me that the solemn, symbolic torch of Hymen has not alone served to lighten your darkness, but that love, the glorious sun of our hearts, pours his rays on you. I come back always, you see, to this midday blaze, which will be my destruction, I fear.

Dear Renée, do you remember how, in your outbursts of girlish devotion, you would say to me, as we sat under the vine-covered arbor of the convent garden, "I love you so, Louise, that if God appeared to me in a vision, I would pray Him that all the sorrows of life might be mine, and all the joy yours. I burn to suffer for you?" Now, darling, the day has come when I take up your prayer, imploring heaven to grant you a share in my happiness.

I must tell you my idea. I have a shrewd notion that you are hatching ambitious plans under the name of Louis de l'Estorade. Very good; get him elected deputy at the approaching election, for he will be very nearly forty then; and as the Chamber does not meet till six months later, he will have just attained the age necessary to qualify for a seat. You will come to Paris—there, isn't that enough? My father, and the friends I shall have made by that time, will learn to know and admire you; and if your father-in-law will agree to found a family, we will get the title of comte for Louis. That is something at least! And we shall be together.

XXVIII.

RENÉE DE L'ESTORADE TO LOUISE DE MACUMER.

December, 1825.

My thrice happy Louise, your letter made me dizzy. For a few moments I held it in my listless hands, while a tear or two sparkled on it in the setting sun. I was alone beneath the small barren rock where I have had a seat placed; far off, like a lance of steel, the Mediterranean shone. The seat is shaded by aromatic shrubs, and I have had a very large jessamine, some honeysuckle, and Spanish broom transplanted there, so that some day the rock will be entirely covered with climbing plants. The wild vine has already taken root there. But winter draws near, and all this greenery is faded like a piece of old tapestry. In this spot I am never molested; it is understood that here I wish to be alone. It is named Louise's seat—a proof, is it not, that even in solitude I am not alone here?

If I tell you all these details, to you so paltry, and try to describe the vision of green with which my prophetic gaze clothes this bare rock—on whose top some freak of nature has set up a magnificent parasol pine—it is because in all this I have found an emblem to which I cling.

It was while your blessed lot was filling me with joy and—must I confess it?—with bitter envy too, that I felt the first movement of my child within, and this mystery of physical life reacted upon the inner recesses of my soul. This indefinable sensation, which partakes of the nature at once of a warning, a delight, a pain, a promise, and a fulfillment; this joy, which is mine alone, unshared by mortal, this wonder of wonders, has whispered to me that one day this rock shall be a carpet of flowers, resounding to the merry laughter of children, that I shall at last be blessed among women, and from my womb shall spring forth fountains of life. Now I know what I have lived for! Thus the first certainty of bearing within me another life brought healing to my wounds. A mighty joy that beggars description has crowned for me those long days of sacrifice, in which Louis had already found his joy.

Self-sacrifice! I said to myself, how far does it excel passion! What pleasure has roots so deep as one which is not personal but creative? Is not the spirit of devotion a power mightier than any of its results? Is it not that mysterious, tireless divinity, who hides beneath innumerable spheres in an unexplored centre, through which all worlds in turn must pass? Sacrifice, solitary and secret, rich in pleasures only tasted in silence, at which none can guess, and no profane eye has ever seen; sacrifice—devotion—jealous God and tyrant, God of strength and victory, exhaustless spring which, partaking of the very essence of all that exists, can by no expenditure be drained below its own level; sacrifice, there is the keynote of my life.

For you, Louise, love is but the reflex of Félipe's passion; the life which I shed upon my little ones will come back to me in ever-growing fullness. The plenty of your golden harvest will pass; mine, though late, will be but the more enduring, for each hour will see it renewed. Love may be the fairest gem which society has filched from nature; but what is motherhood save nature in her most gladsome mood? A smile has dried my tears. Love makes my Louis happy, but marriage has made me a mother, and who shall say I am not happy too?

Selfishness is dead within me.

18

With slow steps, then, I returned to my white grange, with its green blinds, to write you these thoughts.

So it is, darling, that the most marvelous, and yet the simplest, process of nature has been going on in me for five months ; and yet—in your ear let me whisper it—so far it agitates neither my heart nor my understanding. I see all around me happy; the grandfather-to-be has become a child again, trespassing on the grandchild's place ; the father wears a grave and anxious look ; they are all most attentive to me, all talk of the happiness of being a mother. Alas ! I alone remain cold, and I dare not tell you how dead I am to all emotion, though I fib a little in order not to dampen the general satisfaction. But with you I may be frank ; and I confess that, at my present stage, motherhood is a mere affair of the imagination.

Louis was to the full as much surprised as I was by my pregnancy. Does not this show how little, unless by his impatient wishes, the father counts for in this matter? Chance, my dear, is the sovereign deity of maternity. My doctor, while maintaining that this accident works in harmony with nature, does not deny that children who are the fruit of passionate love are bound to be richly endowed both physically and mentally, and that often the happiness which shone like a radiant star over their conception seems to watch over them through life. It may be then, Louise, that motherhood reserves joys for you which I can never know. It may be that the feeling of a mother for the child of a man whom she adores, as you adore Félipe, is different from that with which she regards the offspring of reason, duty, or desperation !

Thoughts such as these, which I bury in my inmost heart, add to the preoccupation only natural to a woman soon to be a mother. And yet, as no family can exist without children, I long to speed the moment from which the joys of Family, where alone I am to find my life, shall date their beginning. At present I live a life all expectation and mystery, except for a sickening physical discomfort, which no doubt serves to prepare a woman for suffering of a different kind. I watch my symptoms; and in spite of the attentions and thoughtful care with which Louis' anxiety surrounds me, I am conscious of a vague uneasiness, mingled with nausea, the distaste for food, and abnormal longings common to my condition. If I am to speak candidly, I must confess, at the risk of disgusting you with the whole business, to an incomprehensible craving for rotten fruit. My husband goes to Marseilles to fetch the finest oranges the world produces—from Malta, Portugal, Corsica—and these I don't touch. Then I hurry there myself, sometimes on foot, and in a little back street, running down to the harbor, close to the Town Hall, I find wretched, half-putrid oranges, two for a sou, which I devour eagerly. The bluish, greenish shades on the moldy parts sparkle like diamonds in my eyes, they are flowers to me; I forget the putrid odor, and find them delicious, with a piquant flavor, and stimulating as wine. My dear, they are the first love of my life! Your passion for Félipe is nothing to this! Sometimes I even slip out secretly and fly to Marseilles, full of passionate longings, which grow more intense as I draw near the street. I tremble lest the woman should be sold out of rotten oranges; I pounce on them and devour them as I stand. It seems to me an ambrosial food, and yet I have seen Louis turn aside unable to bear the smell. Then came to my mind the ghastly words of Obermann in his gloomy elegy, which I wish I had never read: "Roots slake their thirst in foulest streams." Since I took to this diet, the sickness has ceased, and I feel much stronger. This depravity of taste must have a meaning, for it seems to be part of a natural process and to be common to most women, sometimes going to most extravagant lengths.

When my situation is more marked, I shall not go beyond the grounds, for I should not like to be seen under these circumstances. I have the greatest curiosity to know at what precise moment the sense of motherhood begins. It cannot possibly be in the midst of frightful suffering, the very thought of which makes me shudder.

Farewell, favorite of fortune! Farewell, my friend, in whom I live again, and through whom I am able to picture to myself this brave love, this jealousy all on fire at a look, these whisperings in the ear, these joys which create for women, as it were, a new atmosphere, a new daylight, fresh life! Ah! pet, I too understand love. Don't weary of telling me everything. Keep faithful to our bond. I promise, in my turn, to spare you nothing.

Nay—to conclude in all seriousness—I will not conceal from you that, on reading your letter a second time, I was seized with a dread which I could not shake off. This superb love seems like a challenge to Providence. Will not the sovereign master of this earth, Calamity, take umbrage if no place be left for him at your feast? What mighty edifice of fortune has he not overthrown? Oh! Louise, forget not, in all this happiness, your prayers to God. Do good, be kind and merciful; let your moderation, if it may be, avert disaster. Religion has meant much more to me since I left the convent and since my marriage; but your Paris news contains no mention of it. In your glorification of Félipe, it seems to me you reverse the saying, and invoke God less than His saint.

But, after all, this panic is only excess of affection. You go to church together, I do not doubt, and do good in secret. The close of this letter will seem to you very provincial, I expect, but think of the too eager friendship which prompts these fears—a friendship of the type of La Fontaine's, which takes alarm at dreams, at half-formed, misty ideas. You deserve to be happy, since, through it all, you still think of me, no less than I think of you, in my monotonous life, which, though it lacks color, is yet not empty, and, if uneventful, is not unfruitful. And so, God bless you!

XXIX.

M. DE L'ESTORADE TO THE BARONNE DE MACUMER.

December, 1825.

MADAME:—It is the desire of my wife that you should not learn first from the formal announcement, a *billet de faire part,* of an event which has filled us with much happiness. Renée has just given birth to a fine boy, whose baptism we are postponing till your return to Chantepleurs. Renée and I both earnestly hope that you may push on as far as La Crampade, and will consent to act as godmother to our firstborn. In this hope, I have had him placed on the register under the name of Armand-Louis de l'Estorade.

Our dear Renée suffered much, but bore it with angelic patience. You, who know her, will easily understand that the assurance of bringing happiness to us all supported her through this trying apprenticeship to motherhood.

Without indulging in the more or less ludicrous exaggerations to which the novel sensation of being a father is apt to give rise, I may tell you that little Armand is a beautiful infant, and you will have no difficulty in believing it when I add that he has Renée's features and eyes. So far, at least, this gives proof of intelligence!

The physician and accoucheur assure us that Renée is now quite out of danger; and as she is proving an admirable nurse —nature has endowed her so generously!—my father and I are able to give free rein to our joy. Madame, may I be allowed to express the hope that this happiness, so vivid and intense, which has brought fresh life into our house, and has changed the face of existence for my dear wife, may ere long be yours?

Renée has had a suite of rooms prepared, and I only wish I could make them worthy of our guests. But the cordial friendliness of the reception which awaits you may perhaps atone for any lack of splendor.

I have heard from Renée, madame, of your kind thought in regard to us, and I take this opportunity of thanking you for it, the more gladly because nothing could now be more appropriate. The birth of a grandson has reconciled my father to sacrifices which bear hardly on an old man. He has just bought two estates, and La Crampade is now a property with an annual rental of thirty thousand francs. My father intends asking the King's permission to form an entailed estate of it; and if you are good enough to get for him instead of me the title of which you spoke in your last letter, you will have already done much for your godson.

For my part, I shall carry out your suggestion solely with the object of bringing you and Renée together during the sessions of the Chamber. I am working hard with the view of becoming what is called a specialist. But nothing could give me greater encouragement in my labors than the thought that you will take an interest in my little Armand. Come, then, we beg of you, and with your beauty and your grace, your playful fancy and your noble soul, enact the part of good fairy to my son and heir. You will thus, madame, add undying gratitude to the respectful affection of

Your very humble, obedient servant,
Louis de l'Estorade.

XXX.

LOUISE DE MACUMER TO RENÉE DE L'ESTORADE.

January, 1826.

Macumer has just wakened me, darling, with your husband's letter. First and foremost—Yes. We shall be going to Chantepleurs about the end of April. To me it will be a piling up of pleasure to travel, to see you, and to be the godmother of your first child. I must, please, have Macumer for godfather. To take part in a ceremony of the church with another as my partner would be hateful to me. Ah! if you could see the look he gave me as I said this, you would know what store this angel of lovers sets on his wife!

"I am the more bent on our visiting La Crampade together, Félipe," I went on, "because I might have a child there. I too, you know, would be a mother, though, most surely, I should be terribly torn between a child and you. To begin with, if I saw any creature—were it even my own son—taking my place in your heart, I couldn't answer for the consequences. Medea may have been right after all. The Greeks had some good notions!"

And he laughed.

So, my sweetheart, you have the fruit without the flowers; I the flowers without the fruit. The contract in our lives still holds good. Between the two of us we have surely enough philosophy to find the moral of it some day. Bah! only ten months married! there's not much time lost. Too soon, you will admit, to give up hope.

We are leading a gay, yet far from empty life, as is the way with happy people. The days are never long enough for us. Society, seeing me in the trappings of a married woman, pronounces the Baronne de Macumer much prettier than Louise de Chaulieu; a happy love is a most becoming cosmetic. When Félipe and I drive along the Champs-Élysées in the bright sunshine of a crisp January day, beneath the trees, frosted with clusters of white stars, and face all Paris on the spot where last year we met with a gulf between us, the contrast calls up a thousand fancies. Suppose, after all, your last letter should be right in its forecast, and we are too presumptuous!

If I am ignorant of a mother's joys, you shall tell me about them; I will learn by sympathy. But my imagination can picture nothing to equal the rapture of love. You will laugh at my extravagance ; but, I assure you, that a dozen times in as many months the longing has seized me to die at thirty, while life was still untarnished, amidst the roses of love, in the embrace of passion. To bid farewell to the feast at its brightest, before disappointment has come, having lived in this sunshine and celestial air, and well-nigh spent myself in love, not a leaf dropped from my crown, not an illusion perished in my heart, what a dream is there ! Think what it would be to bear about a young heart in an aged body, to see only cold, dumb faces around me, where even strangers used to smile ; to be a worthy matron ! Can hell have a worse torture?

On this very subject, in fact, Félipe and I have had our first quarrel. I contended that he ought to have sufficient moral strength to kill me in my sleep when I have reached thirty, so that I might pass from one dream to another. The wretch declined. I threatened to leave him alone in the world, and, poor child, he turned white as a sheet. My dear, this distinguished statesman is neither more nor less than a baby in my hands. It is incredible what youth and simplicity he contrived to hide away. Now that I allow myself to think aloud with him, as I do with you, and have no secrets from him, we are always amazing each other.

Dear Renée, Félipe and Louise, the pair of lovers, want to send a present to the young mother. We would like to get something that would give you pleasure, and we don't share the vulgar taste for "surprises;" so tell me quite frankly, please, what you would like. It ought to be something which would recall us to you in a pleasant way, something which you will use every day, and which won't wear out with use. The meal which with us is most cheerful and friendly is lunch, and therefore the idea occurred to me of a special luncheon service, ornamented with figures of babies. If you approve of this, let me know at once ; for it will have to be ordered immediately if we are to bring it. Parisian artists are gentlemen of far too much importance to be hurried, they are like the sluggard king. This will be my offering to Lucina.

Farewell, dear wet-nurse. May all a mother's delights be yours! I await with impatience your first letter, which will tell me all about it, I hope. Some of the details in your husband's letter went to my heart. Poor Renée, a mother has a heavy price to pay. I will tell my godson how dearly he must love you.

A thousand kisses, *mon ange.*

XXXI.

RENÉE DE L'ESTORADE TO LOUISE DE MACUMER.

It is nearly five months now since baby was born, and not once, dear heart, have I found a single moment for writing you. When you are a mother yourself, you will be more ready to excuse me than you are now; for you have punished me a little bit in making your own letters so few and far between. Do write, my darling! Tell me of your pleasures; lay on the ultramarine as brightly as you please. It will not hurt me, for I am happy now—happier than you can imagine.

I went in state to the parish church to hear the mass for recovery from childbirth, as is the custom in the old families of Provence. I was supported on either side by the two grand-fathers—Louis' father and my own. Never had I knelt before God with such a flood of gratitude in my heart. I have so much to tell you, so many feelings to describe, that I don't know where to begin; but from amidst these confused mem-ories, one rises distinctly, radiantly—that of my prayer in the church.

When I found myself transformed into a joyful mother, on the very spot where, as a girl, I had trembled for my future, it seemed to my fancy the Virgin on the altar bowed her head and pointed to the infant Christ, who smiled at me! My

heart full of pure and heavenly love, I held out little Armand
for the priest to bless and bathe, in anticipation of the regular
baptism to come later. But you will see us together then,
Armand and me.

My child—see how readily the word comes, and indeed
there is none sweeter to a mother's heart and mind or on her
lips—well, then, dear child, during the last two months I used
to drag myself wearily and heavily about the gardens, not
realizing yet how precious was the burden, spite of all the
discomforts it brought! I was haunted by forebodings so
gloomy and ghastly, that they got the better even of curiosity;
in vain did I reason with myself that no natural function
could be so very terrible, in vain did I picture the delights of
motherhood. My heart made no response even to the thought
of the little one, who announced himself by lively kicking.
That is a sensation, dear, which may be welcome when it is
familiar; but as a novelty, it is more strange than pleasing. I
speak for myself at least; you know I would never affect anything I did not really feel, and I look on my child as a gift
straight from heaven. For one who saw in it rather the image
of the man she loved, it might be different.

But enough of such sad thoughts, gone, I trust, forever.

When the crisis came, I summoned all my powers of resistance, and braced myself so well for suffering, that I bore the
horrible agony—so they tell me—quite marvelously. For
about an hour I sank into a sort of stupor, of the nature of a
dream. I seemed to myself then two beings—an outer cover-
ing racked and tortured by red-hot pincers, and a soul at
peace. In this strange state the pain formed itself into a sort
of halo hovering over me. A gigantic rose seemed to spring
out of my head and grow ever larger and larger, till it enfolded
me in its blood-red petals. The same color dyed the air
around, and everything I saw was blood-red. At last the
climax came, when soul and body seemed no longer able
to hold together; the spasms of pain gripped me like death

itself. I screamed aloud, and found fresh strength against this further torture. Suddenly this concert of hideous cries was overborne by a joyful sound—the shrill wail of the new-born infant. No words can describe that moment. It was as though the universe took part in my cries, when all at once the chorus of pain fell hushed before the child's feeble note.

They laid me back again in the large bed, and it felt like paradise to me, even in my extreme exhaustion. Three or four happy faces pointed through tears to the child. My dear, I was horrified.

"It's just like a little monkey!" I cried. "Are you really and truly certain it is a child?"

I fell back on my side, miserably disappointed at my first experience of motherly feeling.

"Don't worry, dear," said my mother, who had installed herself as nurse. "Why, you've got the finest baby in the world. You mustn't excite yourself; but give your whole mind now to turning yourself as much as possible into an animal, a milch cow, pasturing in the meadow."

I fell asleep then, fully resolved to let nature have her way.

Ah! my sweet, how heavenly it was to waken up from all the pain and haziness of the first days, when everything was still dim, uncomfortable, confused. A ray of light pierced the darkness; my heart and soul, my inner self—a self I had never known before—rent the envelope of gloomy suffering, as a flower bursts its calyx at the first warm kiss of the sun, at the moment when the little wretch fastened on my breast and sucked. Not even the sensation of the child's first cry was so exquisite as this. This is the dawn of motherhood, this is the *Fiat lux!*

Here is happiness, joy ineffable, though it comes not without pangs. Oh! my sweet jealous soul, how you will relish a delight which exists only for ourselves, the child, and God! For this tiny creature all knowledge is summed up in its mother's breast. This is the one bright spot in its world, toward which its puny strength goes forth. Its thoughts cluster round this spring of life, which it leaves only to sleep, and whither it returns on waking. Its lips have a sweetness beyond words, and their pressure is at once a pain and a delight, a delight which by very excess becomes pain, or a pain which culminates in delight. The sensation which rises from it, and which penetrates to the very core of my life, baffles all description. It seems a sort of centre whence a myriad joy-bearing rays gladden the heart and soul. To bear a child is nothing; to nourish it is birth renewed every hour.

Oh! Louise, there is no caress of lover with half the power of those little pink hands, as they stray about, seeking whereby to lay hold on life. And the infant glances, now turned upon the breast, now raised to meet our own! What dreams come to us as we watch the clinging nursling! All our powers, whether of mind or body, are at its service; for it we breathe and think, in it our longings are more than satisfied! The sweet sensation of warmth at the heart, which the sound of his first cry brought to me—like the first ray of sunshine on the earth—came again as I felt the milk flow into his mouth, again as his eyes met mine, and at this moment I have felt it once more as his first smile gave token of a mind working within—for he has laughed, my dear! A laugh, a glance, a bite, a cry—four miracles of gladness which go straight to the heart and strike chords that respond to no other touch. A child is tied to our heartstrings, as the spheres are linked to their creator; we cannot think of God except as a mother's heart writ large. There is nothing visible, nothing perceptible in conception, nor even in pregnancy; it is only in the act of nursing that a woman realizes her motherhood in visible and tangible fashion; it is a joy of every moment. The milk becomes flesh before our eyes; it blossoms into the tips of those delicate flower-like fingers; it expands in tender, transparent nails; it spins the silky tresses; it kicks in the little feet. Oh! those baby feet, how plainly they talk to us! In them the child finds its first language.

Yes, Louise, to feed, to suckle! is a miracle of transformation going on before one's bewildered eyes. Those cries, they go to your heart and not your ears; those smiling eyes and lips, those plunging feet, they speak in words which could not be plainer if God traced them before you in letters of fire! What else is there in the world to care about? The father? Why, you could kill him if he dreamed of waking the baby! Just as the child is the world to us, so do we stand alone in the world for the child. The sweet consciousness of a common life is ample recompense for all the trouble and suffering—for suffering there is. Heaven save you, Louise, from ever knowing the maddening agony of a broken breast which gapes afresh with every pressure of the rosy lips, and is so hard to heal—the heaviest tax perhaps imposed on beauty. For know, Louise, and beware! it visits only a fair and delicate skin.

My little ape has in five months developed into the prettiest darling that ever mother bathed in tears of joy, washed, brushed, combed, and made smart; for God knows what unwearied care we lavish upon these tender blossoms! So my monkey has ceased to exist, and behold in his stead a "baby," as my English nurse calls him, a regular pink-and-white baby. He cries very little too now, for he is conscious of the love bestowed on him; indeed, I hardly ever leave him, and I strive to wrap him around in the atmosphere of my love.

Dear, I have a feeling now for Louis which is not love, but which ought to be the crown of a woman's love where it exists. Nay, I am not sure whether this tender fondness, this unselfish gratitude, is not superior to love. From all that you have told me of it, dear pet, I gather that love has something terribly earthly about it, whilst a strain of holy piety purifies the affection a happy mother feels for the author of her far-

reaching and enduring joys. A mother's happiness is like a
beacon, lighting up the future but reflected also on the past in
the guise of fond memories.

The old l'Estorade and his son have, moreover, redoubled
their devotion to me ; I am like a new person to them. Every
time they see me and speak to me, it is with a fresh holiday
joy, which touches me deeply. The grandfather has, I verily
believe, turned child again ; he looks at me admiringly, and
the first time I came down to lunch he was moved to tears to
see me eating and suckling his grandson. The moisture in
these dry old eyes, generally expressive only of avarice, was a
wonderful comfort to me. I felt that the good soul entered
into my joy.

As for Louis, he would shout aloud to the trees and stones
of the highway that he has a son ; and he spends whole hours
watching your sleeping godson. He does not know, he says,
when he will grow used to it. These extravagant expressions
of delight show me how great must have been their fears and
apprehensions beforehand. Louis has confided in me that he
had believed himself condemned to be childless. Poor fellow !
he has all at once developed very much, and he works even
harder than he did. The father in him has quickened his
ambition.

For myself, dear soul, I grow happier and happier every
moment. Each hour creates a fresh tie between the mother
and her infant. The very nature of my feelings proves to me
that they are normal, permanent, and indestructible ; whereas
I shrewdly suspect love, for instance, of being intermittent.
Certainly it is not the same at all moments, the flowers which
it weaves into the web of life are not all of equal brightness ;
love, in short, can and must decline. But a mother's love
has no ebb-tide to fear ; rather it grows with the growth of the
child's needs, and strengthens with its strength. Is it not at
once a passion, a natural craving, a feeling, a duty, a necessity, a joy ? Yes, darling, here is woman's true sphere. Here

the passion for self-sacrifice can expend itself, and no jealousy intrudes.

Here, too, is perhaps the single point on which society and nature are at one. Society, in this matter, enforces the dictates of nature, strengthening the maternal instinct by adding to it family spirit and the desire of perpetuating a name, a race, an estate. How tenderly must not a woman cherish the child who has been the first to open up to her these joys, the first to call forth the energies of her nature and to instruct her in the grand art of motherhood! The right of the eldest, which in the earliest times formed a part of the natural order and was lost in the origins of society, ought never, in my opinion, to have been questioned. Ah! how much a mother learns from her child! The constant protection of a helpless being forces us to so strict an alliance with virtue that a woman never shows to full advantage except as a mother. Then alone can her character expand in the fulfillment of all life's duties and the enjoyment of all its pleasures. A woman who is not a mother is maimed and incomplete. Hasten, then, my sweetest, to fulfill your mission. Your present happiness will then be multiplied by the wealth of my delights.

23*d*.

I had to tear myself from you because your godson was crying. I can hear his cry from the bottom of the garden. But I would not let this go without a word of farewell. I have just been reading over what I have said, and am horrified to see how vulgar are the feelings expressed! What I feel, every mother, alas! since the beginning must have felt, I suppose, in the same way, and put into the same words. You will laugh at me, as we do at the naïve father who dilates on the beauty and cleverness of his (of course) quite exceptional offspring. But the refrain of my letter, darling, is this, and I repeat it: I am as happy now as I used to be miserable. This grange—and is it not going to be an estate, a family

property?—has become my land of promise. The desert is
past and over. A thousand loves, darling pet. Write to me,
for now I can read without a tear the tale of your happy love.
Farewell.

XXXII.

MME. DE MACUMER TO MME. DE L'ESTORADE.

March, 1826.

Do you know, dear, that it is more than three months since
I have written you or heard from you? I am the more
guilty of the two, for I did not reply to your last, but you
don't stand on punctilio surely?

Macumer and I have taken your silence for consent as
regards the baby-wreathed luncheon service, and the little
cherubs are starting this morning for Marseilles. It took six
months to carry out the design. And so, when Félipe asked
me to come and see the service before it was packed, I suddenly waked up to the fact that we had not interchanged a
word since the letter of yours which gave me an insight into
a mother's heart.

My sweet, it is this terrible Paris—there's my excuse.
What, pray, is yours? Oh! what a whirlpool is society!
Didn't I tell you once that in Paris one must be as the Par-
isians?. Society there drives out all sentiment; it lays an
embargo on your time; and unless you are very careful, soon
eats away your heart altogether. What an amazing masterpiece is the character of Célimène in Molière's " Le Misanthrope!" She is the society woman, not only of Louis
XIV.'s time, but of our own, and of all epochs.

Where should I be but for my breastplate—the love I bear
Félipe? This very morning I told him, as the outcome of
these reflections, that he was my salvation. If my evenings
are a continuous round of parties, balls, concerts, and theatres,

at night my heart expands again, and is healed of the wounds received in the world by the delights of the passionate love which await my return.

I dine at home only when we have friends, so-called, with us, and spend the afternoon there only on my day, for I have a day now—Wednesday—for receiving. I have entered the lists with Mmes. d'Espard and de Maufrigneuse, and with the old Duchesse de Lenoncourt, and my house has the reputation of being a very lively one. I allowed myself to become the fashion, because I saw how much pleasure my success gave Félipe. My mornings are his; from four in the afternoon till two in the morning I belong to Paris. Macumer makes an admirable host, witty and dignified, perfect in courtesy, and with an air of real distinction. No woman could help loving such a husband even if she had chosen him without consulting her heart.

My father and mother have left for Madrid. Louis XVIII. being out of the way, the duchess had no difficulty in obtaining from our good-natured Charles X. the appointment of her fascinating poet; so he is carried off in the capacity of attaché.

My brother, the Duc de Rhétoré, deigns to recognize me as a person of mark. As for my younger brother, the Comte de Chaulieu, this dandy warrior owes me everlasting gratitude. Before my father left, he spent my fortune in acquiring for the count an estate of forty thousand francs a year, entailed on the title, and his marriage with Mlle. de Mortsauf, an heiress from Touraine, is definitely arranged. The King, in order to preserve the name and titles of the de Lenoncourt and de Givry families from extinction, is to confer these, together with the armorial bearings, by patent on my brother. Certainly it would never have done to allow these two fine names and their splendid motto: *Faciem semper monstramus,* to perish. Mlle. de Mortsauf, who is granddaughter and sole heiress of the Duc de Lenoncourt-Givry, will, it is said, in-

19

herit altogether more than one hundred thousand livres a year. The only stipulation my father has made is that the de Chaulieu arms should appear in the centre of the de Lenoncourt escutcheon. Thus my brother will be Duc de Lenoncourt. The young de Mortsauf, to whom everything would otherwise go, is in the last stage of consumption; his death is looked for every day. The marriage will take place next winter when the family are out of mourning. I am told that I shall have a charming sister-in-law in Mlle. de Mortsauf.

So you see that my father's reasoning is justified. The outcome of it all has won me many compliments, and my marriage is explained to everybody's satisfaction. To complete our success, the Prince de Talleyrand, out of affection for my grandmother, is showing himself a warm friend to Macumer. Society, which began by criticising me, has now passed to cordial admiration.

In short, I now reign a queen where, barely two years ago, I was an insignificant item. Macumer finds himself the object of universal envy, as the husband of "the most charming woman in Paris." At least a score of women, as you know, are always in that proud position. Men murmur sweet things in my ear, or content themselves with greedy glances. This chorus of longing and admiration is so soothing to one's vanity, that I confess I begin to understand the unconscionable price women are ready to pay for such frail and precarious privileges. A triumph of this kind is like strong wine to vanity, self-love, and all the self-regarding feelings. To pose perpetually as a divinity is a draught so potent in its intoxicating effects that I am no longer surprised to see women grow selfish, callous, and frivolous in the heart of this adoration. The fumes of society mount to the head. You lavish the wealth of your soul and spirit, the treasures of your time, the noblest efforts of your will, upon a crowd of people who repay you in smiles and jealousy. The false coin of their pretty speeches, compliments, and flattery is the only return they give for the solid gold of your courage and sacrifices, and all the thought that must go to keep up without flagging the standard of beauty, dress, sparkling talk, and general affability. You are perfectly aware how much it costs, and that the whole thing is a fraud, but you cannot keep out of the vortex.

Ah! my sweet dear, how one craves for a real friend! How precious to me are the love and devotion of Félipe, and how my heart goes out to you! Joyfully indeed are we preparing for our move to Chantepleurs, where we can rest from the comedy of the Rue du Bac and of the Paris drawing-rooms. Having just read your letter again, I feel that I cannot better describe this demoniac paradise than by saying that no woman of fashion in Paris can possibly be a good mother.

Good-by, then, for a short time, dear one. We shall stay at Chantepleurs only a week at most, and shall be with you about May 10th. So we are actually to meet again after more than two years! What changes since then! Here we are, both matrons, both in our promised land—I of love, you of motherhood.

If I have not written, my sweetest, it is not because I have forgotten you. And what of the monkey godson? Is he still pretty and a credit to me? He must be more than nine months old now. I should dearly like to be present when he makes his first steps upon this earth; but Macumer tells me that even precocious infants hardly walk at ten months.

We shall have some good gossiping talks there, and "cut pinafores," as the Blois folks say. I shall see, too, whether childbearing "spoils the pattern," as they say.

P. S.—If you deign to reply from your maternal heights, address to Chantepleurs. I am just off.

XXXIII.

MME. DE L'ESTORADE TO MME. DE MACUMER.

My Child:—If ever you become a mother, you will find out that it is impossible to write letters during the first two months of your nursing. Mary, my English nurse, and I are both quite tired out. It is true I had not told you that I was determined to do everything myself. Before the event I had with my own fingers sewn the baby clothes and embroidered and edged with lace the little caps. I am a slave, my pet, a slave day and night.

To begin with, Master Armand-Louis takes his meals when it pleases him, and that is always; then he has often to be changed, washed, and dressed. His mother is so fond of watching him asleep, of singing songs to him, of walking him about in her arms on a fine day, that she has little time left to attend to herself. In short, what society has been to you, my child—our child—has been to me!

I cannot tell you how full and rich my life has become, and I long for your coming that you may see for yourself. The only thing is, I am afraid he will soon be teething, and that you will find a peevish, crying baby. So far he has not cried much, for I am always at hand. Babies only cry when their wants are not understood, and I am constantly on the look-out for his. Oh! my sweet, my heart has opened up so wide, while you allow yours to shrink and shrivel at the bidding of society! I look for your coming with all a hermit's longing. I want so much to know what you think of l'Estorade, just as you no doubt are curious for my opinion of Macumer.

Write to me from your last resting-place. The gentlemen want to go and meet our distinguished guests. Come, Queen of Paris, come to our humble grange, where love at least will greet you!

XXXIV.

MME. DE MACUMER TO THE VICOMTESSE DE L'ESTORADE.

April, 1826.

The name on this address will tell you, dear, that my petition has been granted. Your father-in-law is now Comte de l'Estorade. I would not leave Paris till I had obtained the gratification of your wishes, and I am writing in the presence of the keeper of the seals, who has come to tell me that the patent is signed.

Good-by for a short time!

XXXV.

THE SAME TO THE SAME.

MARSEILLES, *July.*

I am ashamed to think how my sudden flight from La Crampade will have taken you by surprise. But since I am above all honest, and since I love you not one bit the less, I shall tell you the truth in four words: I am horribly jealous!

Félipe's eyes were too often on you. You used to have little talks together at the foot of your rock, which were a torture to me; and I was fast becoming irritable and unlike myself. Your truly Spanish beauty could not fail to recall to him his native land, and along with it Marie Hérédia, and I can be jealous of the past too. Your magnificent black hair, your lovely dark eyes, your brow, where the peaceful joy of motherhood stands out radiant against the shadows which tell of past suffering, the freshness of your southern skin, far fairer than that of a blonde like me, the splendid lines of your figure, the breasts, on which my godson hangs, peeping through the lace like some luscious fruit—all this stabbed me in the eyes and in the heart. In vain did I stick blue cornflowers in my curls, in vain set off with cherry-colored ribbons the tameness of my pale locks, everything looked washed out when Renée appeared—a Renée so unlike the one I expected to find in your oasis.

Then Félipe made too much of the child, whom I found myself beginning to hate. Yes, I confess it, that exuberance of life which fills your house, making it gay with shouts and laughter—I wanted it for myself. I read a regret in Macumer's eyes, and, unknown to him, I cried over it two whole nights. I was miserable in your house. You are too beautiful as a woman, too triumphant as a mother, for me to endure your company.

Ah! you complained of your lot. Hypocrite! What would you have? L'Estorade is most presentable; he talks well; he has fine eyes; and his black hair, dashed with white, is very becoming; his southern manners, too, have something attractive about them. As far as I can make out, he will, sooner or later, be elected deputy for the Bouches-du-Rhône; in the Chamber he is sure to come to the front, for you can always count on me to promote your interests. The sufferings of his exile have given him that calm and dignified air which goes half-way, in my opinion, to make a statesman. For the whole art of politics, dear, seems to me to consist in looking grave. At this rate, Macumer, as I told him, ought certainly to have a high position in the State.

And so, having completely satisfied myself of your happiness, I fly off contented to my dear Chantepleurs, where Félipe must really achieve his aspirations. I have made up my mind not to receive you there without a fine baby at my breast to match yours.

Oh! I know very well I deserve all the epithets you can hurl at me. I am a fool, a wretch, an idiot. Alas! that is just what jealousy means. I am not vexed with you, but I was miserable, and you will forgive me for escaping from my misery. Two days more, and I should have made an exhibition of myself; yes, there would have been an outbreak of " bad form."

But in spite of the rage gnawing at my heart, I am glad to have come, glad to have seen you in the pride of your beautiful motherhood, my friend still, as I remain yours in all the absorption of my love. Why, even here at Marseilles, only a step from your door, I begin to feel proud of you and of the splendid mother that you will make.

How well you judged your vocation! You seem to me born for the part of mother rather than of lover, exactly as the reverse is true of me. There are women capable of neither, hard-favored or silly women. A good mother and a passionately loving wife have this in common, that they both need intelligence and discretion ever at hand, and an unfailing command of every womanly art and grace. Oh! I watched you well; need I add, sly puss, that I admired you too? Your children will be happy, but not spoilt, with your tenderness lapping them around and the clear light of your reason playing softly on them.

Tell Louis the truth about my going away, but find some decent excuse for your father-in-law, who seems to act as steward for the establishment; and be careful to do the same for your family—a true Provençal version of the Harlowe family. Félipe does not yet know why I left, and he will never know. If he asks, I shall contrive to find some colorable pretext, probably that you were jealous of me! Forgive me this little conventional fib.

Good-by. I write in haste, as I want you to get this at lunch-time; and the postillion, who has undertaken to convey it to you, is here refreshing himself while he waits.

Many kisses to my dear little godson. Be sure you come to Chantepleurs in October. I shall be alone there all the time that Macumer is away in Sardinia, where he is designing

great improvements in his estate.   At least that is his plan for
the moment, and his pet vanity consists in having a plan.
Then he feels that he has a will of his own, and this makes
him very uneasy when he unfolds it to me.   Good-by!

XXXVI.

THE VICOMTESSE DE L'ESTORADE TO THE BARONNE DE MACUMER.

DEAR:—No words can express the astonishment of all our
party when, at luncheon, we were told that you had both
gone, and, above all, when the postillion who took you to
Marseilles handed me your mad letter.   Why, naughty child,
it was your happiness, and nothing else, that made the theme
of those talks below the rock, on the "Louise." seat, and you
had not the faintest justification for objecting to them.
Ingrata! My sentence on you is that you return here at my
first summons.   In that horrid letter, scribbled on the inn
paper, you did not tell me what would be your next stopping
place; so I must address this to Chantepleurs.

  Listen to me, dear sister of my heart.   Know, first, that
my mind is set on your happiness.   Your husband, dear
Louise, commands respect, not only by his natural gravity
and dignified expression, but also because he somehow im-
presses one with the depth of his mind and thoughts.   Add
to this the splendid power revealed in his piquant plainness
and in the fire of his velvet eyes; and you will understand
that it was some little time before I could meet him on those
easy terms which are almost necessary for intimate conversation.   Further, this man has been prime minister, and he
idolizes you; whence it follows that he must be a profound
dissembler.   To fish up secrets, therefore, from the rocky
caverns of this diplomatic soul is a work demanding a skillful
hand no less than a ready brain.   Nevertheless, I succeeded

at last, without rousing my victim's suspicions, in discovering many things of which you, my pet, have no conception.

You know that, between us two, my part is rather that of reason, yours of imagination : I personify sober duty, you reckless love. It has pleased fate to continue in our lives this contrast in character which was imperceptible to all except ourselves. I am a simple country viscountess, very ambitious, and making it her task to lead her family on the road to prosperity. On the other hand, Macumer, late Duc de Soria, has a name in the world, and you, a duchess by right, reign in Paris, where reigning is no easy matter even for kings. You have a considerable fortune, which will be doubled if Macumer carries out his projects for developing his great estates in Sardinia, the resources of which are matter of common talk at Marseilles. Deny, if you can, that if either has a right to be jealous, it is not you. But, thank God, we have both hearts generous enough to place our friendship beyond reach of such vulgar pettiness.

I know you, dear ; I know that, ere now, you are ashamed of having fled. But don't suppose that your flight will save you from a single word of the discourse which I had prepared for your benefit to-day beneath the rock. Read carefully then, I beg of you, what I say, for it concerns you even more closely than Macumer, though he also enters largely into my sermon.

Firstly, my dear, you do not love him. Before two years are over, you will be sick of adoration. You will never look on Félipe as a husband ; to you he will always be the lover whom you can play with, for that is how all women treat their lovers. You do not look up to him, or reverence, or worship nim as a woman should the god of her idolatry. You see, I have made a study of love, my sweet, and more than once have I taken soundings in the depths of my own heart. Now, as the result of a careful diagnosis of your case, I can say with confidence, this is not love.

Yes, dear Queen of Paris, you cannot escape the destiny of all queens. The day will come when you will long to be treated as a light-o'-love, to be mastered and swept off your feet by a strong man, one who will not prostrate himself in adoration before you, but will seize your arm roughly in a fit of jealousy. Macumer loves you too fondly ever to be able either to resist you or find fault with you. A single glance from you, a single coaxing word, would melt his sternest resolution. Sooner or later, you will learn to scorn this excessive devotion. He spoilt you, alas! just as I used to spoil you at the convent, for you are a most bewitching woman, and there is no escaping your siren-like charms.

Worse than all, you are candid, and it often happens that our happiness depends on certain social hypocrisies to which you will never stoop. For instance, society will not tolerate a frank display of the wife's power over her husband. The convention is that a man must no more show himself the lover of his wife, however passionately he adores her, than a married woman may play the part of a mistress. This rule you both disregard.

In the first place, my child, from what you have yourself told me, it is clear that the one unpardonable sin in society is to be happy. If happiness exists, no one must know of it. But this is a small point. What seems to me important is that the perfect equality which reigns between lovers ought never to appear in the case of husband and wife, under pain of undermining the whole fabric of society and entailing terrible disasters. If it is painful to see a man whom nature has made a nonenity, how much worse is the spectacle of a man of parts brought to that position? Before very long you will have reduced Macumer to the mere shadow of a man. He will cease to have a will and character of his own, and become mere clay in your hands. You will have so completely moulded him to your likeness that your household will consist of only one person instead of two, and that one neces-

sarily imperfect. You will regret it bitterly; but when at
last you deign to open your eyes, the evil will be past cure.
Do what we will, women do not, and never will, possess the
qualities which are characteristic of men, and these qualities
are absolutely indispensable to family life. Already Macumer,
blinded though he is, has a dim foreshadowing of this future;
he feels himself less a man through his love. His visit to
Sardinia is a proof to me that he hopes by this temporary
separation to succeed in recovering his old self.

You never scruple to use the power which his love has
placed in your hand. Your position of vantage may be read
in a gesture, a look, a tone. Oh! darling, how truly are you
the mad wanton your mother called you! You do not question, I fancy, that I am greatly Louis' superior. Well, I
would ask you, have you ever heard me contradict him? Am
I not always, in the presence of others, the wife who respects
in him the authority of the family? Hypocrisy! you will say.
Well, listen to me. It is true that if I want to give him
any advice which I think may be of use to him, I wait for the
quiet and seclusion of our bedroom to explain what I think
and wish; but, I assure you, sweetheart, that even there I
never arrogate to myself the place of mentor. If I did not
remain in private the same submissive wife that I appear to
others, he would lose confidence in himself. Dear, the good
we do to others is spoilt unless we efface ourselves so completely that those we help have no sense of inferiority. There
is a wonderful sweetness in these hidden sacrifices, and what a
triumph for me in your unsuspecting praises of Louis! There
can be no doubt also that the happiness, the comfort, the
hope of the last two years have restored what misfortune,
hardship, solitude, and despondency had robbed him of.

This, then, is the sum-total of my observations. At the
present moment you love in Félipe, not your husband, but
yourself. There is truth in your father's words; concealed
by the spring flowers of your passion lies all a great lady's

selfishness. Ah! my child, how I must love you to speak such bitter truths!

Let me tell you, if you will promise never to breathe a word of this to the baron, the end of our talk. We had been singing your praises in every key, for he soon discovered that I loved you like a fondly cherished sister, and, having insensibly brought him to a confidential mood, I ventured to say—

"Louise has never yet had to struggle with life. She has been the spoilt child of fortune, and she might yet have to pay for this were you not there to act the part of father as well as lover."

"Ah! but is it possible?——" He broke off abruptly, like a man who sees himself on the edge of a precipice. But the exclamation was enough for me. No doubt, if you had stayed, he would have spoken more freely later.

My sweet, think of the day awaiting you when your husband's strength will be exhausted, when pleasure will have turned to satiety, and he sees himself, I will not say degraded, but shorn of his proper dignity before you. The stings of conscience will then waken a sort of remorse in him, all the more painful for you, because you will feel yourself responsible, and you will end by despising the man whom you have not accustomed yourself to respect. Remember, too, that scorn with a woman is only the earliest phase of hatred. You are too noble and generous, I know, ever to forget the sacrifices which Félipe has made for you; but what further sacrifices will be left for him to make when he has, so to speak, served up himself at the first banquet? Woe to the man, as to the woman, who has left no desire unsatisfied! All is over then. To our shame or our glory—the point is too nice for me to decide—it is of love alone that women are insatiable.

Oh! Louise, change yet, while there is still time. If you would only adopt the same course with Macumer that I have done with l'Estorade, you might rouse the sleeping lion in your husband, who is made of the stuff of heroes. One might almost say that you grudge him his greatness. Would you feel no pride in using your power for other ends than your own gratification, in awakening the genius of a gifted man, as I in raising to a higher level one of merely common parts?

Had you remained with us, I should still have written this letter, for in talking you might have cut me short or got the better of me with your sharp tongue. But I know that you will read this thoughtfully and weigh my warnings. Dear heart, you have everything in life to make you happy, do not spoil your chances; return to Paris, I entreat you, as soon as Macumer comes back. The engrossing claims of society, of which I complained, are necessary for both of you; otherwise you would spend your life in mutual self-absorption. A married woman ought not to be too lavish of herself. The mother of a family, who never gives her household an opportunity of missing her, runs the risk of palling on them. If I have several children, as I trust for my own sake I may, I assure you I shall make a point of reserving to myself certain hours which shall be held sacred; even to one's children one's presence should not be a matter of daily bread.

Farewell, my dear jealous soul! Do you know that many women would be highly flattered at having roused this passing pang in you? Alas! I can only mourn, for what is not mother in me is your dear friend. A thousand loves. Make what excuse you will for leaving; if you are not sure of Macumer, I *am* sure of Louis.

XXXVII.

THE BARONNE DE MACUMER TO THE VICOMTESSE DE L'ESTORADE.

GENOA.

MY BELOVED BEAUTY:—I was bitten with the fancy to see something of Italy, and I am delighted at having carried off Macumer, whose plans in regard to Sardinia are postponed.

This country is simply ravishing. The churches—above all, the chapels—have a seductive, bewitching air, which must make every female Protestant yearn after Catholicism. Macumer has been received with acclamation, and they are all delighted to have made an Italian of so distinguished a man. Félipe could have the Sardinian embassy at Paris if I cared about it, for I am made much of at Court.

If you write, address your letters to Florence. I have not time now to go into any details, but I will tell you the story of our travels whenever you come to Paris. We only remain here a week, and then go on to Florence, taking Leghorn on the way. We shall stay a month in Tuscany and a month at Naples, so as to reach Rome in November. Thence we return home by Venice, where we shall spend the first fortnight of December, and arrive in Paris, *via* Milan and Turin, for January.

Our journey is a perfect honeymoon; the sight of new places gives fresh light to our passion. Macumer did not know Italy at all, and we have begun with that splendid Cornice road, which might be the work of fairy architects.

Adieu, darling. Don't be angry if I don't write. It is impossible to get a minute to one's self in traveling; my whole time is taken up in seeing, admiring, and realizing my impressions. But not a word to you of these till memory has given them their proper atmosphere.

XXXVIII.

THE VICOMTESSE DE L'ESTORADE TO THE BARONNE DE MACUMER.

September.

MY DEAR LOUISE:—There is lying for you at Chantepleurs a full reply to the letter you wrote me from Marseilles. This honeymoon journey, so far from diminishing the fears I there expressed, makes me beg of you to get my letter sent on from Nivernais.

The Government, it is said, is resolved on dissolution. This is unlucky for the Crown, since the last session of this loyal Parliament would have been devoted to the passing of laws, essential to the consolidation of its power ; and it is not less so for us, as Louis will not be forty till the end of 1827. Fortunately, however, my father has agreed to stand, and he will resign his seat when the right moment arrives.

Your godson has found out how to walk without his god-mother's help. He is altogether delicious, and begins to make the prettiest little signs to me, which bring home to one that here is really a thinking being, not a mere animal or sucking machine. His smiles are full of meaning. I have been so successful in my profession of nurse that I shall wean Armand in December. A year at the breast is quite enough ; children who are suckled longer are said to grow stupid, and I am all for old-women sayings.

You must be making a tremendous sensation in Italy, my fair one with the golden locks. A thousand loves.

XXXIX.

THE BARONNE DE MACUMER TO THE VICOMTESSE DE L'ESTORADE.

Your atrocious letter has reached me here, the steward having forwarded it by my orders. Oh! Renée—— but I will spare you the outburst of my wounded feelings, and simply tell you the effect your letter produced.

We had just returned from a delightful reception given in our honor by the ambassador, where I appeared in all my glory, and Macumer was completely carried away in a frenzy of love which I could not describe. Then I read him your horrible answer to my letter, and I read it sobbing, at the risk of making a fright of myself. My dear Saracen fell at my feet, declaring that you raved. Then he carried me off to the balcony of the palace where we are staying, from which we have a view over part of the city; there he spoke to me words worthy of the magnificent moonlight scene which lay stretched before us. We both speak Italian now, and his love, told in that voluptuous tongue, so admirably adapted to the expression of passion, sounded in my ears like the most exquisite poetry. He swore that, even were you right in your predictions, he would not exchange for a lifetime a single one of our blessed nights and charming mornings. At this reckoning he has already lived a thousand years. He is content to have me for his mistress, and would claim no other title than that of lover. So proud and pleased is he to see himself every day the chosen of my heart, that were heaven to offer him the alternative between living as you would have us do for another thirty years with five children, and five years spent amid the dear roses of our love, he would not hesitate. He would take my love, such as it is, and death.

While he was whispering this in my ear, his arm round me, my head resting on his shoulder, the cries of a bat, surprised by an owl, disturbed us. This death-cry struck me with such terror that Félipe carried me half-fainting to my bed. But don't be alarmed! Though this augury of evil still resounds in my soul, I am quite myself this morning. As soon as I was up, I went to Félipe, and, kneeling before him, my eyes fixed on his, his hands clasped in mine, I said to him:

"My love, I am a child, and Renée may be right after all. It may be only your love that I love in you; but at least I can assure you that this is the one feeling of my heart, and that I love you as it is given me to love. But if there be aught in me, in my lightest thought or deed, which jars on your wishes or conception of me, I implore you to tell me, to say what it is. It will be a joy to me to hear you and to take your eyes as the guiding-stars of my life. Renée has frightened me, for she is a true friend."

Macumer could not find voice to reply, tears choked him.

I can thank you now, Renée. But for your letter I should not have known the depths of love in my noble, kingly Macumer. Rome is the city of love; it is there that passion should celebrate its feast, with art and religion as confederates.

At Venice we shall find the Duc and Duchesse de Soria. If you write, address now to Paris, for we shall leave Rome in three days. The ambassador's was a farewell party.

P. S.—Dear, silly child, your letter only shows that you knew nothing of love, except theoretically. Learn then that love is a quickening force which may produce fruits so diverse that no theory can embrace or coördinate them. A word this for my little professor with her armor of corsets.

20

XL.

THE COMTESSE DE L'ESTORADE TO THE BARONNE
DE MACUMER.

January, 1827.

My father has been elected to the Chamber, my father-in-law is dead, and I am on the point of my second confinement; these are the chief events marking the end of the year for us. I mention them at once, lest the sight of the black seal should frighten you.

My dear, your letter from Rome made my flesh creep. You are nothing but a pair of children. Félipe is either a dissembling diplomatist or else his love for you is the love a man might have for a courtesan, on whom he squanders his all, knowing all the time that she is false to him. Enough of this. You say I rave, so I had better hold my tongue. Only this I would say, from the comparison of our two very different destinies I draw this harsh moral—Love not if you would be loved.

My dear, when Louis was elected to the provincial Council, he received the cross of the Legion of Honor. That is now nearly three years ago; and as my father—whom you will no doubt see in Paris during the course of the session—has asked the rank of officer of the Legion for his son-in-law, I want to know if you will do me the kindness to take in hand the bigwig, whoever he may be, to whom this patronage belongs, and to keep an eye upon the little affair. But, whatever you do, don't get entangled in the concerns of my honored father. The Comte de Maucombe is fishing for the title of marquis for himself; but keep your good services for me, please. When Louis is a deputy—next winter that is—we shall come to Paris, and then we will move heaven and earth to get some Government appointment for him, so that we may be able to save our income by living on his salary. My father sits between the Centre and the Right; a title will content him. Our family was distinguished even in the days of King René, and Charles X. will hardly say no to a Maucombe; but what I fear is that my father may take it into his head to ask some favor for my younger brother. Now, if the marquisate is dangled out of his reach, he will have no thoughts to spare from himself.

January 15th.

Ah! Louise, I have been in hell. If I can bear to tell you of my anguish, it is because you are another self; even so, I don't know whether I shall ever be able to live again in thought those five ghastly days. The mere word "convulsions" makes my very heart sick. Five days! to me they were five centuries of torture. A mother who has not been through this martyrdom does not know what suffering is. So frenzied was I that I even envied you, who never had a child!

The evening before that terrible day the weather was close, almost hot, and I thought my little Armand was affected by it. Generally so sweet and caressing, he was peevish, cried for nothing, wanted to play, and then broke his toys. Perhaps this sort of fractiousness is the usual sign of approaching illness with children. While I was wondering about it, I noticed Armand's cheeks flush, but this I set down to teething, for he is cutting four large teeth at once. So I put him to bed beside me, and kept constantly waking through the night. He was a little feverish, but not enough to make me uneasy, my mind being still full of the teething. Toward morning he cried "Mamma!" and asked by signs for something to drink; but the cry was spasmodic, and there were convulsive twitchings in the limbs, which turned me to ice. I jumped out of bed to fetch him a drink. Imagine my horror when, on my handing him the cup, he remained motionless, only repeating "Mamma!" in that strange, unfamiliar voice, which was indeed by this time hardly a voice at all. I took his hand, but it did not respond to my pressure; it was quite stiff. I put the cup to his lips; the poor little fellow gulped down three or four mouthfuls in a convulsive manner that was terrible to see, and the water made a strange sound in his throat. He clung to me desperately, and I saw his eyes roll, as though some hidden force within were pulling at them, till only the whites were visible; his limbs were turning rigid. I screamed aloud, and Louis came.

"A doctor! quick!—— he is dying," I cried.

Louis vanished, and my poor Armand again gasped, "Mamma! Mamma!" The next moment he lost all consciousness of his mother's existence. The pretty veins on his forehead swelled, and the convulsions began. For a whole hour before the doctors came, I held in my arms that merry baby, all lilies and roses, the blossom of my life, my pride, and my joy, lifeless as a piece of wood; and his eyes! I cannot think of them without horror. My pretty Armand was a mere mummy—black, shriveled, dumb, misshappen.

A doctor, two doctors, brought from Marseilles by Louis, hovered about like birds of ill-omen; it made me shudder to look at them. One spoke of brain fever, the other saw nothing but an ordinary case of convulsions in infancy. Our own country doctor seemed to me to have the most sense, for he offered no opinion. "It's teething," said the second doctor. —"Fever," said the first. Finally, it was agreed to put leeches on his neck and ice on his head. It seemed to me like death. To look on, to see a corpse, all purple or black, and not a cry, not a movement from this creature but now so full of life and sound—it was horrible!

At one moment I lost my head, and gave a sort of hysterical laugh, as I saw the pretty neck which I used to devour with kisses, with the leeches feeding on it, and his darling head in a cap of ice. My dear, we had to cut those lovely curls, of which we were so proud and with which you used to play, in order to make room for the ice. The convulsions returned every ten minutes with the regularity of labor pains, and then the poor baby writhed and twisted, now white, now violet. His supple limbs clattered like wood as they struck. And this unconscious flesh was the being who smiled and prattled, and used to say Mamma! At the thought, a storm of agony swept tumultuously over my soul, like the sea tossing in a hurricane. It seemed as though every tie which binds a child to its mother's heart were strained to rending. My mother, who might have given me help, advice, or comfort, was in Paris.

Mothers, it is my belief, know more than doctors do about convulsions.

After four days and nights of suspense and fear, which almost killed me, the doctors were unanimous in advising the application of a horrid ointment, which would produce open sores. Sores on my Armand! who only five days before was playing about, and laughing, and trying to say "Godmother!" I would not have it done, preferring to trust to nature. Louis, who believes in doctors, scolded me. A man is always a man. But there are moments when this terrible disease takes the likeness of death, and in one of these it seemed borne in upon me that this hateful remedy was the salvation of Armand. Louise, the skin was so dry, so rough and parched, that the ointment would not act. Then I broke into weeping, and my tears fell so long and so fast that the bedside was wet through. And the doctors were at dinner!

Seeing myself alone with the child, I stripped him of all medical appliances, and seizing him like a mad woman, pressed him to my bosom, laying my forehead against his, and beseeching God to grant him the life which I was striving to pass into his veins from mine. For some minutes I held him thus, longing to die with him, so that neither life nor death might part us. Dear, I felt the limbs relaxing; the writhings ceased, the child stirred, and the ghastly, corpse-like tints faded away! I screamed, just as I did when he was taken ill; the doctors hurried up, and I pointed to Armand.

"He is saved!" exclaimed the oldest of them.

What music in those words! The gates of heaven opened! And, in fact, two hours later, Armand came back to life; but I was utterly crushed, and it was only the healing power of joy which saved me from a serious illness. Oh, my God! by what tortures do you bind a mother to her child! To fasten him to our heart, need the nails be driven into the very quick? Was I not mother enough before? I, who wept tears of joy over his broken syllables and tottering steps, who spent hours together planning how best to perform my duty, and fit myself for the sweet post of mother? Why these horrors, these ghastly and awful scenes, for a mother who already idolized her child?

As I write, our little Armand is playing, shouting, laughing. What can be the cause of this terrible disease with children? Vainly do I try to puzzle it out, remembering always that I am again with child. Is it teething? Is it some peculiar process in the brain? Is there something wrong with the nervous system of children who are subject to convulsions? All these thoughts disquiet me, in view alike of the present and the future. Our country doctor holds to the theory of nervous trouble produced by teething. I would give every tooth in my head to see little Armand's all through. The sight of one of those little white pearls peeping out of the swollen gum brings a cold sweat over me now. The heroism with which the little angel bore his sufferings proves to me that he will be his mother's son. A look from him cleaves my very heart.

Medical science can give no satisfactory explanation as to the origin of this sort of tetanus, which passes off as rapidly as it comes on, and can apparently be neither guarded against nor cured. One thing alone, as I said before, is certain, that it is hell for a mother to see her child in convulsions. How passionately do I clasp him to my heart! I could walk for ever with him in my arms!

To have suffered all this only six weeks before my confinement made it much worse; I feared for the coming child. Farewell, my dear beloved. Don't wish for a child—there is the sum and substance of my letter!

XLI.

THE BARONNE DE MACUMER TO THE VICOMTESSE DE L'ESTORADE.

PARIS.

POOR SWEET:—Macumer and I forgave you all your naughtiness when we heard of your terrible trouble. I thrilled with pain as I read the details of that double agony, and there seem compensations now in being childless.

I am writing at once to tell you that Louis has been promoted. He can now wear the ribbon of an officer of the Legion. You are a lucky woman, Renée, and you will probably have a little girl, since that used to be your wish!

The marriage of my brother with Mlle. de Mortsauf was celebrated on our return. Our gracious King, who really is extraordinarily kind, has given my brother the reversion of the post of first gentleman of the chamber, which his father-in-law now fills, on the one condition that the escutcheon of the Mortsaufs should be placed side by side with that of the Lenoncourts.

"The office ought to go with the title," he said to the Duc de Lenoncourt-Givry.

My father is justified a hundredfold. Without the help of my fortune nothing of all this could have taken place. My father and mother came from Madrid for the wedding, and return there, after the reception which I give to-morrow for the bride and bridegroom.

The carnival will be a very gay one. The Duc and Duchesse de Soria are in Paris, and their presence makes me a little uneasy. Marie Hérédia is certainly one of the most beautiful women in Europe, and I don't like the way Félipe looks at her. Therefore I am doubly lavish of sweetness and caresses. Every look and gesture speak the words which I am careful my lips should not utter: "*She* could not love like this!" Heaven knows how lovely and fascinating I am! Yesterday Mme. de Maufrigneuse said to me:

"Dear child, who can compete with you?"

Then I keep Félipe so well amused, that his sister-in-law must seem as lively as a Spanish cow in comparison. I am the less sorry that a little Abencerrage is not on his way, because the duchess will no doubt stay in Paris over her confinement, and she won't be a beauty any longer. If the baby is a boy, it will be called Félipe, in honor of the exile. An unkind chance has decreed that I shall, a second time, serve as godmother.

Good-by, dear. I shall go to Chantepleurs early this year, for our Italian tour was shockingly expensive. I shall leave about the end of March, and retire to economize in Nivernais. Beside, I am tired of Paris. Félipe sighs, as I do, after the beautiful quiet of the park, our cool meadows, and our Loire, with its sparkling sands, peerless among rivers. Chantepleurs will seem delightful to me after the pomps and vanities of Italy; for, after all, splendor becomes wearisome, and a lover's glance has more beauty than a *capo d'opéra* or a *bel quadro!*

We shall expect you there. Don't be afraid that I shall be jealous again. You are free to take what soundings you please in Macumer's heart, and fish up all the interjections and doubts you can. I am supremely indifferent. Since that day at Rome Félipe's love for me has grown. He told me yesterday (he is looking over my shoulder now) that his sister-in-law, the Princess Hérédia, his destined bride of old, the dream of his youth, had no brains. Oh! my dear, I am worse than a ballet-dancer! If you knew what joy that slighting remark gave me! I have pointed out to Félipe that she does not speak French correctly. She says *esemple* for *exemple*, *sain* for *cinq*, *cheu* for *je*. She is beautiful of course, but quite without charm or the slightest scintilla of wit. When a compliment is paid her, she looks at you as though she didn't know what to do with such a strange thing. Félipe, being what he is, could not have lived two months with Marie after his marriage. Don Fernand, the Duc de Soria, suits her very well. He has generous instincts, but it's easy to see he has been a spoilt child. I am tempted to be naughty and make you laugh; but I won't draw the long bow. Ever so much love, darling.

CHAPTER XLII.

RENÉE TO LOUISE.

My little girl is two months old. She is called Jeanne-Athénaïs, and has for godmother and godfather my mother and an old grand-uncle of Louis'.

As soon as I possibly can, I shall start for my visit to Chantepleurs, since you are not afraid of a nursing mother. Your godson can say your name now; he calls it *Matoumer*, for he can't pronounce *e* properly. You will be quite delighted with him. He has got all his teeth, and eats meat now like a big boy; he is all over the place, trotting about like a little mouse; but I watch him all the time with anxious eyes, and it makes me miserable that I cannot keep him by me when I am confined. The time is more than usually long with me, as the doctors consider some special precautions necessary. Alas! my child, habit does not inure one to childbearing. There are the same old discomforts and misgivings. However (don't show this to Félipe), this little girl takes after me, and she may yet cut out your Armand.

My father thought Félipe looking very thin, and my dear

pet also not quite so blooming. Yet the Duc and Duchesse de Soria have gone; not a loophole for jealousy is left! Is there any trouble which you are hiding from me? Your letter is neither so long nor so full of loving thoughts as usual. Is this only a whim of my dear whimsical friend?

I am running on too long. My nurse is angry with me for writing, and Mlle. Athénaïs de l'Estorade wants her dinner. Farewell, then; write me some nice long letters.

XLIII.

MME. DE MACUMER TO THE COMTESSE DE L'ESTORADE.

For the first time in my life, my dear Renée, I have been alone and crying. I was sitting under a willow, on a wooden bench by the side of the long Chantepleurs marsh. The view there is charming, but it needs some merry children to complete it, and I wait for you and yours. I have been married nearly three years, and no child! The thought of your quiverful drove me to explore my heart.

And this is what I find there: "Oh! if I had to suffer a hundredfold what Renée suffered when my godson was born; if I had to see my child in convulsions, even so would to God that I might have a cherub of my own, like your Athénaïs!" I can see her from here in my mind's eye, and I know she is beautiful as the day, for you tell me nothing about her—that is just like my Renée! I believe you divine my trouble.

Each time my hopes are disappointed, I fall a prey for some days to the blackest melancholy. Then I compose sad elegies. When shall I embroider little caps and sew lace edgings to encircle a tiny head? When choose the cambric for the baby-clothes? Shall I never hear baby lips shout "Mamma," and have my dress pulled by a teasing despot whom my heart adores? Are there to be no wheel-marks of a little carriage on the gravel, no broken toys littered about the courtyard? Shall I never visit the toy-stores, as mothers do, to buy swords, and dolls, and little tea-sets? And will it never be mine to watch the unfolding of a precious life—another Félipe, only more dear? I would have a son, if only to learn how a lover can be more to one in his second self.

My park and castle are cold and desolate to me. A childless woman is a monstrosity of nature; we exist only to be mothers. Oh! my sage in woman's livery, how well you have conned the book of life! Everywhere, too, barrenness is a dismal thing. My life is a little too much like one of Gessner's or Florian's sheepfolds, which Rivarol longed to see invaded by a wolf. I, too, have it in me to make sacrifices! There are forces in me, I feel, which Félipe has no use for; and if I am not to be a mother, I must be allowed to indulge myself in some romantic sorrow.

I have just made this remark to my belated Moor, and it brought tears to his eyes. He cannot stand any joking on his love, so I let him off easily, and only called him a paladin of folly.

At times I am seized with a desire to go on pilgrimage, to bear my longings to the shrine of some madonna or to a watering-place. Next winter I shall take medical advice. I am too much enraged with myself to write more. Good-by.

XLIV.

THE SAME TO THE SAME.

PARIS, 1829.

A whole year passed, my dear, without a letter! What does this mean? I am a little hurt. Do you suppose that your Louis, who comes to see me almost every alternate day, makes up for you? It is not enough to know that you are well and that everything prospers with you; for I love you,

Renée, and I want to know what you are thinking of, just as I say everything to you, at the risk of being scolded, or censured, or misunderstood. Your silence and seclusion in the country, at a time when you might be in Paris enjoying all the Parliamentary honors of the Comte de l'Estorade, cause me serious anxiety. You know that your husband's " gift of the gab " and unsparing zeal have won for him quite a position here, and he will doubtless receive some very good post when the session is over. Pray, do you spend your life writing him letters of advice ? Numa was not so far removed from his Egeria.

Why did you not take this opportunity of seeing Paris ? I might have enjoyed your company for four months. Louis told me yesterday that you were coming to fetch him, and would have your third confinement in Paris—you terrible mother Gigogne ! After bombarding Louis with queries, exclamations, and regrets, I at last defeated his strategy so far as to discover that his grand-uncle, the godfather of Athénaïs, is very ill. Now I believe that you, like a careful mother, would be quite equal to angling with the member's speeches and fame for a fat legacy from your husband's last remaining relative on the mother's side. Keep your mind easy, my Renée—we are all at work for Louis : Lenoncourts, Chaulieus, and the whole band of Mme. de Macumer's followers. Martignac will probably put him into the Audit Department. But if you won't tell me why you bury yourself in the country, I shall be cross.

Tell me, are you afraid that the political wisdom of the house of l'Estorade should seem to centre in you ? Or is it the uncle's legacy ? Perhaps you were afraid you would be less to your children in Paris ? Ah ! what would I give to know whether, after all, you were not simply too vain to show yourself in Paris for the first time in your present condition ! Vain thing ! Farewell.

XLV.

RENÉE TO LOUISE.

You complain of my silence ; have you forgotten, then, those two little brown heads, at once my subjects and my tyrants ? And as to staying at home, you have yourself hit upon several of my reasons. Apart from the condition of our dear uncle, I didn't want to drag with me to Paris a boy of four and a little girl who will soon be three, when I am again expecting my confinement. I had no intention of troubling you and upsetting your household with such a party. I did not care to appear, looking my worst, in the brilliant circle over which you preside, and I detest life in hotels and lodgings.

When I come to spend the session in Paris, it will be in my own house. Louis' uncle, when he heard of the rank his grand-nephew had received, made me a present of two hundred thousand francs (the half of his savings) with which to buy a house in Paris, and I have charged Louis to find one in your neighborhood. My mother has given me thirty thousand francs for the furnishing, and I shall do my best not to disgrace the dear sister of my election—no pun intended.

I am grateful to you for having already done so much at Court for Louis. But though M. de Bourmont and M. de Polignac have paid him the compliment of asking him to join their ministry, I do not wish so conspicuous a place for him. It would commit him too much ; and I prefer the Audit Office because it is permanent. Our affairs here are in very good hands ; so you need not fear ; as soon as the steward has mastered the details, I will come and support Louis.

As for writing long letters nowadays, how can I ? This one, in which I want to describe to you the daily routine of my life, will be a week on the stocks. Who can tell but

Armand may lay hold of it to make caps for his regiments drawn up on my carpet, or vessels for the fleets which sail his bath! A single day will serve as a sample of the rest, for they are all exactly alike, and their characteristics reduce themselves to two—either the children are well or they are not. For me, in this solitary grange, it is no exaggeration to say that hours become minutes or minutes hours, according to the children's health.

If I have some delightful hours, it is when they are asleep and I am no longer needed to rock the one or soothe the other with stories. When I have them sleeping by my side, I say to myself, "Nothing can go wrong now." The fact is, my sweet, every mother spends her time, so soon as her children are out of her sight, in imagining dangers for them. Perhaps it is Armand seizing the razors to play with, or his coat taking fire, or a snake biting him, or he might tumble in running and start an abscess on his head, or he might drown himself in a pond. A mother's life, you see, is one long succession of dramas, now soft and tender, now terrible. Not an hour but has its joys and fears.

But at night, in my room, comes the hour for waking dreams, when I plan out their future, which shines brightly in the smile of the guardian angel, watching over their beds. Sometimes Armand calls me in his sleep; I kiss his forehead (without rousing him), then his sister's feet, and watch them both lying in their beauty. These are my merry-makings! Yesterday, it must have been our guardian angel who roused me in the middle of the night and summoned me in fear to Naïs' crib. Her head was too low, and I found Armand all uncovered, his feet purple with cold.

"Darling mother!" he cried, rousing up and flinging his arms round me.

There, dear, is one of our night scenes for you.

How important it is for a mother to have her children by her side at night! It is not for a nurse, however careful she may be, to take them up, comfort them, and hush them to sleep again, when some horrid nightmare has disturbed them. For they have their dreams, and the task of explaining away one of these dread visions of the night is the more arduous because the child is scared, stupid, and only half awake. It is a mere interlude in the unconsciousness of slumber. In this way I have come to sleep so lightly, that I can see my little pair and hear them stirring, through the veil of my eyelids. A sigh or a rustle awakens me. For me, the demon of convulsions is ever crouching by their beds.

So much for the nights; with the first twitter of the birds my babies begin to stir. Through the mists of dispersing sleep, their chatter blends with the warblings that fill the morning air, or with the swallows' noisy debates—little cries of joy or woe, which make their way to my heart rather than my ears. While Naïs struggles to get at me, making the passage from her crib to my bed on all fours or with staggering steps, Armand climbs up with the agility of a monkey, and has his arms round me. Then the merry couple turn my bed into a playground, where mother lies at their mercy. The baby-girl pulls my hair, and would take to sucking again, while Armand stands guard over my breast, as though defending his property. Their funny ways, their peals of laughter, are too much for me, and put sleep fairly to flight.

Then we play the ogress game; mother ogress eats up the white, soft flesh with hugs, and rains kisses on those rosy shoulders and eyes brimming over with saucy mischief; we have little jealous tiffs too, so pretty to see. It has happened to me, dear, to take up my stockings to put on at eight o'clock and be still barefooted at nine!

Then comes the getting up. The operation of dressing begins. . I slip on my dressing-gown, turn up my sleeves, and don the macintosh apron; with Mary's assistance, I wash and scrub my two little blossoms. I am sole arbiter of the temperature of the bath, for a good half of children's crying and whimpering comes from mistakes here. The moment has arrived for paper fleets and glass ducks, since the only way to get children thoroughly washed is to keep them well amused. If you knew the diversions that have to be invented before these despotic sovereigns will permit a soft sponge to be passed over every nook and cranny, you would be awestruck at the amount of ingenuity and intelligence demanded by the maternal profession when one takes it seriously. Prayers, scoldings, promises, are alike in requisition; above all, the jugglery must be so dexterous that it defies detection. The case would be desperate had not Providence to the cunning of the child matched that of the mother. A child is a diplomatist only to be master, like the diplomatists of the great world, through his passions! Happily, it takes little to make these cherubs laugh; the fall of a brush, a piece of soap slipping from the hand, and what merry shouts! And if our triumphs are dearly bought, still triumphs they are, though hidden from mortal eye. Even the father knows nothing of it all. None but God and His angels—and perhaps you—can fathom the glances of satisfaction which Mary and I exchange when the little creatures' toilet is at last concluded, and they stand, spotless and shining, amid a chaos of soap, sponges, combs, basins, blotting-paper, flannel, and all the nameless litter of a true English "nursery."

For I am so far a convert as to admit that Englishwomen have a talent for this department. True, they look upon the child only from the point of view of material well-being; but where this is concerned, their arrangements are admirable. My children shall always be barelegged and wear woolen socks. There shall be no swaddling or bandages; on the other hand, they shall never be left alone. The helplessness of the French infant in its swaddling-bands means the liberty of the nurse—that is the whole explanation. A mother, who is really a mother, is never free.

There is my answer to your question why I do not write.

Beside the management of the estate, I have the upbringing of two children on my hands.

The art of motherhood involves much silent, unobtrusive self-denial, an hourly devotion which finds no detail too minute. The soup warming over the fire must be watched. Am I the kind of woman, do you suppose, to shirk such cares? The humblest task may earn a rich harvest of affection. How pretty is the child's laugh when he finds the food to his liking! Armand has a way of nodding his head when he is pleased that is worth a lifetime of adoration. How could I leave to any one else the privilege and delight, as well as the responsibility, of blowing on the spoonful of soup which is too hot for my little Naïs, my nursling of seven months ago, who still remembers my breast? When a nurse has allowed a child to burn its tongue and lips with scalding food, she tells the mother, who hurries up to see what is wrong, that the child cried from hunger. How could a mother sleep in peace with the thought that a breath, less pure than her own, has cooled her child's food—the mother whom Nature has made the direct vehicle of food to infant lips. To mince a chop for Naïs, who has just cut her last tooth, and mix the meat, cooked to a turn, with potatoes, is a work of patience, and there are times, indeed, when none but a mother could, by any possibility, succeed in making an impatient child go through with its meal.

No number of servants, then, and no English nurse can dispense a mother from taking the field in person in that daily contest, where gentleness alone should grapple with the little griefs and pains of childhood. Louise, the care of these innocent darlings is a work to engage the whole soul. To whose hands and eyes, but one's own, intrust the task of feeding, dressing, and putting to bed? Broadly speaking, a crying child is the unanswerable condemnation of mother or nurse, except when the cry is the outcome of natural pain. Now that I have two to look after (and a third on the road), they

21

occupy all my thoughts. Even you, whom I love so dearly, have become a memory to me.

My own dressing is not always completed by two o'clock. I have no faith in mothers whose rooms are in apple-pie order, and who themselves might have stepped out of a bandbox. Yesterday was one of those lovely days of early April, and I wanted to take my children a walk, while I was still able— for the warning bell is in my ears. Such an expedition is quite an epic to a mother! One dreams of it the night before! Armand was for the first time to put on a little black velvet jacket, a new collar which I had worked, a Scotch cap with the Stuart colors and cock's feathers; Naïs was to be in white and pink, with one of those delicious little baby caps; for she is a baby still, though she will lose that pretty title on the arrival of the youngster (whom I feel kicking me) and whom I call my little pauper, for he will have the portion of a younger son. (You see, Louise, the child has already appeared to me in a vision, so I know it is a boy.)

Well, caps, collars, jackets, socks, dainty little shoes, pink garters, the muslin frock with silk embroidery—all was laid out on my bed. Then the little brown heads had to be brushed, twittering merrily all the time like birds answering each other's call. Armand's hair is in curls, while Naïs' is brought forward softly on the forehead as a border to the pink-and-white cap. Then the shoes are buckled; and when the little bare legs and well-shod feet have trotted off to the nursery, while two shining faces (*clean*, Mary calls them) and eyes ablaze with life petition me to start, my heart beats fast. To look on the children whom one's own hand has arrayed, the pure skin brightly veined with blue, that one has bathed, laved, and sponged and decked with gay colors of silk or velvet—why, there is no poem comes near to it! With what eager, covetous longing one calls them back for one more kiss on those white necks, which, in their simple collars, the love-liest woman cannot rival. Even the coarest lithograph of such a scene makes a mother pause, and I feast my eyes daily on the living picture !

Once out of doors, triumphant in the result of my labors, while I was admiring the princely air with which little Armand helped baby to totter along the path you know, I saw a carriage coming, and tried to get them out of the way. The children tumbled into a dirty puddle, and lo ! my works of art are ruined ! We had to take them back and change their things. I took the little one in my arms, never thinking of my own dress, which was ruined, while Mary seized Armand, and the cavalcade reëntered. With a crying baby and a soaked child, what mind has a mother left for herself?

Dinner-time arrives, and as a rule I have done nothing. Now comes the problem which faces me twice every day— how to suffice in my own person for two children, put on their bibs, turn up their sleeves, and get them to eat. In the midst of these ever-recurring cares, joys, and catastrophes, the only person neglected in the house is myself. If the children have been naughty, often I don't get rid of my curl-papers all day. Their tempers rule my toilet. As the price of the few minutes in which I write you these half-dozen pages, I have had to let them cut pictures out of my novels, build castles with books, chessmen, or mother-of-pearl counters, and give Naïs my silks and wools to arrange in her own fashion, which, I assure you, is so complicated that she is entirely absorbed in it, and has not uttered a word.

Yet I have nothing to complain of. My children are both strong and independent ; they amuse themselves more easily than you would think. They find delight in everything ; a guarded liberty is worth many toys. A few pebbles—pink, yellow, purple, and black, small shells, the mysteries of sand— are a world of pleasure to them. Their wealth consists in possessing a multitude of small things. I watch Armand and find him talking to the flowers, the flies, the chickens, and imitating them. He is on friendly terms with insects,

and never wearies of admiring them. Everything which is
on a minute scale interests them. Armand is beginning to
ask the "why" of everything he sees. He has come to ask
what I am saying to his godmother, whom he looks on as a
fairy. Strange how children hit the mark!

Alas! my sweet, I would not sadden you with the tale of
my joys. Let me give you some notion of your godson's
character. The other day we were followed by a poor man
begging—beggars soon find out that a mother with her child
at her side can't resist them. Armand has no idea what
hunger is, and money is a sealed book to him; but I had just
bought him a trumpet which had long been the object of his
desires. He held it out to the old man with a kingly air,
saying:

"Here, take this!"

What joy the world can give would compare with such a
moment?

"May I keep it?" said the poor man to me. "I too,
madame, have had children," he added, hardly noticing the
money I put into his hand.

I shudder when I think that Armand must go to school,
and that I have only three years and a half more to keep him
by me. The flowers that blossom in his sunny childhood
will fall before the scythe of a public-school system; his
gracious ways and bewitching candor will lose their spontaneity. They will cut the curls that I have brushed and
smoothed and kissed so often! What will they do with the
thinking being that is Armand?

And what of you? You tell me nothing of your life. Are
you still in love with Félipe? For, as regards the Saracen, I
have no uneasiness. Adieu; Naïs has just had a tumble, and,
if I run my drama on like this, my letter will become a
volume.

XLVI.

MME. DE MACUMER TO THE COMTESSE DE L'ESTORADE.

CHANTEPLEURS, 1829.

My sweet, tender Renée, you will have learned from the papers the terrible calmity which has overwhelmed me. I have not been able to write you even a word. For twenty days I never left his bedside; I received his last breath and closed his eyes; I kept holy watch over him with the priests and repeated the prayers for the dead. The cruel pangs I suffered were accepted by me as a rightful punishment; and yet, when I saw on his calm lips the smile which was his last farewell to me, how was it possible to believe that I had caused his death by my love. But he *is not*, and I, *I am!* To you, who have known us both so well, what more need I say? These words contain all.

Oh! I would give my share of heaven to hear the flattering tale that my prayers have power to call him back to life! To see him again, to have him once more mine, were it only for a second, would mean that I could draw breath again without mortal agony. Will you not come soon and soothe me with such promises? Is not your love strong enough to deceive me.

But stay! it was you who told me beforehand that he would suffer through me. Was it so indeed? Yes, it is true, I had no right to his love. Like a thief, I took what was not mine, and my frenzied grasp has crushed the life out of my bliss. The madness is over now, but I feel that I am alone. Merciful God! what torture of the damned can exceed the misery in that word?

When they took him away from me, I lay down on the same bed and hoped to die. There was but a door between us, and it seemed to me I had strength to force it! But, alas! I was too young for death; and after forty days, during which, with cruel care and all the sorry inventions of medical science, they slowly nursed me back to life, I find myself in the country, seated by my window, surrounded with lovely flowers, which he made to bloom for me, gazing on the same splendid view over which his eyes have so often wandered, and which he was so proud to have discovered, since it gave me pleasure. Ah! dear Renée, no words can tell how new surroundings hurt when the heart is dead. I shiver at the sight of the moist earth in my garden, for the earth is a vast tomb, and it is almost as though I walked on *him!* When I first went out, I trembled with fear and could not move. It was so sad to see *his* flowers, and *he* not there!

My father and mother are in Spain. You know what my brothers are, and you yourself are detained in the country. But you need not be uneasy about me; two angels of mercy flew to my side. The Duc and Duchesse de Soria hastened to their brother in his illness, and have been everything that heart could wish. The last few nights before the end found the three of us gathered, in calm and wordless grief, round the bed where this great man was breathing his last, a man among a thousand, rare in any age, head and shoulders above the rest of us in everything. The patient resignation of my Félipe was angelic. The sight of his brother and Marie gave him a moment's pleasure and easing of his pain.

"Darling," he said to me with the simple frankness which never deserted him, "I had almost gone from life without leaving to Fernand the Barony of Macumer; I must make a new will. My brother will forgive me; he knows what it is to love!"

I owe my life to the care of my brother-in-law and his wife; they want to carry me off to Spain!

Ah! Renée, to no one but you can I speak freely of my grief. A sense of my own faults weighs me to the ground, and there is a bitter solace in pouring them out to you, poor,

unheeded Cassandra. The exactions, the preposterous jealousy, the nagging unrest of my passion wore him to death.
My love was the more fraught with danger for him because we
had both the same exquisitely sensitive nature, we spoke the
same language, nothing was lost on him, and often the mocking shaft, so carelessly discharged, went straight to his heart.
You can have no idea of the point to which he carried submissiveness. I had only to tell him to go and leave me alone,
and the caprice, however wounding to him, would be obeyed
without a murmur. His làst breath was spent in blessing me
and in repeating that a single morning alone with me was
more precious to him than a lifetime spent with another
woman, were she even the Marie of his youth. My tears fall
as I write the words.

This is the manner of my life now. I rise at midday and
go to bed at seven ; I linger absurdly long over meals ; I
saunter about slowly, standing motionless, an hour at a time,
before a single plant ; I gaze into the leafy trees ; I take a
sober and serious interest in mere nothings ; I long for shade,
silence, and night ; in a word, I fight through each hour as it
comes, and take a gloomy pleasure in adding it to the heap of
the vanquished. My peaceful park gives me all the company
I care for ; everything there is full of glorious images of my
vanished joy, invisible for others but eloquent to me. .

"I cannot away with you Spaniards!" I exclaimed one
morning, as my sister-in-law flung herself on my neck. "You
have some nobility in your souls that we lack."

Ah! Renée, if I still live, it is doubtless because heaven
tempers the sense of affliction to the strength of those who
have to bear it. Only a woman can know what it is to lose a
love which sprang from the heart and was genuine throughout,
a passion which was not ephemeral, and satisfied at once the
spirit and the flesh. How rare it is to find a man so gifted
that to worship him brings no sense of degradation ! If such
supreme fortune befall us once, we cannot hope for it a second

time.   Men of true greatness, whose strength and worth are
veiled by poetic grace, and who charm by some high spiritual
power, men made to be adored, beware of love !   Love will
ruin you, and ruin the woman of your heart.   This is the
burden of my cry as I pace my woodland walks.

And he has left me no child !   That love so rich in smiles,
which rained perpetual flowers and joy, has left no fruit.   I
am a thing accursed.   Can it be that, even as the two ex-
tremes of polar ice and torrid sand are alike intolerant of life,
so the very purity and vehemence of a single-hearted passion
render it barren as hate?   Is it only a marriage of reason,
such as yours, which is blessed with a family?   Can heaven
be jealous of our passions?   These are wild words.

You are, I believe, the one person whose company I could
endure.   Come to me, then ; none but Renée should be with
Louise in her sombre garb.   What a day when I first put on
my widow's bonnet ! When I saw myself all arrayed in black,
I fell back on a seat and wept till night came ; and I weep
again as I recall that moment of anguish.

Farewell.   Writing tires me ; thoughts crowd fast, but I
have no heart to put them into words.   Bring your children ;
you can nurse baby here without making me jealous ; all that
is gone, *he* is not here, and I shall be very glad to see my
godson.   Félipe used to wish for a child like little Armand.
Come, then ; come and help me bear my woe.

XLVII.

RENÉE TO LOUISE.

829.

My Darling :—When you hold this letter in your hands,
I shall be already near, for I am starting a few minutes after it.
We shall be alone together.   Louis is obliged to remain in
Provence because of the approaching elections.   He wants to

be elected again, and the Liberals are already plotting against his return.

I don't come to comfort you; I only bring you my heart to beat in sympathy with yours, and help you to bear with life. I come to bid you weep, for only with tears can you purchase the joy of meeting him again. Remember, he is traveling toward heaven, and every step forward which you take brings you nearer to him. Every duty done breaks a link in the chain that parts you.

Louise, in my arms you will once more raise your head and go on your way to him, pure, noble, washed of all those errors, which had no root in your heart, and bearing with you the harvest of good deeds which, in his name, you will accomplish here.

I scribble these hasty lines in all the bustle of preparation, and interrupted by the babies and by Armand, who keeps crying, "Godmother, godmother! I want to see her," till I am almost jealous. He might be your child!

SECOND PART.

XLVIII.

October 15, 1833.

Well, yes, Renée, it is quite true; you have been correctly
informed. I have sold my house, I have sold Chantepleurs,
and the farms in Seine-et-Marne, but no more, please! I am
neither mad nor ruined, I assure you.

Let us go into the matter. When everything was wound
up, there remained to me of my poor Macumer's fortune
about twelve hundred thousand francs. I will account, as to
a practical sister, for every penny of this.

I put a million into the Three per Cents. when they were
at fifty, and so I have got an income for myself of sixty thousand francs, instead of the thirty thousand which the property
yielded. Then, only think what my life was. Six months
of the year in the country, renewing leases, listening to the
grumbles of the farmers, who pay when it pleases them, and
getting as bored as a sportsman in wet weather. There was
produce to sell, and I always sold it at a loss. Then, in Paris
my house represented a rental of ten thousand francs; I had
to invest my money at the notaries; I was kept waiting for the
interest, and could only get the money back by prosecuting;
in addition I had to study the law of mortgage. In short,
there was business in Nivernais, in Seine-et-Marne, in Paris—
and what a burden, what a nuisance, what a vexing and losing
game for a widow of twenty-seven!

Whereas now my fortune is secured on the budget. In
place of paying taxes to the State, I receive from it, every

(330)

half-year, in my own person, and free from cost, thirty thousand francs in thirty notes, handed over the counter to me by a dapper little clerk at the Treasury, who smiles when he sees me coming!

"Supposing the nation became bankrupt?" I hear you say. Well, to begin with—"'Tis not mine to seek trouble so far from my door." At the worst, too, the nation would not dock me of more than half my income, so I should still be as well off as before my investment, and in the meantime I shall be drawing a double income until the catastrophe arrives. A nation doesn't become bankrupt more than once in a century, so I shall have plenty of time to amass a little capital out of my savings.

And, finally, is not the Comte de l'Estorade a peer of this July semi-republic? Is he not one of those pillars of royalty offered by the "people" to the King of the French? How can I have qualms with a friend at Court, a great financier, head of the Audit Department? I defy you to arraign my sanity! I am almost as good at sums as your citizen king.

Do you know what inspires a woman with all this algebraic wisdom? Love, my dear!

Alas! the moment has come for unfolding to you the mysteries of my conduct, the motives of which have baffled even your keen sight, your prying affection, and your subtlety. I am to be married in a country village near Paris. I love and am loved. I love as much as a woman can who knows love well. I am loved as much as a woman ought to be by the man she adores.

Forgive me, Renée, for keeping this a secret from you and from every one. If your friend evades all spies and puts curiosity on a false track, you must admit that my feeling for poor Macumer justified some dissimulation. Beside, de l'Estorade and you would have deafened me with remonstrances, and plagued me to death with your misgivings, to which the facts might have lent some color. You know, if no one else does, to what pitch my jealousy can go, and all this would only have been useless torture to me. I was determined to carry out, on my own responsibility, what you, Renée, will call my insane project, and I would take counsel only with my own head and heart, for all the world like a schoolgirl giving the slip to her watchful parents.

The man I love possesses nothing except thirty thousand francs' worth of debts, which I have paid. What a theme for comment here! You would have tried to make Gaston out an adventurer; your husband would have set detectives on the dear boy. I preferred to sift him for myself. He has been wooing me now close on two years. I am twenty-seven, he is twenty-three. The difference, I admit, is huge when it is on the wrong side. Another source of lamentation!

Lastly, he is a poet, and has lived by his trade—that is to say, on next to nothing, as you will readily understand. Being a poet, he has spent more time weaving day-dreams, and basking, lizard-like, in the sun, than scribing in his dingy garret. Now, practical people have a way of tarring with the same brush of inconstancy authors, artists, and in general all men who live by their brains. Their nimble and fertile wit lays them open to the charge of a like agility in matters of the heart.

Spite of the debts, spite of the difference in age, spite of the poetry, an end is to be placed in a few days to a heroic resistance of more than nine months, during which he has not been allowed even to kiss my hand, and so also ends the season of our sweet, pure love-making. This is not the mere surrender of a raw, ignorant, and curious girl, as it was eight years ago; the gift is deliberate, and my lover awaits it with such loyal patience that, if I pleased, I could postpone the marriage for a year. There is no servility in this; love's slave he may be, but the heart is not slavish. Never have I seen a man of nobler feeling, or one whose tenderness was more rich in fancy, whose love bore more the impress of his soul.

Alas! my sweet one, the art of love is his by heritage. A few words will tell his story.

My friend has no other name than Marie Gaston. He is the illegitimate son of the beautiful Lady Brandon, whose fame must have reached you, and who died broken-hearted, a victim to the vengeance of Lady Dudley—a ghastly story of which the dear boy knows nothing. Marie Gaston was placed by his brother Louis in a boarding-school at Tours,* where he remained till 1827. Louis, after settling his brother at school, sailed a few days later for foreign parts "to seek his fortune," to use the words of an old woman who had played the part of Providence to him. This brother turned sailor used to write him, at long intervals, letters quite fatherly in tone, and breathing a noble spirit; but a struggling life never allowed him to return home. His last letter told Marie that he had been appointed captain in the navy of some American republic, and exhorted him to hope for better days.

Alas! since then three years have passed, and my poor poet has never heard again. So dearly did he love his brother, that he would have started to look for him but for Daniel d'Arthez, the well-known author, who took a generous interest in Marie Gaston, and prevented him carrying out his mad impulse. Nor was this all; often would he give him a crust and a corner, as the poet puts it in his graphic words.

For, in truth, the poor lad was in terrible straits; he was actually innocent enough to believe—incredible as it seems— that genius was the shortest road to fortune (that will surely make you laugh for hours), and from 1828 to 1833 his one aim has been to make a name for himself in letters. Naturally his life was a frightful tissue of toil and hardships, alternating between hope and despair. The good advice of d'Arthez could not prevail against the allurements of ambition, and his debts went on growing like a snowball. Still he was beginning

* See "La Grenadière."

to come into notice when I happened to meet him at Mme. de Espard's. At first sight he inspired me, unconsciously to himself, with the most vivid sympathy. How did it come about that this virgin heart had been left for me? The fact is that my poet combines genius and cleverness, passion and pride, and women are always afraid of greatness which has no weak side to it. How many victories were needed before Josephine could see the great Napoleon in the little Bonaparte whom she had married?

Poor Gaston is innocent enough to think he knows the measure of my love! He simply has not an idea of it, but to you I must make it clear; for this letter, Renée, is something in the nature of a last will and testament. Weigh well what I am going to say, I beg of you.

At this moment I am confident of being loved as perhaps not another woman on this earth is, nor have I a shadow of doubt as to the perfect happiness of our wedded life, to which I bring a feeling hitherto unknown to me. Yes, for the first time in my life, I know the delight of being swayed by passion. That which every woman seeks in love will be mine in marriage. As poor Félipe once adored me, so do I now adore Gaston. I have lost control of myself, I tremble before this boy as the Arab hero used to tremble before me. In a word, the balance of love is now on my side, and this makes me timid. I am full of the most absurd terrors. I am afraid of being deserted, afraid of becoming old and ugly while Gaston still retains his youth and beauty, afraid of coming short of his hopes!

And yet I believe I have it in me, I believe I have sufficient devotion and ability, not only to keep alive the flame of his love in our solitary life, far from the world, but even to make it burn stronger and brighter. If I am mistaken, if this splendid idyl of love in hiding must come to an end—an end! what am I saying?—if I find Gaston's love less intense any day than it was the evening before, be sure of this, Renée, I should visit my failure only on myself; no blame should attach to him. I tell you now, it would mean my death. Not even if I had children could I live on these terms, for I know myself, Renée; I know that my nature is the lover's rather than the mother's. Therefore, before taking this vow upon my soul, I implore you, my Renée, if this disaster befall me, to take the place of mother to my children; let them be my legacy to you! All that I know of you, your blind attachment to duty, your rare gifts, your love of children, your affection for me, would help to make my death—I dare not say easy—but at least less bitter.

The compact I have thus made with myself adds a vague terror to the solemnity of my marriage ceremony. For this reason I wish to have no one whom I know present, and it will be performed in secret. Let my heart fail me if it will, at least I shall not read anxiety in your dear eyes, and I alone shall know that this new marriage-contract which I sign may be my death-warrant.

I shall not refer again to this agreement entered into between my present self and the self I am to be. I have confided it to you in order that you might know the full extent of your responsibilities. In marrying I retain full control of my property; and Gaston, while aware that I have enough to secure a comfortable life for both of us, is ignorant of its amount. Within twenty-four hours I shall dispose of it as I please; and, in order to save him from a humiliating position, I shall have stock, bringing in twelve thousand francs a year, assigned to him. He will find this in his desk on the eve of our wedding. If he declines to accept, I should break off the whole thing. I had to threaten a rupture to get his permission to pay his debts.

This long confession has tired me. I shall finish it the day after to-morrow; I have to spend to-morrow in the country.

October 20th.

I will tell you now the steps I have taken to insure secrecy. My object has been to ward off every possible incitement to my ever-wakeful jealousy, in imitation of the Italian princess, who, like a lioness, rushing on her prey, carried it off to some Swiss town to devour in peace. And I confide my plans to you only because I have another favor to beg; namely, that you will respect our solitude and never come to see us uninvited.

Two years ago I purchased a small property overlooking the ponds of Ville d'Avray, on the road to Versailles. It consists of twenty acres of meadow-land, the skirts of a wood, and a fine fruit garden. Below the meadows the land has been excavated so as to make a lake of about three acres in extent, with a charming little island in the middle. The small valley is shut in by two graceful, thickly wooded slopes, where rise delicious springs that water my park by means of channels cleverly disposed by my architect. Finally, they fall into the royal ponds, glimpses of which can be seen here and there, gleaming in the distance. My little park has been admirably laid out by the architect, who has surrounded it with hedges, walls, or sunken fences, according to the lay of the land, so that no possible point of view may be lost.

A lovely cottage has been built for me half-way up the hillside, with a charming exposure, having the woods of the Ronce on either side, and in front a grassy slope running down to the lake. Externally the chalet is an exact copy of those which are so much admired by travelers on the road from Sion to Brieg, and which fascinated me when I was returning from Italy. The internal decorations will bear comparison with those of the most celebrated buildings of the kind.

A hundred paces from this rustic dwelling stands a charming and ornamental house, communicating with it by a subterranean passage. This contains the kitchen, and other servants' rooms, stables, and coach-houses. Of all this series of brick buildings the facade alone is seen, graceful in its simplicity, against a background of shrubbery. Another building serves to lodge the gardeners and masks the entrance to the orchards and kitchen-gardens.

The entrance gate to the property is so hidden in the wall dividing the park from the wood as almost to defy detection. The plantations, already well grown, will, in two or three years, completely hide the buildings, so that, except in winter, when the trees are bare, no trace of habitation will appear to the outside world, save only the smoke visible from the neighboring hills.

The surroundings of my chalet have been modeled on what is called the King's Garden at Versailles, but it has an outlook on my lake and island. The hills on every side display their abundant foliage—those splendid trees for which your civil list has so well cared. My gardeners have orders to cultivate sweet-scented flowers to any extent, and no others, so that our home will be a fragrant emerald. The chalet, adorned with a wild vine which covers the roof, is literally imbedded in climbing plants of all kinds—hops, clematis, jasmine, azalea, copæa. It will be a sharp eye which can descry our windows!

The chalet, my dear, is a good, solid house, with its heating system and all the conveniences of modern architecture, which can raise a palace in the compass of a hundred square feet. It contains a suite of rooms for Gaston and another for me. The first-floor is occupied by an anteroom, a parlor, and a dining-room. Above our floor again are three rooms destined for the *nursery*. I have five first-rate horses, a small light coupé, and a two-horse milord. We are only forty minutes' drive from Paris ; so that, when the spirit moves us to hear an opera or see a new play, we can start after dinner and return the same night to our bower. The road is a good one, and passes under the shade of our green dividing wall of woods for some distance.

22

My servants—cook, coachman, groom, and gardeners, in addition to my maid—are all very respectable people, whom I have spent the last six months in picking up, and they will be superintended by my old Philippe. Although confident of their loyalty and good faith, I have not neglected to cultivate self-interest ; their wages are small, but will receive an annual addition in the shape of a New Year's Day present. They are all aware that the slightest fault, or a mere suspicion of gossiping, might lose them a capital place. Lovers are never troublesome to their servants; they are indulgent by disposition, and therefore I feel that I can reckon on my household.

All that is choice, pretty, or decorative in my house in the Rue du Bac has been transported to the chalet. The Rembrandt hangs on the staircase, as though it were a mere daub ; the Hobbema faces the Rubens in *his* study ; the Titian, which my sister-in-law Marie sent me from Madrid, adorns the boudoir. The beautiful furniture picked up by Félipe looks very well in the parlor, which the architect has decorated most tastefully. Everything at the chalet is charmingly simple, with the simplicity which can't be got under a hundred thousand francs. Our first-floor rests on cellars, which are built of millstone and imbedded in concrete; it is almost completely buried in flowers and shrubs, and is deliciously cool without a vestige of damp. To complete the picture, a fleet of white swans sail over my lake at the foot of the lawn !

Oh ! Renée, the silence which reigns in this valley would bring joy to the dead ! One is awakened by the birds singing or the breeze rustling in the poplars. A little spring, discovered by the architect in digging the foundations of the wall, trickles down the hillside over silvery sand to the lake, between two banks of watercress, hugging the edge of the woods. I know nothing that money can buy to equal it.

May not Gaston come to loathe this too perfect bliss ? I shudder to think how complete it is, for the ripest fruits harbor the worms, the most gorgeous flowers attract the insects. Is it not ever the monarch of the forest which is eaten away by the fatal brown grub, voracious as death? I have learned before now that an unseen and jealous power attacks happiness which has reached perfection. Beside, this is the moral of all your preaching, and you have been proved a prophet.

When I went, the day before yesterday, to see whether my last whim had been carried out, tears rose to my eyes; and, to the great surprise of my architect, I at once passed his account for payment.

"But, madame," he exclaimed, "your man of business will refuse to pay this; it is a matter of three hundred thousand francs." My only reply was to add the words, "To be paid without question," with the bearing of a seventeenth-century Chaulieu.

"But," I said, "there is one condition to my gratitude. No human being must hear from you of the park and buildings. Promise me, on your honor, to observe this article in our contract—not to breathe to any living soul the proprietor's name."

Now, can you understand the meaning of my sudden journeys, my mysterious comings and goings? Now, do you know whither those beautiful things, which the world supposes to be sold, have flown? Do you perceive the ultimate motive of my change of investment? Love, my dear, is a vast business, and they who would succeed in it should have no other. Henceforth I shall have no more trouble from money matters; I have taken all the thorns out of my life, and done my housekeeping work once for all with a vengeance, so as never to be troubled with it again, except during the daily ten minutes which I shall devote to my old major-domo, Philippe. I have made a study of life and its sharp curves; there came a day when death also gave me a sharp lesson. Now I want to turn all this to account. My one occupation will be to please *him* and love *him*, to brighten with variety what to common mortals is monotonously dull.

Gaston is still in complete ignorance. At my request he has, like myself, taken up his quarters at Ville d'Avray; to-morrow we start for the chalet. Our life there will cost but little; but if I told you the sum I am setting aside for my toilet, you would exclaim at my madness, and with reason. I intend to take as much trouble to make myself beautiful for him every day as other women do for society. My dress in the country, year in, year out, will cost twenty-four thousand francs, and the larger portion of this will not go in day costumes. As for him, he can wear a blouse if he pleases! Don't suppose that I am going to turn our life into an amorous duel and wear myself out in devices for feeding passion; all that I want is to have a conscience free from reproach. Thirteen years still lie before me as a pretty woman, and I am determined to be loved on the last day of the thirteenth even more fondly than on the morrow of our mysterious nuptials. This time no cutting words shall mar my lowly, grateful content. I will take the part of servant, since that of mistress throve so ill with me before.

Ah! Renée, if Gaston has sounded, as I have, the heights and depths of love, my happiness is assured! Nature at the chalet wears her fairest face. The woods are charming; each step opens up to you some fresh vista of cool greenery, which delights the soul by the sweet thoughts it awakens. They breathe of love.

If only this be not the gorgeous theatre dressed by my hand for my own martyrdom!

In two days from now I shall be Mme. Gaston. My God! is it fitting a Christian so to love mortal man?

"Well, at least you have the law with you," was the comment of my man of business, who is to be one of my witnesses, and who exclaimed, on discovering why my property was to be realized, "I am losing a client!"

And you, my sweet heart (whom I dare no longer call my loved one), may you not cry: "I am losing a sister?"

My sweet, address when you write in future to Mme. Gaston, Poste Restante, Versailles. We shall send there every day for letters. I don't want to be known to the country people, and we shall get all our provisions from Paris. In this way I hope we may guard the secret of our lives. Nobody has been seen in the place during the year spent in preparing our retreat; and the purchase was made in the troubled period which followed the revolution of July. The only person who has shown himself here is the architect; he alone is known, and he will not return.

Farewell. As I write this word, I know not whether my heart is fuller of grief or joy. That proves, does it not? that the pain of losing you equals my love for Gaston.

XLIX.

MARIE GASTON TO DANIEL D'ARTHEZ.

October, 1833.

MY DEAR DANIEL:—I need two witnesses for my marriage. I beg of you to come to-morrow evening for this purpose, bringing with you our worthy and honored friend, Joseph Bridau. She who is to be my wife, with an instinctive divination of my dearest wishes, has declared her intention of living far from the world in complete retirement. You, who have done so much to lighten my penury, have been left in ignorance of my love; but you will understand that absolute secrecy was essential.

This will explain to you why it is that, for the last year, we have seen so little of each other. On the morrow of my wedding we shall be parted for a long time; but, Daniel, you are of stuff to understand me. Friendship can exist in the absence of a friend. There may be times when I shall want you badly, but I shall not see you, at least not in my own house. Here again *she* has forestalled our wishes. She has sacrificed to me her intimacy with a friend of her childhood, who has been a sister to her. For her sake, then, I also must relinquish my comrade !

From this fact alone you will divine that ours is no mere passing fancy, but love, absolute, perfect, godlike ; love based upon the fullest knowledge that can bind two hearts in sympathy. To me it is a perpetual spring of purest delight.

Yet nature allows of no happiness without alloy ; and deep down, in the innermost recess of my heart, I am conscious of a lurking thought, not shared with her, the pang of which is for me alone. You have too often come to the help of my inveterate poverty to be ignorant how desperate matters were with me. Where should I have found courage to keep up the struggle of life, after seeing my hopes so often blighted, but for your cheering words, your tactful aid, and the knowledge of what you had come through? Briefly, then, my friend, she freed me from that crushing load of debt, which was no secret to you. She is wealthy, I am penniless. Many a time have I exclaimed, in one of my fits of idleness: "Oh, for some great heiress to cast her eye on me ! " And now, in presence of this reality, the boy's careless jest, the unscrupulous cynicism of the outcast, have alike vanished, leaving in their place only a bitter sense of humiliation, which not the most considerate tenderness on her part, nor my own assurance of her noble nature, can remove. Nay, what better proof of my love could there exist, for her or for myself, than this shame, from which I have not recoiled, even when powerless to overcome it? The fact remains that there is a point where, far from protecting, I am the protected.

This is my pain which I confide to you.

Except in this one particular, dear Daniel, my fondest dreams are more than realized. I have found the Beautiful without a flaw, the Good without defect. Fairest and noblest among women, such a bride might indeed raise a man to giddy heights of bliss. Her gentle ways are seasoned with wit, her love comes with an ever-fresh grace and charm ; her mind is well informed and quick to understand ; in person, she is fair and lovely, with a rounded slimness, as though Raphael and Rubens had conspired to create a woman ! I do not know whether I could have worshiped with such fervor at the shrine of a dark beauty ; a brunette always strikes me as an unfinished boy. She is a widow, childless, and twenty-seven years of age. Though brimful of life and energy, she has her moods also of dreamy melancholy. These rare gifts go with a proud aristocratic bearing ; she has a fine presence.

She belongs to one of those old families who make a fetish of rank, yet loves me enough to ignore the misfortune of my birth. Our secret passion is now of long standing ; we have made trial, each of the other, and find that in the matter of jealousy we are twin spirits ; our thoughts are the reverbera-tion of the same thunderclap. We both love for the first time, and this bewitching springtime has filled its days for us with all the images of delight that fancy can paint in laughing, sweet, or musing mood. Our path has been strewn with the flowers of tender imaginings. Each hour brought its own wealth, and, when we parted, it was to put our thoughts in verse. Not for a moment did I harbor the idea of sullying the brightness of such a time by giving the rein to sensual passion, however it might chafe within. She was a widow and free ; intuitively, she realized all the homage implied in this constant self-restraint, which often moved her to tears. Can you not read in this, my friend, a soul of noble temper ? In mutual fear we shunned even the first kiss of love.

"We have each a wrong to reproach ourselves with," she said one day.

"Where is yours ? " I asked.

"My marriage," was her reply.

Daniel, you are a giant among us, and you love one of the

most gifted women of the aristocracy, which has produced my
Armande; what need to tell you more? Such an answer lays
bare to you a woman's heart and all the happiness which is in
store for your friend,

MARIE GASTON.

L.

MME. DE L'ESTORADE TO MME. DE MACUMER.

Louise, can it be that, with all your knowledge of the deep-
seated mischief wrought by the indulgence of passion, even
within the heart of marriage, you are planning a life of
wedded solitude? Having sacrificed your first husband in the
course of a fashionable career, would you now fly to the desert
to consume a second? What stores of misery you are laying
up for yourself!

But I see from the way you have set about it that there is
no going back. The man who has overcome your aversion to
a second marriage must indeed possess some magic of mind
and heart; and you can only be left to your illusions. But
have you forgotten your former criticism on young men?
Not one, you would say, but has visited haunts of shame,
and has besmirched his purity with the filth of the streets.
Where is the change, pray—in them or in you?

You are a lucky woman to be able to believe in happiness.
I have not the courage to blame you for it, though the instinct
of affection urges me to dissuade you from this marriage.
Yes, a thousand times, yes, it is true that nature and society
are at one in making war on absolute happiness, because such
a condition is opposed to the laws of both; possibly, also,
because heaven is jealous of its privileges. My love for you
forebodes some disaster to which all my penetration can give
no definite form. I know neither whence nor from whom it
will arise; but one need be no prophet to foretell that the

mere weight of a boundless happiness will overpower you.
Excess of joy is harder to bear than any amount of sorrow.

Against him I have not a word to say. You love him, and
in all probability I have never seen him; but some idle day I
hope you will send me a sketch, however slight, of this rare,
fine animal.

If you see me so resigned and cheerful, it is because I am
convinced that, once the honeymoon is over, you will both,
with one accord, fall back into the common track. Some
day, two years hence, when we are walking along this famous
road, you will exclaim, "Why, there is the chalet which was
to be my home for ever!" And you will laugh your dear
old laugh, which shows all your pretty teeth!

I have said nothing yet to Louis; it would be too good an
opening for his ridicule. I shall tell him simply that you are
going to be married, and that you wish it kept secret. Un-
luckily, you need neither mother nor sister for your bridal
evening. We are in October now; like a brave woman, you
are grappling with winter first. If it were not a question of
marriage, I should say you were taking the bull by the horns.
In any case, you will have in me the most discreet and intelligent of friends. That mysterious region, known as the centre
of Africa, has swallowed up many travelers, and you seem to
me to be launching on an expedition which, in the domain of
sentiment, corresponds to those where so many explorers have
perished, whether in the sands or at the hands of natives.
Your desert is, happily, only two leagues from Paris, so I
can wish you quite cheerfully, "A safe journey and speedy
return."

LI.

THE COMTESSE DE L'ESTORADE TO MME. MARIE GASTON.

1835.

What has come to you, my dear? After a silence of two years, surely Renée has a right to feel anxious about Louise. So this is love! It brushes aside and scatters to the winds a friendship such as ours! You must admit that, devoted as I am to my children—more even perhaps than you to your Gaston—a mother's love has something expansive about it which does not allow it to steal from other affections, or interfere with the claims of friendship. I miss your letters, I long for a sight of your dear, sweet face. Oh! Louise, my heart has only conjecture to feed upon!

As regards ourselves, I will try and tell you everything as briefly as possible.

On reading over again your last letter but one, I find some stinging comments on our political situation. You mocked at us for keeping the post in the Audit Department, which, as well as the title of count, Louis owed solely to the favor of Charles X. But I should like to know how it would be possible out of an income of forty thousand francs, thirty thousand of which go with the entail, to give a suitable start in life to Athénaïs and my poor little beggar René? Was it not a duty to live on our salary and prudently allow the income of the estate to accumulate? In this way we shall, in twenty years, have put together about six hundred thousand francs, which will provide portions for my daughter and for René, whom I destine for the navy. The poor little chap will have an income of ten thousand francs, and perhaps we may contrive to leave him in cash enough to bring his portion up to the amount of his sister's.

When he is captain, my "Pauper" will be able to make a

wealthy marriage and may, perhaps, take a position in society as good as his elder brother's.

These considerations of prudence determined the acceptance in our family of the new order of things. The new dynasty, as was natural, raised Louis to the peerage and made him a grand officer of the Legion of Honor. The oath once taken, l'Estorade could not be half-hearted in his services, and he has since then made himself very useful in the Chamber. The position he has now attained is one in which he can rest upon his oars till the end of his days. He has a good deal of adroitness in business matters; and though he can hardly be called an orator, speaks pleasantly and fluently, which is all that is necessary in politics. His shrewdness and sound knowledge in all matters of government and administration are fully appreciated, and all parties consider him indispensable. I may tell you that he was recently offered an embassy, but I would not let him accept it. I am tied to Paris by the education of Armand and Athénaïs—who are now respectively thirteen and nearly eleven—and I don't intend leaving till little René has completed his, which is just beginning.

We could not have remained faithful to the elder branch of the dynasty and returned to our country life without allowing the education and prospects of the three children to suffer. A mother, my sweet, is hardly called on to be a Decius, especially at a time when the type is rare. In fifteen years from now, l'Estorade will be able to retire to La Crampade on a good pension, having found a place as referendary for Armand in the Audit Department.

As for René, the navy will doubtless land him into diplomacy. The little rogue, at seven years old, has all the cunning of an old cardinal.

Oh! Louise, I am indeed a happy mother. My children are an endless source of joy to me—"*Senza brama sicura ricchezza.*"

Armand is a day scholar at Henri IV.'s school. I made

up my mind he should have a public-school training, yet could not reconcile myself to the thought of parting with him ; so I compromised, as the Duc d'Orléans did before he became— or in order that he might become—Louis Philippe. Every morning Lucas, the old servant whom you will remember, takes Armand to school in time for the first lesson, and brings him home again at half-past four. In the house we have a private tutor, an admirable scholar, who helps Armand with his work in the evenings, and calls him in the morning at the school hour. Lucas takes him some lunch during the play-hour at midday. In this way I am with my boy at dinner and until he goes to bed at night, and I see him off in the morning.

Armand is the same charming little fellow, full of feeling and unselfish impulse, whom you loved ; and his tutor is quite pleased with him. I still have Naïs and the baby—two restless little mortals—but I am quite as much a child as they are. I could not bring myself to lose the darlings' sweet caresses. I could not live without the feeling that at any moment I can fly to Armand's bedside and watch his slumbers or snatch a kiss.

Yet home education is not without its drawbacks, to which I am fully alive. Society, like nature, is a jealous power, and will not have her rights encroached on, or her system set at naught. Thus, children who are brought up at home are exposed too early to the fire of the world ; they see its passions and become at home in its subterfuges. The finer distinctions, which regulate the conduct of matured men and women, elude their perceptions, and they take feeling and passion for their guide instead of subordinating these to the code of society; whilst the gay trappings and tinsel which attract so much of the world's favor blind them to the importance of the more sober virtues. A child of fifteen with the assurance of a man of the world is a thing against all nature ; at twenty-five he will be prematurely old, and his precocious knowledge only unfits him for the genuine study on which all solid ability must rest. Life in society is one long comedy, and those who take part in it, like other actors, reflect impressions which never penetrate below the surface. A mother, therefore, who wishes not to part from her children, must resolutely determine that they shall not enter the gay world; she must have courage to resist their inclinations, as well as her own, and keep them in the background. Cornelia had to keep her jewels under lock and key. Shall I do less for the children who are all the world to me?

Now that I am thirty, the heat of the day is over, the hardest bit of the road lies behind me. In a few years I shall be an old woman, and the sense of duty done is an immense encouragement. It would almost seem as though my trio can read my thoughts and shape themselves accordingly. A mysterious bond of sympathy unites me to these children who have never left my side. If they knew the blank in my life which they have to fill, they could not be more lavish of the solace they bring.

Armand, who was dull and dreamy during his first three years at school, and caused me some uneasiness, has made a sudden start. Doubtless he realized, in a way most children never do, the aim of all this preparatory work, which is to sharpen the intelligence, to get them into habits of application, and accustom them to that fundamental principle of all society —obedience. My dear, a few days ago I had the proud joy of seeing Armand crowned at the great inter-scholastic competition in the crowded Sorbonne, when your godson received the first prize for translation. At the school distribution he got two first prizes—one for verse and one for an essay. I went quite white when his name was called out, and longed to shout aloud: "I am his mother!" Little Naïs squeezed my hand till it hurt, if at such a moment it were possible to feel pain. Ah! Louise, a day like this might outweigh many a dream of love!

His brother's triumphs have spurred on little René, who

wants to go to school too. Sometimes the three children make such a racket, shouting and rushing about the house, that I wonder how my head stands it. I am always with them; no one else, not even Mary, is allowed to take care of my children. But the calling of a mother, if taxing, has so many compensating joys! To see a child leave its play and run to hug one, out of the fullness of its heart, what could be sweeter?

Then it is only in being constantly with them that one can study their characters. It is the duty of a mother, and one which she can depute to no hired teacher, to decipher the tastes, temper, and natural aptitudes of her children from their infancy. All homebred children are distinguished by ease of manner and tact, two acquired qualities which may go far to supply the lack of natural ability, whereas no natural ability can atone for the loss of this early training. I have already learned to discriminate this difference of tone in the men whom I meet in society, and to trace the hand of a woman in the formation of a young man's manners. How could any woman defraud her children of such a possession? You see what rewards attend the performance of my tasks?

Armand, I feel certain, will make an admirable judge, the most upright of public servants, the most devoted of deputies. And where would you find a sailor bolder, more adventurous, more astute than my René will be a few years hence? The little rascal has already an iron will, whatever he wants he manages to get; he will try a thousand circuitous ways to reach his end, and, if not successful then, will devise a thousand and first. Where dear Armand quietly resigns himself and tries to get at the reason of things, René will storm, and strive, and puzzle, chattering all the time, till at last he finds some chink in the obstacle; if there is room for the blade of a knife to pass, his little carriage will ride through in triumph.

And Naïs? Naïs is so completely a second self that I can hardly realize her as distinct from my own flesh and blood.

What a darling she is, and how I love to make a little lady of her, to dress her curly hair, tender thoughts mingling the while with every touch!   I must have her happy; I shall only give her to the man who loves her and whom she loves.   But, heavens! when I let her put on her little ornaments, or pass a cherry-colored ribbon through her hair, or fasten the shoes on her tiny feet, a sickening thought comes over me.   How can one order the destiny of a girl?   Who can say that she will not love a scoundrel or some man who is indifferent to her?   Tears often spring to my eyes as I watch her.   This lovely creature, this flower, this rosebud which has blossomed in one's heart, to be handed over to a man who will tear it from the stem and leave it bare!   Louise, it is you—you, who in two years have not written three words to tell me of your welfare—it is you who have recalled to my mind the terrible possibilities of marriage, so full of anguish for a mother wrapped up, as I am, in her child.   Farewell now, for in truth you don't deserve my friendship, and I hardly know how to write. Oh! answer me, my own Louise.

LII.

MME. GASTON TO MME. DE L'ESTORADE.

THE CHALET.

So, after a silence of two years, you are pricked by curiosity, and want to know why I have not written.   My dear Renée, there are no words, no images, no language to express my happiness.   That we have strength to bear it sums up all I could say.   It costs us no effort, for we are in perfect sympathy. The whole two years have known no note of discord in the harmony, no jarring word in the interchange of feeling, no shade of difference in our lightest wish.   Not one in this long succession of days has failed to bear its own peculiar fruit; not a moment has passed without being enriched by the play of fancy. So far are we from dreading the clanker of monotony in our life, that our only fear is lest it should not be long enough to contain all the poetic creations of a love as rich and varied in its development as nature herself. Of disappointment not a trace! We find more pleasure in being together than on the first day, and each hour as it goes by discloses fresh reason for our love. Every day as we take our evening stroll after dinner, we tell each other that we really must go and see what is doing in Paris, just as one might talk of going to Switzerland.

"Only think," Gaston will exclaim, "such and such a boulevard is being made, the Madeleine is finished. We ought to see it. Let us go to-morrow."

And to-morrow comes, and we are in no hurry to get up, and we breakfast in our bedroom. Then midday is on us, and it is too hot; a siesta seems appropriate. Then Gaston wishes to look at me, and he gazes on my face as though it were a picture, losing himself in this contemplation, which, as you may suppose, is not one-sided. Tears rise to the eyes of both as we think of our love and tremble. I am still the mistress, pretending, that is, to give less than I receive, and I revel in this deception. To a woman what can be sweeter than to see passion ever held in check by tenderness, and the man who is her master stayed, like a timid suitor, by a word from her, within the limits that she chooses? There is a great charm for women in seeing sentiment stronger than desire.

You asked me to describe him; but, Renée, it is not possible to make a portrait of the man we love. How could the heart be kept out of the work? Beside, to be frank between ourselves, we may admit that one of the dire effects of civilization on our manners is to make of man in society a being so utterly different from the natural man of strong feelings, that sometimes not a single point of likeness can be found between these two aspects of the same person. The man who falls into the most graceful operatic poses, as he pours sweet nothings into your ear by the fire at night, may be entirely destitute of those more intimate charms which a woman values. On the other hand, an ugly, boorish, badly-dressed figure may mark a man endowed with the very genius of love, and who has a perfect mastery over situations which might baffle even us with our superficial graces. A man whose conventional aspect accords with his real nature, who, in the intimacy of wedded love, possesses that inborn grace which can be neither given nor acquired, but which Greek art has embodied in statuary, that careless innocence of the ancient poets which, even in frank undress, seems to clothe the soul as with a veil of modesty—this is our ideal, born of our own conceptions, and linked with the universal harmony which seems to be the reality underlying all created things. To find this ideal in life is the problem which haunts the imagination of every woman—in Gaston I have found it.

Ah! dear, I did not know what love could be, united to youth, talent, and beauty. Gaston has no affectation, he moves with an instinctive and unstudied grace. When we walk alone together in the woods, his arm round my waist, mine resting on his shoulder, body fitted to body, and head touching head, our step is so even, uniform, and gentle, that those who see us pass by night take the vision for a single figure gliding over the graveled walks, like one of Homer's immortals. A like harmony exists in our desires, our thoughts, our words. More than once on some evening when a passing shower has left the leaves glistening and the moist grass bright with a more vivid green, it has chanced that we ended our walk without uttering a word, as we listened to the patter of falling drops and feasted our eyes on the scarlet sunset, flaring on the hilltops or dyeing with a warmer tone the gray of the tree-trunks.

Beyond a doubt our thoughts then rose to heaven in silent prayer, pleading, as it were, for our happiness. At times a cry would escape us at the moment when some sudden bend on the path opened up fresh beauties. What words can tell how honey-sweet, how full of meaning, is a kiss half-timidly exchanged within the sanctuary of nature—it is as though God had created us to worship in this fashion. And we return home, loving each other better, always better.

A love so passionate between old married people would be an outrage on society in Paris; only in the heart of the woods, like lovers, can we give scope to it.

To come to particulars, Gaston is of middle height—the height proper to all men of purpose. Neither stout nor thin, his figure is admirably made, with ample fullness in the proportions, while every motion is agile; he leaps a ditch with the easy grace of a wild animal. Whatever his attitude, he seems to have an instinctive sense of balance, and this is very rare in men who are given to thought. Though a dark man, he has an extraordinarily fair complexion; his jet-black hair contrasts finely with the lustreless tints of the neck and forehead. He has the tragic head of Louis XIII. His mustache and tuft have been allowed to grow, but I made him shave the whiskers and beard, which were getting too common. An honorable poverty has been his safeguard, and handed him over to me, unsoiled by the loose life which ruins so many young men. His teeth are magnificent, and he has a constitution of iron. His keen blue eyes, for me full of tenderness, will flash like lightning at any rousing thought.

Like all men of strong character and powerful mind, he has an admirable temper; its evenness would surprise you, as it did me. I have listened to the tale of many a woman's home troubles; I have heard of the moods and depression of men dissatisfied with themselves, who either won't get old or age ungracefully, men who carry about through life the rankling memory of some youthful excess, whose veins run poison and whose eyes are never frankly happy, men who cloak suspicion under bad temper, and make their women pay for an

hour's peace by a morning of annoyance, who take vengeance
on us for a beauty which is hateful to them because they have
ceased themselves to be attractive—all these are horrors unknown to youth. They are the penalty of unequal unions.
Oh! my dear, whatever you do, marry Athénaïs to none but
a young man!

But his smile—how I feast on it! A smile which is always
there, yet always fresh through the play of subtle fancy, a
speaking smile which makes of the lips a storehouse for
thoughts of love and unspoken gratitude, a smile which links
present joys to past. For nothing is allowed to drop out of
our common life. The smallest works of nature have become
part and parcel of our joy. In these delightful woods everything is alive and eloquent of ourselves. An old moss-grown
oak, near the woodman's house on the roadside, reminds us
how we sat there, wearied, under its shade, while Gaston
taught me about the mosses at our feet and told me their
story, till, gradually ascending from science to science, we
touched the very confines of creation.

There is something so kindred in our minds that they seem
to me like two editions of the same book. You see what a
literary tendency I have developed! We both have the habit,
or the gift, of looking at every subject broadly, of taking in
all its points of view, and the proof we are constantly giving
ourselves of the singleness of our inward vision is an ever-new
pleasure. We have actually come to look on this community
of mind as a pledge of love; and if it ever failed us, it would
mean as much to us as would a breach of fidelity in an ordinary home.

My life, full as it is of pleasures, would seem to you, nevertheless, extremely laborious. To begin with, my dear, you
must know that Louise-Armande-Marie de Chaulieu does her
own room. I could not bear that a hired menial, some
woman or girl from the outside, should become initiated—
literary touch again!—into the secrets of my bedroom. The

veriest trifles connected with the worship of my heart partake
of its sacred character.　This is not jealousy; it is self-respect.
Thus my room is done out with all the care a young girl in
love bestows on her person, and with the precision of an old
maid.　My dressing-room is no chaos of litter; on the contrary, it makes a charming boudoir.　My keen eye has foreseen all contingencies.　At whatever hour the lord and master
enters, he will find nothing to distress, surprise, or shock him;
he is greeted by flowers, perfume, elegance, and everything
that can charm the eye.

I get up in the early dawn, while he is still sleeping, and,
without disturbing him, pass into the dressing-room, where,
profiting by my mother's experience, I remove the traces of
sleep by bathing in cold water.　For during sleep the skin,
being less active, does not perform its functions adequately;
it becomes warm and covered with a sort of mist or atmosphere of sticky matter, visible to the eye.　From a sponge-bath
a woman issues forth ten years younger, and this, perhaps, is
the interpretation of the myth of Venus rising from the sea.
So the cold water restores to me the saucy charm of dawn,
and, having combed and scented my hair and made a most
fastidious toilet, I glide back, snake-like, in order that my
master may find me, dainty as a spring morning, at his waken-
ing.　He is charmed with this freshness, as of a newly opened
flower, without having the least idea how it is produced.

The regular toilet of the day is a matter for my maid, and
this takes place later in a larger room, set aside for the purpose.
As you may suppose, there is also a toilet for going to bed.
Three times a day, you see, or it may be four, do I array myself for the delight of my husband; which, again, dear one,
is suggestive of certain ancient myths.　　.

But our work is not all play.　We take a great deal of interest in our flowers, in the beauties of the hot-house, and in
our trees.　We give ourselves in all seriousness to horticulture,
and embosom the chalet in flowers, of which we are passion-

ately fond. Our lawns are always green, our shrubberies as well tended as those of a millionaire. And nothing, I assure you, can match the beauty of our walled garden. We are regular gluttons over our fruit, and watch with tender interest our Montreuil peaches, our hotbeds, our laden wall-fruit, and pyramidal pear-trees.

But lest these rural pursuits should fail to satisfy my beloved's mind, I have advised him to finish, in the quiet of this retreat, some plays which were begun in his starvation days, and which are really very fine. This is the only kind of literary work which can be done in odd moments, for it requires long intervals of reflection, and does not demand the elaborate pruning essential to a finished style. One can't make a task-work of dialogue; there must be biting touches, summings-up, and flashes of wit, which are the blossoms of the mind, and come rather by inspiration than reflection. This sort of intellectual sport is very much in my line. I assist Gaston in his work, and in this way manage to accompany him even in the boldest flights of his imagination. Do you see now how it is that my winter evenings never drag or become wearisome?

Our servants have such an easy time, that never once since we were married have we had to reprimand any of them. When questioned about us, they have had wit enough to draw on their imaginations, and have given us out as the companion and secretary of a lady and gentleman supposed to be traveling. They never go out without asking permission, which they know will not be refused; they are contented too, and see plainly that it will be their own fault if there is a change for the worse. The gardeners are allowed to sell the surplus of our fruit and vegetables. The dairymaid does the same with the milk, the cream, and the fresh butter on condition that the best of the produce is reserved for us. They are well pleased with their profits, and we are delighted with an abundance which no money and no ingenuity can procure in that terrible Paris, where it costs the interest of a hundred francs to produce a single fine peach.

All this is not without its meaning, my dear. I wish to fill the place of society to my husband; now society is amusing, and therefore his solitude must not be allowed to pall on him. I believed myself jealous in the old days, when I merely allowed myself to be loved; now I know real jealousy, the jealousy of the lover. A single indifferent glance unnerves me. From time to time I say to myself: "Suppose he ceased to love me!" And a shudder goes through me. I tremble before him, as the Christian before his God.

Alas! Renée, I am still without a child. The time will surely come—it must come—when our hermitage will need a father's and a mother's care to brighten it, when we shall both pine to see the little frocks and pelisses, the brown or golden heads, leaping, running through our shrubberies and flowery paths. Oh! it is a cruel jest of nature's, a flowering tree that bears no fruit. The thought of your lovely children goes through me like a knife. My life has grown narrow, while yours has expanded and shed its rays afar. The passion of love is essentially selfish, while motherhood widens the circle of our feelings. How well I felt this difference when I read your kind, tender letter! To see you thus living in three hearts roused my envy. Yes, you are happy; you have had wisdom to obey the laws of social life, whilst I stand outside, an alien.

Children, dear and loving children, can alone console a woman for the loss of her beauty. I shall soon be thirty, and at that age the dirge within begins. What though I am still beautiful, the limits of my woman's reign are none the less in sight. When they are reached, what then? I shall be forty before he is; I shall be old while he is still young. When this thought goes to my heart, I lie at his feet for an hour at a time, making him swear to tell me instantly if ever he feels his love diminishing.

But he is a child. He swears, as though the mere suggestion were an absurdity, and he is so beautiful that—Renée, you
understand—I believe him.

Adieu, my angel. Shall we ever again let years pass without
writing? Happiness is a monotonous theme, and that is,
perhaps, the reason why, to souls who love, Dante appears
even greater in the Paradiso than in the Inferno. I am not
Dante ; I am only your friend, and I don't want to bore you.
You can write, for in your children you have an ever-growing,
ever-varying source of happiness, while mine—— No more
of this. A thousand loves.

LIII.

MME. DE L'ESTORADE TO MME. GASTON.

MY DEAR LOUISE :—I have read and re-read your letter, and
the more deeply I enter into its spirit, the clearer does it become to me that it is the letter, not of a woman, but of a
child. You are the same old Louise, and you forget, what I
used to repeat over and over again to you, that the passion of
love belongs rightly to a state of nature, and has only been
purloined by civilization. So fleeting is its character that the
resources of society are powerless to modify its primitive condition, and it becomes the effort of all noble minds to make a
man of the infant Cupid. But, as you yourself admit, such
love ceases to be natural.

Society, my dear, abhors sterility ; by substituting a lasting
sentiment for the mere passing frenzy of nature, it has succeeded in creating that greatest of all human inventions—the
Family, which is the enduring basis of all organized society.
To the accomplishment of this end, it has sacrificed the individual, man as well as woman ; for we must not shut our
eyes to the fact that a married man devotes his energy, his
power, and all his possessions to his wife. Is it not she who

reaps the benefit of all his care? For whom, if not for her, are the luxury and wealth, the position and distinction, the comfort and the gayety of the home?

Oh! my sweet, once again you have taken the wrong turning in life. To be adored is a young girl's dream, which may survive a few springtimes; it cannot be that of the mature woman, the wife and mother. To a woman's vanity it is, perhaps, enough to know that she can command adoration if she likes. If you would live the life of a wife and mother, return, I beg of you, to Paris. Let me repeat my warning: It is not misfortune which you have to dread, as others do— it is happiness.

Listen to me, my child! It is the simple things of life— bread, air, silence—of which we do not tire; they have no piquancy which can create distaste; it is highly flavored dishes which irritate the palate, and in the end exhaust it. Were it possible that I should to-day be loved by a man for whom I could conceive a passion, such as yours for Gaston, I would still cling to the duties and the children, who are so dear to me. To a woman's heart the feelings of a mother are among the simple, natural, fruitful, and inexhaustible things of life. I can recall the day, now nearly fourteen years ago, when I embarked on a life of self-sacrifice with the despair of a ship-wrecked mariner clinging to the mast of his vessel; now, as I invoke the memory of past years, I feel that I would make the same choice again. No other guiding principle is so safe, or leads to such rich reward. The spectacle of your life, which, for all the romance and poetry with which you invest it, still remains based on nothing but a ruthless selfishness, has helped to strengthen my convictions. This is the last time I shall speak to you in this way; but I could not refrain from once more pleading with you when I found that your happiness had been proof against the most searching of all trials.

And one more point I must urge on you, suggested by my meditations on your retirement. Life, whether of the body or the heart, consists in certain balanced movements. Any excess introduced into the working of this routine gives rise either to pain or to pleasure, both of which are a mere fever of the soul, bound to be fugitive because nature is not so framed as to support it long. But to make of life one long excess is surely to choose sickness for one's portion. You are sick because you maintain at the temperature of passion a feeling which marriage ought to convert into a steadying, purifying influence.

Yes, my sweet, I see it clearly now; the glory of a home consists in this very calm, this intimacy, this sharing alike of good and evil, which the vulgar ridicule. How noble was the reply of the Duchesse de Sully, the wife of the great Sully, to some one who remarked that her husband, for all his grave exterior, did not scruple to keep a mistress. "What of that?" she said. "I represent the honor of the house, and should decline to play the part of a courtesan there."

But you, Louise, who are naturally more passionate than tender, would be at once the wife and the mistress. With the soul of a Héloïse and the passions of a Saint Theresa, you slip the leash on all your impulses, so long as they are sanctioned by the law; in a word, you degrade the marriage rite. Surely the tables are turned. The reproaches you once heaped on me for immorally, as you said, seizing the means of happiness from the very outset of my wedded life, might be directed against yourself for grasping at everything which may serve your passion. What! must nature and society alike be in bondage to your caprice? You are the old Louise; you have never acquired the qualities which ought to be a woman's; self-willed and unreasonable as a girl, you introduce withal into your love the keenest and most mercenary of calculations! Are you sure that, after all, the price you ask for your toilets is not too high? All these precautions are to my mind very suggestive of mistrust.

Oh, dear Louise, if only you knew the sweetness of a

mother's efforts to discipline herself in kindness and gentleness to all about her! My proud, self-sufficing temper gradually dissolved into a soft melancholy, which in turn has been swallowed up by those delights of motherhood which have been its reward. If the early hours were toilsome, the evening will be tranquil and clear. My dread is lest the day of your life should take the opposite course.

When I had read your letter to a close, I prayed God to send you among us for a day, that you might see what family life really is, and learn the nature of those joys which are lasting and sweeter than tongue can tell, because they are genuine, simple, and natural. But, alas! what chance have I with the best of arguments against a fallacy which makes you happy? As I write these words, my eyes fill with tears. I had felt so sure that some months of honeymoon would prove a surfeit and restore you to reason. But I see that there is no limit to your appetite, and that, having killed a man, you will not cease till you have killed love itself. Farewell, dear misguided friend. I am in despair that the letter which I hoped might reconcile you to society by its picture of my happiness should have brought forth only a pæan of selfishness. Yes, your love is selfish; you love Gaston far less for himself than for what he is to you.

LIV.

MME. GASTON TO THE COMTESSE DE L'ESTORADE.

May 20th.

Renée, calamity has come—no, that is no word for it—it has burst like a thunderbolt over your poor Louise. You know what that means; calamity for me is doubt; certainty would be death.

The day before yesterday, when I had finished my first toilet, I looked everywhere for Gaston to take a little turn with me before lunch, but in vain.   I went to the stable, and there I saw his mare all in a lather, while the groom was scraping off the foam before rubbing her down.

"Who in the world has put Fedelta in such a state?" I asked.

"Master," replied the lad.

I saw the mud of Paris on the mare's legs, for country mud is quite different ; and at once it flashed through me: "He has been to Paris."

This thought raised a swarm of others in my heart, and it seemed as though all the life in my body rushed there.   To go to Paris without telling me, at the hour when I leave him alone, to hasten there and back at such speed as to distress Fedelta.   Suspicion clutched me in its iron grip, till I could hardly breathe.   I walked aside a few steps to a seat, where I tried to recover my self-command.

Here Gaston found me, apparently pale and fluttered, for he immediately exclaimed: "What is wrong?" in a tone of such alarm, that I rose and took his arm.   But my muscles refused to move, and I was forced to sit down again.   Then he took me in his arms and carried me to the parlor close by, where the frightened servants pressed after us, till Gaston motioned them away.   Once left to ourselves, I refused to speak, but was able to reach my room, where I shut myself in, to weep my fill.   Gaston remained something like two hours at my door, listening to my sobs and questioning with angelic patience his poor darling, who made no response.

At last I told him that I would see him when my eyes were less red and my voice was steady again.

My formal words drove him from the house.   But by the time I had bathed my eyes in iced water and cooled my face, I found him in our room, the door into which was open, though I had heard no steps.   He begged me to tell him what was wrong.

"Nothing," I said ; "I saw the mud of Paris on Fedelta's

trembling legs; it seemed strange that you should go there without telling me; but, of course, you are free."

"I shall punish you for such wicked thoughts by not giving any explanation till to-morrow," he replied.

"Look at me," I said.

My eyes met his; deep answered to deep. No, not a trace of the cloud of disloyalty which, rising from the soul, must dim the clearness of the eye. I feigned satisfaction, though really unconvinced. It is not women only who can lie and dissemble!

The whole of the day we spent together. Ever and again, as I looked at him, I realized how fast my heart-strings were bound to him. How I trembled and fluttered within when, after a moment's absence, he reappeared. I live in him, not in myself. My cruel sufferings gave the lie to your unkind letter. Did I ever feel my life thus bound up in the noble Spaniard, who adored me, as I adore this heartless boy? I hate that mare! Fool that I was to keep horses! But the next thing would have been to lame Gaston or imprison him in the cottage. Wild thoughts like these filled my brain; you see how near I was to madness! If love be not the cage, what power on earth can hold back the man who wants to be free?

I asked him point-blank: "Do I bore you?"

"What needless torture you give yourself!" was his reply, while he looked at me with tender, pitying eyes. "Never have I loved you so deeply."

"If that is true, my beloved, let me sell Fedelta," I answered.

"Sell her, by all means!"

The reply crushed me. Was it not a covert taunt at my wealth and his own nothingness in the house? This may never have occurred to him, but I thought it had, and once more I left him. It was night, and I would go to bed.

Oh! Renée, to be alone with a harrowing thought drives

one to thoughts of death.   These charming gardens, the starry night, the cool air, laden with incense from our wealth of flowers, our valley, our hills—all seemed to me gloomy, black, and desolate.   It was as though I lay at the foot of a precipice, surrounded by serpents and poisonous plants, and saw no God in the sky.   Such a night ages a woman.

Next morning I said—

"Take Fedelta and be off to Paris!   Don't sell her; I love her.   Does she not carry you?"

But he was not deceived; my tone betrayed the storm of feeling which I strove to conceal.

"Trust me!" he replied; and the gesture with which he held out his hand, the glance of his eye, were so full of loyalty that I was overcome.

"What petty creatures women are!" I exclaimed.

"No, you love me, that is all," he said, pressing me to his heart.

"Go to Paris without me," I said, and this time I made him understand that my suspicions were laid aside.

He went; I thought he would have stayed.   I won't attempt to tell you what I suffered.   I found a second self within, quite strange to me.   A crisis like this has, for the woman who loves, a tragic solemnity that baffles words; the whole of life rises before you then, and you search in vain for any horizon to it; the veriest trifle is big with meaning, a glance contains a volume, icicles drift on uttered words, and the death-sentence is read in a movement of the lips.

I thought he would have paid me back in kind; had I not been magnanimous?   I climbed to the top of the chalet, and my eyes followed him on the road.   Ah! my dear Renée, he vanished from my sight with an appalling swiftness!

"How keen he is to go!" was the thought that sprang of itself.

Once more alone, I fell back into the hell of possibilities, the maelstrom of mistrust.   There were moments when I would

have welcomed any certainty, even the worst, as a relief from
the torture of suspense.　Suspense is a duel carried on in the
heart, and we give no quarter to ourselves.

I paced up and down the walks.　I returned to the house,
only to tear out again, like a mad woman.　Gaston, who left
at seven o'clock, did not return till eleven.　Now, as it only
takes half an hour to reach Paris through the park of St. Cloud
and the Bois de Boulogne, it is plain that he must have spent
three hours in town.　He came back radiant, with a whip in
his hand for me, an india-rubber whip with a gold handle.

For the last two weeks I had been without a whip, my old
one being worn and broken.

"Was it for this you tortured me?" I said, as I admired
the workmanship of this beautiful ornament, which contains a
little vinaigrette at one end.

Then it flashed on me that the present was a fresh artifice.
Nevertheless I threw myself at once on his neck, not without
reproaching him gently for having caused me so much pain
for the sake of a trifle.　He was greatly pleased with his ingenuity; his eyes and his whole bearing plainly showed the
restrained triumph of the successful plotter; for there is a
radiance of the soul which is reflected in every feature and
turn of the body.　While still examining the beauties of this
work of art, I asked him at a moment when we happened to
be looking each other in the face—

"Who is the artist?"

"A friend of mine."

"Ah! I see it has been mounted by Verdier," and I read
the name of the store printed on the handle.

Gaston is nothing but a child yet.　He blushed, and I
made much of him as a reward for the shame he felt in deceiving me.　I pretended to notice nothing, and he may well
have thought the incident was over.

May 25th.

The next morning I was in my riding-habit by six o'clock, and by seven landed at Verdier's, where several whips of the same pattern were shown me. One of the men serving recognized mine when I pointed it out to him.

"We sold that yesterday to a young gentleman," he said. And from the description I gave him of my traitor Gaston, not a doubt was left of his identity. I will spare you the palpitations which rent my heart during that journey to Paris and the little scene there, which marked the turning-point of my life.

By half-past seven I was home again, and Gaston found me, fresh and blooming, in my morning dress, sauntering about with a make-believe nonchalance. I felt confident that old Philippe, who had been taken into my confidence, would not have betrayed my absence.

"Gaston," I said, as we walked by the side of the lake, "you cannot blind me to the difference between a work of art inspired by friendship and something which has been cast in a mould."

He turned white, and fixed his eyes on me rather than on the damaging piece of evidence I thrust before them.

"My dear," I went on, "this is not a whip; it is a screen behind which you are hiding something from me."

Thereupon I gave myself the gratification of watching his hopeless entanglement in the coverts and labyrinths of deceit and the desperate efforts he made to find some wall he might scale and thus escape. In vain; he had perforce to remain upon the field, face to face with an adversary, who at last laid down her arms in a feigned complacence. But it was too late. The fatal mistake, against which my mother had tried to warn me, was made. My jealousy, exposed in all its nakedness, had led to war and all its stratagems between Gaston and myself. Jealousy, dear, has neither sense nor decency.

I made up my mind now to suffer in silence, but to keep my eyes open, until my doubts were resolved one way or another. Then I would either break with Gaston or bow to my misfortune; no middle course is possible for a woman who respects herself.

What can he be concealing? For a secret there is, and the secret has to do with a woman. Is it some youthful escapade for which he still blushes? But if so, what? The word WHAT is written in letters of fire on all I see. I read it in the glassy water of my lake, in the shrubbery, in the clouds, on the ceilings, at table, in the flowers of the carpets. A voice cries to me WHAT? in my sleep. Dating from the morning of my discovery, a cruel interest has sprung into our lives, and I have become familiar with the bitterest thought that can corrode the heart—the thought of treachery in him one loves. Oh! my dear, there is heaven and hell together in such a life. Never had I felt this scorching flame, I to whom love had appeared only in the form of devoutest worship.

"So you wished to know the gloomy torture-chamber of pain!" I said to myself. "Good, the spirits of evil have heard your prayer; go on your road, unhappy wretch!"

May 30th.

Since that fatal day Gaston no longer works with the careless ease of the wealthy artist, whose work is merely pastime; he sets himself tasks like a professional writer. Four hours a day he devotes to finishing his two plays.

"He wants money!"

A voice within whispered the thought. But why? He spends next to nothing; we have absolutely no secrets from each other; there is not a corner of his study which my eyes and my fingers may not explore. His yearly expenditure does not amount to two thousand francs, and I know that he has thirty thousand, I can hardly say laid by, but scattered loose in a drawer. You can guess what is coming. At midnight, while he was sleeping, I went to see if the money was still there. An icy shiver ran through me. The drawer was empty.

That same week I discovered that he went to Sèvres to fetch his letters, and these letters he must tear up immediately; for though I am a very Figaro in contrivances, I have never yet seen a trace of one. Alas! my sweet, despite the fine promises and vows by which I bound myself after the scene of the whip, an impulse, which I can only call madness, drove me to follow him in one of his rapid rides to the postoffice. Gaston was appalled to be thus discovered on horseback, paying the postage of a letter which he held in his hand. He looked fixedly at me, and then put spurs to Fedelta. The pace was so hard that I felt shaken to bits when I reached the lodge gate, though my mental agony was such at the time that it might well have dulled all consciousness of bodily pain. Arrived at the gate, Gaston said nothing; he rang the bell and waited without a word. I was more dead than alive. I might be mistaken or I might not, but in neither case was it fitting for Armande-Louise-Marie de Chaulieu to play the spy. I had sunk to the level of the gutter, by the side of courtesans, opera-dancers, mere creatures of instinct; even the vulgar shop-girl or humble seamstress might look down on me.

What a moment! At last the door opened; he handed his horse to the groom, and I also dismounted, but into his arms, which were stretched out to receive me. I threw my skirt over my left arm, gave him my right, and we walked on— still in silence. The few steps we thus took might be reckoned to me for a hundred years of purgatory. A swarm of thoughts beset me as I walked, now seeming to take visible form in tongues of fire before my eyes, now assailing my mind, each with its own poisoned dart. When the groom and the horses were far away, I stopped Gaston, and, looking him in the face, said, as I pointed, with a gesture that you should have seen, to the fatal letter still in his right hand—

24

"May I read it?"

He gave it me. I opened it, and found a letter from Nathan, the dramatic author, informing Gaston that a play of his had been accepted, learned, rehearsed, and would be produced the following Saturday. He also inclosed a box ticket.

Though for me this was the opening of heaven's gates to the martyr, yet the fiend would not leave me in peace, but kept crying: "Where are the thirty thousand francs?" It was a question which self-respect, dignity, all my old self, in fact, prevented me from uttering. If my thought became speech, I might as well throw myself into the lake at once, and yet I could hardly keep the words down. Dear friend, was not this a trial passing the strength of woman?

I returned the letter, saying—

"My poor Gaston, you are getting bored down here. Let us go back to Paris, won't you?"

"To Paris?" he said. "But why? I only wanted to find out if I had any gift, to taste the flowing bowl of success!"

Nothing would be easier than for me to ransack the drawer some time when he is working and pretend great surprise at finding the money gone. But that would be going half-way to meet the answer, "Oh! my friend So-and-so was hard up!" etc., which a man of Gaston's quick wit would not have far to seek.

The moral, my dear, is that the brilliant success of this play, which all Paris is crowding to see, is due to us, though the whole credit goes to Nathan. I am represented by one of the two stars in the legend: AND M M * * . I saw the first night from the depths of one of the stage boxes.

July 1st.

Gaston's work and his visits to Paris still continue. He is preparing new plays, partly because he wants a pretext for

going to Paris, partly in order to make money. Three plays
have been accepted, and two more are commissioned.

Oh! my dear, I am lost, all is darkness around me. I
would set fire to the house in a moment if that would bring
light. What does it all mean? Is he ashamed of taking
money from me? He is too high-minded for so trumpery a
matter to weigh with him. Beside, scruples of the kind could
only be the outcome of some love affair. A man would take
anything from his wife, but from the woman he has ceased to
care for, or is thinking of deserting, it is different. If he
needs such large sums, it must be to spend them on a woman.
For himself, why should he hesitate to draw from my purse?
Our savings amount to one hundred thousand francs!

In short, my sweetheart, I have explored a whole continent
of possibilities, and, after carefully weighing all the evidence,
am convinced I have a rival. I am deserted—for whom? At
all costs I must see the unknown.

July 10th.

Light has come, and it is all over with me. Yes, Renée,
at the age of thirty, in the perfection of my beauty, with all
the resources of a ready wit and the seductive charms of dress
at my command, I am betrayed—and for whom? A large-
boned Englishwoman, with big feet and thick waist—a regular British cow! There is no longer room for doubt. I will
tell you the history of the last few days.

Worn out with suspicions, which were fed by Gaston's guilty
silence (for, if he had helped a friend, why keep it a secret
from me?), his insatiable desire for money, and his frequent
journeys to Paris; jealous, too, of the work from which he
seemed unable to tear himself, I at last made up my mind to
take certain steps, of such a degrading nature that I cannot
tell you about them. Suffice it to say that three days ago I
ascertained that Gaston, when in Paris, visits a house in the
Rue de la Ville l'Evêque, where he guards his mistress with

jealous mystery, unexampled in Paris. The porter was surly, and I could get little out of him, but that little was enough to put an end to any lingering hope, and with hope to life. On this point my mind was resolved, and I only waited to learn the whole truth first.

With this object I went to Paris and took rooms in a house exactly opposite the one which Gaston visits. Thence I saw him with my own eyes enter the courtyard on horseback. Too soon a ghastly fact forced itself on me. This English-woman, who seems to me about thirty-six, is known as Mme. Gaston.

This discovery was my death-blow.

I saw him next walking to the Tuileries with a couple of children. Oh! my dear, two children, the living images of Gaston! The likeness is so strong that it bears scandal on the face of it. And what pretty children! in their handsome English costumes! She is the mother of his children. Here is the key to the whole mystery.

The woman herself might be a Greek statue, stepped down from some monument. Cold and white as marble, she moves sedately with a mother's pride. She is undeniably beautiful, but heavy as a man of war. There is no breeding or dis-tinction about her; nothing of the English lady. Probably she is a farmer's daughter from some wretched or remote country village, or, it may be, the eleventh child of some poor clergyman!

I reached home, after a miserable journey, during which all sort of fiendish thoughts had me at their mercy, with hardly any life left in me. Was she married? Did he know her be-fore our marriage? Had she been deserted by some rich man, whose mistress she was, and thus thrown back upon Gaston's hands? Conjectures without end flitted through my brain, as though conjecture were needed in the presence of the chil-dren.

The next day I returned to Paris, and by a free use of my

purse extracted from the porter the information that Mme. Gaston was legally married.

His reply to my question took the form "Yes, *Miss*."

July 15th.

My dear, my love for Gaston is stronger than ever since that morning, and he has every appearance of being still more deeply in love. He is so young! A score of times it has been on my lips, when we rise in the morning, to say, "Then you love me better than the lady of the Rue de la Ville l'Evêque?" But I dare not explain to myself why the words are checked on my tongue.

"Are you very fond of children?" I asked.

"Oh yes!" was his reply; "but children will come!"

"What makes you think so?"

"I have consulted the best doctors, and they agree in advising me to travel for a few months."

"Gaston," I said, "if love in absence had been possible for me, do you suppose I should ever have left the convent?"

He laughed; but as for me, dear, the word "travel" pierced my heart. Rather, far rather, would I leap from the top of the house than be rolled down the staircase, step by step. Farewell, my sweet heart. I have arranged for my death to be easy, and without horrors, but certain. I made my will yesterday. You can come to me now, the prohibition is removed. Come, then, and receive my last farewell. I will not die by inches; my death, like my life, shall bear the impress of dignity and grace.

Farewell, dear sister soul, whose affection has never wavered nor grown weary, but has been the constant tender moonlight of my soul. If the intensity of passion has not been ours, at least we have been spared its venomous bitterness. How rightly you have judged of life! Farewell.

LV.

THE COMTESSE DE L'ESTORADE TO MME. GASTON.

July 16th.

My dear Louise:—I send this letter by an express before hastening to the chalet myself. Take courage. Your last letter seemed to me so frantic that I thought myself justified, under the circumstances, in confiding all to Louis; it was a question of saving you from yourself. If the means we have employed have been, like yours, repulsive, yet the result is so satisfactory that I am certain you will approve. I went so far as to set the police to work, but the whole thing remains a secret between the prefect, ourselves, and you.

In one word, Gaston is a jewel! But here are the facts. His brother, Louis Gaston, died at Calcutta, while in the service of a mercantile company, when he was on the very point of returning to France, a rich, prosperous, married man, having received a very large fortune with his wife, who was the widow of an English merchant. For ten years he had worked hard that he might be able to send home enough to support his brother, to whom he was devotedly attached, and from whom his letters generously concealed all his trials and disappointments.

Then came the failure of the great Halmer house; the widow was ruined, and the sudden shock affected Louis Gaston's brain. He had no mental energy left to resist the disease which attacked him, and he died in Bengal, whither he had gone to try and realize the remnants of his wife's property. The dear, good fellow had deposited with a banker a first sum of three hundred thousand francs, which was to go to his brother, but the banker was involved in the Halmer crash, and thus their last resource failed them.

Louis' widow, the handsome woman whom you took for your rival, arrived in Paris with two children—your nephews —and an empty purse, her mother's jewels having barely sufficed to pay for bringing them over. The instructions which Louis Gaston had given the banker for sending the money to his brother enabled the widow to find your husband's former home. As Gaston had disappeared without leaving any address, Mme. Louis Gaston was directed to d'Arthez, the only person who could give any information about him.

D'Arthez was the more ready to relieve the young woman's pressing needs, because Louis Gaston, at the time of his marriage four years before, had written to make inquiries about his brother from the famous author, whom he knew to be one of his friends. The captain had consulted d'Arthez as to the best means of getting the money safely transferred to Marie, and d'Arthez had replied, telling him that Gaston was now a rich man through his marriage with the Baronne de Macumer. The personal beauty, which was the mother's rich heritage to her sons, had saved them both—one in India, the other in Paris—from destitution. A touching story, is it not?

D'Arthez naturally wrote, after a time, to tell your husband of the condition of his sister-in-law and her children, informing him, at the same time, of the generous intentions of the Indian Gaston toward his Paris brother, which an unhappy chance alone had frustrated. Gaston, as you may imagine, hurried off to Paris. Here is the first ride accounted for. During the last five years he had saved fifty thousand francs out of the income which you forced him to accept, and this sum he invested in the public funds under the names of his two nephews, securing them each, in this way, an income of twelve hundred francs. Next he furnished his sister-in-law's rooms, and promised her a quarterly allowance of three thousand francs. Here you see the meaning of his dramatic labors and the pleasure caused him by the success of his first play.

Mme. Gaston, therefore, is no rival of yours, and has every right to your name. A man of Gaston's sensitive delicacy was bound to keep the affair secret from you, knowing, as he did, your generous nature. Nor does he look on what you give him as his own. D'Arthez read me the letter he had from your husband, asking him to be one of the witnesses at his marriage. Gaston in this declares that his happiness would have been perfect but for the one drawback of his poverty and indebtedness to you. A virgin soul is at the mercy of such scruples. Either they make themselves felt or they do not; and when they do, it is easy to imagine the conflict of feeling and embarrassment to which they give rise. Nothing is more natural than Gaston's wish to provide in secret a suitable maintenance for the woman who is his brother's widow, and who had herself set aside one hundred thousand crowns for him from her own fortune. She is a handsome woman, warm-hearted, and extremely well-bred, but not clever. She is a mother; and, you may be sure, I lost my heart to her at first sight when I found her with one child in her arms, and the other dressed like a little lord. The children first! is written in every detail of her house.

Far from being angry, therefore, with your beloved husband, you should find in all this fresh reason for loving him. I have met him, and think him the most delightful young fellow in Paris. Yes! dear child, when I saw him, I had no difficulty in understanding that a woman might lose her head about him; his soul is mirrored in his countenance. If I were you, I should settle the widow and her children near the chalet, in a pretty little cottage which you could have built for them, and adopt the boys!

Be at peace, then, dear soul, and plan this little surprise, in your turn, for Gaston.

LVI.

MME. GASTON TO THE COMTESSE DE L'ESTORADE.

Ah! my dear friend, what can I say in answer except the cruel "It is too late" of that fool Lafayette to his royal master? Oh! my life, my sweet life, what physician will give it back to me? My own hand has dealt the death-blow. Alas! have I not been a mere will-o'-the-wisp, whose twinkling spark was fated to perish before it reached a flame? My eyes rain torrents of tears—and yet they must not fall when I am with him. I fly him, and he seeks me. My despair is all within. This torture Dante forgot to place in his "Inferno." Come to see me die.

LVII.

THE COMTESSE DE L'ESTORADE TO THE COMTE DE L'ESTORADE.

THE CHALET, *August 7th.*

MY LOVE:—Take the children away to Provence without me; I remain with Louise, who has only a few days yet to live. I cannot leave either her or her husband, for whose reason I fear.

You know the scrap of letter which sent me flying to Ville d'Avray, picking up the doctors on my way. Since then I have not left my darling friend, and it has been impossible to write you, for I have sat up every night for two weeks.

When I arrived, I found her with Gaston, in full dress, beautiful, laughing, happy. It was a heroic falsehood! They were like two lovely children together in their restored confidence. For a moment I was deceived, like Gaston, by this effrontery; but Louise pressed my hand, whispering—

"He must not know; I am dying."

An icy chill fell over me as I felt her burning hand and saw the red spot on her cheeks. I congratulated myself on my prudence in leaving the doctors in the wood till they should be sent for.

"Leave us for a little," she said to Gaston. "Two women who have not met for five years have plenty of secrets to talk over, and Renée, I have no doubt, has things to confide in me."

Directly we were alone, she flung herself into my arms, unable longer to restrain her tears.

"Tell me about it," I said. "I have brought with me, in case of need, the best surgeon and the best physician from the hospital, and Bianchon as well; there are four altogether."

"Ah!" she cried, "have them in at once if they can save me, if there is still time. The passion which hurried me to death now cries for life!"

"But what have you done to yourself?"

"I have in a few days brought myself to the last stage of consumption."

"But how?"

"I got myself into a profuse perspiration in the night, and then ran out and lay down by the side of the lake in the dew. Gaston thinks I have a cold, and I am—dying!"

"Send him to Paris; I will fetch the doctors myself," I said, as I rushed out wildly to the spot where I had left them.

Alas! my love, after the consultation was over, not one of the doctors gave me the least hope; they all believe that Louise will die with the fall of the leaves. The dear child's constitution has wonderfully helped the success of her plan. It seems she has a predisposition to this complaint; and though, in the ordinary course, she might have lived a long time, a few day's folly has made the case desperate.

I cannot tell you what I felt on hearing this sentence, based on such clear explanations. You know that I have lived in

SHE—— CARRIED ME OFF TO HER PRETTY GARDEN.

Louise as much as in my own life. I was simply crushed, and
could not stir to escort to the door these harbingers of evil.
I don't know how long I remained lost in bitter thoughts, the
tears running down my cheeks, when I was roused from my
stupor by the words:

"So there is no hope for me!" in a clear, angelic voice.

It was Louise, with her hand on my shoulder. She made
me get up, and carried me off to her pretty garden. With a
beseeching glance, she went on:

"Stay with me to the end; I won't have doleful faces round
me. Above all, I must keep the truth from *him.* I know that
I have strength to do it. I am full of youth and spirit, and
can die standing! For myself, I have no regrets. I am dying
as I wished to die, still young and beautiful, in the perfection
of my womanhood.

"As for him, I can see very well now that I should have
made his life miserable. Passion has me in its grip, like a
struggling fawn, impatient of the toils. My groundless jealousy has already wounded him sorely. When the day came
that my suspicions met only indifference—which in the long-
run is the rightful meed of all jealousy—well, that would have
been my death. I have had my share of life. There are
people whose names on the muster-roll of the world show
sixty years of service, and yet in all that time they have not
had two years of real life, whilst my record of thirty is doubled
by the intensity of my love.

"Thus for him, as well as for me, the close is a happy one.
But between us, dear Renée, it is different. You lose a loving
sister, and that is a loss which nothing can repair. You alone
here have the right to mourn my death."

After a long pause, during which I could only see her
through a mist of tears, she continued:

"The moral of my death is a cruel one. My dear doctor
in petticoats was right; marriage cannot rest upon passion as
its foundation, nor even upon love. How fine and noble is

your life ! keeping always to the one safe road, you give your husband an ever-growing affection ; while the passionate eagerness with which I threw myself into wedded life was bound in nature to diminish.   Twice have I gone astray, and twice has Death stretched forth his bony hand to strike my happiness. The first time, he robbed me of the noblest and most devoted of men ; now it is my turn, the grinning monster tears me from the arms of my poet husband, with all his beauty and his grace.

"Yet I would not complain.   Have I not known in turn two men, each the very pattern of nobility—one in mind, the other in outward form?   In Félipe, the soul dominated and transformed the body; in Gaston, one could not say which was supreme—heart, mind, or grace of form.   I die adored— what more could I wish for?   Time, perhaps, in which to draw near the God of whom I may have too little thought. My spirit will take its flight toward Him, full of love, and with the prayer that some day, in the world above, He will unite me once more to the two who made a heaven of my life below.   Without them, paradise would be a desert to me.

"To others, my example would be fatal, for mine was no common lot.   To meet a Félipe or a Gaston is more than mortals can expect, and therefore the doctrine of society in regard to marriage accords with the natural law.   Woman is weak, and in marrying she ought to make an entire sacrifice of her will to the man who, in return, should lay his selfishness at her feet.   The stir which women of late years have created by their whining and insubordination is ridiculous, and only shows how well we deserve the epithet of children, bestowed by philosophers on our sex."

She continued talking thus in the gentle voice you know so well, uttering the gravest truths in the prettiest manner, until Gaston entered, bringing with him his sister-in-law, the two children, and the English nurse, whom, at Louise's request, he had been to fetch from Paris.

"Here are the pretty instruments of my torture," she said, as her nephews approached. "Was not the mistake excusable? What a wonderful likeness to their uncle?"

She was most friendly to Mme. Gaston the elder, and begged that she would look upon the chalet as her home; in short, she played the hostess to her in her best de Chaulieu manner, in which no one can rival her.

I wrote at once to the Duc and Duchesse de Chaulieu, the Duc de Rhétoré, and the Duc de Lenoncourt-Givry, as well as to Madeleine. It was time. Next day, Louise, worn out with so much exertion, was unable to go out; indeed, she only got up for dinner. In the course of the evening, Madeleine de Lenoncourt, her two brothers, and her mother arrived. The coolness which Louise's second marriage had caused between herself and her family disappeared. Every day since that evening, Louise's father and both her brothers have ridden over in the morning, and the two duchesses spend all their evenings at the chalet. Death unites as well as separates; it silences all paltry feeling.

Louise is perfection in her charm, her grace, her good sense, her wit, and her tenderness. She has retained to the last that perfect tact for which she has been so famous, and she lavishes on us the treasures of her brilliant mind, which made her one of the queens of Paris.

"I should like to look well even in my coffin," she said with her matchless smile, as she lay down on the bed where she has lingered for the past two weeks.

Her room has nothing of the sick-chamber in it; medicines, ointments, the whole apparatus of nursing, is carefully concealed.

"I am making a good death, am I not?" she said to the Sèvres priest who came to confess her.

We gloated over her like misers. All this anxiety and the terrible truths which dawned on him have prepared Gaston for the worst. He is full of courage, but the blow has gone home.   It would not surprise me to see him follow his wife in the natural course.   Yesterday, as we were walking round the lake, he said to me—

"I must be a father to those two children," and he pointed to his sister-in-law, who was taking the boys for a walk.   "But though I shall do nothing to hasten my end, I want your promise that you will be a second mother to them, and will persuade your husband to accept the office of guardian, which I shall depute to him in conjunction with my sister-in-law."

He said this quite simply, like a man who knows he is not long for this world.   He has smiles on his face to meet Louise's, and it is only I whom he does not deceive.   He is a mate for her in courage.

Louise has expressed a wish to see her godson, but I am not sorry he should be in Provence; she might want to remember him generously, and I should be in a great difficulty.

Adieu, my dear friend. ·

August 25th (her birthday).

Yesterday evening Louise was delirious for a short time; but her delirium was the prettiest babbling, which shows that even the madness of gifted people is not that of fools or no-bodies.   In a mere thread of a voice she sang some Italian airs from "I Puritani," "La Somnambula," "Moïse," while we stood round the bed in silence.   Not one of us, not even the Duc de Rhétoré, had dry eyes, so clear was it to us all that her soul was in this fashion passing from us.   She could no longer see us!   Yet she was there still in the charm of the faint melody, with its sweetness not of this earth.

During the night the death agony began.   It is now seven in the morning, and I myself have just raised her from bed. Some flicker of strength revived; she wished to sit by her window, and asked for Gaston's hand.   And then, my love, the sweetest spirit whom we shall ever see on this earth departed, leaving us the empty shell.

The last sacrament had been administered the evening before, unknown to Gaston, who was taking a snatch of sleep during this agonizing ceremony; and after she was moved to the window, she asked me to read her the *De Profundis* in French, while she was thus face to face with the lovely scene, which was her handiwork. She repeated the words after me to herself, and pressed the hands of her husband, who knelt on the other side of the chair.

August 26th.

My heart is broken. I have just seen her in her shroud; her face is quite pale now with purple shadows. Oh! my children! I want my children! Bring me my children!